THE SINAI ARTIFACT

THE SINAI ARTIFACT

Howard Gleichenhaus

ARPress
ILLUMINATING IDEAS
EMPOWERING VOICES

ARPress
45 Dan Road Suite 5
Canton MA 02021

Hotline:1(888) 821-0229
Fax:1(508) 545-7580

Ordering Information:
Quantity sales. Special discounts are available on quantity purchases by corporations, associations, and others. For details, contact the publisher at the address above.

Printed in the United States of America.
ISBN-13:   Paperback   979-8-89330-471-8
                eBook   979-8-89330-472-5

Library of Congress Control Number: 2024902535

Contents

Gretchen Bell perched on a metal stool in front of a microscope and nervously turned toward a glass-faced cabinet, one of several mounted to the walls that lined the laboratory's perimeter. Petite with short blonde hair, the Harvard graduate student wore a short miniskirt that fell to mid-thigh. Shoulder length blonde hair framed a pretty face younger than her actual age.

She paid little attention to what was under the lens, her mind instead focused on one thing, the priceless artifact she'd been trying to steal.

For Bell, time was running out. She'd taken risks all summer trying to secure the priceless rock, an innocuous looking piece of granite the Smithsonian was not even aware it possessed. On one occasion, she sneaked back into the building late using a master key lifted from her boss's key ring.

Curator Dimitri Kastianich had a penchant for downing copious amounts of Russian vodka and passing out on the couch of his suburban Virginia apartment.

Bell had spent hours in the Smithsonian's storage areas, poking through boxes and crates, until finally she found it, mislabeled in a crate of pottery shards. Six inches wide, and heart-shaped, its curved top tapered to a point at the lower edge with small inward and outward projecting notches. Lettering in an alphabet Bell did not recognize covered one side.

Bell's Russian handler, Hans Richter, a German national working for the FSB, Russia's secret service, had been correct about the artifact being lost somewhere in Smithsonian's bowels. How Richter knew, and where she needed to look, Bell never asked. Questioning Hans Richter was not a wise career move, or so she'd been warned.

Twice, with the relic secure in her briefcase, Bell managed to reach the only unalarmed exit door in the entire building, but a guard, 24/7, occupied a desk a few feet away and he seldom left his post without a backup to take his place. Both times she needed to stash the relic in the microscopy lab and return to Kastianich's apartment before he woke up. On her second failed try she'd stashed the priceless object in plain sight—inside the glass-faced cabinet a few feet away from her workstation. Today was her last chance. Richter provided the customized attaché case that sat right under her desk.

Bell turned, startled when she heard a key in the locked door. She slipped a glass slide under the microscope lens and leaned in, feigning work.

Dimitri Kastianich, bear-size of a man, was the curator of the Smithsonian's Forensic Antiquity Division. He locked the heavy door behind him and Bell recognized the look on his face. The fifty-year-old archeologist slid a hand across her shoulder and held it there for several seconds, his fingers stroking the fabric of her blouse.

Bell stiffened. The last thing she wanted, especially today, was dealing with the old letch's advances. Even now, at 11:00 a.m., she smelled the vodka on his breath—there was always vodka. Bell had poured the old man a stiff vodka an hour earlier. Supplied by Hans Richter, she was assured it would keep him out of her way for hours. It didn' work.

Outside the lab, her summer intern colleagues waited for the curator's final remarks before they all left Washington and returned home to wait. Only two of the current interns would be offered post-doctoral fellowships at Georgetown—an academic plum, compliments of the United States government. Bell had no interest in Georgetown's academic plums, or any academic plums for that matter; her plan, Richter's plan, was far more ambitious.

The horny Russian was easy pickings for the sensuous twenty-year-old. Richter's briefing on Kastianich's proclivity for young blondes assured it. It was the reason he'd recruited her.

Seducing the fool took little effort. From May, when Bell first arrived to begin the summer program, she found ways to be alone with her boss. She hacked his personal e-mail account and his daily calendar. She knew where he'd be at any given time, day or night, often showing up as if by coincidence. Flattered by the young woman's attention, Kastianich, predictably, took a special liking for the Harvard grad student and within a week offered 'special mentoring,' but once in his apartment very little mentoring took place. After each tryst Bell spent an hour soaking in a bathtub, ridding herself of the creepy feeling.

Kastianich came up behind her. His meaty hands encircled her waist, his face buried in her neck. He ignored her feeble protests and moved an arm over her shoulder, reaching down for the top button of her green silk blouse. With the finger dexterity of a surgeon he popped one button, then another.

Standing, Bell turned and faced him. "Please, Dimitri, not now. There are people outside. Someone may come in."

She tried humor, but the window of opportunity for getting the artifact into her attaché case was closing. Once she left the lab and the good-bye ceremonies started, there would be little chance to gain reentry and retrieve her prize.

Kastianich's hand slid under the hem of her skirt. He caressed her inner thigh, then moved his fingers higher, his lips still pressed to her neck.

Bell stared at the Harvard class ring on her finger. *Veritas*, etched on a heraldic shield, surrounded gold garlands, with the word 'Harvard' engraved below. Her instructions on how the ring worked came with a dire warning. Only as a last resort, Richter had said, but she was out of options, her mission about to be compromised if she did not act.

She pressed a thumb hard on the ring's top surface. The crimson stone slid sideways revealing a tiny, sharp, hollow needle.

Kastianich barely felt it slide across the back of his neck below the hairline, scratching the skin's surface. She was now in uncharted territory, playing for time, a less than eager participant in Kastianich's clumsy dance of grope and feel. She waited for whatever was in the ring to take effect, information Richter failed to share, but knowing him, Bell expected something terrible.

A high-pitched whine filled Kastianich's ears. "What is that?" he mumbled, his words slurred. He fixed his gaze on one of the storage units mounted on the wall across the room. "And what is that glow?"

Bell turned. There was no glow, or high-pitched whine. She stepped out of reach.

"What is in there?" he said more forcefully.

"They are pottery chards, Dimitri. They arrived last week, from Egypt, I think. I told you about them."

Beads of sweat formed on his face. He ran a sleeve across his forehead. "Why it is so hot in here?"

Humor him, Bell thought—keep him occupied until whatever is in the ring takes full effect. She pointed. "Do you mean those glass cabinets?"

She inched farther away. There were still no sounds or glowing auras from any place, the room dead silent. It was all in Kastianich's head.

"Only pottery?" he bellowed. "Pottery can wait," He reached for her.

Bell slipped away, surprised at how easily he yielded. "Don't you think we should find out? It might be important, Dr. Kastianich."

"So now is doctor, is it?" His words slurred together.

A few more seconds, she hoped.

"Please, Dimitri, I beg you. There are people out there. They saw you come in."

His voice grew louder, more insistent, more agitated, unaware he was now shouting. "*Nyet!*" he roared. "Is not important who is there. The door is locked."

"Yes Dimitri, it is important."

"No, I say is not important. Come *Myshka*, we have better things to do than argue."

Bell closed her eyes. She could not believe that in the throes of being poisoned he still had the twisted notion that he wanted to, or could, perform sexually. On his best night, it had been slam-bam-thank-you-ma'am, over in minutes, that is when vodka did not have the final word.

"I will come to your apartment tonight," she pleaded. "I promise. Just not here, not now."

Kastianich ignored her pleas, took her hand and shoved it into his crotch, and then stopped, a look of frozen terror on his face. He backed away.

Bell watched, her mouth agape.

Palms tight against his ears, the Russian stumbled, his gait halting and unsteady. He could barely navigate the distance from Bell's lab bench to the glass cabinets across the room.

"What are these?" he asked, lifting a plastic compartment-tray from a shelf. "From where do they come?"

Bell watched horrified as Kastianich traced his finger across the piece of odd-shaped granite. She held her breath, afraid that in his current state he would drop the priceless artifact onto the ceramic tile. "I told you, Dimitri, they're part of a shipment that arrived last week. Please. Be careful. Here, let me have it."

"You say it came last week and you told me so? No. You said to me no such thing," he snapped at her, not remembering what she'd said to him seconds before.

"Please, Dimitri, I've been sorting and preparing them for carbon dating and chemical analysis. I have the work order you signed in my desk. They're ordinary pieces of pottery, parts of oil lamps, water pitchers, and earthen plates."

Kastianich held the stone close to his eye; he blinked several times and moved the artifact back and forth trying to focus.

"This is not pottery," he said, lifting the triangular shaped stone with its rounded top.

Bell held her breath again. The pig had the prize, her prize, in his shaky fingers, the most important historical artifact on the planet according to Richter. Twice she gasped when the fragile stone slipped, almost falling to the floor.

"I do not feel so good," he mumbled again, gagging as waves of nausea rolled over him.

She took the stone from his trembling fingers. "You are right, Dimitri, it is not pottery," she said, humoring him.

Struggling to stay on his feet, Kastianich snatched the sample from Bell and slid it under the microscope, but no matter how many times he twirled the focusing knob the image remained blurred.

"You must look for me," he said. "I also do not see so good," he added, moving behind her.

Bell felt his crotch against her lower back. He was flaccid. She kept her eyes on the microscope lens. Odd shapes and bands of color came into focus. Gold flecks on the stone's surface fluoresced. "Here," she said. "You look."

Beads of sweat on Kastianich's neck coalesced into larger droplets. One at a time they rolled down his neck and disappeared into his shirt collar. The small scratch where she'd run the needle had turned red. Tiny drops of blood made a prominent stain. His breathing, more labored, now came in gasps. He tore at the collar, popping a row of buttons on the sweat-drenched garment.

Kastianich stood up, turned and faced her. Broken blood vessels wormed through the sclera of both his eyes, their pupils wide open, unresponsive to the room's bright fluorescent lighting. He reached for her, grasping, trying to maintain his balance.

Both arms outstretched, Kastianich stumbled headlong into the glass cabinet. Bell, unable to move, stared in horror. Whatever was in that ring Richter gave her, Kastianich's violent reaction to the poison made her cringe.

Thin cracks appeared in the glass followed by spider-like veins spreading down and sideways before cracking. Hundreds of jagged glass beads crashed to the laboratory floor.

Bell's attention went to the door. For the first time, she realized that people were banging their fists. She needed a plausible story, and fast.

First inside was a fellow intern, Faruq Abdalla, a six-foot-tall Egyptian grad student from Cairo University. He took one step into the room, stopped, and stared at Bell's open blouse and disheveled hair. She turned away, her back to the incoming crowd, and straightened her clothing. People stormed in behind Abdalla, gawking at the mayhem.

Faruq Abdalla focused on the broken glass strewn across the floor, and then at Kastianich's body face down, sprawled under a table.

"He… he attacked me, Faruq." Bell's eyes welled up and she began to sob.

CHAPTER TWO

FBI agent Ted Lansing, asleep, stirred at the ringtone coming from a cell phone. Groggy and jet-lagged from a long overnight flight from Hawaii, his eyes remained closed as he reached for the nightstand, sweeping an iPhone into his palm.

"Lansing," he mumbled. There was no response. It continued to ring. He opened one eye and squinted, trying to focus on the readout. He felt for his reading glasses, more and more a necessity since he'd turned forty-five. It wasn't his phone making the noise. His head dropped back onto the pillow. "It's for you, Felicia," he whispered across the bed. The ringtone continued. "Felicia?" he said louder.

Bare-chested, Lansing sat up. His wife of two weeks, or was it twenty years, was not in bed. He could hear the sound of running water coming from the bathroom. He slid an arm across to her side. The sheets felt warm. He grabbed the ringing cell phone and hit receive.

"I'm sorry to wake you so early on your first day back director, but..."

Lansing recognized the voice, Pearly Weaver, Felicia's assistant. "I'm sorry to wake you, Director Albreda, but..."

"No, I'm sorry, Miss Weaver, it's Ted. The director is in the shower. We lost track of time this morning."

"Oh, I am so sorry, sir. I apologize. It's almost nine o'clock, and by the way, congratulations to you both—a second wedding, getting remarried on a starlit beach on Maui, sooo romantic. When did you get in?"

"Last night—late. We landed after 1:00 a.m."

"Again, I'm so sorry to wake you but I need to speak with the director. It's urgent."

Aren't FBI matters always urgent? Lansing thought. He slid out of bed, knocked once on the bathroom door and went inside.

Felicia Albreda, forty-two-years old, stepped naked from the smoked glass enclosure. She draped a bath towel around her as water droplets beaded over her toned body and glowing bronzed shoulders. Wet, limp hair clung to her face. Lansing handed her the phone thinking to himself how beautiful she looked, and how lucky he was to have his old life back.

Albreda listened for several seconds before motioning for a pad and pen, all the while repeating, "uh-huh... got it..." and then, "He will be there in an hour."

Lansing pulled her against his bare chest and felt her tight, muscular body, the result of an almost fanatical routine every morning in the Hoover building's workout facility. He kissed her on the neck. "That *me* you just volunteered is me—right?"

"Afraid so, Teddy. Duty calls—honeymoon's officially over."

He admitted to himself that this time, this honeymoon, had been a hell of a lot better than their first one, over twenty years ago.

She kissed his cheek, pulled away, let the towel fall and walked naked into the bedroom as he watched her hips sway from side to side, her calves tightening with every step.

"Do you remember that no-tell motel outside Annapolis," Lansing said following her to the bedroom. "The Rendezvous something, I think?

"Oh, yes, I remember they spelled it Randy-Views. How could I ever forget that place? The mattress sagged to the floor underneath us, and that horrible rock band partied all night in the next room." Without turning, she laughed. "If memory serves, Agent Lansing, you weren't much in the mood for sleep that night anyway."

She reached into an armoire drawer, pulled out a pair of white panties and stepped into them.

Lansing spun her around. "Yep, young and stupid, that was us, babe. Why'd we ever get divorced?"

She gave him a sly look. "Mmmm, I wonder? What was her name again? Or is that their names?"

"Yeah, but I was really cute back then. Right?"

"Don't press your luck lover boy."

They both laughed. When his hand slid up her back she closed her eyes before kissing him sensually, their tongues intertwined.

Lansing winked. "Touché, c'mon, let's crawl back into bed. By my calculations, we're still on our honeymoon for another twelve hours."

"Sorry Teddy, but you have to get over to the Smithsonian, and I need to get to my office. There's been an incident. Details are sketchy, but Walters," she said, referring to the director of the FBI, "received a call from State. Does the name Kastianich mean anything to you?"

"Yeah, isn't he that that Russian, a scientist or something. I remember reading about him. Speculation had him as ex-KGB."

"Alleged KGB," Albreda said. "We could never pin anything on him."

"Okay, alleged. So, sue me. I didn't get that memo. He's that ex, I mean alleged ex, KGB agent who landed some big job at the Smithsonian—curator of something or other."

"Antiquities, but close enough—yes, the very same."

Lansing pulled on a pair of dark gray slacks. "What'd he do?"

"He's dead, possibly murdered. Metro is on the scene, and they already have a person of interest. The lead detective is named Arlen Drew. He's waiting for you."

"If it's Metro's case, why are we involved?"

"The usual, Ted. Politics. The Russian ambassador called the White House, the White House called State, who called the AG, who called the director who…"

"Right." He laughed. "I got it. Kastianich was a VIP."

Since Lansing's transfer to Washington from the New York Office, a promotion from special agent, he now headed a new division, Special Crimes, headquartered out of the Hoover Building in DC. The team of agents for the new division had been selected from across the country. Lansing's long-time partner, Jennifer Fallana, promoted to special agent in charge, had been transferred to the San Francisco office after they broke up a conspiracy plot to blow up the national mall. He planned on selecting a new partner from the newly assembled team, but so far, no perfect fits. Felicia was on him to make a choice.

Lansing missed nothing about his once out-of-control bachelor life in Manhattan after the divorce. A new intimacy between him and Felicia felt right this time, and reconnecting with their son, Joshua, now a graduate student in aeronautic engineering at MIT, was the icing on his cake. His hours were more regular now, or as regular as an agent who still did considerable amounts of fieldwork could be regular. Ted Lansing, old school, and hands-on, hated being cooped up in an office if he could help it.

The transfer to Washington came with a significant bump in both pay and grade, and whenever discussions about possible candidates for assistant director level promotions came up, the name Theodore Lansing always sat atop a very short list. Felicia swore she had nothing to do with it.

Chapter Three

Lansing entered the Smithsonian's castle building through an arched entrance on Jefferson Drive near the National Mall between the Capitol and the Washington Monument. He made his way to the South Hall's central rotunda where a uniformed guard directed him to a bank of employee elevators. Two floors down he exited onto a narrow corridor. A sign affixed to the wall identified the Antiquities Division with an arrow pointing down a winding hallway.

At the first bend, Lansing heard voices, loud and confrontational, all shouting at once. He moved to investigate, stopping in front of a door with an opaque, glass panel marked *Staff*. Whoever was inside arguing, a male and a female kept repeating one name over and over— Gretchen. Lansing opened the door a few inches and eavesdropped.

The female voice shouted, "Get real, Faruq. Who else but that Ivy League bitch could have, or would have done it? And who had better motive? She was in the damn lab alone with him for God's sake. And, don't tell me you don't know what was going on in there. Hell, you know it, we all knew."

The best Lansing could tell from the accusations, and whomever this Gretchen person was, she'd spent a lot of her time screwing somebody's brains out, and at least according to the speaker got what she deserved and then killed her boss in a fit of rage.

"Yes, she is a conniving little opportunist," the male voice said. "But murder? No way. I don't buy it." The voice spoke in flawless English with an accented flair, British, Lansing thought, but not quite.

"Give me a break, Faruq." The female was speaking again. "That sneaky little bitch is crazy. Do you think she really believed Dimitri wanted anything more than a piece of ass? She was a summer diversion for Christ's sake! She was all over him from day one."

"My point exactly," the Faruq character interrupted. "Why kill a goose that's about to lay a golden egg?"

"I'll tell you why, because it's our last day, and he finally blew her off. Maybe he told her she wasn't getting that fellowship and she freaked. Maybe the little slut believed that by fucking the disgusting letch he'd give her one of the positions out of love, or out of pity—who the hell knows what goes on in that devious brain of hers? I always thought there was something odd about her. She was never in the running. I knew it, you knew it, and so did every other intern. The girl is a fucking idiot! I know more archeology in my pinky finger than she knows in her entire brain."

Lansing opened the door enough to peek in, to get a look at who was speaking, making lurid accusations one after the other. The girl, he guessed, couldn't be more than twenty with short dark hair and large breasts. She had on a tartan kilt with green tights, and a sleeveless blouse.

Lansing nodded to her, closed the door and continued down the hall. He took his cell phone from a pocket and whispered into a recording app, "Gretchen? Faruq? Plus, one zaftig brunette. ID ASAP." At a door marked *Director of Antiquities - D. Kastianich, Ph.D.*, Lansing grabbed the knob and went inside.

In the center of the room, an African American man in a tweed sports coat and jeans was making copious notes in a small notebook. Lansing assumed he was the Metro detective Felicia had mentioned.

Clean-shaven with thinning hair, he looked to be in his mid-thirties, at least ten years younger than Lansing. Even in his cop-clichéd, baggy sports coat, it was clear this detective was in good shape. Instinctively, Lansing's hand went to his own mid-section. He definitely needed to put more time in at the gym.

"Arlen Drew?" he asked.

The detective nodded.

Taller than Lansing's six feet, Arlen Drew's casual blue knit shirt reminded him of detectives out of Metro and the NYPD he'd worked with before, and he wondered if dressing down was now a job requirement.

"It's Detective Drew," he said. "My chief said to expect you. You're Lansing, right? FBI?"

Lansing showed his ID. "What do you have so far, Detective?" he said, his tone all business.

Drew opened his notebook. "I've got a dead Russian named Kastianich. He ran the place. I also have a hysterical girl, maybe in her twenties, name is Gretchen Bell. I've got her cooling her heels in a conference room down the hall. Best I could get out of her so far is that she was in a lab with Kastianich when he just up, collapsed and died—her words."

Lansing moved a chair in front of Kastianich's desk and sat down. "Any signs of foul play?" he asked.

"Hard to say," Drew answered. "The lab is a mess, something sure happened, but without forensics, it's too soon to tell what. Right now all I have is a he said-she said, and he's dead."

"Tell me about those interns down the hall. When I passed they were giving each other their candid opinions on what happened, and who's responsible. And by the way, where is the victim's body? I need to have a look."

"I got to tell you, Lansing, I'm not even sure we have a crime scene yet. Despite the fact that there are a million things in that lab, potential weapons, the forensic team's initial examination showed no certain signs of foul play on the victim's body. He wasn't shot or stabbed, or bludgeoned with some heavy object."

"Anything out of the ordinary when you interviewed the Bell girl?" said Lansing.

Drew thought for a second. "No, except that she cries a lot. Strange."

"Strange, how so?"

"Didn't sound genuine."

"Why not?"

"Listen, Lansing, I've been questioning murder suspects for over five years now. I get a pretty good read on people. Believe me when I tell you the girl is hiding something."

It was not Drew's words that made the veteran FBI agent bristle, but his tone. Lansing was not accustomed to his judgment being questioned, especially by local law enforcement, but from experience, he knew that little would be gained by antagonizing the locals. "Sorry, Detective, but I had to ask. Where is the victim?"

"The M.E. has him at the morgue, they're waiting on someone from the Russian embassy before they can start a formal autopsy. The Russians I'm told were quite adamant about it."

"Did this Kastianich have diplomatic status?"

"I don't think so," Drew answered. He turned to a uniformed officer near the door. "Carson, go check Kastianich's diplomatic status for me."

***

Gretchen Bell sat curled up on a leather couch in a conference room. Arms wrapped tight around her chest, the Harvard graduate student rocked back and forth. When she saw Lansing at the door, his

ID wallet flapped over a breast pocket of his suit jacket, she started to sob again, pleading. "I didn't do it, kill him… I swear to God I never touched him."

Lansing pulled a chair close, introduced himself and sat facing her.

"Gretchen Bell is it?"

The girl nodded between sobs.

Lansing sized her up making notes in his book—5'2", hair blonde, short, almost boyish, attractive. He noticed her clothing, disheveled, with a button missing on her blouse.

"Let me assure you, Miss Bell, nobody is accusing you of anything. I know you told it all to Detective Drew here, but, please, humor me." He placed a silver recorder on a coffee table. "I am going to record this interview if that is all right with you. Once more, what exactly happened this morning inside that locked laboratory?"

Through stifled cries, Bell repeated everything that transpired prior to her boss's death, artfully omitting anything about their summer-long affair or the Harvard ring still on her finger. The more Lansing listened, the more he knew that Drew might be right. Something about the way Gretchen Bell spoke was off. She cried at all the right times and on the correct cues, but something was wrong and he could not put his finger on it.

Lansing shut off his recorder and motioned to Drew. They stepped into the corridor. "I need to see the crime scene."

Drew led Lansing to the microscopy lab where he tore away yellow tape from across the door. "Metro CSI left everything in place," Drew said. "It's all precisely where they found it, except for Dr. Kastianich."

Lansing walked the room's perimeter with a digital camera. He snapped a dozen photographs from every angle before moving in close to the beads of glass scattered about. He took several more pictures from several different angles making verbal notes concerning the scatter patterns. He walked the room a second time photographing everything on exposed counter tops, table surfaces, and anything visible through the glass-front cabinets affixed to the walls.

Lansing focused attention on a rolling cart and a plastic tray with molded compartments. Each slot contained pieces of what appeared to be shards of old pottery.

"Before you got here, Lansing, Bell told me something about things being out of place, but I'm not sure what she meant. As soon as she said it though, she clammed up, claimed it wasn't important. I think she lied."

Lansing slipped on a pair of surgical gloves and lifted each shard from its compartment in the tray.

Drew opened his notebook. "The crime scene team cataloged everything in the lab." He flipped several pages. "Nothing jumped out at them either. The vic didn't have a mark on him, except for a small scratch on his neck."

"You mean except for being dead." Lansing laughed. "I'm bringing one of our forensic units in. Those interns down the hall know a hell of a lot more than they're willing to share. After the autopsy, we'll know for certain if we have a crime scene here or not. For all I know, the poor bastard could have keeled over and croaked from a damn heart attack or a stroke. How old was he anyway?"

Drew looked at his notes again. "Late forties, but a stroke or a heart attack are definite possibilities. First responders, DC EMTs, noted Kastianich as grossly overweight, and everyone I've questioned pretty much described him as a heavy smoker and a heavy drinker—expensive Russian vodka his drug of choice according to…" Drew flipped to a new page. "An intern named Faruq Abdalla."

"Faruq?" Lansing said. "He's the one I heard defending Bell when I first came in?"

"Yes," Drew answered, "the very same, and it wouldn't be the first time a trifecta of tobacco, food, and booze put someone into the ground before his time, but yes, that Faruq character, Egyptian I think, I don't trust him."

Lansing scanned the glass beads scattered on the floor, focusing his gaze on a shattered microscope. "Something violent sure as hell happened."

"Like I said, Lansing, except for the fact that Kastianich is dead, there was not a mark on him."

Lansing started for the door. "None of those interns can leave DC, detective."

"That may be a problem," Drew said. "Keeping them in Washington I mean. Today was supposed to be their last. They're all scheduled to leave by tomorrow night or the day after—LA, Boston, Cairo, London—who knows where else?"

"Break it gently, detective. Nobody is going anywhere. At least not until we have a confirmed COD on our dead professor."

CHAPTER FOUR

Outdoor tables set with long picnic benches wet from a mid-morning shower sat empty at a small cafe on Berlin's *Dirksenstrasse*. Out of habit, Hans Richter parked his Mercedes across the street and waited. He peered up at an apartment building diagonally across the wide avenue and scanned a row of balconies overlooking the restaurant. Nothing out of the ordinary caught his eye, but suspicion and paranoia did not die easily for the former East German operative now in the employ of the FSB, Vladimir Putin's latest incarnation of the KGB.

He scanned a slip of paper in his palm—"wooden tables, long picnic benches, an elevated railroad track across the street." It was the right place, but where was his contact? Richter leaned back into the plush leather seat and checked his watch for a third time.

Thirty minutes later, his contact still a no show, Richter sent a text. *"No sign yet. It is now… 1:00 p.m."*

About to pull away, he glanced into his rear-view mirror. A black and white Ducati motorcycle was speeding toward him. The rider stopped in front of the cafe, dismounted and set the kickstand. Richter pointed his cell phone camera in the rider's direction and snapped off several photographs.

The rider, a woman, looked familiar. Tall, angular and bony, she wore a black leather biker's jacket with multiple zippers and pockets, and skn tight leather motorcycle pants. On her head, a blue helmet with an opaque visor hid the woman's face.

Richter enlarged the phone image. From her body language and movement, he recognized her.

The woman looked around for several seconds, glanced up and down both sides of the street, and removed her helmet. Richter squinted for a better look. When the rider shook out a head of salt and pepper hair, it fell to mid-cheek with pageboy bangs; very different from what he remembered when they'd last met, more than twenty years before.

Irina Kazakov, Russian linguist, was a world-renowned expert in biblical archeology with PhDs from Oxford and Harvard. Richter first met her in Berlin. His Russian handlers at the time set up the introduction. She'd been his mark.

Richter shuddered, remembering how they ordered him to seduce her, and secure a Matisse oil painting expropriated from the Hermitage at St. Petersburg. He'd spent three days and three nights trying to seduce her in a posh Moscow hotel, complete with room service, pounds of Beluga caviar, French champagne, and sex, a lot of sex. It got him nothing but a huge hotel bill and dismissal from the case. Kazakov played him, something Hans Richter did not learn for weeks and never forgot. A scar on his cheek fro Kazakov's knife reminded him every day. He still harbored a ill feelings even after twenty years.

Richter observed her for several minutes until a waiter approached the table. He exited his car and started across *Dirksenstrasse*.

Kazakov looked up as he approached. Without emotion, Richter lied, "It is good to see you again, Irina."

She nodded. "*Guter Tag Hans.* Yes, is *gut.*" Kazakov lied too.

Richter was certain that while he did not know whom to expect, she did. "Yes, it has been a long time," he answered.

"At least twenty years," she replied without making eye contact.

"*Ya*," he answered dispassionately. "We have much to speak about," he said. "There is a situation, a problem."

"What kind of problem?"

"Dimitri, he is dead."

If Richter expected a reaction, he did not get one. Kazakov and Kastianich were colleagues, friends for years, but from her voice inflection on hearing of his death, her affect was flat. "That is too bad," she said, again without making eye contact.

Richter evaluated her reaction. Yes, the bitch was cold but he was equally certain she already knew about the events in Washington.

He slid into a bench across from her. "There is something else you need to know."

He started to speak but stopped when the server returned with a pot of tea and remained, hovering, a pad and pencil in hand, waiting for Richter to order.

He scowled, and with the flick of his wrist gave the man a terse, "*Nichts für mich*—nothing for me."

He turned back to Kazakov. "As I was about to say, Irina…"

Her demeanor, already cold and distant, became even colder. "You will address me as *Frau Doktor*."

It took the German spy by surprise. *Arrogant bitch*, he thought, *nothing has changed*. He decided against a confrontation. He needed her and what she could bring to his mission. "Whatever you wish," he answered. "From what I have learned, *Frau Doktor*," he said, stressing doktor for affect, "Dimitri was killed as he was about to acquire…" He stopped, and looked behind him at a couple sitting at a nearby table. "That thing he was supposed to secure. I am told you know of what I speak."

Kazakov leaned toward him and whispered, "You do know who has it now Do you not?"

Richter remained silent. He marveled at her self-control, knowing she knew more than she was willing or able to say.

Slowly, with measured words, Kazakov whispered, "The mate to that piece in Washington awaits my arrival in Rome, without it I cannot proceed. If I were you, Hans, I would go to Washington at once and recover the second artifact."

Richter grinned, the kind of grin that says you are a lying bitch. "If one did not know better, *Frau Doktor*, one might think you want to send me on a fool's errand while you go off to Rome by yourself. How do I know that you do not already have the Washington artifact?"

"Do as you wish, Hans, it is no matter to me."

Kazakov smiled inwardly. She had learned what she needed. Richter was not yet aware that Faruq Abdalla had lifted the stone before the police arrived at the Smithsonian. His coded text message arrived with a single word, *safe*.

Richter slid from the bench, crossed the street and got back into the Mercedes. He punched a number into his cell phone. "*Da*," said a voice in Russian.

"A waste of time. She was useless and I do not trust her," Richter said. "But I must go to see for myself. Book me on the next flight out of Berlin to Washington DC."

Kazakov remained at the table, sipping tea, waiting for Richter to drive away before she took out her own cell phone. "I bought us some time. The filthy German will go to Washington—I am certain of it. I leave for Rome in the morning. Send someone to Washington to secure the second artifact. Faruq Abdalla is your contact."

Chapter Five

Father Antonio DeLarussa felt his cell phone vibrating in the pocket of his cassock. Anxious, he'd waited days for the call. He saw the readout and smiled. It was Faruq at last.

"It is me, Father," said a voice, with an English accent tinged with Egyptian Arabic.

"Please tell me you are safe. When you did not arrive in Jerusalem, I was all worried."

"I am well, Father, but something has happened, something most unfortunate."

"What has happened, my son?"

"Kastianich was murdered."

DeLarussa held his breath. "Oh, dear Jesus, tell me you have it."

"Yes, Father, I do. Someone got to it before me, but in the chaos of Dimitri's murder I recovered it and removed it from the Smithsonian lab. It is safe now."

Concerned there were others chasing the relic, DeLarussa blurted, "Do you know who first took it?"

"Yes, Father. There is a woman here, a fellow intern, I believe she stole it, and then hid it in plain sight."

DeLarussa waited several seconds, mulling over what needed to be done, what could be done.

"Listen to me," said the priest. "I was scheduled to leave Jerusalem tomorrow and return to Rome. I am to meet a woman there, an expert in biblical archeology. She knows where the second artifact is. With both stones, we can at last begin the search."

"How do I get the artifacts out of the country?" Abdalla asked.

"Remain where right where you are fr now," DeLarussa said. "I will come to Washington. It will be easier for a priest to carry it through security."

"I could not leave if I wanted to. The American authorities have named me a person of interest in Dimitri Kastianich's death. Is it possible to have the Vatican intercede on my behalf?"

Father DeLarussa moved into a doorway on the street. "No, that is not possile. Forgive me, but I must ask. Did you…"

"No, no, of course not, Father. I would never do such a thing—commit murder, a mortal sin against God. You taught me better."

DeLarussa, relieved, took a long deep breath. "It is not prudent for the Holy See to make inquiries at this time, not with Dimitri Kastianich dead under suspicious circumstances. It would send warning signals to the wrong people. For now, remain in Washington, but say nothing to anyone."

"But the FBI, Father."

"Speak to no one, Faruq, especially the FBI."

DeLarussa reached the front entrance of St. Bartholomew Church, walked up two concrete steps and entered the sanctuary. He hurried down the center nave to the altar rail, knelt, made the sign of the cross and quickly rose. At a table of votive candles set at the foot of St. Bartholomew's statue, DeLarussa lifted a wax taper, lit a candle and offered a prayer petitioning Saint Bartholomew, a martyred disciple of Jesus, to intercede.

The priest turned At the sound of footstep and nodded to an elderly cleric coming toward him. "*Buongiorno Monsignore*," he said, "I have an urgent request. I must leave Jerusalem tomorrow."

"Are you returning to Rome? It has been several years."

"No, *Monsignore*, I go to Washington."

"America? Why? Has something happened to Faruq?"

"No, *Monsignore*, the boy is well, but something has happened."

"Please, Antonio, assure me it has nothing to do with the death of that horrid Russian archeologist?"

DeLarussa said nothing.

Chapter Six

A ntonio DeLarussa, wearing a cheap, black suit, sans Roman collar, nursed a glass of red wine as the El Al 747 made its way across the Atlantic. His clothing, dated, was the only non-clerical garb he owned, already out of fashion when he bought it ten years ago. The phone call from Washington so unnerved him that he had little time to prepare or purchase more modern apparel.

DeLarussa flew coach thinking it would draw less attention than a first-class ticket, but from the second the plane took off the fifty-year-old priest knew booking the crowded coach section had been a mistake. He wanted peace and quiet, time to think and plan what he would do in Washington, but a woman sitting next to him never stopped bending his talking.

The woman, Gertrude Singer, lived in Tel Aviv. She was on her way to a grandson's Bar Mitzvah in Maryland, or was it Virginia? He paid little attention to what the insufferable woman said.

He introduced himself as Antonio, a silver merchant from Jerusalem. The woman reminded him of his own mother, right down to a quaint laugh that rose and fell a few octaves at the end of every sentence. She never put down her knitting and appeared nervous about flying. She kept herself well lubricated through the entire flight with white wine in small bottles, insisting DeLarussa join her—her and toast her grandson.

She droned on endlessly about her the boy's big day, but interspersed in her enthusiasm were seemingly innocuous questions asking details about his visit to Washington. She asked him if he had family there, where he was staying and for how long. After his fourth glass of Chablis, DeLarussa, thankfully, dozed off—a two-hour respite.

By the time they landed in DC Father Antonio DeLarussa knew more about Gertrude Singer than he ever wanted or needed to know, and she knew a great deal about him as well. Once during the flight, she'd called him Father. DeLarussa, with a considerable amount of wine still clouding his head, could not remember if he'd mentioned the priesthood. He dismissed the idea as paranoia.

DeLarussa walked down the jet-way at Washington's Reagan National. He pulled a carry-on bag down the international concourse eying his reflection in shop windows and understood why Mrs. Singer thought he was a priest. *Sweet Jesus, I look like a priest, even without the damn collar.*

He stopped at a Brooks Brothers store on the airport's main promenade where he overpaid for a knit golf shirt with a small alligator logo on the breast and a pair of khaki slacks that almost fit.

Outside the terminal, Washington oppressive summer heat, heavy air, and humidity descended over him like a pawl. Cars and buses, their horns blaring, jockeyed for positions at the curb. Limos with diplomatic plates idled in a coned off section and liveried chauffeurs held printed placards scanning the crowds exiting the terminal. An acrid smell of exhaust fumes permeated everything. In a minute, DeLarussa's new shirt was soaked through with sweat and clinging to his clammy skin.

DeLarussa heard a voice from inside a dark green Jetta stopped along the curb in front of him. "Antonio. Over here, Father! Quickly, get in."

DeLarussa ducked low to see the driver's face. "Thank God, Faruq. It is you. I am so glad that..."

The driver cut him off. "Yes, Father. It is me. Please hurry. I believe that I was followed."

DeLarussa settled into the front seat, luxuriating in the Jetta's air conditioning. "Followed?" he said, alarmed. "How is that possible? I told no one I was coming."

"No one, Father?" the driver asked.

"Only *Monsignore* Allegretti. He used the church's credit card to book my flight."

Is it possible someone have monitored the credit card transaction?

Faruq Abdalla took the first airport exit onto the George Washington Memorial Parkway. Immediately he spotted a silver, late model SUV in his rear-view mirror. Each time he changed lanes, sped up or slowed down it was still there, matching his every move.

Abdalla made another rapid lane change; he wove in and out of line in the heavy afternoon traffic. The Jetta swerved around slower moving vehicles, Abdalla's eyes looked into the mirror and back to the road. The silver SUV, ten cars behind him, stayed right there. It continued to maintain the distance between them, not closing the space.

DeLarussa saw the change in Abdalla's demeanor—an intense look of concentration, his body rigid, on high alert. Both hands gripped the steering wheel—each dangerous maneuver smooth and calculated, executed as if driving like this was second nature.

"What is happening?" DeLarussa said, panic now in his voice. He turned and looked back through the rear window and began to speak, but Abdalla, oblivious, remained in a different place. He took the Volkswagen into the far right-hand lane. Ahead of them an overhead sign read, *Exit - Jefferson Davis Highway - Two Miles*.

Abdalla removed a black automatic handgun from his belt and placed it in the center console. He ignored DeLarussa's pleas to slow down. They sped past a pickup loaded down with scrap metal. Five cars behind him the tail moved back into line. Ahead, another overhead sign read, *Exit – Quarter Mile*.

Abdalla accelerated. The distance between him and the nearest trailing vehicle increased. Without warning, he swerved right, cutting across two lanes of traffic. Father DeLarussa heard the screech of tires as drivers behind them slammed their brakes to avoid a pileup. The Jetta cornered, skidding sideways onto the exit ramp. The trailing SUV, boxed in, too close to react, shot by them.

DeLarussa's entire body started to shake. He reached for the rosary beads in his pocket and stared across the seat, incredulous. "What is happening Faruq? You are going to get us both killed."

Traffic behind them showed no sign of their pursuers. Abdalla slowed, eased left and passed a line of slower moving cars. Relieved, he placed the handgun back into his belt.

A hundred yards behind the Jetta a non-descript, black sedan matched Abdalla's speed but remained far enough behind to go unnoticed. The driver pressed the call button on his steering wheel. One ring and a woman's voice came on. "Target acquired. He outmaneuvered our Russian friends."

"We suspected as much," the woman answered in English with an Israeli accent. "We knew the boy was good."

"He may have lost the Russians, but I have him in my sights now."

"Unless you are certain do not engage at this time. We know where he goes."

"I copy that, Aviya." The Israeli agent signed off.

DeLarussa watched his young protégé's furtive glances into the side mirror every few seconds. Between the gun secure in Abdalla's belt and his maniacal driving, the priest remained silent, speechless, his throat parched, not knowing this young man he'd trusted. The young man he'd raised since the boy was twelve.

Faruq entered a cloverleaf and merged onto a limited access roadway. The speedometer again climbed and the priest,s fingers gripped the center console, his knuckles white.

Delarussa could not help but gawk at the passing landscape he'd only seen in books and on television. As the Jetta crossed the Potomac at the 14th Street Bridge Washington's alabaster monuments came into view on the National Mall. In the distance, the Washington Monument towered above everything, the Lincoln Memorial to their left.

Abdalla speds past the wrought iron fence that surrounded the south lawn of the White House, continued north onto Massachusetts Avenue, and then to Dupont Circle. He turned onto a quiet residential street lined with posh townhomes.

"We are here, Father," Abdalla said, stopping in front of a brownstone with a concrete stoop leading up to a fancy oak door painted bright red.

The black sedan following them continued past the tony house and parked fifty yards up the street. "Quarry has landed," the driver said to a faceless voice on the other end of his cell phone. "I can do it now," he said.

"No," came a sharp reply. "We know where he is. You can take your time, plan, do it with less risk. We have no positive intel that it is there someplace in the house."

CHAPTER SEVEN

Hans Richter made his way along the cobblestones of the river-walk. He stopped, leaned over a retaining wall and stared into the black water of the Moskva River. He lit a *Sobranie*, placed it between his lips and took a long drag. Spitting, he flipped the horrid tasting Russian cigarette into the fast-moving current.

The German operative now working for Russia's FSB glanced first at his wristwatch, and then turned and looked up into a reddening afternoon sky. The orange ball of a setting sun lit the gold onion-dome of a nearby church. It appeared to be surrounded by a halo. In the far distance, the Kremlin's spires glowed. A chill wind blew off the water forcing Richter to reach for his coat collar and pull it tight. Even though still officially summer, it portended the coming Russian winter. Ironic, Richter thought.

Curious and more than a little nervous about why he'd been summoned back to Moscow instead of proceeding on to Washington from Berlin, Richter felt uneasy. Being summoned in the middle of a mission was never a good thing. Well past the age when most operatives were either retired or dead, out of habit he felt for the gun in his shoulder holster.

Until this assignment to recover the stone artifacts came along, his Russian handlers hadn't called upon his unique skill set in over two years. His kind of work, specialized, seldom came up any more in a world where tact and diplomacy replaced brute force—tact and diplomacy were talents Richter possessed in very small doses. He told himself that he had not reached the age of sixty-three by not being paranoid—a job requirement in his line of work.

A taller, much younger man in an expensive camelhair topcoat, carrying a thin leather briefcase, came toward him. They made eye contact as the younger man passed. Richter nodded. Ten meters farther down the river-walk the man in the topcoat stopped, turned and looked out at the dark water. "I believe winter comes early this year."

Richter moved to the wall, his eyes straight ahead. "Yes," he said. "Is it a good time to be in Crimea. Are you Anton?"

The man nodded. "Come, Hans. Walk with me."

They moved along the river until the man in the camel hair coat pointed to an empty bench, and in Russian, said. "*Sidet.*" Sit.

Richter watched him place the briefcase on his lap, open it and remove a single sheet of paper.

"What is that?" Richter asked.

"I was hoping you could tell me," the man answered, never turning in Richter's direction.

The German looked at it for several seconds. "It appears to be a map or at least a copy of a map."

After several more seconds, his finger began to trace the contour of shapes displayed on the chart. "This is the Gulf of Aqaba and here is the Gulf of Suez, which makes the land mass between them the Sinai Peninsula. A child of ten would recognize it."

When he looked up the man was smiling. "Excellent."

Richter felt relief until he spoke again.

"I told them you were the right person for this assignment." His voice dripped sarcasm. "So smart… you can even recognize the Sinai from a crudely drawn map."

Richter ignored his mocking tone. "And who are they?" He tried to mask his uneasiness with a false show of bravado. "Any idiot could recognize those land formations."

"Yes, that is true, and you appear to be just such an idiot. Be careful with your questions, Herr Richter. Who they are is not important. You have not exactly ingratiated yourself with the Kremlin. Work is work. Do you not agree?"

Richter nodded.

"Can you read any of the writing on the map?"

Richter stared at the paper again. "No. I do not even recognize the alphabet. What language is it?"

"That is what we need you to find out," he said. "Can you do it?"

"Possibly, but I first need to locate an old colleague from my Stasi days."

"You refer to Irina Kazakov I presume?"

Not sure what the Russians knew about his meeting with Irina Kazakov in Berlin, he feigned surprise but managed to keep his nerves in check. He understood why he alone had been selected for this mission, and why he'd been sent to Berlin. It was the woman—that bitch, Irina Kazakov.

"Yes, I refer to Kazakov. You met with her in Berlin, did you not? Why do you lie?"

They knew.

Irina Kazakov's extensive translations of the Dead Sea Scrolls had garnered her enough gravitas to be welcomed by the Vatican as a visiting scholar with unfettered access to its massive library and its collection of rare manuscripts.

"Listen to me, Hans, and listen well. We have learned that Irina Kazakov is already on her way to Rome. She works with an old priest named Angelico. He works in a little known and clandestine workshop in the catacombs below Saint Peter's Basilica."

That lying bitch, Richter thought. *I knew she wanted to send me on a wild goose chase.* He grew bolder.

"Tell me, how do you come to know of Irina Kazakov's current whereabouts?"

"That is not important. What is important is that you learn on what she is working."

"I am listening," said Richter, still not sure where the conversation was headed.

"She and that old priest are researching a second stone artifact."

Richter played the ignorance card. "And what is the nature of this second artifact?"

"Like the one in Washington it is made of stone, granite, ten, maybe fifteen centimeters long by thirty centimeters wide. We are not certain about the measurements because no one in the Kremlin has yet seen it."

"So, you are sending me to Rome for a piece of old stone?"

The Russian handler nodded. "Precisely. You are a fast learner my German friend."

"Your cryptic talk is not helpful," said Richter. "I asked what is so special about this second artifact?"

"It is believed by some that the stone she and Angelico are researching is a piece of…" He stopped, looking for the right words, almost embarrassed to say them aloud. "The original tablets."

Richter laughed, loud and long. "I beg your pardon, but did I hear correctly? It sounded like you said tablets. What kind of tablets? Aspirin tablets?" Richter laughed out loud, stopping abruptly when he saw the man's scowl. He was serious.

Composing himself, Richter blurted, "Please tell me that when you say the original tablets you do not refer to the original Hebrew Commandments."

When he got no reply, it evoked another laugh. "You are serious!"

"Oh, I am, Hans, as serious as cancer. There are those in my government, fools though they may be, who believe there is great power in the tablets of the Jewish Law."

"They are delusional. They want me in Rome to locate Irina Kazakov and steal the stone tablets of the original Ten Commandments? Are you insane? This is Russia. Who believes in such nonsense?"

"No one in my government truly believes it. It is a ruse. You are going to retrieve something far more valuable to us. Buried somewhere in the Sinai is a canister containing something we left there over forty years ago. It was entrusted for safekeeping to a Greek Orthodox priest named Petrakis. We have paid him handsomely for forty years."

"I do not see the problem," Richter said.

"The problem is that this priest, Petrakis, died a year ago without revealing where he put the damn canister that belongs to us."

"What do these stone artifacts have to do with a canister hidden by an old priest?"

"They are the key to finding where Petrakis stashed the damn thing. I assure you, Herr Richter, there are more than a few powerful men within my government who are serious, dead serious, about the matter. That is why we meet here by this *chert vozmi,* goddamn river instead of in my office at the Kremlin. But it is not to Rome that you are going. You go to Washington."

"Why to Washington?" Richter asked, knowing full well why. It had something to do with Dimitri Kastianich's death and Irina Kazakov.

"There is a second stone artifact, very much like the one in Rome that Kazakov seeks," the Anton said. "Without it, she cannot proceed. Are you familiar with the name Kastianich?"

Tell me something I do not already know, Richter thought. He did everything he could to contain his composure and not show his true contempt for his Russian superiors. Whoever this Anton person was, Richter was just as certain he had no idea that he'd been active on this case for months and remained silent. The Russians, obviously, still did not talk to each other. Nothing had changed since the Cold War ended. Everyone was still paranoid. He decided to play along.

"Yes, I know of this Kastianich."

Anton produced several 8 x 10 inch black and white photographs. "These are graduate students who arrived in Washington for summer internships at the Smithsonian Institution."

On the back of each picture, short bios of the candidates contained names, ages, and the schools they attended along with other personal data.

Richter flipped through them, stopping for several seconds at the picture of a young woman in her early twenties. On the back, it said, *Gretchen Bell, 22, Harvard University*. Her address and telephone number were both listed.

"I thought that face would get your attention."

A broad grin formed on Richter's face.

"Good. You do see the resemblance?" said Anton.

Richter could barely contain himself.

"Uncanny, do you not agree?" the Russian said.

Richter closed his eyes. *Gretchen Bell my German ass*, he thought— *if this imbecile only knew.*

CHAPTER EIGHT

The short drive from the FBI building to the Medical Examiner's office took Ted Lansing down Pennsylvania Avenue, where he turned left on 4th Street SW and crossed the National Mall. His dashboard clock said 9:00, but his appointment with Dr. Robert Altschuller, Washington's Chief Medical Examiner, wasn't until 10:00. He pulled in front of a busy café near a Metro station, placed an FBI ID placard on the dashboard, got out and sat at an outdoor table. He opened a folder to review the notes he'd taken at the Smithsonian, highlighting questions about the dead curator he hoped Dr. Altschuller could answer.

A short stocky man in his early fifties, Frederick Altschuller greeted Lansing, acknowledging that he too shared concerns about the death of Dimitri Kastianich. The ME led him to an elevator leading to a state-of-the-art forensics lab situated off the morgue. Altschuller swiped his ID and then placed a fingertip on a biometric reader. The morgue's double door swung open. A receptionist at the front desk nodded to Altschuller. "Doctor Anapour is waiting in forensics, sir."

"Doctor Anapour?" Lansing asked.

Altschuller smiled. "Best kept secret around here, agent Lansing, I may be head honcho, the one with the title, but Raj, Doctor Rajeesh Anapour, is as good as a forensic investigator gets. Wait until you meet him but try not to show too much surprise."

"Surprise?" Lansing laughed. "Why? Does he have two heads?"

Altschuller laughed. "No, not two heads. Let's just say that surprise is the usual reaction I get whenever someone meets Rajeesh Anapour for the first time."

The morgue, adjacent to the forensics lab, looked to Lansing like every other autopsy room he'd ever seen, the kind he'd been in more times as an agent than he wanted to count. He hated the smell, a combination of embalming fluid and body decomp. Overly bright fluorescent lights gave the skin of the living a greenish hue, and made the cadavers laid out on stainless steel tables with their huge overhead surgical lights a sickly combination of greenish gray.

Rajeesh Anapour recognized the expression on Lansing's face, but before Lansing could say a word, he nodded, extended a hand.

"I'll be twenty in January."

"Was I that obvious?" Lansing said.

"Yes, but I'm used to it. I left Mumbai at twelve, completed my undergrad degree at Yale by fourteen, Med School at seventeen, residency in pathology at eighteen. I've been here a year.

"Impressive, but what can you tell me about the dead Russian?"

"All business I see," Anapour said. "I like that, Agent Lansing."

The young forensic physician pulled open a refrigerated crypt and slid out a tray with Kastianich's corpse. Two morgue assistants moved him to a stainless-steel autopsy table.

"Come have a look," Anapour said. "I'll walk you through it, but there's not much to see, externally that is."

Anapour reached above his head and brought a CCTV camera down close to Kastianich's right eye. "Look up at that screen," he said, pointing to a monitor above the table where Kastianich's eyeball was magnified eight times.

"See those faint red lines running through the sclera. They're petechial hemorrhages. In most instances, markers indicating COD as some type of asphyxiation, manual or chemical. On examination of the eye's interior I found signs of more extensive bleeding in both retinas."

"You said, in most instances, Doctor Anapour. Are you saying not this time? Why not asphyxiation?" Lansing asked.

Anapour picked up on Lansing's hesitation. "Even though the forensics suggests it as a cause of death, I do not believe he was manually asphyxiated."

"Interesting, what makes you so hesitant?" asked Lansing.

"First responders at the Smithsonian reported only one other person in the room with Kastianich. The only one with opportunity was a young woman, Gretchen Bell. This Bell woman I am told is barely 5'1" and weighs no more than a hundred to a hundred ten pounds."

"Yes, that is correct. I've met Miss Bell."

"Then you must realize there is no possible way someone her size could overcome a man the size of Kastianich, and without a weapon I might add. Coupled with no evidence of chemical asphyxiation, and not enough alcohol in his system to be overcome by a small woman, strangulation makes no sense here."

Anapour checked his notes again. "Except for the hemorrhaging in the optical capillaries, I found no other signs of asphyxiation."

"And what would they be?" Lansing asked. "Short and sweet. Please."

"Cell abnormalities. I would expect to see changes in the victim's respiratory tissues. They were absent in this case."

"Could he have choked on something?"

"No, he did not choke nor was he strangled. If something like a garrote was used there would be ligature marks and there were no indications in his esophagus that anything had been lodged tight enough for him to suffocate." Anapour pointed to body's neck area.

"What about poison?" Lansing asked. "Something injectable."

"Again, a dead end. I examined every square inch of the body—between his toes, in body folds. Nothing. The man was not injected, but I did find something interesting."

Anapour rolled the corpse sideways revealing a scratch on the back of the neck.

He brought the CCTV camera down again. "Something scratched the skin surface right here. I excised a small sample and sent it to forensics, but whatever scratched the skin left no trace of anything. If this in fact is a poison injection site and not a simple scratch from a pin or a shirt label or even a fingernail, I will have to wait for the complete toxicology report to come back."

Anapour scanned down the current report. "Every standard poison protocol, including a few exotics, so far have come back negative. But this is a Russian we're talking about. The lab is still testing for more exotic poisons, especially considering the candy store of possibilities found in that lab of his. But for now, there is nothing I can rule out definitively as COD."

"Well, something sure as hell killed the poor bastard," Lansing said, his voice tinged with frustration. "Was it a heart attack, a stroke, some underlying medical condition that we're not aware of? The man's medical history does indicate heavy smoking and drinking."

"That may be all well and good," Anapour added. "And I did factor it in. I need you to look at this."

Lansing examined a medical report from George Washington University Hospital. Kastianich had been a patient from June 1st of the previous year until June 4th, admitted through the ER for severe abdominal pain, with laparoscopic surgery performed the next morning by a C. Wilton, MD. "What's a cholo... ecyst... ectomy?" Lansing asked, butchering the pronunciation.

"They removed his gallbladder," said Anapour.

Lansing continued reading, understanding little of what it meant.

"The short version," Anapour said, "even with his poor personal life choices, the vodka, the cigarettes, his pre-surgical workup at Georgetown, and my autopsy showed little serious damage to his heart or lungs. The man had no heart disease to speak of - no cancer and no vascular abnormalities that would indicate an impending CVA."

"CVA?"

"A stroke. His coronary arteries were clean. There were no brain malformations or AVMs, a kind of abnormal connection between the arterial and venous circulation that could prove fatal. Given another ten years, however, I suspect any one of those factors could come into play, but Kastianich was in his fifties, good genes, I guess. I was about to declare COD as DUO."

"Translation."

"Death by Unknown Origin."

"You said, about to?"

Anapour pressed the button of a remote and a diagram of the human heart appeared on screen above the autopsy table. Lansing thought it looked like a chicken roasting on a vertical spit. The model turned in a 360-degree circle. Anapour pressed another button and the model's outer skin peeled away showing the heart's interior.

With a laser pointer Anapour placed a tiny red dot on the screen near the midpoint of the heart model.

"This area is called the Bundle of His. It is a collection of cardiac muscle specialized for electrical conduction. Histology found some interesting changes in the cell structure that might account for a sudden arrhythmia. The physiology is a bit complicated."

"You said the cell changes were interesting. How so?"

"I use the word interesting for lack of a better term."

"I'm sorry, Doctor Anapour, but I'm not following."

"Interesting in the sense that neither I, nor any of my colleagues have ever seen them before, and that particular abnormality has never been reported in any medical literature that I am aware of."

Lansing left his phone number with Dr. Anapour and returned to his office in the Hoover Building where he faxed a copy of the autopsy notes to several medical experts he'd worked with at the NIH in Bethesda hoping for a more plausible cause of death, but by 5:00 p.m. he was no closer to an answer than he'd been that morning.

CHAPTER NINE

A yellow taxi slowed and stopped under the covered portico of the Washington Hilton. A bellman opened the car door and extended a hand to the lone passenger. "Afternoon, ma'am. Welcome to the Washington Hilton. Will you be checking in with us?"

The passenger, a woman in her sixties, short with gray hair and a pear-shaped body, slid forward in the rear seat.

"Why, yes, thank you, young man," she said.

"May I take your luggage?"

"That would be just lovely," she answered, smiling before handing the taxi driver a bill in her hand. Realizing she'd given him a Shekel note, the woman stuffed it quickly into her purse and reached instead for a US ten-dollar bill from a stack of crisp new bills in a zippered compartment.

At the front desk, she presented an Israeli passport, along with a MasterCard in the name of Gertrude Singer. Ten minutes later, Gertrude Singer, tourist from Tel Aviv, followed the bellman's cart to a bank of elevators.

Alone in her hotel room, Singer removed a small silver device from her handbag. She extended an antenna and switched it on. A green LCD readout blinked on and off for several seconds as it powered up and a cursor began to flash a zero. She moved to the center of the room and turned in a three-sixty arc aiming the device at the walls and ceiling, her eyes focused on the blinking icon. The zero remained. Moving to a telephone on the nightstand she unscrewed the mouthpiece and checked for a listening device. She did the same to a second telephone in the bathroom before returning to the room and lifting three cheap reproduction prints away from the walls. Satisfied the room was clean she took out her cell phone and punched in an overseas number.

A male voice, in Hebrew, answered, "Shalom, Colonel Heifetz. The line is secure and encrypted. You may speak freely."

"I am in Washington, registered as Gertrude Singer at the Hilton on Connecticut Avenue. I spoke to the assigned agent in Washington. He has Abdalla and the priest, DeLarussa, under surveillance. They are currently at a townhouse off Dupont Circle. I need to speak with Ari."

"That will take a few minutes, Colonel, but first, did you engage the priest, get anything from him during your flight?"

"No," Heifetz said. "DeLarussa either knows nothing or is very good at keeping his mouth shut. He seemed frightened."

"One more thing, Colonel. Your birthday present has been delivered to the hotel. Expect it momentarily."

Heifetz ended the call, went to the bed, opened a suitcase and laid out an array of photographs—Hans Richter, Irina Kazakov, Monsignor Alonso Allegretti, and Faruq Abdalla looked back at her from the bed.

She turned suddenly, startled, at a soft knock on the door.

"Who is there?"

"Concierge."

Heifetz peered through the peephole. An Asian man in a blue blazer with a Hilton logo on its breast pocket held a large gift-wrapped box tied with a red bow and ribbon that read, *Happy Birthday*.

"One moment please, "the Mossad colonel answered, hurridly returning to the array of photographs, shoving them into a dresser drawer.

"Mrs. Singer?" the concierge asked as she opened the door.

Heifetz nodded.

"This arrived by messenger a few moments ago, and if I may, allow me on behalf of the Washington Hilton family to extend a happy birthday as well. Enjoy your stay, ma'am."

Heifetz took the box with *Happy Birthday* printed along its length and handed the concierge a five-dollar bill. As she closed the door her cell phone started to ring.

The readout showed a single character, one Hebrew letter—an *aleph*. A voice in Hebrew asked if the room was to her liking.

Heifetz answered, "Yes, it is light and airy."

"Thank-you… please hold for ben Yehuda."

Ari ben Yehuda, the lead Mossad agent on the case, came on the line. "I trust your flight went well?" said a deep male voice in Hebrew.

"Yes and no, Ari. I was not able to engage the priest, DeLarussa, on anything meaningful—thirteen hours and nothing. But on the plus side, I am certain he did not suspect, at least not until that debacle of a car chase at the airport."

"That was not our people in the silver Mercedes, Aviya. We were there, but far behind, following at a safe distance. As soon as I am certain Abdalla and the priest have left the townhouse, Laufer will go in."

"Yes, Ari, I know. But inform him that Abdalla knows his cover is blown. He will be hyper vigilant for anything suspicious. Speed is crucial. Where are we with the others?"

Heifetz could hear Ari ben Yehuda, a senior agent with the IISO, Institute for Intelligence and Special Operations, Mossad, shuffle through a report.

"Irina Kazakov landed in Rome an hour ago and Richter is currently inbound to Washington from Moscow aboard Lufthansa flight 865 due in at 11:30 p.m. tonight, your time. We have an agent on board who has the German under surveillance. He will be handed off to another agent after he lands in Washington. Expect him. This Richter is a player."

"And what of the Egyptian, the student intern, Faruq Abdalla?"

"Intelligence has amassed quite a dossier on Mr. Abdalla. First, he is not twenty-years old, nor is he a student of archaeology at Cairo University."

"Is Abdalla even his real name?" Heifetz asked.

"No," came ben Yehuda's quick reply. "Since he was ten years old his legal name has been Josef Tomasso, but he now goes by his given Egyptian name. He was born Adahm Faruq Abdalla to a Muslim father, Adahm, and a mother, Fadalla. His parents separated soon after the boy was born. At four, an automobile accident killed the father. The mother converted to Christianity soon after but died of cancer a few years later. We believe that is when he began a lifelong, almost father-son, relationship with a young Roman priest who…"

Heifetz interrupted, "Father Antonio DeLarussa?"

"Yes. Antonio DeLarussa baptized him into the faith and began his Catholic education at a convent outside Jerusalem. When the boy turned thirteen DeLarussa sent him to a boarding school in England, the Thomas Moore Academy in Leeds, and then to Our Lady of the Sacraments University near Dorchester for one year before moving on."

"I am familiar with Our Lady of Sacraments. It is an institution that prepares students for religious vocations. When did he study archeology?" Heifetz asked.

"He didn't. DeLarussa's protégé did not spend the summer at the Smithsonian Institution learning about antiquity from Dimitri Kastianich. In fact, Abdalla's interest, or knowledge of archeology, does not extend beyond acquiring the stone."

"Send me a full report," Heifetz said.

"You should already have it on your phone."

Heifetz scrolled down her iPhone screen, opened a PDF file and began to read Abdalla's curriculum vitae amassed by Mossad. *Pontifical University of Saint Thomas Aquinas, Angelicum—studied for the priesthood—no record of final vows. Travel Visas—Vatican City, United States, Ukraine, and Israel.* Heifetz signed off the call but continued reading the download.

She paid particular attention to a single entry. While Abdalla was in Israel he traveled frequently from Jerusalem to Egypt, specifically the Sinai Peninsula. He'd spent three nights at an upscale Four Seasons Resort in *Sharm El Sheik* and visited the monastery of Santa Katerina at the foot of Mt. Sinai several times. The images of his hotel signature cards were attached to the PDF file.

Several other more interesting Jpegs accompanied the transmission. One, in particular, showed an elderly, distinguished-looking man with white hair sitting with Abdalla in a corner of a Four Seasons hotel bar deeply engrossed in conversation. A footnote identified the man as Guillermo Cardinal Bertolini of Padua.

Farther down the page was another image that appeared to be taken at a symposium of some kind. Ornate chairs in a Baroque style filled a room with paintings covering the walls, each with Renaissance theme. The room appeared to be a grand salon like one of many such rooms Aviya Heifetz had seen in the Vatican.

She enlarged the image. Sitting in the front row, three figures from the left, was a familiar face—Irina Kazakov.

Heifetz put down her phone, went to the bed and unwrapped her birthday package. Nestled between layers of nondescript clothing lay a .45 caliber automatic pistol with an extended barrel threaded for sound suppression. Secreted in a shoe bag along with a silencer were two boxes of ammunition.

"The Father and I are leaving for a while," Abdalla said to a tall man in a simple white caftan that flowed to the floor.

Matteo Pentangelo, part of Abdalla's security team guarded the townhouse on a rotating basis, nodded.

"I will be upstairs in my room," he said in Italian.

"Remain alert, Matteo," Abdalla warned. "After what happened on the ride from the airport I am concerned. If there is anything suspicious call my cell phone at once."

Abdalla stood on the top step of the townhouse stoop. He held up a hand for DeLarussa to wait inside until it was safe. He peered down both sides of the street, and, not seeing anything suspicious, took the priest's arm and led him to the VW Jetta parked in front.

Halfway up the street, fifty feet from the Jetta, the driver of a black SUV spoke Hebrew into his cell phone. "They are leaving. I can be in and out in ten minutes. If the stone is there, I will find it."

"You are a go," came the response.

The Israeli agent remained in his vehicle, watching the Jetta move up the street, turn the corner and disappear before he got out and made his way to an alley alongside the townhouse. He took a small black case with a set of lock picks from his pocket, inserted two of them and in under five seconds gained access. He entered what he believed was an empty house and started for the back stairs.

Reading on the bed of his second-floor room, Matteo Pentangelo heard sounds coming from downstairs. He depressed the button on a panic switch, sending a short text to Abdalla's cell phone and reached for a semi-automatic pistol under his pillow. He moved silently to the door and pressed an ear against the wood.

Turning onto K Street, Abdalla heard three short beeps from his cell phone.

DeLarussa saw a sudden change in Abdalla's facial expression. "What is wrong, my son?"

"Matteo tripped the alarm. Something is wrong. We must return at once."

The Mossad agent crept along the second-floor hallway. He peered into an empty bedroom, entered and began to rummage through drawers, looking under the bed and opening a closet door. Finding nothing he moved to the next room.

Inside a walk-in closet, he spotted a trapdoor in the ceiling, the opening just large enough for the body of a small man to fit through. Too high to reach, Mossad Laufer poked at it with a clothes hanger, but hearing a sound from behind him, he turned.

Matteo Pentangelo, his automatic weapon aimed at the Mossad agent's head, was grinning.

"Get out of that closet… *now*!" Pentangelo ordered. "Get on your knees—hands behind your head. Do it or I will shoot you where you stand." The agent dropped to his knees, never taking his eyes from Pentangelo's weapon.

Afraid to turn his head away from the Israeli agent, Pentangelo continued moving backwards until one leg brushed against a wooden table. He groped for the table's edge, triying to push it sideways, but the flowing caftan snagged a piece of wood jutting from the table.

Pentangelo's head turned, all the opening the Mossad agent needed. Still on his knees, he pulled a gun secured to an ankle holster. Before Pentangelo could react, he fired three rounds from the kneeling position. A tight cluster of bullet holes circled the caftan mid chest, spreading bright crimson across the white linen.

Abdalla, caught in late afternoon traffic north of Dupont circle, took more than a half hour to reach the townhouse. By the time he and DeLarussa arrived a pair of Metro patrol cars were parked in front. An ambulance stood nearby with its rear doors open. He continued past the house without slowing down.

Ted Lansing picked up his ringing desk phone.

"Ted." It was Felicia Albreda. "R Street, 3467, off Dupont Circle. It's a townhouse. There was a shooting two hours ago. One victim is dead. I need you over there, right now, Ted."

"I'm afraid to ask," Lansing said, reaching for his suit coat. "Who and what?"

"The house is leased to a Faruq Abdalla, but neighbors told Metro that Abdalla doesn't actually live there."

"Abdalla? The same Faruq Abdalla I interviewed two days ago in connection with the Kastianich case?"

"The very same."

"For Christ's sake, Felicia, he's a twenty-something summer intern working over at the Smithsonian. He told me that he and the other interns live in some dormitory style hotel near the museum that the institute leases for them—no charge. How in hell does a kid, a college student, an intern, afford a townhouse in that part of the city?"

Albreda, about to say coincidence, stopped. In her head, she could hear Lansing's credo—there are no coincidences, just connections we haven't made.

"How sure are you of that, Ted? I mean about the interns living in a hotel."

"We're still doing backgrounds on all of them, but nothing in the Smithsonian's personnel records contradicted Abdalla's story."

Lansing heard Albreda shuffling papers. "Abdalla, Faruq. Ah, here it is. Six feet—dark hair and dark eyes—about 170. Is that him?"

"Sounds about right," said Lansing.

"Ted, the Faruq Abdalla who rented that townhouse is over thirty years old, and no intern or any other kind of student. Our friends over at Langley, if it's the same guy, say he's connected to the Vatican, some sort of operative."

"Vatican operative?" Lansing was incredulous. "Since when does the Vatican have operatives?"

"That I don't know," Albreda said. "I'm waiting on surveillance footage from Reagan National. For some reason, Abdalla picked up a Catholic priest named DeLarussa, who arrived from Tel Aviv via El Al."

"I'm on it," Lansing said.

"Oh, and one more thing, Ted, a Metro detective, Arlen Drew, is meeting you at the townhouse. Officially this is still their case, so play nice. I'm running down an incident report about a high-speed chase on the GW Parkway between a Jetta containing two passengers and a silver Mercedes with tinted windows. A couple of witnesses to the chase described the Jetta's driver to Metro's traffic control. It could have been Abdalla."

Chapter Ten

A yellow Fiat sped along Corso Vittorio Emanuele, the ramparts of Castel Sant'Angelo visible in the distance. Irina Kazakov drove her rental car across the Ponte Sant'Angelo Bridge above the Tiber and turned onto Via Della Conciliazione toward Vatican City.

Past the entrance to Bernini's, Plaza San Pietro, the Fiat merged onto a narrow road taking her around and behind Michelangelo's great dome soaring above St Peter's Basilica.

Kazakov followed the directions written on a slip of paper taped to her steering wheel continuing on to where the road narrowed to a single lane. At 7:00 p.m., with daylight fading, she reached her destination, *Giardini Vaticani*, the Vatican Gardens.

Kazakov gathered her bearings and found the landmark, a small elevation—*Mons Vaticanus,* a gentle rise whose name was as ancient as Christianity itself. Sunk partially below the surface of the loamy soil was a stone bunker with a tangled web of ivy growing over its faded gray stone. A weathered copper door gave it the look of a crypt.

Kazakov came up the incline and lifted an ornate doorknocker in the shape of a cross hanging from a copper ring. She slammed it three times and waited as she'd been instructed.

The heavy door opened. There, hidden in shadow and wearing a Franciscan robe with a cowl neck and a knotted, white-corded belt hanging from its waist, stood a tall man with a shaven head. He spoke in Italian.

"You are Doctor Kazakov?"

Who is he, she wondered, a novitiate, a monk, a priest? There was never any mention of anyone remotely like him.

With a nod, he bade her to enter. "I am Brother Jeremiah," he whispered. "Please follow me. Father Angelico awaits your arrival."

Wary, Kazakov followed.

The narrow poorly lit passageway, had a low ceiling illuminated by a series of low wattage bulbs spaced fifteen meters apart, each one secure in a caged metal housing. She took one step down and stopped.

Jeremiah turned, extending his hand. "Please, Doctor Kazakov, we must hurry," he warned. "Father Angelico does not have much time. The Holy Father expects him for canonical hours."

Kazakov, claustrophobic since childhood, felt lightheaded in the confining space.

Ten meters farther down the passage they came to another metal door. Jeremiah reached into a pocket of his robe, his hand emerging with a tarnished key. She recognized the symbol imprinted on one end, two Greek letters, Chi and Rho. The first two letters of the word Christ were superimposed one atop the other, an early depiction heralding the coming of Christianity.

Jeremiah started down a steep, narrow stone staircase. When Kazakov reached the top step, she stopped. It was barely wide enough for one person, her lightheaded feeling intensified.

She stood frozen. Her temples throbbing, her heart rate increasing with beads of sweat formed on her forehead.

Alternating between opening and closing her eyes, she started down, a coping mechanism learned from her father, an eminent Russian psychiatrist.

Hands outstretched against the centuries-old stone of the Vatican catacombs; she made her way to the bottom.

Still unsure, Kazakov followed Jeremiah until they reached yet another door, this one hewn from rough oak.

Father Angelico's workshop, a series of interconnected rooms with walls covered in white tile from floor to ceiling, looked modern, an anachronism, she thought, compared to the hand carved, stone of the catacombs. Bookcases overflowed with ancient papyri, bound and unbound manuscripts, and dozens of codeci.

At a round table in the center of the room, Father Angelico, wearing a simple gray smock over black pants and a black shirt with a Roman collar, held a wizened hand on an ornate, wooden box. Carved into the lid, was *Fidelus Deus Sempiturnus*—faithful to God for all eternity. A bowl of fresh fruit, loaves of bread, and a carafe made of Venetian glass, filled with wine, sat on the table. The old priest looked frailer than she remembered.

"It has been too long, my friend," she said, embracing the priest.

Father Ignacio Angelico smiled. "Yes, Irina, far too long. Thanks be to God, you are finally here."

"Is that it?" she said, pointing to a box in his hands.

Angelico made the sign of the cross and nodded. "Yes, my child."

"If I may," she asked, feeling the tightness in her chest dissipate, replaced by a tingling sensation of anticipation.

Father Angelico opened the lid and removed a black velvet bag. He pulled on the drawstring and removed a piece of granite.

Kazakov felt her breath coming in spurts. The relic, fifteen centimeters wide, rounded at the top with its lower end tapered in a V shape, had two notches carved into the stone, one on each side of the V. She stared at the lettering carved along the rounded top edge.

Expert in liturgical Latin, biblical Hebrew, and ancient Aramaic, Kazakov had seen writing like it before. Angelico handed her a magnifying glass.

As she studied the faded letters, Kazakov tried to imagine the second stone, the missing artifact, now somewhere in Washington. Did it have notched outcroppings that fit into the stone in her hand? Were they keys to the original commandments' location?

She moved the magnifying glass closer to the surface and brought her face an inch from the relic. *Strange*, she thought, *the lettering is painted, not etched into the granite.*

Kazakov was certain that this artifact and the one Faruq Abdalla looked for in Washington were key to finding the tablets.

"It is beautiful, Father," she whispered. "But we must act quickly before Hans Richter, who is already on his way to Washington, gets his hands on the mate."

Angelico took the stone and returned it to the box. He closed the lid and placed his lips on the carved inscription, *Fidelus Deus Sempiturnus*.

"I entrust this to your safe keeping, Irina," he said. "Guard it with your life."

Jeremiah, silent through it all, stood up and shouted, "No, Father. I will not allow it!"

Kazakov, confused, faced Jeremiah. "Who is this man, Father?

"He is Brother Jeremiah Vesticci," said Angelico. "He is my assistant."

"How long has Brother Jeremiah been your assistant, Father?"

Angelico came out of his chair. "A month, Irina. Cardinal Bertolini came to me and asked if I needed help. When I said yes, he offered Jeremiah."

Her attention went back to the tall, head shaven monk.

"Who do you think you are to make such demands? You do not allow it? This matter does not concern you." A .32 caliber Walther came from her pocket. "I am in no mood for this, and I do not have the time. Move, now, or I will shoot."

"Irina!" Angelico shouted. "Stop. Jeremiah is a good man, only confused."

"No, Father, he is not confused. You are not aware, but there are forces who want this discovery for their own ends, and I believe Jeremiah was placed here for just such a purpose."

She moved closer and glared. "You work for Hans Richter, don't you? Father, he has no more a religious vocation than I do. Brother Jeremiah my ass."

"Irina, please," Angelico begged.

When her attention turned back to Angelico, Jeremiah slapped the gun from her hand. It went skidding across the tile floor.

Angelico pleaded with Jeremiah. "We have spoken of this, my son. I truly understand your desire to keep the artifact here, but Monsignor Allegretti awaits its arrival in the Holy City, and for Father DeLarussa to bring the complementary piece to him from Washington."

Jeremiah backed away. "No! It does not go to Jerusalem. It goes with me, to Moscow."

"Moscow? Why Moscow? Think, Jeremiah, your holy vows."

Kazakov laughed. "You waste your breath, Father. He has made no vows to anyone or anything. Jeremiah is not a Franciscan. He does the bidding of those who would destroy the church."

Angelico tried to reason with him. "With both pieces, both artifacts, Irina can unlock the secret and all the world will know that the God of Abraham is the true God, and Jesus Christ is his son."

Angelico lifted the box and held it at arm's length. "May the Lord be with you, Irina. May he bless and protect both you and your holy mission."

"No," Jeremiah shouted again. He snatched the box from the priest's outstretched arms. "I will not allow it."

Angelico reached for the box, too late. Jeremiah stepped back out of reach.

"Who are you, Jeremiah? Why are you doing this?"

Jeremiah remained silent. The box in hand, he started for the door, but when he moved past Kazakov she grabbed for his robe and held fast. Jeremiah slapped her hand, broke free, and pulled a knife protruding from an apple on the table.

Dagger in hand, Jeremiah flailed. Kazakov jumped away, avoiding the blade. She made several attempts to reach for the box, but Jeremiah continued to lash out, menacing. She stumbled backward, falling, her head slamming against the wall. Angelico snatched the box from Jeremiah's grasp.

Jeremiah shoved the old priest with a flick of his wrist. He grabbed the box and pulled it from his outstretched arms. With a rapid lunge, he lashed out, cutting Angelico's hand. The priest cried out, blood pouring from the wound as he grappled with Jeremiah. They rolled onto the floor, Angelico no match for the younger, stronger Jeremiah.

Angelico came to his feet, looked down at his bloodstained smock, and charged headlong into Jeremiah's outstretched hand. The knife blade pierced his abdomen to the hilt and the old priest fell, gasping.

Writhing in pain, the old man tried to stand again, to follow Jeremiah, but his steps were halting and unsure. Their eyes locked for a brief second.

Angelico mouthed a single word, "Please."

Jeremiah bolted for the stairs as Kazakov came to her feet and started after him, the Walther in her hand.

She spotted him halfway up the narrow steps, dropped to one knee, grasped the gum in both hands and fired twice.

The deafening report echoed off the walls in a decreasing crescendo. Jeremiah clutched his side, turned and looked down the stairs at Kazakov. One stifled gasp, his knees buckled, and he fell, landing at her feet. The wooden box lay open on the ground, the black velvet bag exposed.

Kazakov heard a choking sound from behind her. When she turned, Father Angelico, lying on the ground, his back to the catacomb wall, tried to sit up. He fell backward and motioned for her to sit next to him.

His head cradled in her lap; Irina Kazakov pressed a palm against the wound in Angelico's abdomen. It did little to stem the blood flow.

"Please," she begged, "you must remain still, Father. I will go and find help."

Through lips barely moving, the priest whispered in a soft voice, an almost serene look spreading across his face. "No, my dear Irina… there is no time… it does not matter any longer. I do not fear death. Soon I will be healed, sitting at the right hand of our Lord and Savior… Go… now, before someone comes and finds the box. Do not let it from your sight until you are safely in Jerusalem with the *monsignore*. He alone knows what you are to do next."

Kazakov squeezed the old priest's hand and made the sign of the cross. "*Vade in pacem*, go in peace." Father Angelico was dead.

She lowered him gently and came to her feet, picked up the box with her blood-soaked hands, tucked it under an arm, and stepped over Jeremiah's broken form. She started up the narrow, concrete steps feeling her chest begin to tighten in the confining space.

Outside in the cool night air, the stone artifact in hand, Irina Kazakov got back in her Fiat and headed out of Rome.

Wounded, the pain radiating down his shoulder, Jeremiah opened his eyes. He saw Angelico, half sitting, his back against the wall, his eyes closed. There was blood everywhere but no sign of the woman. He came partway to a standing position when a sharp pain in his leg made him stop. He tried again to stand, this time using the wall for support.

On his knees, Jeremiah climbed from the catacomb. For a while, he lay on his back in the soft, wet grass before he pulled a cell phone from his pocket. "She was here, Hans. The bitch shot me and took off with the stone. I need your help to get out of here. I can barely stand."

CHAPTER ELEVEN

Lansing drove from his office at the Hoover Building to the townhouse murder scene on R Street. A crowd of onlookers along with several DC Metro vehicles with roof lights flashing made it difficult to navigate. He maneuvered into a parking spot along the curb, got out and came up the concrete stoop. A uniformed officer positioned at the door gave a cursory look at his FBI credentials and waved him through.

Inside a large front room, Lansing recognized the African American detective examining papers and documents on a roll-top desk. A gold shield on a lanyard hung around his neck.

The detective looked up. "Lansing," he called from across the room. "Over here… Arlen Drew… Metro Homicide… we met a few days ago at the Smithsonian."

Lansing nodded. "Yes, detective, the Kastianich case."

Lansing ran a hand across the polished wood surface of the antique rolltop and whistled. "Louis XIV?"

"Impressive," said the detective. "I wouldn't know a XIV from a XVI."

"Don't be so impressed," Lansing laughed. "Louis XIV is the only name I know. My wife is the expert."

"Think it's genuine?" Detective Drew asked.

Lansing laughed again. "Who knows? That's well above my pay grade."

Drew placed the papers back on the desk and turned to Lansing. "When this case hit, and I saw the name Abdalla come up in conjunction with this house… my captain said to expect you."

Drew pointed around the lavishly appointed sitting room with what appeared to be original artwork on the walls. "Swanky digs for a lowly intern, don't you think, Lansing?"

"Yeah, I was thinking the same thing," he answered.

"A pair of stiffs, days apart, in two different locations, and the same name, Abdalla, comes up in both cases. What are the odds?"

Lansing scoffed. "Not a coincidence. Only connections we haven't made - yet. This whole intern bullshit makes no sense."

Aware the State Department and the Russian Embassy were poking their noses into Dimitri Kastianich's death, Lansing decided it best not to share that particular bit of information with Arlen Drew. It was only a matter of time before the bureau took the case out of Metro's hands anyway—SOP when foreign embassies are involved, especially if the victim is a VIP. It depended on what forensics uncovered and how it tied in with events at the Smithsonian.

Lansing followed Drew to a second-floor bedroom, one of three, where a body had been discovered. Drew told him that a neighbor made the 911 call about a stranger lurking in an alleyway between the two houses in the upscale neighborhood.

Drew walked a circular path around a chalk outline and pointed. "The victim is one Matteo Pentangelo. We identified him from fingerprints. Pentangelo is, was, an Italian national in the US on a temporary work visa. His occupation is listed as a security officer. The responding uniforms found him with three gunshot wounds to the chest. The neighbor who called it in…" Drew stopped and opened his notebook. "was out walking his dog on the street at the time, about 2:00 p.m. The man told the responding officers he observed a white male, in his thirties, light brown hair, over six feet tall with an athletic build, come from the alley between houses. The man hurried past him with a gun dangling at his side."

Lansing pointed to a dry bloodstain in the center of the chalk outline. "Where are the forensics collected by Metro's CSI team?"

"Everything went downtown. Agent Lansing"

"Did the witness say anything else about this guy with a gun?" Lansing asked.

Again, Drew went to his notes, 'The man blew past me and got into a black vehicle, possibly a Chevy Suburban with DC plates."

"Did he get a good look at the guy?"

Drew shook his head. "Said he was more concerned that his dog would get trampled, some little frou-frou thing. Suspicious, he entered the house and called out to see if anyone was at home." Flipping a notebook page Drew kept reading. "He made his way up the stairs to this room and found the body. The victim's name is on a passport in that fancy desk."

"A US Passport?" Lansing asked.

"I wish," said Drew. "The passport was issued by the Vatican. Never saw one of those before and I've been a detective in DC for over ten years."

"The Vatican?" Lansing asked. "I wasn't aware they issued their own passports."

"It seems they do, at least for diplomats. Vatican City is officially a European microstate not included in the US Visa Waiver Program. Instead, they issue their own diplomatic documents."

"So, this Matteo was a diplomat?"

"Not sure, Lansing. I haven't had time to do a full search of the name, but so far, nothing on local or state DMV records indicates diplomatic status. Dealing with embassies is always problematic."

Lansing took out his cell phone and called his office. "Barbara," he said. "I need an expedited check with State, ASAP. The name is Pentangelo, Matteo Pentangelo, Italian national with Vatican credentials. See if he comes up as a registered diplomat with their Mission."

"You Feds sure do cut to the chase," said Drew. "That inquiry would take a month from my office."

Drew went back to his notebook. "The first thing I observed on the body was one very tight cluster of gunshot wounds to the chest. Whoever killed the poor bastard knew what he was doing."

"Any indication if it was a robbery gone south?" Lansing asked.

"I doubt it," Drew said. "Pentangelo had an expensive watch on his wrist, a Phillipe Patek, and his wallet contained over five hundred dollars, along with several credit cards, including an Amex Silver. No, Lansing, this was no random act by some amateur looking for a quick score." He glanced at his notes again. "The crime scene team had that gunshot cluster with less than a ten to fifteen-millimeter separation between entry wounds, dead center above the sternum. Son of a bitch was dead before he hit the floor. I'm thinking a pro."

Lansing moved around the room opening drawers, feeling under clothing and behind artwork on the walls. He knelt, looked under the bed, and pulled out a pair of brown wingtips. "GJ Cleverley & Co, size 12, pretty expensive footwear."

"There's another bedroom down the hall," Drew said.

In the second bedroom, an unmade bed had rumpled sheets. "What's behind that door?" Lansing asked, pointing to an alcove in the corner.

"A closet," Drew answered.

Lansing opened the door and slid several hangers apart, separating five pairs of expensive men's slacks neatly hung along with two suits, both size 48-Regular. A dozen freshly laundered dress shirts with initialed French cuffs, MP, hung neatly. A second pair of shoes, same size and equally expensive, sat on the closet floor with wooden shoetrees inserted into each one.

"Everything in here is a perfect fit for the victim," Lansing said. "Right down to the initial engraved cuffs. This was Pentangelo's bedroom."

Lansing ran a palm up and down the closet's interior walls. Then, moving the back of his hand from place to place, he tapped his Naval Academy ring on the wall listening for hollow sounds. Above his head, a small attic access door was slightly ajar. "Anybody looked up there?"

"No," said Drew, embarrassed at missing such an obvious clue.

Lansing said nothing about the mistake. He'd missed enough things himself. He pulled a chair from behind a writing desk and carried it into the closet.

Standing on the chair, Lansing reached above his head, gripped the edges of the rectangular opening and chinned, lifting his face to eye level. The crawl space was dark. He lowered himself back onto the chair. "I need a flashlight."

A mini flashlight gripped in his teeth; Lansing chinned up again. There were several boxes and portable file carriers beyond his reach. He looked down over his shoulder. "Drew, get someone up here, someone small enough to fit through this goddamn opening."

The phone in Lansing's pocket started to ring. He listened for several seconds before ending the call and turning to Drew. "It's confirmed. There is a Matteo Pentangelo listed as part of the Vatican Mission. He's on their security detail. Don't take this personally," he said, "but those boxes in that crawl space are coming with me. This is now officially an FBI case. The decision came down from Justice a few minutes ago. I'm headed over to the ME's office now. There's a new development they want to show me."

"Can I tag along?" Drew asked.

From experience, Lansing knew working with locals had its upside and its downside, but there was something about this Detective Drew that gave him a good feeling. He nodded. "Okay. I'll drive."

At the ME's office, Rajeesh Anapour in starched blue scrubs met Lansing and Drew in his office off the morgue. When Drew extended a hand to the young ME, Lansing recognized the look—the same look he'd had the first time he met the Cracker Jack forensic physician who looked like a teen.

Lansing placed a hand on Drew's back as they started for the autopsy lab with Anapour leading the way. "How old is he?" Drew whispered. Both he and Anapour laughed at the same time.

"The doc and I go back a long way. Right, Raj?" said Lansing, a grin on his face.

"Yes, a very long way." Anapour chuckled. "At least forty-eight hours."

Matteo Pentangelo's body was laid out on a stainless-steel table, his head supported by a plastic headrest. A small towel covered his genital area, and a classic vee-shaped cut ran from Pentangelo's shoulders, meeting mid-chest down the centerline of his abdomen.

Anapour explained that the body had been thoroughly washed and cleaned after his autopsy. All trace materials from under the victim's fingernails, inside nasal cavities and ear canals, were being analyzed in the forensics lab.

Without blood obscuring the gunshots, Lansing saw just how efficient the killer had been. Three clean hits, two practically on top of each other with less than ten millimeters separation from a third. Drew was right. This was not a robbery gone bad.

"Unless something extraordinary pops up, Agent Lansing, COD could be any one those three entry wounds," said Anapour. "All three were kill-shots. They tore up his chest pretty good. .22s tend to do that.

They don't have enough firepower to go through and through. Instead, they tend to rattle around inside, ricocheting off bone, doing a lot of secondary damage.

"I received a call right after the body arrived here. Actually, there were two calls, five minutes apart. The Russian Embassy is pressing hard for answers on whether this case is connected to Dimitri Kastianich's death."

"If they weren't connected that would be some strange coincidence," said Drew.

"That's not all," Anapour added. "Not two minutes later I received a third call from the FBI, an Assistant Director Albreda, I think she said. She informed me that this case had top priority and no information could be released to the Russians or anyone else, especially the press. And, until I spoke to you, and even then, not until I got clearance from the FBI. Here, let me show you something interesting."

Anapour inserted a thin metal rod into an entrance wound. He took Lansing's hand, placed it gently at the end of the rod, and guided his fingers. "Now, Lansing, gently, I want you to push inward, slow but steady. When you feel resistance, stop, don't force it."

Lansing felt the resistance at once. The rod would not penetrate more than an inch or two into Pentangelo's wound. Then, with Anapour's hand guiding his again, he changed the rod's angle, fifteen degrees toward the victim's head, and pushed downward. He met the same resistance.

Anapour then moved the upper end of the rod in the opposite direction, toward Pentangelo's feet. Lansing pushed again. This time the rod slid easily into the chest cavity. "He was shot from a low angle!" Lansing said, an 'aha' moment.

"Very good," said Dr. Anapour. "Yes, a very low angle, maybe as much as forty-five degrees upward trajectory. Whoever killed him was either very small, child-size, or on the ground at a distance of at least five to ten feet away, because I found no GSR on the victim's clothing or hands. But that's not the most interesting thing I found."

Anapour brought over a Petri dish with a badly crushed bullet.

"A .22?" Lansing asked.

"It is," Anapour answered. "And I've seen only one like it before. It's for a Beretta, Model 70, and the functionally identical Model 71."

"Okay then," Lansing said. "We have a dead Vatican diplomat killed with a Beretta wielded by someone who's an ace marksman and can hit his target from a prone position with dead-on precision. What am I missing?"

Anapour opened a loose-leaf book with plastic pages. "If I am right, Lansing, the weapon in question, the Beretta, is the signature pistol used by Mossad agents and carried almost exclusively by Israeli Sky Marshals. It is the perfect weapon for confined spaces, or assassination. Put sound suppression on the barrel and you could shoot up a library and nobody would hear a thing."

CHAPTER TWELVE

The Kastianich murder still without a real suspect or a definitive cause of death had Lansing no closer to solving the Russian's murder, or Matteo Pentangelo's for that matter. The fact that both events were related had Lansing talking to himself.

For a week he'd spent a good deal of his time contacting prominent researchers at the NIH and his contacts at Langley hoping one of them might shed some light on the coroner's findings.

He'd faxed copies of Dr. Anapour's autopsy notes to his Interpol contacts in Paris and New York asking if there was a plausible explanation for the dead archeologist's heart abnormalities discovered during the autopsy. All came up zero. He'd struck out. None of the NIH scientists had ever seen or even read about the kind of cell abnormalities Dr. Anapour found deep in the dead Russian's heart muscle. One hypothesized a previously undetected congenital defect, going so far as to request tissue samples, which Lansing messengered to his lab in Bethesda, and then heard nothing back. Another contact, a Nobel Prize-winning virologist in Paris, postulated something he called a prion, a sub-viral particle known to be the causal factor for a disease he referred to as Creutzfeldt-Jakob, akin to Mad Cow.

Dr. Anapour smarted from one arrogant comment that the abnormalities on the tissue slides weren't real and he, Doctor Anapour, was an incompetent who somehow contaminated the tissue harvesting. In a phone call to Lansing, the man went on to offer his services for consultations with the FBI—at a hefty fee of course.

Lansing pressed the C key on his computer keyboard. His calendar for the day opened. He had one interview scheduled for the next morning at 9:00 a.m. with Gretchen Bell.

The cell phone on the desk dinged an incoming text. The readout said, Felicia. "Please stop at Baccus on your way home. Pick up a bottle of Prov-Pomerol. Frederick will know which one. Big surprise waiting at home. Text me if you can't do it – Luv F."

A wall clock said 6:30 and he'd been at it since 2:00 that afternoon. A flickering overhead fluorescent fixture wasn't helping the headache he'd felt since lunch, like a band tightening around his skull. In front of him, the list of NIH scientists still had several more names to contact. Felicia's text was all the excuse Lansing needed to call it quits. He'd pick up on the list tomorrow.

A $150 bottle of Château Provénce Pomeról 2010 sat on the front seat of Lansing's SUV. He wondered what surprise, or what dinner guest on a Thursday night, merited such an expensive Merlot, Felicia's favorite, but only for special occasions. He couldn't have missed their anniversary because they'd been married, or was it remarried, for less than a month now. Even counting the years of separation during their divorce, their original anniversary was in May and Felicia's birthday not until mid-July. His father-in-law, Javier, happy as a Cuban clam lived in Taos, at what was more a golf resort than a retirement village, was not expected for his next visit until September, and besides, if Javier Albreda were coming, Felicia would have mentioned it. But, at this moment, Ted Lansing didn't care. Georgetown and home were twenty minutes away if traffic cooperated, and the evening weather exquisite.

Snug in the cocoon of his luxury SUV, Lansing settled into the plush leather, marveling at how letting go like this would have been out of the question only a year ago when he was single, divorced and living in Manhattan, commuting to Georgetown every other weekend. He reached above his head for the moon roof switch.

The panel slid back, and a rush of warm evening air enveloped him. The National Mall whizzed past, his satellite radio filling the interior with soft jazz sounds of Dave Brubeck. By the time he reached his street the day's frustrations, Dimitri Kastianich and Matteo Pentangelo, had melted away.

From a half block away, Lansing spotted a fire engine red Honda Civic parked in his driveway. Pulling in he saw the window decal with alternating vertical and horizontal bars of gray and maroon that spelled MIT if you imagined the bars connected at the top. His son, Joshua, was home.

Good thing or bad thing, Lansing wondered as the garage door went up. Neither he nor Felicia expected to see Josh so soon after his wedding he and Felicia's remarriage in Hawaii. Serving as Lansing's best man, Joshua had been with them in Maui but stayed on to go sailing with friends before flying back to Cambridge. In his third year of graduate school, working toward a doctorate in aeronautics, Joshua Lansing's major area of study was robotics, specializing in unmanned aero-technology applications—drones.

Felicia and Joshua were engrossed in conversation on a leather sofa in the downstairs den, or what Felicia now called his man-cave. It had a 65"-inch flat screen on the far wall in front of a pair of massive leather recliners with receptacles for drinks. Each had tray tables built into the arms. A collection of photographs from Lansing's playing days at Annapolis adorned the paneled walls along with his Navy jersey, #23, that he'd worn during his final Army-Navy game. It was framed in a shadow box alongside the game ball. On a side table sat a pair of photographs of Lansing and his best friend and teammate at the academy, It held a prominent place.

Joshua jumped from the couch, came across the room and embraced him, clasping both arms around his neck, double tapping his back.

Lansing grinned. "I ove ya, but those cool back taps are okay for your buds, but in my world, dads always get a kiss to go with the hug."

Joshua Lansing, at 6' 2" taller than his father, gave him a quick peck on the cheek.

Sniffing the air, Lansing looked at his wife. "Whatever that is, it smells really good. What has Rosaria cooked up for dinner?" he said, referring to their long-time housekeeper.

"FYI, Mr. Special Agent know-it-all, I gave Rosaria the night off because I am the chef tonight." She laughed, giving him a quirky look. "Yes, I do remember how to cook, and that exquisite aroma is my world-famous Chicken Kiev. I'll also have you know, my dear man, because you've been so good about your diet lately, and stayed away from that junk food crap you love to shove down your throat whenever…" Felicia stopped mid-sentence and grinned. "I bought us a decadent dessert."

Lansing's attention went to his son. "So, kiddo, the million-dollar question, what brings you home?"

Felicia jumped in. "Sorry boys, but business can wait until we're all at the dining room table." She winked at her son. "Right Josh?"

"Uh oh," said Lansing. "The dining room table on a Thursday night—sounds ominous. Do I need something stronger than a merlot, even an expensive one?"

"Maybe yes and maybe no." Felicia laughed. "You go wash up, and Josh, that bottle of wine your father brought home is in the kitchen. Why don't you open it so it can breathe a while? Table's set, salads are chilling, and the Chicken Kiev is just about ready." She put her arms around Lansing and her son. "It's not often these days that I get to sit down with my two favorite men at the same time."

Lansing smiled, catching a fast wink from his wife. Something was definitely up.

At the dining room table, Felicia lifted her wine glass. "A toast to Joshua, headed for great things."

Lansing took a sip and placed the glass back onto the white, embroidered linen tablecloth that once belonged to Felicia's mother. Another odd touch he thought for a weekday night. He looked suspiciously at both of them. "Okay. You two are up to something and I still don't have a clue what this obviously contrived and hastily planned celebratory dinner is all about… Is there something I'm supposed to know but don't? Is someone getting married?" He turned to Joshua. "Maybe won a lottery?"

Josh laughed. "No dad. Sorry, no weddings and no millions." He slid an envelope across the table.

Lansing read silently, and then looked up. "Wow," he said, placing the letter back on the table. "This is fantastic. When did it happen, and how?"

"Remember Professor Wineborn?"

Lansing nodded, even though the name meant nothing to him.

"I co-authored a paper with Dr. Wineborn, the one on unmanned aerial aircraft… drones. I sent you a copy last year, in May I think."

Lansing still didn't remember.

"Well, Professor Wineborn submitted it to a panel of leading UAV engineers, and I've been invited to present the original paper at a symposium."

Josh's graduate school thesis an impressive research paper, was titled, *Applications of Low Altitude Unmanned Aerial Vehicles in Mixed Terrain.*

"Okay, I know those looks," Lansing said. "What's the kicker here? You two are holding something back. I see it on your faces. Don't forget, I'm an FBI profiler at heart… sort of."

"It's not the what, Dad, it's the where. The symposium is in Israel, Haifa, at Teknion, the Israel Institute of Technology."

"Okay, no big deal," Lansing said. "So it's half way around the world and I suspect a great honor to be asked. But—"

Josh stopped him. "The small honorarium doesn't begin to cover costs for food, or airfare or incidentals. Dr. Wineborn arranged for me to stay with a Dr. Abraham Erlich. Dr. Erlich is a top administrator at Teknion."

"So, you're home to hit up the old man for some cash?"

"When you put it that way," Josh started to say, his head down, "I've already checked every major carrier, including El Al. A ticket is over a thousand, and I'm figuring maybe another couple of hundred for…"

He looked up to see his father grinning. "This thing, this symposium, it's a big deal, right?"

Joshua nodded. "It doesn't get much bigger, Dad. Professor Wineborn says they've never invited a student to present a paper before, even a graduate student."

Lansing picked up his wine glass. "Okay then, Joshua. Make us proud." He took another sip. "We'll go online after dinner and book a flight."

Chapter Thirteen

H ans Richter landed at Reagan National just after 9:00 a.m. A thirty-minute cab ride took him to a nondescript one-story ranch house in a Northern Virginia suburb, where for the first time he saw the place first hand that he'd rented over the Internet a year ago when the Russians first tasked him for the mission.

A young woman in a flowery sundress, that billowed out above her shapely legs, and close-cropped blonde hair answered the door. Seeing Richter, she tensed.

Darya Bargova, thirty-one, looked nineteen, the reason Richter recruited her. She led him through a narrow hallway to a bedroom with an attached sitting room. She patted the comforter and sat down.

"I did not expect you, Hans" Bargova said, and then stopped, hoping for an explanation of why he'd come—one that did not end with her being dead. None was forthcoming.

"I believe you will find the accommodations quite adequate," Bargova said in German. "How long will you be here?" she added, afraid of what he would say, but still more frightened of why he'd come in the first place.

He admonished her for speaking German. "We have come too far for you to break cover now, Darya, even with me. You are to speak only in English from now on and drop the German accent. Always remember who you are, Miss Gretchen Bell."

Bargova came across the room and lifted a can of club soda from a teacart, poured it into a glass, added ice and faced him. In a nasal voice, sounding like a moronic American teenager, she blurted, "Would'ya like a soda, sweetie. Don'tcha just love how them bubbles tickle your nose. How's about I call and order us up a pizza pie from Dominos."

Richter, not amused at Bargova's sarcasm, reached for her wrist. "Do not mock *Meine Liebe.* Is not good for your health," he said, quickly followed by a threatening laugh. He removed a pack of English Ovals from his inside jacket pocket, lit an unfiltered cigarette and took a long drag, exhaling through his nose. "I will tell you why I am here."

Silent for several seconds, Richter erupted. "I gave you one fucking thing to do, one job—find that goddamned stone."

"Please, Hans, it is not for lack of…"

He inched closer, his face ugly and contorted. "*Genug*! Enough! I am tired of excuses. You were sent to retrieve the stone and you failed."

Bargova tried to defend herself until Richter lifted a hand as if to strike. She ducked, moving her hands to her head to fend off the coming blow, but he stopped and walked away.

"Irina Kazakov is now in Rome," he said. "She may have already secured the second artifact."

Bargova, calmer, asked for a cigarette. Richter placed one between his lips and lit it and handed it to her. Feeling bolder, Bargova asked, "If Kazakov is now in Rome, why are you not there, and where was that wunderkind of yours, Jeremiah?"

Richter weighed his options—kill the incompetent bitch now, cut his losses, or continue to use her. If Bargova could not secure the artifact, then it must be with the Egyptian, Faruq Abdalla, he thought, and Bargova was still his best option for finding the missing Egyptian intern. He decided to read her in, for now, tell her everything he knew, or thought he knew.

"Do you know the name Heifetz, Aviya Heifetz?" he asked.

"Yes, I know the name. She is Mossad."

Richter went to the window, his back to Bargova, and stared out at the tree-lined street. "And what of that intern, Faruq? Are you aware that his mentor, a Catholic priest named DeLarussa, is here, now, in Washington?"

Ted Lansing buzzed his assistant. "Has Gretchen Bell arrived yet?"

"No sir, she has not, but oddly, I have her father on line 2 right now. His name is Franklin Bell."

"Gretchen Bell's father? How could he possibly… What does he want?"

"I don't know, sir, but it's the second time he's called today."

"Why wasn't he put through?"

"There was a mix-up. Best I can tell, his initial call wound up in White Collar Crime."

"Put him on."

Franklin Bell rambled incoherently. He had not heard from his daughter, Gretchen, in weeks. He'd called her cell phone a dozen times today, always going to voicemail assuring him that she was busy with work but fine. Last week he contacted her service provider, Verizon, who informed him that service had been terminated.

Gretchen had broken a two-year contract, agreeing to pay hefty early termination charges, and Verizon agreed to have a voice mail message remain on her line for six months. She paid the fee with a VISA card in the name of F. Bell, the same Visa card Franklin Bell gave his daughter before she left Harvard for Washington.

The longer Franklin Bell spoke the crazier it all sounded. The man described a young woman, accomplished and confident of herself. But the girl Lansing spoke to at the Smithsonian on the day Kastianich died, not so much. He checked his interview notes from that day.

Gretchen Bell. Female-Early twenties-5'2"-blonde hair-blue eyes. He'd made a notation in the margin that she acted frightened, at times almost in tears. It took him a few seconds to decipher another margin scribble. *Like a scared rabbit,* the perfect description of the girl he'd met in the Smithsonian lounge, not the one Franklin Bell described.

A copy of Bell's Massachusetts driver's license, along with a photograph he took the day he met her, stared out from the folder. Her height, her hair color, and eye color matched what he'd jotted down during the initial interview.

Franklin Bell kept rambling. He told Lansing that the manager of her residence hotel told him nobody named Gretchen Bell had ever been a resident. Desperate, unable to argue with the hotel manager, it had to be a mistake. He knew she lived there from June to August during her internship. Franklin Bell had contacted the Smithsonian. Other than giving him the same hotel address and phone number, they were unable to help. The Intern program had ended, and the candidates already returned to their respective universities.

"Mr. Bell," said Lansing, "Gretchen was due here in my office at nine o'clock this morning."

Lansing heard a deep exhale. "Thank God!" Bell said. "So, you know where she is?"

"No, I'm afraid not, sir. I'm sorry, but Gretchen did not show up."

"Oh dear God," Bell cried, the panic back in his voice.

"The last time I spoke to my daughter was two days after her boss's death."

Lansing paused, tried to make up his mind how far he should go telling Franklin Bell the details of the murder, and his daughter's alleged sexual relationship with a man more her father's age. He decided the matter was too urgent to play cat and mouse with a distraught father.

"Mr. Bell. Your daughter was the last person to see Dimitri Kastianich alive, and there are still a lot of unanswered questions about a…" He paused again. "Let's call it a more personal relationship between Gretchen and Dr. Kastianich."

Franklin Bell pressed the issue. "Do you have children, Agent Lansing?"

"Yes, sir, a son close to your daughter's age."

"Then you know, or at least can commiserate, about what I'm feeling. This personal relationship you spoke of, was it of a sexual nature?"

This is no time to play coy, Lansing thought. *If it were my kid, he'd want all his cards on the table.* "Yes Mr. Bell, based my preliminary investigation, Gretchen did have a sexual affair with her boss."

Lansing, open-mouthed, did not to know what to make of Franklin Bell's response—he broke out in laughter.

"Excuse the laugh, Agent Lansing, but that is not possible."

"But Mr. Bell…"

"No, Agent Lansing, allow me to repeat myself. That is not possible. The idea that Gretchen was screwing anybody, especially some fifty-year-old Russian man, is preposterous. My daughter is gay, Agent Lansing. She came out to her mother and me back in high school."

Lansing sat stunned.

"Please," Bell said. "Something is very wrong here. This makes no sense. I can feel it. I haven't heard from Gretchen, at least not in person, since she left in June for that goddam internship."

"June, Mr. Bell? That's over three months ago. You're saying you haven't heard from your daughter since June?"

"Yes, and I've been beating myself up over it for weeks, but Gretchen insisted. All of our communication during her internship has been by email and text. The one time I spoke to her, she sounded strange. She keeps a Facebook page and there were a few posts, mostly about how excited she was and the work challenging. She never mentioned this Kastianich."

Lansing jotted, *sounded strange,* on a small pad followed by a huge question mark. "What do you mean by sounded strange?"

"Her voice. It didn't sound like her, more nasal, a bit deeper. I asked and she laughed it off. Said she was getting over a nasty cold, and I was being an overprotective dad."

"What about your wife? Has Gretchen had any contact with her mother?

"We're divorced, Agent Lansing. Lillian and I have been apart for over a year. She lives on the Cape and hasn't heard from Gretchen either, except for emails or texts. We're both afraid something terrible has happened to our baby."

Lansing jotted, *missing,* on the pad with another huge question mark.

"A week ago, Lillian and I received the same voice message from Gretchen. It said she'd been cleared of involvement in that awful business with her boss's murder and she was coming home. Lillian expected her at the Cape a week ago, but she never arrived. She made several calls to her cell phone that went unanswered like all the others."

Lansing added the words *cell service* to the notepad, again with a giant question mark—a reminder to contact Verizon.

"I'll need a contact number for your ex-wife, Mr. Bell. Can I reach you at this number?"

"Yes, Agent Lansing, it's a cellphone, but I'm staying in Washington for now," said Bell. "I am at L'Enfant Plaza. It's a few blocks from where Gretchen worked. I thought…"

Lansing cut him off and pushed back from his desk. "Wait for me right there, sir. I'll be at your hotel in ten minutes."

Lansing ended the call and punched in an extension. "Luchinsky, Ted Lansing. I'm sending you a cell phone number. I need a complete dump of all calls in or out for the last three months, and the metadata too. Look for correlations—numbers in common, people in common, anything out of the ordinary, especially foreign calls. Service has been terminated so go directly to the carrier, Verizon. I need to know when service was terminated, how and by whom, and I need it ASAP."

A line of taxis idled outside Washington's L'Enfant Plaza Hotel. They formed a gauntlet as Lansing maneuvered around and between them and entered the hotel lobby. Businessmen in suits were queued in a snaking line at multiple check-in desks along with casually dressed tourists with cameras dangling around their necks.

At the concierge desk, he identified himself to a pretty Asian woman in a green blazer and asked for Franklin Bell's room number. She directed him to a sitting area off the main lobby. "Mr. Bell is that gray-haired gentleman in the blue blazer, Agent Lansing. He said to expect you."

In his early fifties with salt and pepper hair and a receding hairline, Franklin Bell paced nervously. Every few seconds, he glanced up at a clock above a bank of elevators.

"Franklin Bell?" Lansing asked.

"Thank God. Are you the agent I spoke to on the telephone?"

Lansing showed his ID. "May I see an ID, Mr. Bell," said Lansing.

"There's a coffee shop one floor down," Bell said, "It's more secluded. We can talk there."

In a booth at the rear of the coffee shop, Lansing took note of a slight tremor in Bell's left hand as he lifted a glass of water to his lips. The man's stress level and breathing rate were sky high.

Lansing began his interview by asking Franklin Bell what he knew for certain, from the sparse communications he'd had with his daughter during the summer.

All Bell could do was repeat that Gretchen sent an email to him the day after Kastianich's murder. She told him her boss had an apparent heart attack but until the Medical Examiner completed his autopsy, she and the other summer interns had to remain in Washington. She made no mention that she'd been in the room with him when he died. She'd told her father she was going to do some sightseeing at the Capitol before flying back home to Boston.

"I've been a fool, Agent Lansing. You try your best as a parent to do the right thing. You know what I'm talking about. Don't you?"

Lansing's thought flashed on Josh, but he said nothing. Bell, distraught, needed to vent.

"The time comes, a time every parent dreads. A time when you have to let go, trust them, even when alarm bells are going off in your head."

"When was the last time you actually saw Gretchen face to face, Mr. Bell?

Bell removed a cell phone from his pocket and accessed his calendar. "May 17th. I drove to Boston from Providence."

"Rhode Island? I thought you lived in Boston."

"No, Agent Lansing, I'm sorry if I gave you the wrong impression. When Lillian and I separated I kept the house in Providence, and she moved into our vacation home outside of Provincetown on the cape. I met Gretchen at the Bristol, it's in the Four Seasons on Boylston Street."

Bell brought up a photograph on his phone, an image of himself and Gretchen at lunch in the hotel restaurant. "Look how pretty she looked," he said, sliding the phone across the table.

Lansing stared at the image, blinked, but held his composure. The face looking back did have a striking resemblance to the girl he'd interviewed in the Smithsonian lounge the day Kastianich died.

The overall body shape was similar as was her hair and eye color, but whoever the girl in the photograph was, it was not the Gretchen Bell he'd spoken with.

Lansing slid from the booth. "Mr. Bell. I need you to do something for me."

Bell nodded. "Whatever you want, Agent Lansing, just ask."

"I need you to stop trying to locate your daughter or to trace her movements, who she met with or spent time with in the past six weeks. And whatever you do, do not contact anyone at the Smithsonian. I will keep you in the loop, but for now, there are some things I need to check on first."

Chapter Fourteen

Monsignor Alonso Allegretti set a silver chalice and paten plate on the altar of St. Bartholomew Church. He turned to see a tall, reed-thin woman in a black skirt with a scarf pulled tightly around her head hurrying down the center nave. Bright backlight from a stained-glass window behind her made it difficult to see the woman's face, but when she reached the altar rail, knelt and made the sign of the cross, Allegretti smiled, nodding, relieved.

Irina Kazakov; the stone artifact she'd taken from the Vatican garden was secure in a canvas messenger bag, its strap slung over her shoulder. She'd made the drive from Ben Gurion airport to Jerusalem in under an hour. The canvas bag had not left her side since she fled up the catacomb steps.

Allegretti, animated with anticipation, unable to wait a second longer, called out, "Thanks to God, Irina, you are here and safe. Please, tell me you have it."

Kazakov nodded, offering a helping hand to the old priest coming down the altar steps. "Yes, Father, it is right here." She patted the bag.

He saw an odd look on her face. "What is wrong?"

"I bring sad news," Kazakov said. She waited several seconds, searching for the right words. "Father Angelico is dead, *Monsignore*, murdered in front of my eyes."

Allegretti's shoulders sagged, the joy he felt only seconds before now gone. He steadied himself on a pew back, his head bowed. "Ignacio was a dear and faithful friend. I thought him like a brother. How? Who would do such a thing?"

Kazakov sat in a front pew. "Do you know a young priest called Jeremiah?"

"I know of him, Irina. Ignacio wrote to me that he had taken on an assistant, a promising young novice," he said. "The position was arranged by Cardinal Bertolini."

"Jeremiah was a fraud, Father."

"A fraud? I do not understand."

"I do not believe he was even a priest."

"How is that possible, Irina? Cardinal Bertolini would never—"

Kazakov stopped him. "I have an idea how, Father, and who, but I cannot yet prove it."

She reached for the canvas bag, undid the snaps and removed the artifact Angelico died protecting this. She held it for the monsignor to see.

A look of rapture came over his face. "Never in my life dared I believe I would hold such a treasure."

He pressed it to his chest and closed his eyes as the ecstasy descended over him. He appeared to not breathe until emerging from the transcendental state, his finger tracing faded markings on the stone's rough surface.

He mumbled a prayer.

"In what language were you praying, Father?" Kazakov asked, not certain he even heard her.

"Was I praying?"

"Yes, Father. As you traced the markings you spoke first in Latin, and then a tongue I never heard before. Do you recognize these letters on the stone?"

Allegretti stared down at it. "Many years ago, when I was a boy, perhaps thirteen, living with my mother and father near Galilee, a stranger visited our meager house. This man had a parchment, ancient, that he offered to sell. My father, a poor man, had little money so he offered a lamb from our flock in exchange. The stranger said he had no use for sheep, but in the morning after he was gone, the parchment lay on a table with a letter. I carry it with me always."

Allegretti removed a yellowed envelope from a pocket in his cassock.

"May I?" Kazakov asked.

She read aloud. "'I have traveled long and far brother Allegretti, and now fear that I can go no farther. My life will soon be at an end. I entrust this to you. It is a great treasure, one that will reveal the word of God.'"

The monsignor took the paper from Kazakov's fingers. "It was not signed, nor did I ever lay eyes on him again."

He folded it gently and placed it back into his pocket. "The next day my father made arrangements for me to go to Rome where I began my studies for the priesthood, a ward of his childhood friend, Ignacio Angelico, Father Angelico. He saw to my education and ordination, and I never saw my father or my mother again."

"Did Father Angelico know of the parchment?"

"Yes, Irina. I caried it with me to Rome. My father believed that Ignacio would know what it meant. For thirty years, it became his life's work to decipher the words in hopes of discovering the secret of what now sits in that bag of yours."

Kazakov now more excited blurted, "Did he succeed?"

Allegretti remained silent, pondering, deciding if he should place all of his trust with Irina Kazakov but if the second artifact, now somewhere in Washington DC, were to find its way home to Jerusalem it was the only way—he had no choice but to trust her.

Allegretti took both of Kazakov's hands in his. "Come, Irina, to my apartment in the rectory."

In the bedroom of Allegretti's private quarters, the monsignore reached under the front edge of an antique wardrobe and pressed a hidden button. A compartment slid open revealing a leather tube thirty centimeters long. He donned a pair of white cotton gloves, unscrewed the top with agonizing care and slid a fragile parchment from its sheath.

Dry and cracked with an odor of a musty bookshop, Allegretti unrolled the delicate goatskin, placing a small stone at each corner to hold it flat.

Using a jeweler's loupe Kazakov peered at the document. In the center, faded but recognizable, was a crude map. The writing looked similar to eighth century Aramaic, something she was intimately familiar with, but this lettering was strange, more rudimentary. "Please, Father, a pencil, and paper."

For an hour, Kazakov made jots, copying letters, juxtaposing symbols, trying to translate words written below the map. "Has the parchment's age been authenticated?" she asked.

"Yes, Irina, but it was inconclusive. If authentic I believe it dates to the first century."

When she looked up again, Allegretti was beaming. "Let me show you something my father wrote many years ago."

Allegretti lifted a leather-bound diary from a desk drawer. The brittle pages were dog-eared. He read aloud from an entry.

"'December 10th Anno Domini 1950. I received a letter from Ignacio today. He writes that many in Rome are not yet believers, but the author of this parchment speaks of the Word of God, The Lord's Commandments, of that he is certain.'"

Kazakov turned to face him. "Father Angelico wrote this?"

"Yes Irina, just before my own father died." Allegretti became animated, his hands moving as he spoke. "He wrote to me in Rome that he was coming for a visit and wanted to meet with Allegretti."

"Did he ever come?"

"Sadly no."

"I must apologize, *Monsignore*, but when and how did your father die?"

"He died in 1970, at the age of 90, and no, Irina, my father was old, but he was not sick either. I believe he had many years of life ahead of him and we were to be soon united, but he was struck and killed by a hit and run driver. He lived for two days but never regained consciousness, and the driver was never located. After his funeral, before I returned to Rome, my mother gave this diary to me."

She returned the leather-bound book. "I am afraid, Father, that without provenance the parchment and your father's diary are but another oddity in a long line through the ages that will meet with skepticism, or outright rejection by any but the most faithful."

Kazakov placed a gloved finger on the lower left edge of the parchment and peered through the jeweler's loupe. "Here is an oddity," she said. "The word, *Mafkat*, referring to the Sinai, should not be here."

Allegretti's facial expression changed. "I do not understand."

She stared at the parchment again; the crude map was clearly present-day Sinai. Her finger touched the surface. "This word, Father, *Mafkat*, it is the ancient name for the Sinai where the Egyptians mined turquoise at two locations in the days of the pharaohs—Wadi Maghareh and Serabit el-khadimin in the southwestern Sinai Peninsula."

The monsignor's face took on an odd look. "I do not understand why you question the parchment's authenticity?"

"Wadi Maghareh means Valley of Caves and has been the accepted translation for centuries. However, the word *Mafkat* for the region is not correct in this context."

"*Mafkat?*" Allegretti asked.

"Yes Father, *Mafkat* spelled like this first appeared in a treatise by a Russian named Ilya Zelijko in 1975. I met Ilya shortly before his death in 2004. In every document I have ever seen the word *Nekhel* appears for this location, not *Mafkat*. *Nekhel* is located along the southern border of the North Sinai Governorate, once part of an Egyptian Empire, part of the province *Du Mafkat* once the capital of the entire Sinai. The region supplied the empire with minerals, turquoise, gold, and copper. I find it strange that the word appears on a parchment purported to be as old as this one."

Kazakov's eyes focused on a faint marking in the lower corner of the parchment. On a small pad, she copied the faint image. "This is a guess at best," she said. "The scribe who wrote this is called *Rashem*. Has that name appeared in any form your father might have stumbled over in his travels? It could help in establishing provenance. Are there any other documents like this in your possession?"

"You believe the parchment is a forgery, an elaborate ruse?"

"Yes, Father. That is possible."

"Who would do such a thing, and why?"

Before she could answer, he and Kazakov turned at the sound of someone in the vestibule outside the apartment. "Are you expecting anyone?" she said.

"No; quickly," Allegretti said, "place the parchment back into its scabbard and please be careful."

The knocking became more insistent. The priest turned and whispered, "Is the parchment safe?"

Kazakov nodded, sliding it back into the hidden compartment in the wardrobe.

"Who is there?" Allegretti said to whoever was on the other side of the door.

"Please, Father, let me in. I bring good news."

"It is Father Sentini, my assistant curate."

Kazakov placed the tone artifact back into her messenger bag.

In the doorway, breathless, Sentini choked out, "I received a message from Antonio, *Monsignore*. Both he and Faruq eluded the authorities and made it out of Washington safely. They are en route to Jerusalem as we speak."

Kazakov interrupted.. "Did he say anything about a second stone?"

"Yes. The news is good. The second artifact is secure. I do not have details,sbut it had something to do with the murder of Faruq's director, a Russian named Kastianich."

"How did they elude the authorities?" Allegretti asked.

"This I do not know, but the message said to expect them in two days."

Chapter Fifteen

D etective Arlen Drew sat in a straight-back chair outside Ted Lansing's office in the Hoover Building. His fingers played with a visitor's ID attached to his suit coat. His wife, Camille, just before he'd left the house that morning, said she thought the FBI was going to offer him a job. Drew laughed it off. "That's a bit of a stretch, don't you think?"

Driving to the Hoover Building he remembered what Lansing said to him about working the Kastianich case together, but at the time he'd brushed it off as idle chatter, not an offer of anything, certainly not a position at the FBI.

An early morning call from Metro's Chief of Detectives ordered him to be at FBI headquarters by 10:00 A.M. Camille insisted he wear the new suit he'd bought for special occasions. "Every successful man needs at least one good suit to make a good impression," she'd said. Drew thought his new blue worsted, far too expensive for a cop, looked like something you get buried in, but the interview, according to his wife, was one of those special occasions. Arlen Drew's work clothing preferences ran to comfortable sports coats, the kind he'd worn every day since he made detective five years ago. He had a closetful, but who was he to argue with Camille?

At 11:00, Lansing's assistant apologized for her boss's lateness. She offered the detective a bottle of water or a cup of coffee, which he declined.

This was not the first time the FBI ran him in circles with nothing to show for it. His mistake this time was telling Camille, already making plans for an addition on their house.

"Sorry I'm late," Lansing said as he stepped off the elevator. "Love the suit. New?" he aasked as he passed the detecrive without slowing down. "Come into my office. We'll talk."

"Camille got to you? Right, Lansing?"

"Who is Camille?" Lansing answered.

"The suit…" said Drew. "Nevermind.

Lansing's office, furnished for functionality, not meant to impress, did precisely that. Drew looked around before taking a seat in front of a generic gray metal, steel desk.

"Don't laugh," said Lansing. "Not a word… I inherited it, every piece of crap. The last agent who occupied the space did the decorating."

"When?" Drew laughed, pointing to a lava lamp on a bookshelf. "Circa 1960?"

"Yeah, I know." Lansing chuckled, as he plopped down into an expensive desk chair, the one thing he'd ordered personally for his new office. His back demanded it. "You should have seen my workspace in New York," Lansing laughed. "A cubicle like the ones out there. I have a budget for swanking up this place if I ever get around to it. I have until March 14th at the stroke of midnight."

Drew laughed. "Stroke of midnight? Witching hour? What happens at 12:01? The place turns into a pumpkin?"

"Who knows," Lansing said, "maybe. Go figure - bureaucracy."

"Look, Agent Lansing, I…"

"Call me Ted."

"Okay, Ted. My chief left a cryptic message with my wife last night. I've got a shitload of cases on my desk, including the Kastianich murder, so, if you tell me the real reason I'm here on a Monday morning instead of there, I'll get on with my day and go catch bad guys."

"How do you like cubicles?" Lansing asked.

"Like? You mean that I have a special affinity for small, sterile, cramped spaces?"

"I suppose." Lansing laughed again. "What have they got you in over at Metro?"

"For us kick-ass detectives, cubicles without the walls. One big room, open space with a lot of desks."

"Difference without distinction," Lansing mocked, sliding a folder across to Drew.

Drew saw his name in bold lettering on a tab. He opened it. Two pages, side by side, had signatures at the bottom, Director of the FBI and the Attorney General of the United States. Below each signature, a blank line with his name typed underneath. "What is this?"

"That my friend is a temporary appointment. Yours if you want it. The one I argued and lobbied for last week and again this morning. It's the reason I'm late."

"How is this even possible? I mean… 'borrowing' a DC Metro detective?"

"I thought the same thing, Arlen, but best I can tell from the legal mumbo-jumbo, the Bureau does have authority to deputize any state or local law enforcement to assist in the investigation of violations of Federal law."

Drew shook his head. "If you say so, Ted."

"Not me, Arlen, the AG. Kastianich dying at the Smithsonian made it a federal case."

Lansing slid open a drawer and placed two leather wallets on the desk in front of the detective. "Like I said, yours if you want it."

Drew opened both wallets. One held an ID with FBI in large letters, his name below and the words Special Assistant; the second held a gold shield, Special Projects Liaison. "All they need is your photo," Lansing added. "Impressed?" Lansing joked, failing to include the actual lengths he'd gone to for the appointment to pass muster with his superiors and the not too small part his wife, Assistant Director Albreda had played.

"If you accept the job, you still get your regular salary paid by Metro, plus an FBI stipend. You'd be working here, with me. It's nothing to sneeze at Arlen. The initial appointment is for one year."

The intercom on Lansing's desk buzzed. "I have a Doctor Rajesh Anapour on line 2—he's with the Medical Examiner's office."

Mentally reconstructing his last conversation with Doctor Anapour, Lansing picked up his phone. "Good to hear from you again Raj. I was hoping you'd call."

"It's about the Kastianich case, Agent Lansing. I may have found a possible COD."

"May have?

"Not definitive—yet."

"I'll take whatever you have doc."

"Can you get over here? I'd rather not discuss it on the phone."

He looked at Drew. "Give us twenty minutes."

"Us?" Anapour asked.

Lansing placed a hand on the mouthpiece. "What do you say, Arlen? Ready to be a G-man?"

Chapter Sixteen

Lansing displayed his ID to a receptionist at the ME's office and looked at Arlen Drew nervously adjusting his tie.

"Relax." Lansing laughed. "You'll do fine. Stop worrying. You're not a rookie, Arlen."

Drew lifted his newly minted credentials from an inside pocket and flipped it with a flourish. Lansing laughed again and patted his arm. "Not so eager, partner."

Drew nodded and followed him to an elevator.

When the elevator door opened on basement level the young pathologist was already waiting at the end of a long corridor outside the morgue's swinging doors. "Look at the doc there, Arlen. Tell me what you see," Lansing asked.

"He's excited," Drew whispered. "There's something he can't wait to tell you."

The pathologist's index finger tapping the cover of a blue file folder at his side as he started toward them. "He's chomping at the bit to show us whatever is in that thing," Drew said. "I think he found something he believes no one else on earth could have uncovered except him."

"Not bad, Arlen, not bad at all."

In a conference room, on a long table, were a half dozen textbooks held in place by a pair of cheap aluminum bookends. Anapour lifted a large volume from the row of books, opening it to a color plate. "*Hapalochlaena lunulata*," he announced, beaming, his palm flat on the page.

"Hapa what?" asked Lansing

"*Hapalochlaena lunulata*, gentlemen, the slayer of your Russian archeologist."

"What is it?" Lansing asked.

"Common name, the Greater Blue Ringed Octopus."

The ME grabbed a medical text, *The Biochemical Etiology of Systemic Poisons,* and laid it open to a page on venemous ocean predators.

Lansing scanned the effects of octopus venom, picking up on nausea, gross motor paralysis, blindness, heart failure, and death and hallucinations. "What's a tetrodotoxin?"

"Nasty stuff, Lansing; real nasty. Despite *Hapalochaena's* size, 12 to 20 centimeters, it carries enough venom to kill a dozen humans. Victims often do not even realize they have been poisoned until respiration slows and paralysis starts to set in. There is no known anti-venom."

"How sure are you?"

"Sure as I can be. I reanalyzed the cardiac samples from Kastianich's autopsy, this time looking for specific cell receptors on the surface of the director's heart muscle—it was positive for the toxin. I missed it the first time because there is no standardized test or any toxicology screen we'd ordinarily include when COD is an infarct, a heart attack."

"Any chance of accidental ingestion?" Drew asked.

"Anything is possible, but in my considered opinion, no. If he'd been in, let's say, Australia, diving off the Great Barrier Reef, maybe.

But powerful neurotoxins like the kind produced by this cephalopod cannot be purchased anywhere in the United States, at least not without a license, and a license request triggers state and federal scrutiny."

"What about a foreign government?" Drew asked.

Anapour nodded. "That is a game changer."

"So, you're one hundred percent positive there's no possibility of accidental poisoning?" Lansing asked.

"Nothing's a hundred percent," Anapour stressed. "But no, this was not an accident. This thing might kill you accidentally if you spend time on the Barrier Reef, but the Bell woman, Gretchen if I remember, said Kastianich had auditory and visual hallucination just before he died. Even toxins in *Blue Ring Octopus* need to be distilled and concentrated to a higher level to have that effect. Besides, the stuff has a nasty taste in concentrated form, even a few drops in a drink, especially alcohol, would not be disguised completely."

"Enough of a taste for Kastianich to notice?" Drew asked.

"Maybe yes, maybe no," Anapour answered, "but that is not how he was poisoned. The last time you were here I showed you a small scratch mark on the back of his neck. I went back to re analyze the tissue samples from that scratch—also positive for the neurotoxin. Under the scanning microscope, a minute scratch mark is clearly visible. A pin, maybe a needle of some kind, had been drawn across the skin surface to introduce the toxin. He was definitely poisoned, and the vehicle was *Hapalochlaena lunulata* toxin. I am amending the autopsy report. COD by cardiac arrest brought on by a neurotoxin. I wish I still had his body here."

Lansing closed his notebook. "Not going to happen, doc. The body was flown back to Moscow for cremation."

Halfway back to the Hoover building Lansing took a call from Assistant Albreda. "Where are you now Ted?"

"On our way from the ME's office. I have a confirmed COD. Kastianich was poisoned using an exotic toxin. Definitely a homicide."

"Listen, Ted, I need you and Drew to head over to a place called Huntley Meadows Park. It's a wetland preserve a few miles south of Alexandria, out near Groveton—less than an hour. Take US 1."

"What am I rolling into?"

"A pair of hikers stumbled over a decomposed body—a young woman—dead for months, maybe longer. This could be the real Gretchen Bell."

"What ties the body to the Bell woman?" Lansing asked.

"The body was stripped naked and dumped into a pond. Whoever dumped it tried very hard to make her unidentifiable—fingerprints were burned off, post mortem, beyond recognition, and the body nude except for a pair of lace thongs. But the killer missed something. There was a tiny label sewn into the waistband of the panties with the initials GB."

Lansing ended the call, made a quick U-turn and started south toward Virginia.

The road inside Huntley Park narrowed to a single lane ending at a rustic log cabin reception center. A woman, mid-twenties, wearing a loden jacket, matching green slacks, and a Smokey the Bear hat, drove toward them in a golf cart.

"Susan Michaels," she said, extending a hand. "Are you Special Agent Lansing?"

Lansing nodded.

"Been expecting you. I'm the head park ranger. It's usually not busy mid-week, but finding that corpse, poor girl, put a damper on what visitors we do get. We're going in about a half-mile, so hop on. The Groverton police chief, that would be Daniel Thomas, is on the scene with a couple of detectives and the county coroner."

Lansing and Drew held fast to the seat grips as Michael's golf cart rumbled over loose, gray, boardwalk slats that ringed the hiking trail. Lansing eyed the terrain running past them on both sides, fields of wildflowers, colorful ponds, and swamps. "Perfect for a body dump."

A temporary shelter with four aluminum stakes supported a blue canopy. A man in a blue nylon jacket with CORONER printed on the back was kneeling alongside a partially covered, almost naked, badly decomposed body.

"Dr. Jenkins?" Lansing asked.

"And who you would be?"

"Ted Lansing FBI. This is my associate, Arlen Drew."

Lansing knelt down for a closer look at the woman's body. "Small caliber gunshot to the right temple," he said.

"Yes, Agent Lansing, a .22, and from the looks of it the gun barrel was pressed up against her skull. I'll know more when I get her on my table. Any idea who she is?"

Lansing made a decision. "I think it best, Dr. Jenkins, that the autopsy is done in DC," he said, ignoring the county ME's question. He took the phone from his jacket, called Albreda and then Rajeesh Anapour.

On the drive back to Washington, Lansing remained quiet, almost sullen. Drew asked about it, but all Lansing would say was that he dreaded the coming conversation with Franklin Bell.

"You hungry, Ted?" Drew asked.

Lansing's eyes went to the dashboard clock. "Sure, pick a place but somewhere fast, in and out. We need to get back to my office."

"Okay then, you my friend are in for a treat. Ever try soul food?

Daddy Long Legs on the corner of Maryland and 8th Street had a small outdoor seating area with two umbrella tables in a cramped brick courtyard. Inside the restaurant, even smaller in area, were a counter, three more tables, and a large burly black man in a BBQ-sauce stained apron. Drew gave him a loud hello.

"Earl, I want you to meet my new partner, Ted Lansing."

Earl 'Daddy Long Legs' Monroe grinned wide, exposing a gold tooth, his voice deep and resonant, reminiscent of James Earl Jones. "Any friend of my man Arlen here is okay in my book. What can I get you boys?"

"Your choice, Earl, surprise us."

Settling at an outdoor table, Lansing loosened his tie and relaxed for the first time since they'd left the office. When Earl brought over two bottles of a beer called, Surly Lager, with a hardened red wax cap, a brand Lansing had never seen before, he waved him off. "Sorry, Earl, you too Arlen, but we're on the clock, bureau rules, no alcohol."

"Then it's sweet tea comin' right up," Earl said. He looked at Drew.

"Make it two, Earl."

The aroma of pulled pork, steaming cornbread, and collard greens had Lansing salivating before Earl even set the plate in front of him. After one mouthful, Lansing leaned back in his chair. "Okay, Arlen, listen up. What I'm about to tell you never leaves here."

"Don't you worry, Ted. I am the epitome of discretion. I never share my cases with anyone outside law enforcement."

Lansing started to howl, and then stopped. "I wasn't talking about the case."

"Then what?" asked Drew, confused.

"The day will come, Arlen, probably sooner than later, when you are going to meet Felicia, my wife, and both our bosses."

"Both our bosses?" Drew was now more confused.

"You know the name Albreda?"

"You mean like in Assistant FBI Director Albreda?"

"Yep, that would be correct, Felicia Albreda, as in Mrs. Lansing, the mother of my kid. Me, you, both of us, will never speak of Daddy Long Legs BBQ in front of her. If you do, I'm sorry, but I will deny ever being here or knowing you—and I might just have to kill you."

Drew laughed. "So, you have one of them at home too? Camille thinks I stop for lunch at some diner every day and order a salad."

CHAPTER SEVENTEEN

Mossad colonel, Aviya Heifetz's return flight to Israel was over two hours late, a minor inconvenience she thought compared to the missing artifacts, which still eluded her. The botched attempt at recovering the artifacts at the Dupont Circle townhouse, however, had become a major headache for Israel's clandestine service. In addition, the FBI taking over the investigation made things even more difficult.

Heifetz's hastily prepared trip to Washington which was meant to deflect attention from Mossad's actual mission, securing the stone artifacts, coupled with the killing of a foreign diplomat with ties to the Vatican, needed explaining up the chain of command.

Faruq Abdalla and his priest-mentor, DeLarussa, were now the wind and that meant months of covert work had gone for nothing—wasted time. She'd reviewed it in her head a dozen times during the flight home to Tel Aviv. The American's would have to be brought into the entire operation, something neither she nor Mossad wanted.

From the outside, the nondescript three-story building in a Tel Aviv suburb, a Mossad off-site satellite, looked like an ordinary medical arts building, complete with a lobby directory of non-existent doctors. Set back fifty yards from the road, surrounded by an ornamental fence, the top floor of the structure housed an array of satellite dishes that collected data from all over the world.

Inside the front entrance, a security guard in civilian clothing wore an open-collared, khaki shirt and slacks. An Uzi was slung over his shoulder and a communications device in his ear. He informed Colonel Heifetz that the meeting had been rescheduled for the atrium, a secure inner courtyard in the building's interior.

Bright sunlight filtered through the atrium euphemistically called the Tea Garden by the staff. It had a translucent skylight, but from ground level it appeared to be an open-air space, an effective illusion. The curved dome had a projected image that mimicked the outside. At night a starlit sky, by day, sunny or cloudy, depending on the actual weather—a sort of indoor, outdoor. The space was surrounded on all four sides by sophisticated electronics, and landscaped with colorfully tiered flowerbeds, the space had the look of a small bistro. No outside listening devices could penetrate the high-tech security network that enclosed the entire garden.

Etan Perz, Director of Operations, stood when Heifetz entered through an archway.

"Ah, good, you are finally here Aviya. Welcome home. Your flight was satisfactory, I hope?"

"Yes, please, Etan, sit," she said. "The business at hand is urgent."

The director nodded. "Yes, I agree. I read your report. How could such a mistake happen?

"There is no excuse," Heifetz said. "I take full responsibility. My team had the townhouse under surveillance for three days and never once saw, or even suspected, the operative now identified as Matteo Pentangelo was providing armed security. It was most unfortunate, but…"

"There are no buts, Aviya." Perz pointed to a pot of tea on a round metal table. "May I?"

"Yes, please," she answered, "no sugar."

"Unfortunate is perhaps a better word to describe it… Yes, I think that will work," the director said as he poured steaming liquid into a tall glass. "We have not heard the last of this matter."

Heifetz smiled. "You do know me, Etan."

"Yes I do, Aviya—more than most. How long has it been?"

"Nearly thirty years, my friend."

"Had this operation gone sideways we would have a…" he stopped. "Thank God it did not come to that."

Perz leaned back. "You are right," he said. "I mean about DeLarussa and Abdalla. They are not, however, as you said, in the wind. They are both here, now, in Israel." Perz opened a laptop and tapped the play button. "This was captured by our security at Ben Gurion, yesterday at 11:23 a.m. The audio is not good, too much background noise."

Heifetz slipped a pair of headphones over her ears. A garbled voice, female, coming from a PA system in the background, announced incoming flights and passenger information requests in Hebrew.

Perz stopped the recording and pointed at the screen. "That is Father Anthony DeLarussa, age fifty-one. He is a Catholic priest currently assigned to St. Bartholomew Church in Jerusalem—he is an assistant pastor. The priest in charge is one Monsignor Allegretti."

"Your agents here have done well," Heifetz said.

Perz moved his finger to the younger man at DeLarussa's side. He carried a metal case, not by its handle but tightly under an arm. "That is Josef Tomasso, age 27, born Faruq Abdalla, Egyptian, the name given by his parents. His mother was a Muslim convert to Christianity when Faruq was a child."

"Impressive," Heifetz said. "What else do we know about this Abdalla?"

Perz looked down at an open dossier. "DeLarussa presided over the boy's conversion to Christianity. The best we can glean is that his parents sent him to live with DeLarussa in Rome. He was thirteen at the time. DeLarussa was assigned, and resided at the time, at Sacro Cuore Immaculata, a titular church in Rome."

"Titular church?" Heifetz asked. "I am not familiar with that term."

"It is a church assigned to a cardinal. Because of their extensive duties at the Vatican, these titular cardinals are assigned mostly in name. A pastor who presides over a titular church has authority to speak for the diocese, much as a bishop or a monsignor might do."

"Did Abdalla and DeLarussa fly directly from Washington?" Heifetz asked.

"No, their flight originated in Washington but made a two-hour stopover in Athens."

"Did either of them contact anyone while in Athens?" she asked.

Perz handed off a ringed binder. "Look at page three. There is a transcript of a single cell phone call DeLarussa made from the airport in Athens. It was to an unlisted number in Israel. The number was blocked but we were able to determine who received the call."

A woman answered who identified herself as an employee of St. Bartholomew Church. The calldes spoke for less than a minute, the conversation, although mundane, included his ETA at Ben Gurion."

Standing, Perz said. "Come, Aviya, walk with me. When I sit too long these days my legs cramp up."

Both Perz and Heifetz walked the perimeter of the courtyard. "DeLarussa raised the boy, had him baptized and changed his name to Josef Tomasso. He saw to the boy's education, going so far as to encourage him to the priesthood, but the vocation idea never took, nor the Christian name. He began using his his Muslim name "

Heifetz read aloud from the dossier. "Undergraduate degree at Cambridge, graduating Summa Cum Laude—he will be twenty-seven years old in…" She stopped and lifted another document from the dossier. "This can't be right, Etan." She held up a birth certificate. "This says he is twenty-two."

"Yes Aviya, an excellent forgery Abdalla used to enter the intern program at the Smithsonian. His transcript from Cairo University is also a forgery, albeit a very good one as well. Somebody quite adept went to great lengths creating a persona for Abdalla as a twenty-two-year-old graduate student in archeology."

Heifetz turned when a young female aide appeared at the atrium door.

"Come, Marlena," said the director.

The woman leaned in and whispered into Perz's ear. He looked up at her and nodded.

"Have him wait. Aviya and I will go to my office."

Seated behind his desk, Perz pressed an intercom button, "Send him in now, Marlena."

A tall man in a well-tailored blue Italian pinstripe suit stood in the doorway. His expensive haircut, perfectly styled salt and pepper hair, and deep tan made Heifetz think he looked like a movie star.

Perz rose to meet the man halfway into the room. "Colonel Heifetz, allow me to introduce Carlo Cilazzo. Captain Cilazzo heads the criminal investigative unit in Vatican City."

All Heifetz could think was Pope Police.

"Ah, good day, Colonel Heifetz, the Italian said. Your reputation precedes you." He spoke in Italian, before switching to English, apologizing for a lack of fluency. "I am so glad to have this opportunity so I will get to the point of why I am here. And I thank you, Director Perz, for seeing me on such short notice. I believe we have, how you say, *una problema*."

Cilazzo handed a pair of photographs to Heifetz. She stared at the first one, a snapshot of a young man, his head shaven, wearing a Franciscan robe. A second photograph was a formal portrait of an elderly priest.

"Do you know either of these two men?"

Heifetz shook her head.

"The younger man is Jeremiah Vesticci. We do not believe it is his real name. He purported to be a novitiate studying for the priesthood. The older man was a priest, a renowned biblical scholar, Father Ignacio Angelico."

"You said he was a priest, Signore Cilazzo?"

"Yes, Father Angelico was murdered in his workshop at the Vatican— we believe by that man, Jeremiah Vesticci. We have ascertained that Jeremiah is not a priest nor does he study for the priesthood. We believe he is a Russian operative named Jaroslav Vasiliev recently recruited by an FSB agent named Richter, Hans Richter."

Cilazzo handed Heifetz another photograph. "Do you know this woman?"

Heifetz took the photograph. "Yes, this one I do recognize. It is Irina Kazakov. She is Russian by birth, a linguist—an expert in ancient languages. There is a rumor she had a romantic relationship with an East German operative named Richter, a very disagreeable man indeed."

Perz caught Heifetz's attention, his head shaking. She knew what he meant, play it close, let Cilazzo talk.

"It is most interesting you say that *Colonnello*." Cilazzo produced a second photograph of Kazakov that showed her sitting at an outdoor café. "The man across the table none other than Hans Richter."

"How old is this picture?"

"It was taken only a few weeks ago, in Berlin."

"I must have your assurances, Director Perz," Cilazzo added, "that we are not being recorded, because what I am about to tell you must not leave this room."

Perz lied. "I assure you, *capitan*, we do not record anything said here in my office."

Cilazzo handed Heifetz a silver flash drive.

The first image on the drive showed a steep, narrow stone staircase descending into the blackness below. "These were taken in the *Giardini Vaticani* while my men investigated Ignacio Angelico's murder."

"I am familiar with the Vatican gardens, captain," Heifetz said.

"Those steps," said Cilazzo, "lead to a labyrinth of tunnels that run under the gardens and go all the way to the *Basilica di San Pietro*, emerging through a door below the main altar."

The second image showed an elderly man in a black robe sprawled under a hedge. "That is Father Angelico's body."

According to Captain Cilazzo, the dead priest had been discovered above ground, near an entrance to the underground tunnels, but another set of images taken inside the passageway told a different story. Angelico had been stabbed to inside his workshop, a small, modern room off the main tunnel; his body was then moved above ground. Blood covering the workshop walls told a horrid story of bloody mayhem.

"Somebody wanted Angelico found, and quickly," Cilazzo said. "There is one more image you need to see, *Colonnello*"

The image, a silhouetted woman illuminated by a single lamppost,showed little detail. The woman, tall and thin, almost gaunt, was getting into a subcompact car. "Not many women are built like that, *Colonnello* Heifetz. I now believe that is Irina Kazakov fleeing the Vatican."

"You said Father Angelico had a workshop in the catacomb," Heifetz asked with no emotion in her voice, hoping additional detail of the investigation would be forthcoming.

"*Si*." Cilazzo nodded.

"Do you know what Father Angelico was working on?" Heifetz asked, knowing full well that Cilazzo knew.

"For certain, no," the Italian answered.

Heifetz glanced across at Perz who nodded, almost imperceptibly. Cilazzo was holding back not to be trusted.

"When Ignacio Angelico was found, and my men discovered his workshop below ground, we made many inquiries, but *ho colpito una parete di pietra*."

"English please," said Heifetz.

"Ah, *scusi*," Cilazzo answered. "We ran into a stone wall. The Vatican's silence was deafening on the matter."

Perz smiled and extended a hand. "*Grazie il signore Cilazzo*. You have been most enlightening. My aide will show you out."

Once alone, Heifetz said, "The Vatican takes these rumors of the artifacts quite seriously, Etan. Of that I am certain. We need to learn more about this Jeremiah."

"And Hans Richter," Perz added.

Heifetz scowled. "Yes, and Richter."

Etan Perz took a file folder from a drawer. "Cardinal Adriano Alba, one of the Pope's most trusted representatives to the Roman Curia, is scheduled to be in Jerusalem early next week. Intelligence says that he is meeting with members of the Chief Rabbinate Council."

"Do we know the nature of the meeting?"

"No, but considering what we now know I have a good idea, Aviya."

Settling into a plush sofa Heifetz sipped a glass of ice water. "If the boy, Faruq, rejected DeLarussa's attempts to bring him into the priesthood, then what is his involvement in all of this?"

"Again, Aviya, and this is only conjecture, I believe DeLarussa, a long time ago, discovered the boy possessed a unique skill-set and a morality, or lack thereof, to go along with it. In short, Faruq Abdalla will do whatever is necessary, and whatever DeLarussa orders him to do."

"Is he still a practicing Catholic?"

The director nodded. "I believe so, but…"

"But what, Etan?"

"DeLarussa, his immediate superior, *Monsignore* Allegretti, certain members of the Vatican's most secret inner circles, and now the orthodox rabbinate here in Israel have all bought into a hoax."

"You are certain that it is a hoax, Etan?" Heifetz said, a serious look on her face.

Director Perz laughed. "I see your sense of humor remains intact, Aviya."

"Black humor, Etan, very dark. Richter is our first priority," she added, closing the folder. "If there is nothing else…"

CHAPTER EIGHTEEN

Eluding security at Ben Gurion, Richter drove to the Russian Embassy in Tel Aviv. He'd been ordered to seek out an embassy attaché identified only as Anton, no last name. Certain that Darya Bargova's body had already been discovered on the golf course where he'd dumped her in Washington, Richter knew he needed to hurry. Killing Bargova was unfortunate, but necessary. There could be nothing left in Washington tying him to Kastianich's murder.

He'd staged her killing to look like a suicide by placing a .38 caliber revolver in her hand, pressing her finger to the trigger and firing one round into her head, ensuring gunshot residue on the skin and clothing. He hoped the single kill shot to her head would send local law enforcement in another direction. But he knew at best it would only buy him enough time to leave the country.

He stood in front of wrought iron gate surrounding the Russian Embassy and engaged a young military sentry. He showed his Russian passport and asked the guard to call upstairs for Anton.

"Who is this Anton?" the guard asked. "I do not know of anyone any Anton." The sentry said.

At a loss, Richter repeated, "Anton," the only name he knew.

Richter extended his passport again and and a Russian driver's license.

"You said his name is Anton? Anton?"

"*Da*," Richter answered.

The sentry took the documents to a small guardhouse, returning a few minutes later with a nasty look on his face. He shoved the papers back across to Richter. "Go! There is no one here called Anton. Leave now or I will have you removed."

Richter dropped his passport just inside the locked gate. "Please, young man," he called out in perfect Russian. "If you will please hand me my papers I will be on my way."

The sentry reached down and picked up Richter's passport, reached through the fence bars and handed him the document.

Richter grabbed the man's wrist and pulled his face tight against the bars. His other hand reached in and wrapped around the sentry's neck, pulling him tighter, cutting off his air supply.

Richter's mouth inches from the guard's ear, snarled, "I say this to you only one time. You will find this Anton now! Open this fucking gate and call whomever you are supposed to call and find him… Do it now or I will snap this scrawny chicken neck of yours like a twig." He increased the pressure until the guard's knees started to buckle.

The sentry reached into a uniform pocket and pulled out a two-way radio.

A soft metallic clank followed by a series of tones sounded as the gate in front of the guardhouse swung open.

"Remain where you are," a voice from a loudspeaker above his head boomed down in Russian.

Two armed soldiers appeared from a side door, their guns drawn. Richter's hands went up. They shoved him against the wrought iron bars, forced his legs apart and did a pat-down.

"You will come with us."

Sitting alone in an office on the third floor of the Russian embassy, Richter marveled at the décor, not what he remembered from his days as a Stasi operative. Nothing austere or threatening about this place—the furniture, comfortable and modern, artwork on the walls and to his left a bar with premium liquors on an antique rolling cart.

He glanced at the ceiling and his old fears returned. In one corner of the room, partially obscured by an artificial tree, a surveillance camera watched everything—a second camera, diagonally across, provided full coverage of the entire room. *Once Russian, always Russian,* Richter thought. He smiled into the lens, turning when he heard the door open. A man, over six feet tall, with dark hair and eyes and a small blemish on his cheek, came in.

"Hello Hans."

"You," said Richter staring into the eyes of the same man he'd met in Moscow along the Moskva River.

The man now spoke English with a British accent, his classic pinstripe suit and silk tie expensive.

"Do not allow my speech pattern to fool you, Herr Richter," Anton said as he sat behind a mahogany desk and opened a thick folder. "I am also fluent in Hebrew, English, and French. My name is Anthony Dustman, but do not let the accent or my clothing fool you. Here in the embassy, you will refer to me only as Anton. It is not important that you know more, but be assured I know much about you, your past, what you are capable of and to some degree your future, or lack thereof."

Richter stood up and began to pace.

Anton stopped him. "Remain seated," he said.

"When I agreed to accept this mission," said Richter, returning to his chair but not sitting, "I did not for one second think I would be kept in the dark as to what I was chasing and why."

"Sit," Anton said, more an order than a request.

Richter did as he was told.

"Very good then, I will tell you why you are chasing after two pieces of what appear to be worthless rocks."

Anton wove a story that Richter found incredulous, especially from a godless Russian bureaucrat in a designer suit. The longer Anton rambled about stone artifacts and the original tablets of the Ten Commandments, the more Richter was convinced the man, and possibly the entire Russian clandestine service, had gone insane.

"Suppose for one second that I do believe what you are saying about these chunks of granite or what you claim them to be, so what. How does one go about even establishing provenance? They are merely pieces of stone, for God's sake, inert pieces of rock."

"Are they?" said Anton. "Are you certain they are merely worthless pieces of rock? How certain are you, enough to bet your life on it?"

"I assure you, Anton, I am not a believer in the supernatural, in faeries or poltergeists. I understand why the Catholics and the Jews would want these stones if they are in fact pieces of history—but why is Moscow so interested?"

"Ahhh, so now we come to the crossroad." Anton grinned and pushed a photograph toward Richter.

"What is this?" he asked.

"That, Herr Richter, is why we have sent you around the world."

Anton handed another document across the desk. "Do you know this person?"

Richter examined the photograph, a faded black and white Polaroid.

"I recognize the face, Vasily Babkin," Richter said, tapping a finger on the image. "He was a Russian spy who worked for Stalin in the fifties. I knew him by reputation only, the man was a legend, and also a linguist I believe. He has been dead for over thirty years."

Anton nodded. "You are correct. Which brings me to this translation he made. Look again at the first photograph. Do you see the picture of an old parchment or a piece of a parchment? We believe now that a priest called DeLarussa has it in his possession."

Richter sat up straight and stared at the image for several seconds. The photograph, though faded, printed in a deep sepia, was identical to the black and white reproduction he'd been shown the day he walked along the Moskva River with Anton.

"Do you know the current whereabouts of this priest, DeLarussa?" Richter asked.

"Do not play me for a fool," Anton mocked. "DeLarussa is why you are in Israel, is it not? Look at Babkin's translation."

Anton slid a piece of paper across the desk. Richter read aloud. "'He who shall take this key to his heart shall have eternal life.' Babkin wrote this?"

Anton nodded.

Richter sat quietly, and then burst into laughter. "And you believe those words are literal?"

"It is not what I believe that matters, Herr Richter."

"Then you are, Anton, a fool. There are a thousand interpretations I can think off that do not entail the supernatural."

"Yes, Hans, you are correct on that matter. It is all bullshit."

"Then what am I chasing?"

Anton smiled. "Good, now we can cut to the chase."

"And you are going to let me in on your little secret?" Richter mocked.

"You are correct, Hans, we are not in search of biblical artifacts, certainly not stones that lead to the Ten Commandments. How stupid do you believe we are?"

Richter said nothing, holding his contempt for the Russian in check.

"Then what is it I look for?"

"A weapon, Herr Richter, a deadly weapon that belongs to Russian government."

"A weapon? What kind of weapon—if I am allowed to even know such a thing?"

Anton frowned, his eyes glaring at the German. "I do not like your tone," he snarled. "Remember where you are."

Richter knew precisely what Anton meant and became contrite, nearly choking on an apology.

"Good," said Anton. "Now that we understand each other, I will tell you what you are searching for. My superiors, and yours as well, believe the stone artifacts and the rest of that parchment will lead you to a biological weapon hidden in the Sinai desert by our military fifty years ago."

Richter asked the obvious question, if the Russians stashed the weapon themselves, why did they need him to find it?

"The weapon, Hans, was placed in the hands of a priest for safe keeping during World War II. He is or was abbot of a monastery in the Sinai. He and his band of religious fanatics were paid handsomely for this."

"And he double-crossed you?"

"No, Richter, the abbot at the time did not betray us, he died. The new abbot of the monastery is the traitor. The key to the weapon's location is in those stones—what was hidden by the abbot before his death is what you now seek. Find Irina Kazakov, Faruq Abdalla, and that meddlesome priest, DeLarussa. Follow them, they truly believe the elaborate myth of the Commandments and will lead you to it."

Anton handed Richter a slip of paper. "Go to this address in Jerusalem. It is not far. I believe your answers can be found there."

Richter looked at the paper—St. Bartholomew Catholic Church.

CHAPTER NINETEEN

Lansing picked up the telephone on his desk. It was the medical examiner's office.

Does the name Darya sound familiar, agent Lansing?

"Dr. Anapour? It's not even eight o'clock for God's sake. I haven't had my third cup of caffeine yet. Is Darya spelled with an 'ia' or 'ya'?" said Lansing as he reached for a memo pad. "Do you live in that lab?"

"No rest for the weary, Lansing."

"Touché, and no, to answer your question, I never heard the name before. Who is she? She is a she, is she not?"

"Yes, she's a she, and it's Darya with spelled with a 'ya'."

Lansing looked up to see detective Drew standing in the doorway of his office with a flash drive in his hand. He motioned for Drew to sit.

Never comfortable with unanswered questions on his autopsy table, Anapour made a dozen inquiries about the dead woman found in a water-filled sand trap on a local golf course. A dozen agencies, from Interpol to Canada's RCMP, all came up blank on both fingerprints and DNA. He then sent the fingerprints, tissue samples, a physical description, and a photograph taken prior to autopsy. A hit came back from France's *Police Nationale*.

"I'm sending it all to you as soon as I hang up," said Anapour.

Lansing downloaded the file, a fifteen-page PDF.

A clear picture of the dead woman emerged—Russian national, twenty-eight. Recruited at eighteen directly out of Lomonosov, Moscow State University, and began work in their Foreign Intelligence Service right after graduation.

Lansing scrolled through page after page with background information on Darya Bargova's childhood and education, as well as a few sparse details of her work for Mother Russia. "Busy woman," he said to Drew.

Each time a new photograph appeared Bargova looked different—hair color and length, eye color altered with contacts, and in one, twenty pounds heavier and ten years older with the magic of creative makeup, costuming and well-placed padding.

"A regular chameleon," said Drew.

"And deadly," Lansing added. "Two confirmed kills in France alone, at least that's what the French authorities believe."

Lansing put his feet up on the desk. "Okay, Arlen, what do we know about her time here in Washington, and what part, if any, she played in Kastianich's death or the real Gretchen Bell's murder for that matter?"

The phone on Lansing's desk started to ring.

"Dr. Anapour is online on line 1 again, sir."

Anapour words came so fast that Lansing needed to slow him down. He was rambling about a belt buckle he'd overlooked during Bargova's initial autopsy.

After undressing the body, a lab assistant boxed up her personal effects. He logged in a cheap, ornamental belt buckle with an engraving of the US Capitol, the kind of junk tourists purchase for a few dollars at any souvenir shop on the mall. Earlier that day while cataloging the inventory again, another tech noticed an obscure thumbprint on the rear side of the belt buckle and no corresponding notation of a thumbprint on the evidence log. She brought it immediately to Anapour's attention.

"The print got a hit, Lansing. It matches an ex-East German operative named Hans Richter, aka Albrecht Reuter, Lentz Romanov among others. A search of each alias, as well as the name Richter, came back with multiple hits—most were the wrong Hans Richter. One, however, had a strange two-letter computer link—the initials AH." Lansing moved the cursor over the link and clicked.

A man's face appeared with a highlighted notation—*Richter, Hans, agent, KGB, formerly East German Stasi, now believed to be FSB.* Under the name was a list of known aliases, followed by, *possibly deceased* and a telephone number. Lansing dialed. A short, terse, voice message answered the call.

"You have reached Heifetz. Call on a secure line."

Lansing waited but there was nothing more, not even a tone to leave a message. "Heifetz?"

Lansing typed the name Heifetz into a Google browser—page after page of names came up. He began to scroll down. On the third page, one name in particular caught his attention. *Aviya Heifetz, Israeli.* He grabbed his phone and called the FBI's National Name Check Program that disseminated information from bureau files in response to requests received from Federal agencies.

"Lansing here," he said, supplying his FBI access code to the records clerk. "I need a quick check on a Heifetz, first name, Aviya. Cross-reference it with anything having to do with Israel, Israeli, or the Middle East. Link it to keywords like Russian, Operative, or Intelligence. Check it against the Universal Index. I need all instances of that individual's name appearing in both main and reference files."

No sooner did Lansing hang up, his phone started to ring again.

Drew, from across the room, pouring coffee, laughed out loud. "Now that is what I call fast service. How do you do it?"

"Lansing here," he said into the phone.

"Please hold for the assistant director."

Felicia came on the line. "Whatever you have planned for this morning, Ted, cancel it. I need to see you and your new partner at 11:00."

"I was about to follow up on something. Is it possible to reschedule…"

Albreda cut him off. "No, Ted. Whatever you and Drew are up to, cancel it for now. Eleven o'clock sharp."

Before Lansing could plead his case Albreda was gone. He placed the phone back on its cradle. "Something's up, Arlen. That was the AD. We've been summoned to a meeting at 11:00. It sounded serious."

Ten minutes later, AD Albreda's confidential assistant knocked twice on Lansing's office door. She entered without waiting for a response and handed him a sealed envelope. *Biltmore Café. E-Street entrance. 11:00.*

"Not her office," said Lansing. "We're meeting across the street."

***

The Biltmore Cafe, directly across from the Hoover Building, open only for breakfast and lunch, had a dozen booths arranged along its perimeter. Whenever Albreda needed to take a meeting away from her office she arrange to have a secluded booth out of earshot in a back corner of the restaurant.

Behind the counter, a fry-cook with a hair net feverishly prepared e-mailed lunch orders for pick up later in the day.. Lansing and Drew started toward a back booth where two women sat huddled over coffee. Felicia sat facing him, but the second woman was a mystery.

The woman's hair, gray, perfectly coifed. Drew thought she looked like someone's grandmother.

Lansing slid in next to Albreda, Drew alongside the gray-haired woman in black pants who remained expressionless. Lansing had no idea who she was, or how she was connected to the case.

"Agent Lansing, Detective Drew, allow me to introduce Aviya Heifetz," Albreda said, and added, "Colonel Aviya Heifetz, of Israeli intelligence, Mossad."

Lansing looked across at Drew, whose facial demeanor had not changed. He knew instinctively to allow the AD Albreda to continue before jumping in with what they'd learned from Dr. Anapour that morning.

"Shalom," Heifetz said. "You as well detective Drew. It is my pleasure to meet you both."

She spoke English with a familiar cadence Lansing recognized from past interactions with Israelis speaking English.

"May I assume, Agent Lansing, that it was you who accessed a secure website at..." Heifetz stopped and looked down at the cell phone in her lap. "At 8:22 a.m. today."

Lansing nodded.

"When I was informed the inquiry came from the FBI, I thought it best I speak personally with you about that call. The web link you accessed is not supposed to be available to anyone except my operatives, but somehow it wound up as an open-source link. It has been deleted."

Lansing, incredulous, sat up straight. What is not right with this picture, he wondered. A Mossad colonel flying all the way to the United States about a murder at an American museum seemed a bit over the top. From the look on Drew's face, he wondered the same thing.

For twenty minutes, without notes, relying on memory, Lansing went over everything he remembered about the murder of Dimitri Kastianich. From Kastianich's death to an ersatz Gretchen Bell, Heifetz listened intently, nodding occasionally and looking down into her cell phone.

"What I am about to tell you, Agent Lansing, must remain here, with us, for now at least. I have already discussed this matter with Director Albreda."

Lansing looked warily at his wife, who nodded her agreement.

"In fact," Heifetz added, "I believe that if you attempt to repeat it to anyone, they would think you demented."

"Hear Colonel Heifetz out," Albreda said.

"There are people, Agent Lansing, not necessarily part of my government, but who, none the less, carry a great deal of influence in Israel, who believe that Dimitri Kastianich was murdered for a small piece of granite that is the key to finding the original tablets of the Ten Commandments."

Arlen Drew did a double take. "Pardon me, Colonel Heifetz, but you are talking about *the* Ten Commandments, Moses, Sinai, wandering the desert for forty years, rocks that spew water?"

"That is precisely what I am saying, detective. I did not say I believed it, but there are those who do and are willing to kill to obtain it. Do you know the name, Hans Richter?"

Returning to AD Albreda's office, Lansing and Drew settled into a sofa.

"Let me ask you both a question," she said. "That story Heifetz told, about stone tablets, eternal life, Moses, biblical mountains, the whole ball of wax, did you buy any of it?"

"Of course not," said Lansing. "But whether I believe it or not, or even if Heifetz does, it's irrelevant. We have a prominent scientist dead under suspicious circumstances, an innocent nineteen-year old Harvard grad student murdered, and the woman who killed her found dead, shot, her murder made to look like a suicide."

He stopped for a second, and added, "And let's not forget about that shooting over at Dupont Circle, a Vatican security officer. Somehow, some way, the Russians and the Israelis are both involved."

"What about you, Arlen?"

"I don't need any religious mumbo jumbo, ma'am, I mean as an inducement to go after whoever is behind this." Drew leaned forward. "You are looking at a lapsed Southern Baptist here, one who hasn't been to church in so long I 'spect the Lord forgot all about me. Like Ted, my main focus is finding who and what's behind this, but to answer your question, no. I don't believe a word of it."

Albreda walked to the window, looked out for several seconds, then turned and faced them. "Okay," she said. "This Richter, this ex-GDR spy, ex-KGB, FSB and all-around asshole, according to Colonel Heifetz, is currently in Israel. Two days ago, Mossad identified him arriving at Ben Gurion on a flight from Reagan, which pretty much squares up with what Heifetz told me and fits perfectly with our timeline on Darya Bargova's murder."

"What ties Richter to the Russians?" Lansing asked.

"Two hours after he arrived in Tel Aviv, they had him on surveillance video causing a disturbance outside the Russian embassy. From where I sit, at this point, he's our best lead, which is why I'm sending both of you to Tel Aviv. Two Mossad agents will meet you at the airport. Heifetz arranged it. Find Richter and bring him back sto Washington. Heifetz assures us there will be no problem with his... uh... deportation."

Chapter Twenty

Father Antonio DeLarussa and Faruq Abdalla huddled over the goatskin parchment, open and unrolled on a table in front of them, alongside it a current geological map of the Sinai Peninsula. They compared known distances on the geological survey to present day landmarks in relation to *Jabal Mūsa*, as the Arabs called it, the Mountain of Moses, Mt. Sinai.

DeLarussa laid a small, leather-bound book on the table, its yellowed pages written meticulously in a calligraphic hand.

"What is this?" Abdalla asked.

"It is a log of sorts,"

He slipped on a pair of white cotton gloves and moved a finger down to the bottom of an entry. The salutation read, 'In Christ, Fr. S. Koshenko.'

"Who is Koshenko, and where did you get this?"

"It once belonged to a Serafim Koshenko, an Orthodox priest. In 1933 he accompanied a man, a British peer, Sir Nigel Fitzwalter, and a Russian soldier of fortune named Petya on an expedition into the Sinai. Both died in a cave in. Daphne Fitzwalter, Sir Nigel's wife, died in 1958. Shortly thereafter, this book, Koshenko's diary of the expedition, came into my possession by the will of God."

"Will of God? I do not understand," Abdalla said.

"In 1958, newly ordained, just out of the seminary, I accompanied my mentor, Bishop Francis Murdoch, to a Vatican II conclave in Rome. It was there I first met Father Koshenko. In his seventies by then, I met with him several times at Bishop Murdoch's hotel. It was there he first learned of the expedition, the cave-in, and the death of his companions."

"But the diary, Koshenko just gave it to you?"

DeLarussa shook his head. "Bequeathed is a better word."

"I still do not understand."

"Many years later, the book you see arrived in Jerusalem. Koshenko left instructions for the diary to be delivered here to me. There was a letter in Father Koshenko's hand saying I would know how to proceed, how to succeed where others had failed."

Abdalla and DeLarussa turned at a sound coming from the staircase leading down into the church basement. Irina Kazakov, fighting her claustrophobia, eased down the steps one at a time and settled into a chair at the table.

"Were you successful, Irina?" asked Abdalla. "Did you find the old man, and can he help us?"

She took a breath, smiled, nodded, and reached into the messenger bag she carried over her shoulder, "I have, and he did."

She'd spent the past two days tracking down a biblical scholar, an Israeli professor of antiquity, Binyamin Gershon. She found him in a nursing home near Netanya on the Mediterranean coast.

"I was fortunate," she said. "The staff at the facility were kind, but not certain Professor Gershon could be of much help. He had, in their words, good days and bad days. He suffers from dementia and has few visitors any longer."

"You said you were lucky?" asked DeLarussa, eager to hear what Gershon revealed.

"When I first entered Binyamin's room, he was alone, sitting in a wheelchair on the balcony of his apartment, staring out at the ocean. The aide who escorted me tapped the old man on the shoulder and asked if he was up for a visitor. To my amazement, when Gershon turned and saw me, without a second's hesitation he smiled and in Hebrew said, "*Boker tov*, Irina. It has been a long time. Where have you been?"

"He recognized you?" asked DeLarussa.

"Yes, thirty-five years ago I was on a summer fellowship at Princeton, Professor Gershon was the Archeologist in Residence, and I was only a schoolgirl with a crush. I did not think I made much of an impression at the time."

"And he still recognized you after all these tearse, and with dementia no less? How is that possible?"

"In Gershon's mind, it was thirty-five years ago. The mind is a mysterious thing, Father. I caught him on a good day, and when I showed the learned professor the full-size copy of our parchment, he became agitated. If I did not know better, I would say he was moved to tears. Here, let me show you what Professor Gershon saw on the parchment that we all missed."

She leaned over the goatskin. "See these markings." Her finger moved over a pair of odd images near the bottom. "We assumed these glyphs were distance measures, but according to Professor Gershon, it is a name." She removed a slip of paper from her bag and passed it to Abdalla. "*Che-Na-Niya*, Gershon called him. Does it mean anything to either of you?"

"Yes Irina," DeLarussa said, his voice growing excited. "It makes sense. From its position on the parchment, I believe Gershon was correct. *Chen-Na-Niya* is the map's author. There was a prolific scribe by that name who lived some time before the third century BCE."

DeLarussa placed a clear grid on top of the parchment. "Without an accurate translation of the distance units, it is not possible to determine how far from *Jabal Mūsa* or even in what direction to start our search."

"Is it possible the distances indicated by the map are what we today call miles?" asked Abdalla.

Kazakov looked up. "No, Faruq, not in the sense that we understand the word today. Our mile derives from the Old English, *mīl*, which is based on the Roman *milia passuum*. It refers to the distance a Roman soldier traveled after taking one thousand steps. Other translations of the etymology make it *miliarium spatium*, one thousand intervals. Whichever is correct, *passuum or spatium*, it provides only a rudimentary measure of distances indicated on the parchment."

Kazakov removed a small recorder from her bag and hit play. The voice of an old man, barely audible, spoke in Hebrew. "Come, look, liebchen."

"That is Professor Gershon's voice," she said, tapping the eraser end of a pencil to the parchment. "And this is what the professor was pointing to when he said it, come look."

Abdalla placed the grid over the parchment.

"Look closely," Kazakov said, "Do you see this tiny marking?"

Abdalla peered through a jeweler's loupe. "Yes, I saw it weeks ago but believed it to be a flaw in the goatskin. You say Gershon recognized it?"

"Yes," she said, spinning the parchment one-hundred-eighty degrees and moving the pencil eraser to a second mark, identical to the first. Closer inspection showed that each mark contained a flourish, a stylized arrow made by a rudimentary stylus—one pointed east, the other west. On the eastern side of the map, the Gulf of Aqaba, to the west, the line ended at the Monastery of Santa Katerina, at the foot of *Jabal Mūsa*, the mountain of Moses.

"I believe he was not shocked when I first showed him the parchment," she said. "He kept repeating over and that he'd always believed the map was real and someday he would find it."

Growing impatient, Abdalla blurted, "Enough history. Did Gershon tell you where to look? Where the cave-in that killed Fitzwalter and Petya is located?"

"No, Faruk. Gershon's good day ended right there. He looked at me, and then at the map spread across the table. It was as if a dark cloud had descended over him. He asked his aide who I was, and why I was there. When I tried to calm his agitation and explain, he became angry, no, more than angry, irate, combative. It was then that his aide intervened, said it was time for me to leave because the professor would probably not be back anytime soon."

DeLarussa stood up and walked away. "Then we are still no closer."

Kazakov smiled. "No, Father, I am now certain where we must begin our search."

Two hundred meters from St. Bartholomew Church Hans Richter pulled his Mercedes to the curb. The austere black suit and boxy shoes were gone, replaced by a flowery, short sleeve shirt, khaki slacks, sunglasses, and sandals. A cheap camera dangled from a strap around his neck, and for added effect, a Star of David hung on a thin gold chain—the perfect tourist. He stood for several seconds snapping photographs of the church before climbing the steps and going inside.

In the dimly lit sanctuary, Richter peered down the nave, past the transepts to the apse and the altar, before sliding into a rear pew. From the shadows, his eyes adjusted, focusing on a door adjacent to the altar. Three figures emerged. He recognized Kazakov at once. Behind her were two men, the younger one tall and dark, the second, an older man, wore a Roman collar. That had to be the meddlesome DeLarussa he thought.

All three started up the center aisle of the church. Richter snatched a missal from a pew back and buried his head in the musty book.

Once they'd passed, he reached to his ankle, feeling for the gun secured in a leg holster. He got up and followed them until they left the church.

From the top step of the portico, Richter watched a blue Fiat drive away. He took a cell phone from his pocket and punched in a number. "I found them, Jeremiah."

CHAPTER TWENTY-ONE

Arlen Drew dozed with his head resting on a pillow against the plane's window. Next to him in the aisle seat, with his eyes closed, headphones nestled over his ears, Ted Lansing felt a soft tap on his shoulder. The El AL cabin steward handed him a folded slip of paper.

"It's from the captain, sir. He requests you come to the flight deck."

Lansing read the note—*Communication for you from Washington.*

Drew stirred, turned and watched Lansing get up. He asked in a whisper what it was about.

"Go back to sleep," Lansing whispered. "I'll take care of this."

At the cockpit door, a sky marshal in a gray blazer and dark blue slacks asked for Lansing's ID. The marshal spoke into a hand-held radio and the cockpit door clicked open.

El AL Captain Davíd Nathan extended a hand. "Shalom, Agent Lansing. "There is a radio transmission for you from Washington, Felicia Albreda. It came on a secure coded military channel.

Captain Nathan gave Lansing a set of headphones and a microphone. "Press and speak normally."

"Felicia?" Lansing said.

"Ted, listen carefully. Early this morning I received a call from Mossad Colonel Heifetz. She's returned in Tel Aviv and Mossad has eyes on Hans Richter in Jerusalem. He was spotted nat a church called St. Bartholomew."they flagged him on street surveillance video after they lost him at the Russian embassy. When you land a Mossad agent will meet you at Ben Gurion. Look for a uniformed driver from a company called Mila Transport. He'll brief you. Tomorrow, 9:00 a.m., you are meeting with a team of Mossad agents. They'll fill you in on the details. I've arranged for a SAT phone. Colonel Heifetz will have it when you arrive, along with weapons for both you and Arlen."

Albreda reminded him their son Joshua was leaving Cambridge on Sunday for the conference in Haifa.

"I'll text you his international cell phone number once I have it. Josh knows you're in Israel on assignment. He won't call you, but if you get the chance…"

Lansing cut her off. "Yes, Felicia. I will call if I have the chance."

Hans Richter left Tel Aviv in a late model Mercedes, compliments of the Russian embassy, and started back toward Jerusalem. He scanned through several radio stations before settling on a German language broadcast, but was soon bored with the caterwauling rock and roll.

Programmed into the Mercedes' GPS navigation was the Church of the Ascension, seventy kilometers away on the West Bank. Beyond the old city and the Temple Mount, the Church of the Ascension, a landmark tourist attraction, stood above the site where Mohammed, it is believed by Muslims first ascended into heaven. The drive, would take just over an hour. He turned off the radio, turned up the air conditioning and continued driving in silence.

At the Church of the Ascension, Richter got out and blended in with a crowd of European tourists exiting a tour bus. Dressed as a tourist Richter thought he looked as stupid and clueless as the crowd of elderly men and women snapping photographs at every turn on a winding gravel path leading to the shrine's main entrance. He followed the tourists to a visitors' reception area.

Through an arched gate, fifty meters from the church's dome, the tour guide stopped and raised a hand, her fingers twirling for everyone's attention. She stepped up onto a large flat stone and began a lengthy monolog about the church's long historic past.

Like most restorations o the West Bank, this one had Arab, Christian, and Jewish roots, none of which Richter gave a damn about. He had more important business. He stared down at his watch, and then back at the crowd.

The tour group started to move again, and Richter found himself inside a walled enclosure, an open rounded space that encircled the chapel. One by one group members passed through the narrow archway where again the guide began to go on about the three major religions taking credit for the site's rich history. He remained at the periphery of the group and listened, growing more impatient by the second. Where was Jeremiah?

Sensing someone behind him he turned. Jeremiah in a Franciscan robe was grinning at him.

"You are slipping, Hans. I have been behind you since you first got out of that fancy car."

They separated themselves from the crowd and Richter noticed Jeremiah's pronounced limp.

"You are hurt," he said, stating the obvious as Jeremiah slid into the passenger seat of the Mercedes.

Settling into the supple leather, Jeremiah winced, a hand rubbing at his side. "I had the damn stone in my hands," he blurted, "when that fucking witch shot me. I am lucky to be alive."

"Yes, you are my boy. Irina Kazakov can be a hellion, and I have scars to prove it."

He reached behind him and pulled a canvas sports bag from the rear seat. "Here," he said, holding up a brown, short-sleeved shirt.

"Take it. It should fit but we will have to make a stop." He reached into the bag again and pulled out a pair of black pants. "These will be too small, you will look like an Amish farmer."

Richter continued west to the HaMenuchot Jewish cemetery. "It is quiet and secluded here." Richter said. "We need to talk."

Through the cemetery's main gate, Richter followed one narrow road after another until with graves on either side.

Turning in his seat, Richter's demeanor changed. "*Sie sind ein idiot*," he snarled. "Tell me how you failed to secure the stone," he shouted, louder, surprising Jeremiah with his sudden outburst. "We spent countless hours making you believable. Great lengths were gone to, to place you at the Vatican with that fool, Angelico. And you still you failed."

"It was that woman, Hans—Kazakov."

"I do not want to hear your excuses. It is my ass on the line, not yours."

"It was not my fault, Hans. I was led to believe, by you, that Kazakov was one of us."

Richter reached for the gun in his belt. "Tell me why I should not kill you right here, leave your body to rot with the rest of this Jewish vermin. You are of no use to me now."

"That would be foolish," Jeremiah said with more confidence as Richter lowered his weapon.

He was right, and Richter knew it. He needed a second pair of eyes, eyes that would recognize Kazakov. He could not proceed alone.

Past Israeli customs at Ben Gurion, Lansing caught sight of their driver. A man in a black suit held a white card above his head—Mila Transport. Under Lansing's name, in bold marker, National Dynamics Inc.

Lansing and Drew settled into the back seat of an Audi. The driver eased his way from the curb into traffic. "I am Avi Lichter," the driver said over his shoulder. "Is it Mister Lansing, or do you prefer Agent Lansing?"

"Either is fine, Avi, but let's go with Ted for now. This is Arlen Drew, my partner."

After a fifteen-minute drive, Lichter pulled the Audi onto a narrow side street, a street whose name in Hebrew was on a small green sign, rusted and beat up to the point of being almost unreadable, a fact Lansing suspected was no accident.

Ahead, a building, also without a street number, had a caduceus symbol above the front entrance. This was no medical arts building.

In the air-conditioned lobby, Lansing looked around at the shiny marble and stone. On a far wall, a directory listed a dozen names followed by MD, DDS, and Ph.D. He doubted any of them were real. Inside an elevator, etched onto the floor, in Hebrew letters.

"What does it say?" Lansing asked.

Avi Lichter answered. "Where there is no guidance, a nation falls, but in an abundance of counselors there is safety.' They are words we live by at Mossad"

The two Americans followed Lichter to a door at the far end of a long hallway. Inside a woman Lansing recognized wore a black pantsuit and a white blouse. He saw the bulge in her jacket and the edges of a leather holster.

Aviya Heifetz looked up from her desk. "Ah, Agent Lansing, Detective Drew, you have finally arrived. Welcome to *Eretz Yisrael.* Come, sit," she said. "We shall get right down to business." She handed Lansing a thick file.

On page one, was a glossy 8x10 inch photograph of a man and underneath it a name—Hans Richter.

Lansing showed the photograph to Drew, and then turned back to Heifetz. He thumbed pages of the large folder like a deck of cards. "Do you have some coffee, Colonel? This could take a while."

CHAPTER TWENTY-TWO

Joshua Lansing fidgeted with his bowtie and looked down at his name in a ceremonial program.

Mr. Joshua Lansing – The Massachusetts Institute of Technology:

Applications of Ground Penetrating Infra-Red in Low Altitude Unmanned Aerial Vehicles Over Mixed Terrain.

Recipient of the Abraham Karem Medal for UAV Technology

The seat next to him was empty. Joshua hoped his father would reach Haifa in time to see him receive the prestigious award, but he knew it was a long shot at best. He turned and peered back as the auditorium lights began to dim as a movie screen descended on stage.

Joshua sat back and watched, enthralled, at a series of complex aerial maneuvers by unmanned aircraft combined with melodic sounds of Johann Strauss filled the auditorium. His doctoral thesis project at MIT involved ground penetrating Infra-Red sensors mounted on small boxy drones, nothing like the exotic, mantis-like robots armed with missiles flying on the screen in front of him.

Joshua's four-foot-square drone had on-board cameras capable of producing image outlines of objects below ground. The project was a combined effort of MIT's aeronautics lab and his area of expertise was groundbreaking, but it carried no weapons, guns, or missile firing capabilities.

Friederich Altschuller, Director of the Unmanned Flight Experimental Center in Haifa, came to center stage accompanied by rousing applause.

"My friends, sitting in the front row tonight is a bright light, the future of unmanned aircraft technology. In past years, several of you have been recipients of the Karem medal, but no engineer this young has ever reached the level of achievement of this year's recipient. The young man I am about to introduce will be among us and doing amazing things for many years to come. So, at this time I am most proud to introduce the winner of this year's Karem Medal for Unmanned Aerial Vehicle Technology—ladies and gentlemen, from the Massachusetts Institute of Technology in Cambridge Massachusetts, Mr. Joshua Lansing."

Amid the applause, Joshua turned to look back again hoping to see his father, but the now darkened auditorium made it impossible to see anything behind him. His mother called earlier in the day to remind him that his father was there in Israel, but he knew that for Ted Lansing, the assignment always came first.

A dozen rows back his host family, Dr. Abraham Erlich, Erlich's wife Greta, and their pre-teen son Aaron, sat with their twenty-year-old daughter, Hana. She held a video camera in her lap. On leave from the IDF, she'd volunteered to record Joshua's big moment.

For Joshua Lansing, more important than the money he'd saved by passing on a hotel in Haifa and accepting Doctor Erlich's invitation, was twenty year old Hana a corporal in the IDF. She and Joshua had become close in the few weeks he'd been in Israel.

Before getting up, Joshua shut his eyes, determined to savor the moment. He saw Hana's pixie-like brown hair, her dark eyes, and smooth olive skin. They'd spent the last two weeks going to clubs, dancing, listening to music, seeing many of Israel's historic sites, or just lying on the white sand of Haifa's beautiful beaches.

Jarred from his reverie, Joshua heard his name being called. When he looked up, Dr. Altschuller stood alongside the podium at center stage. Altschuller held a gold medal with a powder blue and white ribbon draped over his forearm. In the awkward few seconds of silence between Altschuller calling his name and Joshua realizing he was being summoned to come up on stage, a voice from behind shouted into the near silent auditorium, "Joshua, get up already."

"Hana?" he mumbled to himself.

The audience broke out in laughter.

On stage with the Karem Medal around his neck, Joshua moved in behind the lectern and pulled a stack of notecards from his inside jacket pocket. He took a deep breath and stared out at the audience.

A thousand eyes stared back. Notes he'd meticulously prepared were blurry and appeared to move on the cards. Beads of sweat dripped into his eyes. He took another long breath, composed himself and started to speak, but when he looked out again, the seat next to his was occupied. Ted Lansing, smiling, thumbs up, had made it to Haifa.

In the lobby outside the banquet hall, Lansing embraced his son. "You were sensational, kiddo. I was so damn proud I almost busted a gut in there. I didn't understand much about what you said, but by the applause, all those really smart people in the audience sure did." Lansing pointed at two men in tuxedos disappearing into the banquet hall. "Like them."

Joshua turned to see who they were "Yeah, I'd say smart is an understatement, Dad. The one on the left won a Nobel Prize in Physics."

"You are staying for the dinner, aren't you?" Josh asked. "I made sure there were empty seats at our table just in case you or mom made it. Besides, I want you to meet the Erlichs."

Josh saw a change on his father's face.

"What?" he asked.

"Remember when they called your name to go up on stage?"

Timidly, Joshua shook his head.

"Do you remember hearing, 'Josh get up already?'"

His face reddened.

"Sorry, kiddo, the jig is up. I met Hana Erlich right after the closing comments. You have excellent taste in women. Kind of like your old man." He laughed. "You like her, huh?"

Joshua nodded. "Yeah, Dad, a lot."

Come inside, I'd love for you meet Dr. and Mrs. Erlich."

"Maybe one quick drink," he said. "I convinced a certain Israeli colonel to get me a ride on a military chopper from Jerusalem to Haifa, but the ride isn't open-ended."

"But you hate helicopters."

"Not as much as I'd have hated not seeing you get this award. You know if your mother wasn't so caught up in work she'd be here too."

Lansing checked his watch. It was almost 10:30. "I have wheels up in an hour, way over on the other side of town. If I'm not there when the chopper leaves I walk."

Lansing felt a soft vibration in his pocket and excused himself, returning to the table a few minutes later with a worried look.

"What's wrong?" Joshua asked.

"I apologize, but I have to go now." He turned to Dr. Erlich. "Allow me to thank you and Mrs. Erlich for the hospitality you've shown Josh."

"Please," Dr. Erlich said. "Call me Abraham, and not another word about being sorry. "Having a fine young man like Joshua as our house guest has been a pleasure—just ask my Hana."

Hana's face reddened. "*Abba!* How could you?" She blushed deeper.

"Abraham, if you and your family are ever in Georgetown, Josh's mother and I would love to have you as our houseguests. Washington is a beautiful city."

Joshua followed his father down an escalator and onto the street. Before sliding into a cab, Lansing embraced his son. "You take care of yourself now and be careful. This is Israel and…"

"I know, Dad. Go or you'll miss your ride."

In the cab's back seat Lansing leaned forward and tapped the driver's shoulder. "Haifa Naval Base." He held up a US twenty. "And make it fast."

CHAPTER TWENTY-THREE

Hana Erlich reached across a small bistro table, took Joshua's hand, and smiled, the kind of smile that says to a boy, you are special to me. "It nice, being alone for once without Aro to pester me."

"You don't really mean that do you?"

"Yes, of course I mean it. What girl wants her kid brother around all the time, especially when she is on a date?"

"And I thought it was all about me."

"Joshua we have not had a moment to ourselves."

Joshua put his hand over hers and squeezed. "I know, but Aaron's not so bad. I kind of like him. I'm an only child and I've always wondered what it would be like to have a kid brother, pest or not."

"Oh, believe me, it is not all fun and games with that one. A twelve-year-old tagging along, no matter how much you like the little *nudnik*, is not so much fun for me."

"Yes, I suppose it is a date with a soldier. I do not usually go out in uniform when I am at home on leave. Tell me it is not too much?"

"This is not Cambridge, Joshua." Her tone grew more serious. "This is Israel. You never know."

"Okay," he said, finishing the milky-white liquor swirling in his glass, his third, making things around him fuzzy at the edges. "What do you call this stuff again?"

"Arak, a favorite if one wants maximum effect for minimum cost. One hundred percent Israeli, but you still have not answered my question."

"What question was that?"

"My uniform."

"Hana Erlich," he said, staring into her eyes. "Whether you are in khakis or that sexy dress you wore to the awards banquet, I think you are beautiful."

She blushed.

"Tell me," he said. "Were you born in Israel? I know there's a word for that, but I can't remember it. One more Arak and I may even forget my own name."

"Sabra," Hana answered. "The name comes from a desert plant, the prickly pear, a cactus with a thick skin that conceals a sweet, soft interior. It is often compared to native Israelis, tough on the outside, but delicate and sweet on the inside." She pressed a finger to a dimple in her cheek. "Like me. But no, I am not native born. My *Abba* and *Ema* made *Aliyah* from Brooklyn, in New York City. They came when I was eight and Aaron just a baby."

"Aliyah?" Joshua asked.

"It is what you call it when you pack up everything and emigrate to *Eretz Yisrael*. It is my country now. I would die in her defense."

Joshua took her hand and helped her from the table. "No more talk of dying. We are here to have fun."

Outside the club, arm in arm, they strolled past clubs filled with couples their age, boys with girls, girls with girls, and boys with boys, many, like Hana, in uniform, some had a weapon visible.

The carnival atmosphere on the street was not much different from Boylston Street in Boston, sans military getups. Kids from Harvard, MIT, Boston College, and Tufts roamed from club to club on Saturday nights much like the Israeli kids here in Haifa. Blaring sounds filtered out of one bar, fading away until the next one on the street picked up the slack. Passing a barker shilling outside a club, the man palmed a coupon into Josh's hand.

"Two for one drinks? Why not?" Josh grinned, leading Hana inside.

They settled at a table in front of a raised platform, a terrible cover band played the worst sounds either of them had ever heard.

"Two of your very finest, Araks my good man," Josh said in his best broken Hebrew to a bored waiter hovering over them in the smoke-filled room.

The waiter scoffed as he walked away. "Very finest Arak? American idiot!"

"Is this music bad or is it the booze?" Josh laughed out loud, finishing the milky-white anise flavored drink.

"Oh yes, they are terrible," said Hana. "The band and the drinks."

"Come," he said. "Let's get out of here. I have a better idea."

Standing in the neon street glow, Joshua took both of Hana's hands. "Want to play with my drone?" He stopped, hearing what he'd just said. "No, that came out wrong. I meant…"

She kissed him. "I know what you meant."

In front of a large building in an industrial section of Haifa, their taxi driver turned to face his two young fares cuddling in the back seat.

"Are you two sure about this?" the driver asked. "It looks deserted."

"Are we sure, Hana?" Joshua joked. "The man wants to know if we're sure." They broke into giddy laughter as Josh slid from the back seat.

Alone on the deserted street, Hana tapped Joshua's shoulder. "Okay, mister drone expert," she said, slurring her words. "Now what?"

The building resembled a huge airplane hangar. Above the entrance, it said 'University of Haifa.'

"To be truthful, Corporal Erlich, I don't know. You should have thought this through."

"Me?" she said "It's your drone. Maybe they left a key under the doormat."

Josh, hysterical, fell on the wet grass, the back of his shirt soaked from the dewy sod. Hana fell on top of him, still laughing out of control, but the laughter stopped when she leaned down, her lips over his.

"Didn't see that one coming," Joshua said, pulling away and standing up.

Hana took his hand. "Then I take it back."

He pulled her closer, kissing her again. "No backsies! Come on, follow me."

At the far side of the massive building, Josh pulled a plastic key card from his wallet. "Shhhhhh," he said. "I forgot. I have a key."

"It was nice of them to give you a key."

"Who?" Joshua asked.

"I don't know who, the *droners*, or do you call them *dronians*?"

Her laughter started him laughing again, and then, stopping suddenly, a finger pressed to his lips, he said, "Quiet... somebody will hear you."

Hana looked up and down the empty street. "Who?"

"Shhhhh," Joshua said again. "Somebody."

Hana, serious for a second, broke into laughter again. "The government? Isn't this a secret hush-hush place?"

Joshua thought for second. "I don't think so. It's part of Haifa University. Here, you try the lock," he said, handing her the key card.

Hana swiped it through a slot on a reader affixed to the door. She heard a click. "It works."

Joshua pulled on the door handle.

"It is dark in here, I can't see a thing," Hana whispered.

"You are right, it is dark. I think it's because there are no lights."

"A regular rocket scientist," she mocked, kissing him on the lips.

"Not rockets, drones," he said. "Follow me, and I'll show you my drone."

"Ooh, I have never seen a boy's drone before. I cannot wait to play with it. I can, can't I?"

Josh led her down a corridor to a door marked, *Flight Lab – Do Not Enter When Red Light Is On.*

Hana pointed to an unlit bulb above the door. "I guess that means we can go in." The alcohol-fueled giddiness returned.

Joshua threw a wall switch and Hana got her first look at the UAV test area. The flight-lab, over one hundred meters long, had a ceiling she estimated to be at least twenty meters. "Impressive," she said. "Now where is that drone of yours, the one you promised I could play with?

"Oh no, I said you could look, not play."

She punched his shoulder. "You are no fun, Joshua Lansing."

He opened a storage cabinet against a far wall. "Behold, m'lady, my creation; Solomon Grundy, who was born on a Monday."

"Who is Solomon?"

"Grundy, Solomon Grundy, haven't you ever… Never mind. My parents didn't get it either."

Hana stared at the strange device. Gunmetal gray and box-like, about a meter square, it had two arms protruding outward on both sides. At the end of each arm, a propeller swiveled 180 degrees. Mounted in a cage below the UAV's main body was a camera, also able to swivel 180 degrees.

"I thought drones looked like giant flying bugs, flying robots," Hana said. "This looks like a child's toy. I have seen ones like it in the Hammacher catalog."

"Hammacher catalog?" Josh said, grabbing his chest and feigning an arrow to the heart. "You, Corporal Erlich, have cut me to the quick. Solomon, I will have you know is a programmable unmanned aerial surveillance vehicle, PUAV—no weapons. He's not armed."

"Oh, so she's a he?" Hana started to laugh again. "How appropriate, like Mata Hari, and you named her Solomon. Sneaky, sneaky, sneaky boy." She giggled, kissing his cheek. "You are strange, Joshua Lansing, but I like you anyway."

Joshua carried his UAV to a small circle painted with a cross on the smooth concrete floor in the middle of the vast hangar. "Follow me," he said. "The control room is over there in that glassed-in area."

Joshua entered a passcode into a computer terminal and the drone's outboard propellers made soft humming sounds as it lifted off the painted circle, stopped at five meters and hovered. With a deftness belying the alcohol clouding his brain Joshua manipulated a joystick and took the UAV up near the ceiling, and into a series of slick roll maneuvers.

Hana oohed and aahed. "That is amazing," she cried, moving in behind him. "Can I try? Please. Please, pretty-please."

They exchanged places at the console. Hana's hand gripped the joystick with Joshua's fingers over hers. "It's tricky," he whispered into her ear, his lips brushing against her neck. "Very delicate—small movements get maximum response. You like?"

"If you mean your lips on my neck, yes, I like it very much," she murmured, her head leaning back onto his chest.

Joshua flipped a series of switches on the console. "Look at the monitor," he said, pointing to the screen.

Hana saw the top of her own head. She craned her neck upward. The UAV was hovering in place above them, static, near the ceiling. Josh scribbled some words on a slip of paper with a black, felt-tip marker. "No peeking," he said. "Hold it flat on top of your head, words facing up."

Craning her neck again, she looked up, and then back at the monitor.

"Watch," he said, his fingers pushing the control stick forward. The monitor screen filled with the white slip of paper, the edge of one black letter just visible. "Keep watching." He dialed back the magnification and the onboard camera zoomed out until the entire piece of paper filled the monitor. He'd written, 'Drones are for Lovers!' with an exclamation mark and little heart.

Hana turned on the stool, her lips pressed against his.

"What was that?" she said, pulling away from him. "Did you hear that? Someone is here, Joshua."

He hit the light switch and the hangar went dark, the only sound a soft whirr from the drone hovering above them.

"Can you make it land before they get here?"

"I can do better than that."

He flipped a pair of toggles and the hum stopped. "It has a silent run mode. Look up again." The monitor in the console was still on and Hana saw herself in an eerie green light.

"It has thermal night vision too," he bragged.

The hangar door opened and a burst of light from the hallway spilled into the dark test area. Joshua took Hana's hand and pulled her down under the console.

"You forgot to turn off the computer screen," she whispered.

Eyes glued to the glowing monitor; they held their breath as a security guard moved into range of the UAV's camera. Hana's fingers dug into Joshua's arm. Neither was laughing now. "The monitor," she whispered again. "He will see it."

Josh reached up, switched off the monitor and crawled back to Hana.

When he looked up again the guard was standing over them. "Mr. Lansing is that you? What are you doing here at this hour?"

"Busted!" Joshua said, holding a hand in front of his face to shield his eyes from the guard's flashlight. The man moved his light to Hana's face.

"Hana? Hana Erlich? Does your *Abba* know that you are here?"

Chapter Twenty-Four

Hans Richter parked on *Shvil Hatsuk* Street with a direct line of sight to St. Bartholomew's front entrance. He shut off the Mercedes' engine and waited. Soon, Faruq Abdalla emerged, got into a blue car and drove off only to return an hour later, still alone. For two days Richter saw no sign of the priest, DeLarussa, or his real quarry, Irina Kazakov.

On the fourth morning of the stakeout, fighting sleep, Jeremiah taking over for Richter was roused by the sound of a car door opening. In the soft morning light, he glimpsed a woman in the driver's seat of a black SUV, and a male figure emerging from a side door. The man approached the vehicle and handed an envelope through an open window.

Jeremiah peered at them through binoculars and zeroed in on the driver. She turned in his direction, her face partially obscured by a fine mist covering the windshield. Even through the clouded glass, he recognized her, the woman who tried to kill him as he fled Angelico's workshop in the Vatican catacomb. He fought the urge to kill her right there, Richter's voice screaming in his head. "Do not engage Kazakov." When he looked again, she was counting a roll of bills.

Jeremiah focused on the man standing alongside the vehicle and watched for several seconds before laying the binoculars on the front seat and picking up a camera. He snapped off a half dozen images, and propped a folder against the steering wheel and removed a glossy 8x10. He compared his camera's digital image with the picture in the folder. He called Richter.

"She is here, Hans, right now, at the church, Abdalla as well. I believe they are about to leave."

"What of that priest, DeLarussa?" asked Richter, his voice rising with anticipation. "Is he there as well?"

"I do not know. There is no sign of him. Do you want me to maintain my position or follow her?"

Richter, silent for several seconds, weighed his options. "Follow her," he decided. "Without the priest, Kazakov will not go far, or for long. I will be there in fifteen minutes to continue the surveillance. Call me when you know where she is going."

Jeremiah eased away from the curb, following at a safe distance. Kazakov's circuitous route confused him.

She wove in and out of side streets, changed directions, retraced already traveled paths. Was she being cautious, or did she know he was following her?

The sky grew lighter and morning rush hour traffic built as Jeremiah switched on the car's GPS to get an idea of where he was, but soon found himself leaving the old city and heading north. Twenty minutes later he passed a road sign that read, *Rockefeller Archeological Museum – 2 Km.*

Outside the museum's rear gate, Jeremiah pulled into a parking spot and watched Kazakov lean from the window and hand something to a parking attendant. After a cursory glance, the man waved her through to an inner parking area.

Jeremiah followed, stopping to show his ID, an Israeli driver's license compliments of the Russian embassy. It bore an alias, Jonas Winkler Ph.D. He placed it into the guard's outstretched hand.

"Good morning, Dr. Winkler. Is your business today tourism or professional. I do not see your name on the visitors' log?"

"Business," he answered. "I am here to meet an art restorer named Karpinski, Ludmilla Karpinski."

"Very good then. Shall I call ahead to Doctor Karpinski's office and inform her that you are here?"

Jeremiah smiled at the man. "That will not be necessary. Ludmilla is a dear friend. I want to surprise her. She does not expect me until next week."

"You may park in the rear, ahead on your right, sir. Put this placard on your dashboard. There are several visitor spaces. When you enter the building, please sign in at the desk and wait. Someone will come to escort you to Doctor Karpinski's office."

Jeremiah stepped from his vehicle, straightened his necktie and put on the suit jacket Richter had purchased for him. With one last look at his appearance in the car's side-view mirror he placed a black kippah on his bald head, another detail Richter insisted upon.

Inside a narrow vestibule, prepared to bluff his way into the museum he found the sparsely furnished area had no security, not even a receptionist. At the far end, a second door with a call button had a card scanner attached to the wall. He looked at it warily. Pressing it would summon somebody who might ask questions. He'd hoped for a real person, a lowly receptionist he could bluff.

Without warning the door flew open and three young women came through. Each wore a green blazer with the museum's logo prominent on its breast pocket. From their banter, a mixture of English and Hebrew, Jeremiah made them to be docents.

He nodded and smiled. "Shalom ladies." A pretty redhead returned the greeting and smiled flirtatiously as she held the door open for him.

***

Willem Halschtein, the museum's assistant curator, looked up from his desk. "Ah, Irina. I was not informed that you were coming, but it is a pleasure nonetheless. Come, sit. May I offer you a cup of tea, or perhaps some sherry? To what do I owe this visit? I was not even aware that you were in Israel."

"Thank you for your kind hospitality, Willem," she said. "I must decline because I am in a hurry today, but I thank you for seeing me without an appointment. You have always been a good friend."

The curator stood up. "No, it is I who must thank you, it is not every day we have someone of your reputation visit the museum. I am only sorry that Director Isaacs is not here. He will regret missing you when I tell him."

Kazakov, well aware that the museum director, Milton Isaacs, was in Paris, took his hand. "You are too kind."

Halschtein set his coffee cup on the desk. "What is it I can do for you?"

Her cover story prepared, Kazakov spoke of a dig near the tip of the Sinai Peninsula, and an old papyrus the archeologists on site needed translated.

"Ahh," Halschtein said, "you must speak of Wolfgang Schatz and the group from Vienna. There has been talk of a major find at Thebes, the Middle Kingdom."

Without a clue to what Halschtein was talking about, she bluffed. "I have been found out, Willem. I could never fool you. Yes, Schatz and his expedition are digging in what they believe is the lost tomb of Mentuhotep I."

She elaborated on the lie, telling Halschtein she'd traveled from Washington to Egypt, and then to Israel where she'd assembled a small cadre to accompany her into the Sinai to assist the Austrians.

Halschtein, hearing mention of Washington, became excited. "Were you there in Washington when Dimitri was murdered?"

Stupid, she thought, *why did I say Washington?* She scolded herself, hoping she had not opened a conversation she did not want to have.

"I only ask, Irina, because of that awful business. We were both shocked and saddened to learn of Dimitri's death under… how shall I put it, such disturbing circumstances? It is a terrible loss to our small community. Were you there when it happened?"

It was almost 10:00, no time for meaningless discussions about Dimitri Kastianich. "No Willem, I was not. I arrived in Washington a week after Dimitri's death. No one at the Smithsonian would speak about it, and when I asked they would only say that the authorities forbade it. I did not press the issue."

"All right then," Halschtein said, visibly disappointed. "Why do we not see about outfitting you properly for that trek into the Sinai. How many did you say will be going with you?"

"Three, plus two additional support people to do the heavy work, pack, unpack, set up tents, and prepare food."

Willem started for the door. "Support people, Irina—really? Is that what you call them now."

***

Jeremiah stepped into an alcove and waited.

Kazakov and the assistant curator came out into the hall. "What can I say, Willem? In my old age, I have come to like my creature comforts, even in the field."

Jeremiah followed them to a stairwell.

In a small storage room, one floor down from Halschtein's office, Kazakov read from a list. "I will need tents, at least three, several boxes of water purification tablets, MREs for a week, and portable heaters. It gets cold in the desert at night."

Halschtein assured her that everything she needed was there and hers for the asking.

Jeremiah heard all he needed to hear. He eased away and hurried back up the stairs.

***

Twenty minutes later a pair of maintenance men carried Kazakov's borrowed equipment to the parking area and packed it all into her vehicle. She thanked Halschtein and drove off, never seeing the green Volkswagen pull in behind her. The Mossad agent spoke into a cell phone. "She is on her way back to the church."

***

"Where are you?" Richter asked Jeremiah. "Do you know who Irina went to see?"

"I do," he answered. "She met with a curator named Halschtein."

"Halschtein? It makes sense that she would seek assistance from that narcissist. He fawns over her, always has. I've known him for many years. He and Kazakov were once colleagues. I believe the preening peacock had a hard on for her back in the day, probably still does. There is no accounting for taste. Ach! The woman disgusts me. But, tell me, what did you learn?"

"Halschtein is outfitting her for an expedition."

"*Gut!*" Richter said. "It is just as I expected. Return here now, we have much planning to do if we are to follow them into the desert."

CHAPTER TWENTY-FIVE

A makeshift office on the third floor of Mossad's Tel Aviv listening post was the best Ari ben Yehuda could put together on short notice. Two small desks faced each other in what Lansing thought had once been a windowless storage space. There were several faded marks visible where steel shelving once sat against a wall. An overhead fluorescent fixture gave everything in the tight space, including Lansing and Drew, a sickly pallor.

Arlen Drew stared down at the screen of a laptop. A web page displayed information about the Rockefeller Museum. Lansing, sitting across, tapped a finger idly on a photograph of the museum's logo when Ari ben Yehuda appeared in the open doorway. "What are you thinking?" he asked.

Lansing looked up. "Someplace inside this museum is someone who can help us, or at least point us in the right direction."

The Mossad agent sat on the edge of Lansing's desk. "Do not waste your time my friend. I sent an agent there yesterday afternoon. The museum's director, a Dr. Friedrich Isaacs, inventoried everything we believe was given to Kazakov. The list is extensive."

He handed Lansing a copy of the report.

"I don't see anything about where they might be headed with all that equipment," Lansing said.

"That is true. Isaacs was not helpful, even standoffish. He claimed to know nothing about Kazakov's destination and swore to my agent he had not spoken personally with her in years."

"Do you believe him?" Lansing asked.

"In a word, no."

Lansing pointed to a second name highlighted in blue marker. "Who is Willem Halschtein?"

"Halschtein is Isaacs' number two at the museum."

"Could he be the one who outfitted Kazakov?" Drew asked. "Without Isaacs' knowledge?"

"Not according to Isaacs, and certainly not without his permission," ben Yehuda answered. "We never got the chance to speak with Dr. Halschtein, or even see him."

"Tell me Ari, and please be candid, would it be overstepping if Arlen and I took a run at Isaacs, maybe even get a chance to interview Halschtein? He could be the key to finding Kazakov, and if we find her, we find Richter."

"If you think it will get us closer, then Mossad has no objections. We are not at cross-purposes here."

At the Rockefeller Museum Lansing proffered a story to Director Isaacs about being in Israel on temporary assignment with Interpol. He told him they had tracked an elusive art thief from Athens to Rome and then here, to Jerusalem. He used a well-publicized open Bureau case about recently stolen Greek statuary, taking advantage of Isaacs' known affection for Irina Kazakov and the danger she might face if the art thief caught up to her before the authorities.

Isaacs took the bait. "If you allude to the statues recovered from the Temple of Artemis, now part of our permanent collection, I assure you, Agent Lansing, they were acquired legally. The Rockefeller does not traffic in stolen antiquities."

Lansing interrupted. "No, sir. We aren't here about those statues."

"Then what business brings the Federal Bureau of Investigation to Israel? And please do not waste my time with your made-up stories. I had a visit from Mossad only a day ago," Isaacs said, his voice resonant and assured. "There is more here than meets the eye."

Even with Isaacs' emphatic denial, Lansing's behavioral training told him he had rattled the man. Beads of perspiration formed above Isaacs' lower lip and his breathing became more rapid. Not making direct eye contact was another sure tell.

Isaacs claimed he had not seen or spoken to Irina Kazakov, but realizing phone records and visitor logs could easily prove him a liar he tensed, his shoulders tightened and his lips pursed against his teeth. He remained silent for several seconds before blurting out, "Willem Halschtein is the man you need to speak with, Agent Lansing."

Lansing recognized the long delay, coupled with absently fumbling a stack of papers on the desk, a delaying a tactic. Isaacs was buying time to either get his story straight or figure a way to warn Halschtein that he was there.

"I must apologize, Agent Lansing, but as I told that agent from Mossad Dr. Halschtein is currently on leave and cannot be reached. It is a family matter, an emergency I believe, and I do not interject myself into my colleagues' personal lives."

"Please, Doctor Isaacs," said Drew, continuing to bait the man. "This is urgent, and any help you can provide will be appreciated."

Isaacs' mood changed, his voice tinged with annoyance. "Did you not hear what I said? Again, Willem is on leave and I cannot, no, I will not disturb him while he deals with his own urgent business."

Isaacs pointed to the door. "Now if you will, gentlemen, I am a very busy man."

Drew touched Lansing's shoulder. "You heard him, Ted, he's very busy. We can come back another day when he has more time. Isn't that right Dr. Isaacs?"

Isaacs nodded but said nothing.

Drew reached into a pocket and covertly removed a small digital recorder. He placed it on his chair out of Isaacs' line of sight and stood up. "Come on Ted. Leave the man to his business."

Outside in the hallway, Drew stopped. "Wait here for a couple of minutes."

Drew went back into the office, strode past the objections of Isaacs' startled assistant and burst into his private office.

Startled, a cell phone pressed to his ear, Isaacs looked up. Flustered, he feigned outrage. "Was I not clear a few moments ago? Agent Drew is it?"

"It's Detective Drew, sir, and yes you were quite clear, but I seem to have dropped my ID wallet while I was here."

On the chair in front of Isaacs' desk Drew's recorder light blinked. He scooped the miniature device into his palm, and with his back turned to the director, slipped it into his other hand, exchanging it with his ID wallet. He turned to face the curator. "Whew—found it. You can't imagine how much trouble I'd be in if I lost this thing. I apologize again for the interruption, sir."

"Well then," Isaacs said, still annoyed but now composed. "Please leave and do not come back. Our business is concluded."

***

In a stairwell outside the office, Drew hit PLAY. The director's voice came on. "*Willem, they are back. I told them you were out on extended leave. I do not know if they believed me but whatever you do, remain in your office and lock the damn door. They will be gone soon.*"

Lansing grinned. "You sneaky bastard, wish I'd have thought of it. Now how do we find Halschtein?"

Drew pointed to a building directory affixed to the wall. "There," he said. "Eight names down—Willem Halschtein, Asst. Curator – B22. We'll take the stairs."

On the basement level Drew and Lansing found Suite B22 at the end of a long hallway. The door was locked. "Now what?" Drew asked. "Pick it?"

"I don't think it'll come to that," Lansing said. He grasped the door handle, rattled it two or three times, and then, in a loud voice, said, "I've almost got it. A little longer and we're in." He turned to Drew and whispered. "Give it a few seconds."

Fifty feet down the narrow corridor a door opened and a short, slightly built man in a tweed sports coat started toward the elevator.

"Dr. Halschtein!" Drew shouted.

The man turned, looked back, but kept going. His pace quickened.

Lansing shouted, "Doctor Willem Halschtein?"

Halschtein started to run for the elevator with Drew in pursuit. He made it halfway before Drew grabbed his collar and pulled him to the floor.

"Please don't hurt me," the curator cried, cowering at Drew's feet. "I know nothing of Irina Kazakov's whereabouts. I have done nothing illegal."

"Did I mention the name Kazakov?" Drew asked, mocking him.

"Not that I recall, partner," said Lansing.

Drew pulled Halschtein upright.

Lansing took a cell phone from his pocket and called ben Yehuda. "We're at the museum and have the good Doctor Halschtein right here with us. He tried to make a quick exit. Once he's out of this building, Ari, the man is gone."

Lansing moved out of the curator's earshot and whispered into his phone. "Ari, I don't think I exactly have any legal right to make an arrest here, or even take an Israeli citizen into custody for questioning.

And besides, Halschtein, and Isaacs for that matter, haven't committed any crime, unless outfitting a world-renowned archeologist is a crime in Israel."

"So what do you suggest, Lansing?"

"Interrogating the man, even off the books, would be helpful. We're on the basement level. Get someone over here to pick him up. He knows where Kazakov went. I'm sure of it."

Chapter Twenty-Six

In the front seat of an old Range Rover assigned to Richter from an aging embassy motor pool, Richter turned to Jeremiah and shouted, "There! Below that rise—stop."

They'd followed Irina Kazakov from St. Bartholomew Church in Jerusalem, south to Ashqelon on the Mediterranean coast, and then east to Be'er Sheva. From there she led them to Nitzana on the Israeli-Sinai border.

A shower of fine sand billowed up from the dry ground and settled over Richter's Range Rover. He reached for the open sunroof and pulled himself upright, his head protruding out through the opening. "Go up ahead and see what is on the other side of this rise," he ordered.

Jeremiah lay prone at the top of the rise, binoculars pressed tight to his face. Ahead, shimmering like a mirage, a tiny object came into view. He twirled the focus ring, but undulating heat waves emanating from the desert floor made it impossible to make out who or what it was. He bounded back down to a waiting Hans Richter.

"Whoever is out there, they are too far off to make a definite identification."

Richter glanced at his watch, and pulled a small notebook from his pocket. He found the data entry he needed—a set of GPS coordinates. "We have twenty minutes," he said. "You must hurry."

Jeremiah climbed on top of the vehicle and reached down as Richter lifted a small satellite dish for him to set up on the roof of their vehicle. He spread the built-in tripod legs and secured the suction cups. Using Richter's notebook readings, Jeremiah then aligned the dish before running a pair of wires through an open window where Richter secured a USB connection to a laptop computer. He looked at his watch, again, for the third time—two minutes.

At 11:55 a grainy image appeared on the computer screen. Transmitted from a satellite three hundred kilometers above, compliments of the Russians, it scanned the desert for a hundred kilometers in all directions. The image began to sharpen. Perigee and maximum clarity were in six more minutes.

Richter began a screen-capture program, hitting AUTOSAVE every thirty seconds until the satellite passed out of range and the computer screen went dark.

Richter scrolled through the captured Jpegs. A pair of blurred objects in the lower right-hand corner of one image stood out from the surrounding light-colored sand. He punched in a three-key sequence and a grid with a vernier scale superimposed itself over the screen. A quick calculation determined the objects were precisely 20.23 kilometers away. He entered a second set of keystrokes and the image zoomed to maximum magnification. He could make out the shape of a vehicle, possibly two, but they were too blurred to make out anything for certain.

"That has to be them," Jeremiah said, looking over Richter's shoulder.

"You are probably right. But where do they go? There is nothing but sand, snakes, and scorpions for a thousand kilometers, a few oases, small towns, but mostly dry riverbeds and mountains."

"We could outflank them, Hans, be on them before they know we are even here."

"No, I do not yet know what Kazakov learned about the stones or where she is going. Even if we do catch them and take the map there is no guarantee she will cooperate. No, Jeremiah, killing them will not get us to where we must be. Without Irina's cooperation, I cannot decipher whatever is on that *Gott verdammt* parchment she carries. I know her, Jeremiah, more than I want to, believe me. She is stubborn as a mule, a nasty one at that. For now, it is best we wait and we follow. For the next two days, there is a small window near midday to track them by satellite if they venture too far off."

Richter closed the laptop, disconnected the cables and stepped from the Range Rover. He made his way back up the rise and stared across the shifting terrain of undulating sand. Silent, thinking what his next move should be, he made his way back down to Jeremiah.

"Pack it all up," he ordered. "We go now."

Brushing sand from his hair and clothing Richter climbed back inside the Rover. "There are several more hours of daylight. Once darkness comes we will shorten the distance between us."

***

Irina Kazakov stared into a deep wadi and pointed west. "Over there, Father, to the left."

DeLarussa cupped a palm over his eyes and squinted into the bright orange ball of a setting sun.

"Do you recognize it?" she asked.

"Of course I recognize it, Irina. I have visited Santa Katerina on many occasions. Father Petrakis, the abbot for decades, was a dear friend. Sadly he died a few years ago, well into his nineties at the time. The new abbot is called Androlitis. I have not yet met him."

"Then it is time you did."

"You know this Androlitis?"

"I do," she answered. "Constantine Androlitis is a renowned scholar. Long before he was posted at Santa Katerina we collaborated on a paper in Athens. He is quite the expert on ancient scrolls and documents. He speaks several languages, from the Romances to Aramaic. I am certain he can help us."

"When do I meet this learned scholar? There are so many things I wish to speak with him about."

"Soon, Father. Tonight we camp outside the monastery wall. After dark, you and I will make our way down to meet with Father Androlitis. It has all been arranged."

"How much does he know, Irina, about our reason for being here?"

"He knows only that we are in search of an important archeological dig site that may bring clarity to the existence of the man antiquity calls Moses."

CHAPTER TWENTY-SEVEN

In an unmarked hangar a mile away from the passenger terminals at Ben Gurion Airport, an Israeli Air Force preflight briefing-room devoid of Air Force personnel sat empty. On the tarmac, Lansing and Drew, both in non-descript khaki flight suits, exited an unmarked sedan. Ari ben Yehuda greeted them.

Drew smoothed the legs of his tan nylon fabric. "Nice outfits," he said.

Ari ben Yehuda laughed. "Compliments of the Israeli Air Force no doubt my friend—a fashion statement to be sure."

All markings, flag, and rank were gone from the generic flight suits.

"We have excellent seamstresses at the IDAF. You and Lansing do not exist, at least not officially."

Lansing tapped Drew's shoulder. "So, Ari here has never existed. How long is the flight?" Lansing asked, referring to Yotvata, forty kilometers north of Eilat; the staging area for their jump-off into the Sinai.

"Not long, under an hour," ben Yehuda answered.

The door to the preflight room opened and ben Yehuda motioned to a man in the doorway. "Come Elon, I want you to meet Ted Lansing, Special Agent, FBI, and Arlen Drew, Detective, Metro Police, Washington DC."

Elon Bilboz extended his hand. He wore an identical khaki flight suit.

"Is he Mossad?" Lansing asked.

Ari ignored the question.

"This trek we are taking into the Sinai, is it a covert operation or not?" Lansing asked.

"Not covert, not in the strict sense, Ted."

"Then why all the secrecy, removal of flag and rank designations, landing first at an out of the way airfield in the Negev. Hans Richter is a stone-cold assin, not ane international terrorist with political repercussions on the line."

"True, Ted. But your CIA has its limitations as well as Mossad, does it not?"

Without waiting for Lansing to answer he added, "The CIA and FBI have similar restrictions. You are after Richter, a murderer, but I have a more sensitive mission. If we are mutually beneficial to each other's ends, so much the better. But make no mistake, after we cross into the Sinai, not exactly friendly territory, we are in Egypt."

"I thought..." Lansing started to speak, but ben Yehuda stopped him.

"Some history my friend. The 1978 treaty demilitarized the peninsula, and only by God's will has the Egyptian peace held. I assure you Tel Aviv wants nothing to jeopardize that agreement. The last thing anyone, Israeli or Egyptian, needs is an incident involving a covert Mossad operation in their territory."

"So, you're saying if we are caught out there we're basically screwed, disavowed, on our own?" Drew asked.

Ari ben Yehuda smiled. "You read too many Le Carré novels my friend. No, we would not be disavowed, nor left to languish in some Egyptian prison. There would, however, be serious international repercussions followed by the usual diplomatic outrage. Better we look like anything but Israeli military or clandestine service."

Lansing left the preflight area and made his way through a massive hangar where a pair of F-15 fighter jets sat side by side as a crew of mechanics worked on the engines. Painted in desert camouflage, both planes had Israeli markings. Lansing stopped to admire the warplanes he'd not seen up close since he left the Navy.

Lansing slipped on a pair of mirrored aviator sunglasses, looked out and groaned, "Oh geeze, no."

"What's wrong?" Drew asked.

"That's what's wrong." Lansing pointed.

Fifty yards from the hangar door a blue and white helicopter stood parked, on its side Arabic lettering. "What does it say, Ari?" Lansing asked.

"Eilat Desert Tours Inc."

"You aren't fond of those things?" Bilboz laughed seeing Lansing's pained expression.

"Long story, but no, I mean yes. I hate them."

Bilboz placed an arm on Lansing's shoulder. "I promise to be gentle, my friend." He laughed and walked away.

Ben Yehuda came up alongside Lansing. "Sorry, Ted. It is the best Colonel Heifetz could do, the chopper I mean."

The SA-Eurocopter flew a southeast course passing Be'er Sheva. Lansing, his palms gripping the seat arms every time Bilboz took them into a banking maneuver. He closed his eyes to stave off he vertigo he knew was coming.

The farther south into the Negev they flew, the sparser the terrain below, now a uniform sea of tans and browns punctuated by swaths of green, oases, settlements, and villages. In under an hour, Bilboz set the helicopter down in Yotvata, fifty kilometers north of Eilat on Israel's southern border where the Gulf of Aqaba separates the tiny nation from its neighbors, not always friendly, Egypt, Jordan, and the vast Arabian Desert.

Lansing climbed from the chopper and looked around. They were a quarter mile from a passenger terminal. A ground crew in green coveralls started to unload equipment from the helicopter's cargo bay. Bilboz pointed to a Jeep Cherokee coming toward them. "Our next ride."

Sliding into a seat behind the driver, Lansing questioned why they were going in the opposite direction from the terminal.

"We start early tomorrow, Ted, very early," said ben Yehuda. "I have arranged a billet for the night. Once we are in the Sinai it will be bare bones, few creature comforts, but tonight good food, a comfortable bed, and a hot shower, compliments of the Israeli Air Force.

Towel around his waist, Lansing stepped from the small shower enclosure in his room. He picked up a phone only to hear a woman's voice before he could say a word. "How may I assist you, Agent Lansing?" She spoke English with an Israeli accent.

"I'm impressed," he said to the disembodied female voice at the other end. "Not even one ring. Are you monitoring me?"

"How may I assist you, Agent Lansing?" He thought she might be a recording.

"Ari ben Yehuda, please."

"Thank you," the disembodied voice answered.

Ari picked up. "Dinner in a half hour, Ted—Officers' Mess. Turn left from your room and follow the green stripe on the floor."

"Not why I called, Ari. I need a favor or at least some information. My son, Joshua, is in Haifa for a conference. I have a satellite phone in my duffle, and I'd like to call him before we shove off tomorrow at 0600. What's the protocol on outgoing communication?"

"As long as we are within Israel's borders, a SAT phone call to Haifa is okay, but be careful of what you say to him. No hint as to where you are or what we are doing. Once we cross over into Egypt and certainly when we are deep in the Sinai, absolutely no outside communications that are not on secure military channels. The Egyptians routinely monitor radio and telecom traffic. Somebody will be listening, bet on it. If we encrypt, it is a dead giveaway that we are here for no plausible reason."

Lansing placed the receiver back on its cradle and took the satellite phone from his duffle.

y idea when you'll be headed back home to Cambridge?"

Lansing turned at a knock on his door. It was Drew. "Ted, I'm heading to the mess hall."

"Go on ahead, Arlen. I'll meet you there

Lansing ended the call to his son and looked at the expensive watch Felicia hgave him before he left for Israel. He scrolled through a list of cities, stopping at Washington. The time changed to 3:30 pm.

Chapter Twenty-Eight

A million stars flickered above the desert floor. Irina Kazakov looked out into the Sinai and mused. "This is exactly how it must have looked when God delivered his sacred laws to Moses."

She made her way toward Father DeLarussa's tent. Faruq and the Egyptians they'd hired slept nearby in another pair of tents.

"It is time, Antonio," she whispered. "We must go now."

Shev led DeLarussa down a boulder-strewn path to the twenty-foot high outer wall of Santa Katerina. She looked for an arched opening and a hand carved wooden door on the eastern side of the monastery.

On a ridge overlooking Santa Katerina, Jeremiah peered through binoculars at a pair of lights descending on a path toward the monastery. He noted the time, twelve fifty-five. The flickering lights continued on a downward trajectory to the outer wall and disappeared. The silhouette of Santa Katerina's bell tower, barely visible against a purple sky, melded with Mount Sinai's peak, a ghosted image in the distance. Jeremiah turned at the sound of approaching footsteps.

"You could not sleep either, Hans?" he said to Richter.

The German stood behind him with a down jacket zippered to his neck, its collar turned up. He knelt alongside Jeremiah. "This god-forsaken wind, how could anyone sleep?"

"Perhaps God speaks to you," Jeremiah said. "Maybe He is angry at all the horrible things you have done."

Richter scowled. "*Wer fragte Sie?* Who asked you?"

"A light, Hans. It came from over there." Jeremiah pointed to a rise a a kilometer away.

"Was it Kazakov?"

"I do not know." Jeremiah stood up, binoculars dangling from a strap around his neck. "It is too dark. But if I had to guess, I would say yes. They are already in the monastery."

"*Gut*," Richter answered. "*Gekommen. Wir gehen.* We go. It is time we learn what she knows."

Awakened by a ringing telephone, Christavo Demos leaped from his bed. The call he dreaded, but expected, had come. Barely able to close the long row of buttons of his clerical habit, and place the velvet *skufos* on his head, the thirty-five-year-old priest sprinted across the open courtyard to the arched doorway leading into Santa Katerina's library behind the church's main altar. His thumb and forefinger grasped the gold, three-barred eastern cross that hung on a chain around his neck as his robe flew open.

Curator of the monastery's rare book collection, Demos had been awakened by a call warning that strangers were making their way down the ridge overlooking the monastery.

He burst through the library door where sAbbot, Constantine Androlitis, stood. Demos saw the look on Androlitis' face. "You know?" he said.

"Yes, Christavo, I did not think she would come, at least not this soon, before we had time to plan. We need more time."

"They are almost at the gate. Do you think she suspects?"

"If she does not suspect now, she soon will. Send Brother Tsakalidis. Tell him to bring them here."

Kazakov and Father DeLarussa reached the easternmost wall of the monastery. A waiting novice embraced her. "I am Brother Tsakalidis. Follow me, please, quickly."

Irina Kazakov nodded.

"Father Androlitis waits for you in the chapel."

A row of lights set flush on a concrete path wound its way toward the chapel of the Church of the Transfiguration, Santa Katerina's basilica. Construction of the monastery began in 548; one of the oldest in the world, it housed an impressive array of unique books and artifacts, including the *Syriac Sinaiticus.*

Entering the darkened sanctuary, Tsakalidis led them down three polished marble steps, each inscribed with Greek letters spelling *Lakobos,* James, an apostle of Jesus. The steps lead to the Narthex, an elaborate wooden door, leading to the three-aisled interior of the church.

Starting down the central nave DeLarussa stopped to admire the mosaics and icons that lined the walls. From one of the earliest known depictions of Jesus, the *Christ Pantocrator,* to the transfiguration, centuries old chalices and reliquaries held remains of martyred Christians. They filled niches from the Narthex to the apse.

In front of the altar, Tsakalidis stopped, turned and urged DeLarussa to follow. "Please, Father, there is no time. We must hurry."

DeLarussa and Kazakov followed him up three marble steps, and onto the church's main altar. Behind it was a small chapel the faithful believed to be the site where Moses first heard God speak.

The walls of the chapel, clad in blue Damascene, surrounded a silver plate embedded in the floor that marked the spot where God appeared to Moses. Tsakalidis knocked twice before entering.

Constantine Androlitis stood at a reader's lectern poring over an old tome, its leather cover cracked and dry, with a fading icon, a Roman cross, visible through a patina formed by a thousand hands examining the sacred text for a thousand years.

"Is that…" Kazakov said, her voice rising an octave with a slight quiver. She recognized the book open on the altar, the *Syriac Sinaiticus*, the oldest preserved manuscript of the Bible, dated to the fourth century.

Androlitis beckoned her to come closer. "I thought you would be interested in seeing this, Irina"

"I believed it disappeared from Santa Katerina in the eighteenth century only to reappear a short time later in St. Petersburg."

"You know your history well, Irina. The tsars were not shy about acquiring things they had no business acquiring. Cossacks first stole it, but the British, also not known for their better judgment, later acquired it. It collected dust in a British museum for decades until it was returned to us. But first, if I may, allow me to see this map, this parchment you wrote about in your email."

Hans Richter, gun in hand, came through a small door at the rear of the cathedral. He knelt in darkness, hidden from view. Jeremiah followed close behind him. Halfway down the nave, the Russian operative ducked behind the Bishop's Throne, *a cathedra,* a large, ornate chair, the symbol of a bishop's authority, a fixture in classical cathedrals for centuries.

Richter unfolded a hand drawn diagram and pointed to the altar bathed in a surrealistic blue light.

"There, behind the altar," Richter whispered. "There is a chapel and the Sacristy. Remain here in the shadows."

A voice from the darkness called out, "Who are you and why are you skulking about at this hour?"

Richter's first instinct was to brandish his gun, end the threat with one silenced round. A gunshot h would give away his position, his element of surprise, and bring people running. From the corner of his eye, he spotted Jeremiah in the shadows, hidden by the Bishop's Throne.

"I think I am lost," Richter said. The gun remained out of sight at his side. "I am here for the conclave… and I could not sleep. I wanted to see the basilica for myself before morning prayers."

"I am Father Demos," the priest said. "I know nothing of a conclave, tomorrow or any other day. I think it best I walk you back to your room. What is your name, my son?"

A sliver of light from the altar illuminated Demos' face.

Jeremiah sprang from behind the Bishop's Throne. He reached his forearm around Demos' neck. Choking sounds came from deep inside the priest's throat as Jeremiah took a switchblade knife from his pocket and plunged the thin blade into Demos' side. Jeremiah lifted him off the ground, the knife protruding from the stunned man's ribs.

Demos flailed, thrashing, kicking, gasping for air, but he was no match for the powerful Jeremiah. Soon, the thrashing and choking noises stopped. Jeremiah and Richter dragged the dead priest into the shadows under a pew.

Richter whispered, "Whatever Kazakov may or may not learn from Androlitis we cannot remain here any longer. It is too dangerous. When she is ready to leave, we will follow her."

DeLarussa pulled the parchment with its map from the protective sheath and laid it flat on a table. Androlitis placed a finger on the parchment before peering in close through a huge magnifying glass. "Is this the original document?" he asked. "Has it been carbon dated?"

"Yes," Kazakov answered. "Between 1200 and 1300 BCE."

"That is good," he said. "Hebrew scripture places Moses' birth around 1270 BCE."

Androlitis moved his finger to a section of text below the faded map. "This does not appear to be Hebrew or Aramaic. Very curious." He turned to her. "Do you know the term language extinction?"

"Of course, Father. It occurs when there are no native speakers and the spoken word disappears into antiquity."

"Yes," Androlitis said. "Dead languages are most difficult to translate. Their idioms and dialects are lost, and rarely do we find any written word. I have never seen this language before. I do not believe I can be much help."

A loud, piercing scream came from the cathedral. A voice, or was it several, Androlitis could not tell, were wailing and crying in the basilica. Over and over the word, "*phoneús,*" murder, reverberated through the church.

Kazakov started for the chapel door.

"Wait!" Androlitis screamed. "It is not safe for any of you. Let me go."

In a side aisle halfway up the center nave three young men in *Rassaphores,* the Eastern Orthodox habit of a novice priest, were kneeling, cradling Father Demos in their arms. "He is dead! He is dead. Father Demos has been murdered."

Androlitis bent down and felt for a pulse; there was none. "Did anyone see who did this?"

"No, Father, God forgive us. We came to prepare for morning mass. I was there." He pointed to a wall of icons and religious paintings, iconostases that separated the nave from the sanctuary.

"I heard a noise, a moan. I looked but saw nothing." The young man made the sign of the cross. "Only when we were leaving did I see poor, dear Father Demos."

"Go quickly, my son. Call the authorities," said Androlitis.

Androlitis hurried back to the chapel. "Roll the parchment and follow me. You all must leave… now. It is no longer safe for you to be here."

***

"Pick up, damn it, pick up." Ben Yehuda impatiently spoke to himself. A digital bedside clock said four-thirty a.m. On the fifth ring, a sleepy voice answered.

"Lansing here. This better be good."

"Get your ass out of bed, wake up your partner and get over to the preflight lounge ASAP."

"Ari?"

"Yes. We got a break, a coded message from a Mossad operative in Cairo who monitors Egyptian police bands. There's been a murder. A priest named Demos."

"Who?" Lansing asked.

"Not who, Lansing, where."

"Ari, stop playing games."

"This dead priest, Father Demos, was murdered, stabbed, and very professionally I might add. Have you ever heard of a monastery called Saint Catherine, Santa Katerina?"

Lansing did not answer.

"It is at the foot of Mount Sinai—a community of Orthodox priests—a tourist destination for religious pilgrims."

"And you think Richter is responsible?"

"We will know when we get there."

An hour before first light Lansing and Drew left their billet and started for the tarmac. Instead of a fixed wing aircraft, Lansing looked out at a Ford Explorer parked where the Piper Aztec chopper had been the day before. Elon Bilboz, their pilot, was supervising a crew, loading equipment into the Explorer's tailgate.

"No plane?" Lansing asked.

"There has been a modification," ben Yehuda answered. "Two, as a matter of fact. We first drive to Santa Katerina to investigate what happened to that priest, Demos, but there is no place near the monastery to land a fixed wing aircraft. Elon does not think it wise to fly. The place will be crawling with Egyptian police or military.

But more serious is the chatter Mossad picked up from the Egyptian military. They are beefing up patrols in the Sinai. Mossad ais not sure if it is related to the murder or some other internal matter. Who knows with those idiots? Better we are not in the air with the Egyptian Air Force active. From Aqaba, it is only one hundred fifty kilometers. If we hug the coastline there will be paved roads much of the way."

Chapter Twenty-Nine

Lansing got his first look at Santa Katerina from a sand dune overlooking it from the west. A narrow path twisted down to the walls surrounding the monastery. Mt. Sinai was framed in the distance beyond.. "So that's God's Mountain," Drew said.

"Yes, my friend," ben Yehuda said. "*Jubal Musa,* as the Bedouins call it."

"You know, Ari, as a kid I heard so many songs in church about the grandeur of Mt. Sinai, I thought it would look a little more…"

At the outer wall of Santa Katerina, Elon Bilboz pulled the Ford Explorer alongside a vehicle with Egyptian police markings. A crowd of Italian tourists and a female guide, the all-business type in crisp blue slacks with an embroidered logo on the breast pocket of her blazer that reas, *Giri delle Terre Sante di Rendazzo*, Rendazzo Holy Land Tours. The woman stood alongside a tour bus grumbling to an Egyptian police officer in Italian.

Ari approached the apoplectic tour guide ranting about the stupidity and manhandling ofr tour group endured at the hands of these Egyptians. "*Tre ore attendiamo,* three hours in that bus and now this," she cried. "We are so *in ritardo,* behind schedule." Ben Yehuda, his Italian passable, sympathized. He asked her what was wrong.

"*Stupido, stupido, stupido,*" she shouted. "*Il posto maledetto è chiuso.*"

"What did she say?" Lansing asked.

"Signora Capella here says the monastery is closed—no tourists in or out by order of the Egyptian authorities. She is angry because nobody bothered to contact her or the tour company. They spent the better part of a day getting here only to find that the police closed the place."

Ari ben Yehuda approached the Egyptian officer, and in perfect Arabic asked the reason for the delay. After a short exchange, he returned to the vehicle. "The man could not, or would not, provide details except to say we had better turn around because no one will be admitted for the foreseeable future."

An elderly Arab in a white *dishdasha* with a knitted *keffiyeh* on his head approached, his weight supported by a crude walking stick. "You are the one called ben Yehuda?" he asked in a whisper. Lansing shook his head and pointed to Ari.

"I am Mollach, Agent ben Yehuda. Please, to follow me."

The old man led them around the monastery wall to a solitary steel door. He rapped his cane three times and waited. The door opened.

A priest greeted them with a simple nod. "I am Brother Odonio." He reminded ben Yehuda about the police presence.

"That is a beautiful name, Odonio. In Hebrew it means God." The Mossad agent recognized Adonio's recent tonsure and outer cassock, a *rasson*, with its wide sleeves and *paramandyas*, a square cloth worn on the back, embroidered with the instruments of the Passion connected by leather ties

Odonio led them past an outdoor chapel, through a second door and down a flight of concrete steps, the ceiling so low that Lansing and Drew both needed to duck their heads in the confining space, a narrow passage lined with white tiles. They emerged in the church library.

"Please," Lansing said with urgency. "We don't have a lot of time. May we speak with Father Androlitis as quickly as possible so we can be on our way? The matter is very important."

Odonio smiled again. "And you must be the American that Father Androlitis spoke of. Are you not?"

"Yes, but…"

"Why are you Americans always in such a hurry, running everywhere, going no place?"

Ben Yehuda took Lansing off to the side. "Let me do the talking, Ted. They have their ways of doing things. We cannot rush them."

CHAPTER THIRTY

"I believe the authorities are gone, but I must first be certain before we can proceed," Father Odonio whispered.

No Ben Yehuda said "

The Orthodox priest touched ben Yehuda's arm. "It is not only we in the brotherhood who will suffer if the Egyptian authorities find you here. They will accuse us of murdering Father Demos. We have had our problems with the authirities in the past."

Reluctantly, ben Yehuda agreed.

Lansing and Drew remained behind in the chapel, while ben Yehuda, a hand firmly on his weapon, went out to the sanctuary and crouched behind the altar.

He watched Odonio make his way up the center nave. Midway he reached the Bishop's Throne, cordoned off with yellow police tape to mark the spot where Father Demos' body had been discovered.

Genuflecting, Odonio continued to the Narthex, and then down a short flight of marble steps to the cathedral's front door. He peered into a courtyard.

Two Egyptian police officers speaking Arabic, cigarettes dangling from their lips, were enveloped in a cloud of gray smoke. Odonio watched them toss the half-smoked butts onto the ground, get into a rusted Jeep and drive toward the monastery gate. Only then did he lift the hem of his robe and hurry back up the nave, motioning for ben Yehuda to summon the others.

At the Bishop's Throne, Lansing stopped. Three rows of pews were cordoned off by yellow tape. He ducked underneath and moved to the far side aisle where a chalk outline of a body extended under a pew. Dark stains of dried blood were everywhere. The outline of the body showed the victim's legs bent at the knees, one arm straight out, pointing down along the torso, the other arm outstretched above its head as if reaching for something.

Drew shined a flashlight on the chalk outline. A pencil-thin beam of light followed the contours of an outstretched arm. He stared at it for several seconds, thinking, before turning to Odonio. "Was Father Demos face up or face down when they found him?"

"Upward," Odonio answered, "on his back. I shall never forget his eyes, open, stared at me. He was dead. I see them now when I close my eyes."

"What are you thinking, Arlen?" Lansing asked.

"Look at that," said Drew, pointing to a scattering of small brown wood flecks on the floor.

Kneeling, he dabbed at them with his fingertip. "Wood shavings?" he said, lifting a piece of shiny metal lodged in the leg of the pew.

Lansing took it from him. "It's a damn paper clip."

Drew sat on the floor, stretched onto his back and slid underneath the pew, his flashlight pointing upward. On the underside were words scratched into the underside of the bench.

"Give me your camera," said Drew.

Aiming the camera's lens at the underside of the bench Drew snapped a dozen digital pictures.

Something had been etched into the underside of the pew. "Can you read this, Odonio?"

The priest squinted at the tiny image on the camera's viewing screen.

"It is, the word for 'lower' but there are letters missing."

Drew brought up a second image. Odonio identified the etched word as 'map.'

Examining a third image, Odonio, translated it as, 'under the rose.'

Lansing started to brainstorm. "Under the rose on the lower map? A map with a rose at the bottom? Look under the rose? Do you have any idea what map Father Demos referred to?"

Odonio's face went ashen. "Oh, dear God, yes, yes, of course, it was that map."

"That map?" ben Yehuda asked. "What map?"

Odonio's entire body shook. "That is what she came for, why they were here. She came asking for the Abbot's help."

"Who is she?" Lansing asked.

Odonio spit out the words. "That horrid Russian woman, Kazakov. She is the reason Father Demos is dead."

Drew pulled Lansing aside. "Richter is here someplace, and close by."

Lansing took the young priest's arm and turned him around. "Please, Father Odonio, what map were you referring to? This is very important."

"Forgive me. Just before Father Demos was murdered, we were all gathered in the rectory."

"All? Who is all?" Lansing said.

"That Russian woman, Kazakov, a Catholic priest from Jerusalem called DeLarussa, a young man, Egyptian I believe, and our Abbot, Father Androlitis. The Kazakov woman had a parchment unrolled on a table. It had a map with inscriptions… on the lower portion."

"Did the parchment have a rose?"

"I know nothing of any rose. The language was one we had never before seen. It was then that Father Demos suddenly left the rectory."

"Do you know why he did that, or where he went?"

"He needed to find something in our library archives, but did not say what. A half hour later we heard the screams coming from the sanctuary."

Lansing pulled ben Yehuda to aside. "Richter must have followed them here from Jerusalem, sneaked into the church looking for Kazakov and surprised Demos, or maybe Demos surprised him."

"If you're right, Ted, Richter has at least a twenty-four-hour head start. Kazakov and her gang, even more."

Lansing asked ben Yahuda if Mossad could be of help.

"Maybe," ben Yehuda said.

He took a satellite phone from his pocket.

"Is that a good idea?" asked Lansing.

"I must chance it if we are going to catch up to them. It's not perfect but if the call is short…" He stopped when a voice came on the line.

"It is me," he said to a faceless female voice. "I need a secure line to Mother, and I need it now. I do not care where she is—find her."

Across the courtyard, inside the priest's private residence, Odonio closed the door to his room. He lowered a window shade, reached into a pocket and removed a cell phone with one pre-programmed number.

"Odonio?" The voice was Father Androlitis'.

"Yes, Father, it is me."

"Thank God. Have the police left the monastery?"

"Yes, but I am here with two Americans. They are from the FBI. Also, there is an agent from Mossad called ben Yehuda."

"Do they know where I went?"

"No. I told them nothing, but I do have news that could prove helpful. Father Demos left a cryptic message before he died. It was etched into the wood on the underside of the pew where we found his body. The black FBI agent, the one called Drew, discovered it. He is quite the clever detective. On that parchment you took with you, there is a rose."

"A rose? Are you certain you heard this detective correctly?"

"Yes, Father.. That is all I know. Do not allow the Russian woman to find it. It may be the final clue she needs to discover our secret. I await your return."

Odonio hurried back to the rectory where five priests of the order, each dressed in black woolen robes with cowls pulled over their heads, waited for him.

"The day has come, my brothers, the day we have dreaded, but a day we are prepared for. We do not have much time. Father Androlitis cannot keep them at bay forever."

Led by Odonio, they walked in single file to the church's main altar. Odonio leaned a shoulder against a marble table. It slid away revealing a stone staircase leading downward. A row of lights built into the wall came on illuminating the steps.

***

Ari ben Yehuda peered at the readout on his satellite phone. One word appeared, 'Mother.' "Aviya?"

"Yes, Ari."

"Do you know where we are right now?"

"Yes," she said, careful not to say anything to give away his position if the Egyptian authorities were listening. From descrambled GPS data on his satellite phone, Heifetz knew precisely where her agents were at all times.

"Can you help?" he asked.

"Maybe. I am looking at real-time images from an American satellite."

"American satellite images? How did you acquire them?"

"For that, you must thank your friend Lansing. I spoke with his superior in Washington. She was quite helpful and quite solicitous about both he and Arlen Drew. "The Americans have eyes looking down at most of the Sinai, Yemen, Saudi Arabia, and Syria, but that is no secret to anyone. Do you have a timeline for me to narrow my search? These images and videos are all time-stamped. There are thousands of files."

Ben Yehuda gave his best estimate of when Kazakov fled after Demos' murder.

In less than a minute Heifetz came back. "I have a pair of relevant videos taken forty-one minutes apart. The satellite position at the time was directly above your current location. It shows two vehicles traveling from a rise on the east side of the complex heading west into the desert. There is a second clip with a third vehicle traveling in the same direction on the same trajectory, also due west. Both clips are less than fifteen seconds long. Both are traveling at a rapid speed."

"Any idea where they went?"

"No. Only that they were traveling southwest."

"Were traveling?

"Yes, for some reason the first two vehicles turned around and started back."

"Back to where?"

"From what I can tell, back to you."

Ben Yehuda looked at Lansing, a perplexed expression on his face.

"One more thing," Heifetz said, "weather satellites indicate a huge dust storm rolling in from the west. They are going to run right into it. Stay put for now. I will contact you after it clears."

"We must wait," he said to Lansing. "There is a powerful storm headed in our direction."

"Are you certain?" Lansing asked.

"Yes, my friend. The images were provided by your government, compliments of your boss."

"My boss? In Washington?"

"Yes, Ted. An FBI Director, a Felicia Albreda. Is she not your boss?"

"Oh yeah, Ari, she's my boss all right. In more ways than you will ever know."

Chapter Thirty-One

"There! Up ahead," Faruq Abdalla riding point in the first SUV shouted into a two-way radio.

In the second SUV, a quarter mile behind him, Irina Kazakov and Androlitis, absorbed in conversation about the translations on the parchment, paid little attention to what Abdalla said, or the ominous sky looming in the distance.

Abdalla leaned closer to the windshield and shouted again, "*Come in damn it! What is that?*"

Androlitis looked up from the text in his lap. "Oh dear God. Irina, we must find shelter. That is an oncoming *habūb*. If we do not find a place out of the wind it will cut us to pieces—sandblasted into eternity."

A gigantic wall of swirling sand covered the horizon like a black curtain rushing toward them.

Abdalla's voice came back again. "*We must turn around. Irina, do you hear what I am saying?*"

Androlitis took the microphone. "No, Faruq. We cannot outrun it." He turned back to Kazakov. "Find something, anything that will stand between us and storm. It is our only chance."

Kazakov stopped, got out, climbed atop the SUV and peered through a pair of binoculars. The terrain was flat, no place to shelter from an oncoming windstorm. She turned in a circular arc, stopping at a dark cluster of objects in the distance, and focused her binoculars. "Over there, to the east," she said, pointing to the grouping of circular stone structures rising from the desert floor five kilometers away.

Androlitis placed his foot on the SUV's front bumper and climbed onto the hood.

"Over there." Kazakov pointed and handed him the binoculars.

"Yes, I see them. What are they?"

Shimmering in the rising heat waves, a cluster of three rounded structures came into focus. "They are called *nawamis*," she said.

Abdalla drove up alongside her. "What did you call them?"

Kazakov jumped from the roof and ordered everyone back into their vehicles. "They may just save our lives, Faruq. Quickly, there is no time to waste."

***

The rounded stones sticking up from the desert floor were man-made. Hollow, constructed of hand-hewn stone, they were believed to have been in the Sinai for thousands of years. Their entrances, for some unknown reason, always faced east, toward the rising sun. Arab legend had it that *Musa*, Moses, and the fleeing Israelites constructed them as shelters from swarms of ravenous insects during their forty years wandering, but no one knew for certain what they were, or who had actually built them, or what they were used for by ancient nomads.

The approaching *habūb* now appeared to be a wall of night in the rear-view mirror, less than a half-mile behind them. The roaring sound of oncoming wind sounded like a bombardment.

Kazakov shouted over the roaring storm. "Go to the opposite side from the oncoming dust!" She turned to DeLarussa, still shouting. "Somewhere on the eastern side there is an opening into the structure. It will be a block of stone with a carving, most likely a scimitar. Find it!"

Razor-sharp grains of sand and tiny jagged stones swirled around DeLarussa forcing him to wrap a bandana over his mouth and nose. It was difficult to inhale, with choking sand filling his airway. Kneeling, he rocked the scimitar inscribed stone at the base of the *nawami*. His fingertips shredded and bleeding, he pulled it free, until the opening was large enough to crawl inside.

Kazakov clutched the leather tube that held the parchment map, dropped to her knees and followed him inside, Abdalla went next, and then DeLarussa and their Arab bearers. Androlitis was last.

Androlitis reached out through the opening, and with Abdalla's help, pulled the oblong stone back into place, sealing them inside.

Kazakov switched on a lantern illuminating the interior walls as the howling windstorm descended over them. "The *nawamis* have withstood Sinai's dust for millennia," she said, her voice reassuring. "We will be safe here until it passes."

The others were not so sure.

Shadows from Kazakov's lantern danced across the stones covered in graffiti. The lettering appeared to be Arabic. Androlitis ran a finger over them. "This is *Nabataean*. It records names, short simple statements, and sometimes prayers. It could be as much as two thousand years old, Irina."

Or last week, she mused. She examined the lettering details. "Yes, at some *nawamis* one can find Egyptian hieroglyphics, Roman, Greek, and old Arabic script, plus inscriptions from early European travelers, etched into the walls. Little of it, before the first century, has been authenticated. In other places the writing is just scribble, vandalism by careless tourists to the Sinai."

Sitting with her back against a wall, Kazakov opened the hollow leather tube, slid the parchment from its sheath and spread it across the sand. Abdalla, DeLarussa, and Androlitis sat in a circle around her.

"Look closely," Kazakov said, pointing to the parchment.

"For what?" Abdalla asked.

"Somewhere, hidden in this document, is a rose, perhaps the written word, perhaps a drawing, I do not know which."

Androlitis moved a finger along the parchment. He stopped at a grouping of letters in an alphabet Kazakov did not recognize. "Father Demos for the past year has studied several texts in our collection at the monastery. Some go as far back as the second century."

"What were those texts, Father?" DeLarussa asked.

"Do you know of a Pope called *Antacletus the First*? His pontificate went from 79 AD to 90 AD?"

"I do," DeLarussa answered. "There is a painting of him at the Vatican, outside the Sistine Chapel. I saw it on my last visit to Rome, over twenty years ago."

The Roman priest made the sign of the cross. "Martyred, he lies entombed beneath Santa Pietro. He is depicted on a throne with a long sheet of paper or possibly a parchment trailing onto the ground at his feet."

"Enough nonsense," Abdalla said. "What does a martyred two-thousand-year-old pope have to do with anything?"

DeLarussa, a hand on Abdalla's arm, spoke softly. "Please, have patience."

"What do you see in that grouping of letters?" DeLarussa asked Androlitis.

"It resembles the Aramaic word *Sangui*, blood, but I do not have any idea, nor hold any theory as to its meaning."

Again, Abdalla cried in disgust. "In the name of Jesus, is anyone certain of anything? What does this have to do with a dead pope?"

"Think hard, Father," Kazakov said. "That sheet of trailing paper in Antacletus' lap, could it be a parchment? This very parchment?"

Kazakov pulled a magnifying glass from her pocket.

***

Hans Richter, twenty kilometers behind his quarry, stood alongside his Range Rover staring up at the sky. Dust had already begun to swirl and fine sand adhered to Jeremiah's day-old stubble and a layer of sweat.

The dark wall stretched skyward, blocking the sun, giving the desert a look of approaching night. "Where do we go, Hans? If we do not find shelter soon this wind will kill us."

"Quickly," Richter ordered. "Push as much sand as you can around the entire vehicle. Pack it tight. Leave no daylight penetrating, and only enough space for us to crawl underneath on one side. Hurry, we do not have much time before it is on us."

Secure under the Rover, Richter shoved a blanket at Jeremiah. "Cover your eyes, mouth, and nose, and keep your face down."

***

Faruq Abdalla kicked away the stone guarding the entrance to the *nawami*. He crawled out and looked around. It was night, and the wind no longer howling, the air clear with a bright moon illuminating the desert. The others, one by one, emerged behind him.

Both SUVs, although protected by the circular chimney structures. were still intact, but sand covered them up to their door handles. Pockmarks dotted the uncovered surfaces where good size pieces of detritus had struck like a fusillade of bullets, in several places the paint stripped away, the metal surface sandblasted clean down to bare metal.

Twenty kilometers away Richter clawed his way out from under the Range Rover. Its windshield was gone, beads of glass were strewn on the seats, and the metal window frame, contorted, hung limply on the dashboard. Fine stones that were propelled at high speeds by the fierce wind had shredded a left-front tire.

Richter barked, "Check our supplies, especially the water. Get rid of that windshield. We will have to do without. I will see if I can start the engine."

"Do you think Irina was also caught by the storm?" Jeremiah asked.

Richter shook his head. "If she was, then what we seek may be gone, forever. Irina Kazakov could be a pile of dead flesh. They were not that far ahead of us. The faster I get this piece of junk running the faster we can be on our way. Then we will know."

Richter stared at the shredded tire. "Get the damn spare and change that thing, right now. Leave the old rim."

CHAPTER THIRTY-TWO

The storm past and the Egyptian authorities gone, the monastery's priests and brothers were busy sweeping sand and debris from pathways and courtyards. Spared from the *nawami's* full force, Santa Katerina still needed a lot of work if the faithful were to soon return for guided tours up the slopes of Mt. Sinai.

Elon Bilboz thanked Odonio and readied the SUV to go out after Richter. With information gathered from satellite imagery, compliments of the United States military, and at the urging of Director Albreda, they would head toward the Gulf of Aqaba. Best guess from the satellite images, Richter, or Kazakov, or both, were going in that direction—fifty kilometers as the crow flies. Because of the Sinai's mountainous terrain they needed to first drive north along the Nuweiba road, tripling the distance to the gulf.

Lansing and ben Yehuda dozed in the rear seat as Bilboz drove. He gave Arlen Drew sitting next to him a running commentary on the Sinai's history and Israel's long-standing problems, both military and political with Egypt's ever-changing government, and ever-changing regulations concerning the Jewish state.

Lansing sensed the vehicle slow down. He opened his eyes. "Where are we?"

"We approach *Qesm Saint Katrin*, and we may have a problem," Bilboz said.

Ben Yehuda stirred. "What do you see, Elon?"

"An Egyptian checkpoint."

Directed by a police officer they pulled off into a siding with three small, ramshackle buildings. Bilboz slowed the SUV and stopped. Mossad had provided each with what Lansing believed to be impeccably forged documents; their cover, a cultural trip with details left sketchy.

The identification papers identified Drew and Lansing as professors of antiquity visiting Egypt from a small Midwestern Christian college—Bilboz and ben Yehuda, colleagues from Tel Aviv University.

Lansing's uneasy quotient went up when Bilboz and ben Yehuda were led away and separated from him and Drew, but as the Egyptians led them across the compound, ben Yehuda turned and nodded to Lansing, motioning with his hand that the situation was under control. It did little to ease Lansing's angst.

In a windowless room in an adjacent building not much larger than a small hut, Drew and Lansing sat alone. Painted drab green, the sparsely furnished space had two hard plastic chairs, a single overhead fan, and wobbly metal table.

Lansing leaned in and mouthed, "They could be recording." Drew nodded. He remained silent, rehearsing the cover story in his head.

The door opened and a middle-aged, overweight police officer with a day's stubble on a deeply tanned and lined face came in. Sweat stains spread downward under each armpit, and he smelled even worse than he looked. There were sergeant's chevrons on each shoulder board, the left chevron detached, hanging loose. He had Lansing's identification papers in his hand.

"There are discrepancies in your documentation…" The man looked up. "Dr. Lansing, is it?"

"What discrepancies?" Lansing asked.

The guard answered, his voice louder, "Discrepancies!"

Drew started to speak, but Lansing held up a hand. "With all due respect, Sergeant, I do not know to what discrepancies you refer."

The Egyptian officer leaned closer, grinning, close enough for Lansing to recoil from an overpowering stench of garlic emanating from the man's mouth, sans one front tooth.

"Do not be so smug, Professor Lansing. You are not in the United States now." He looked back at Lansing's papers again. "You think this is… "*Yip… Yipo… Yipo-so-lanty, Mich-a-gun?*" he said, butchering Ypsilanti, and not much better with Michigan.

He turned in Drew's direction. "I will ask you then. Why are you here in Egypt with those Israeli professors? If they really are professors."

Lansing nodded to Drew. "Like my colleague said, it's a cultural mission. We are touring archeological sites in the Sinai. The Israelis are our guides."

"You test my patience, Professor Drew."

Drew started to answer, but another glance from Lansing convinced him not to take it any further. He sensed a growing anger in the policeman's tone, hoping for a quick confession—but a confession for what, Lansing had no idea.

The door opened and another police officer came inside. Unlike the sergeant, this one was all spit and polish.

The sergeant stood, saluted, and moved behind Lansing and Drew. He placed a meaty hand on each one's neck. "Lock these two in a cell. Perhaps a few days in a hot room without food or water will convince them to talk."

"Release them, Sergeant. Captain's orders."

***

Emerging from the windowless room, both Lansing and Drew squinted in the bright sunlight as they made their way across the compound to the Ford Explorer still parked where they'd left it. Bilboz was already behind the wheel, ben Yehuda next to him in the front seat.

Lansing slid in back. "What the hell was that all about? And how in God's name did you convince them we're legit?"

Laughing, Bilboz eased the Explorer forward.

"I say something funny?" said Lansing.

"No, my friend," ben Yehuda answered. "Nothing about this is funny. There were no discrepancies, as they called it, with our papers. I assure you they are the best forgeries Mossad could make, certainly good enough for a couple of morons looking for a bribe."

"A what?" Drew exclaimed.

"Money, Arlen. Nothing more."

"Are you telling me this whole thing was a shakedown?"

Bilboz laughed.

"How much money?" asked Lansing.

"For this type of… uh… transaction, two hundred dollars US, give or take. I had six hundred in a money belt under my waistband."

"Going rate?" Drew asked.

"Yes, my friend, the going rate, the cost of doing business with Arabs. It was anticipated. In Egypt, and in most places in the Middle East, unless you grease the wheels nothing gets done."

Drew caught a glimpse of himself in the rearview mirror and laughed. The face staring back virtually screamed cop. He looked at Lansing. If Lansing's face said anything it sure wasn't professor of antiquity. Ben Yehuda was right. *These Israelis know what they are doing. Dealing with Arabs is a whole other world.*

CHAPTER THIRTY-THREE

Irina Kazakov emerged from her tent and cursed aloud.

"What is wrong?" DeLarussa asked. She pointed.

One of their vehicles was gone, along with everything inside it. Also gone, the Egyptians they'd hired to do the work. "We have been robbed by those bastards Faruq hired."

Loading everything into the remaining SUV, Kazakov and DeLarussa climbed into the rear, Androlitis drove and Abdalla rode shotgun alongside him.

For hours they drove through dry riverbeds and wadis, checking and rechecking their calculation, crisscrossing the same barren landscape. Each time Androlitis maneuvered back over terrain he'd already covered Kazakov, from the rear seat, eyed him suspiciously. She leaned over and whispered to DeLarussa, "Something is not right. I think Androlitis is taking us in circles."

"Where are we?" DeLarussa asked.

She checked a handheld GPS locator. "28.121 Latitude, by 34.185, precisely where we are supposed to be, and sure enough to know that this is not where Nigel Fitzwalter first unearthed the artifacts in 1933.

"Father," she said to Androlitis. "Stop, please. I need to recheck our position."

With DeLarussa next to her, Kazakov unrolled the parchment onto the hood of the vehicle. Androlitis stepped between them.

"These symbols," he said, "I believe they are part of a description that places Mt. Sinai, not above the monastery of Santa Katerina, but the actual Sinai, *Jubal Musa*, the place where God spoke to the Hebrew prophet, Moses. *Jubal Musa* is sixty kilometers southeast of Mt. Sinai."

"I see no mountain," said Kazakov.

She stared off through a pair of binoculars.

"What do you look for?" Androlitis said.

"I am haunted by an entry in Nigel Fitzwalter's diary, '*To look under the rose*.' I am more certain than ever that if we determine what Sir Nigel meant we will find the grotto's location."

She went back to the tailgate, pulled out a canvas rucksack and reached inside for the Fitzwalter diary.

"'Amid strewn boulders, I discovered a pair of broken chunks of granite, each less than eight inches wide and one inch thick. They match exactly the rounded indentation in the niche. There is a rumbling now emanating from somewhere deep inside the cavern. Pieces of stone are beginning to fall from the cave roof, one struck Petya.'

"It appears the grotto collapsed on them." Her finger ran farther down the page. "They made it back to the place where they first rappelled down into the cave."

"When did Fitzwalter find the time to write all this amid the collapse?" asked DeLarussa.

Kazakov turned a page. "Entry 65: 'Koshenko is not there. The rope we need to escape this place is also gone. We are trapped and the sound of collapsing stone grows louder.'

"Entry 66: 'Without warning, a light shone from above. It is Koshenko. He has returned from God knows where. Petya insists I go first.'"

DeLarussa's eye went from the diary to the parchment and back again. "Look closer," he said, removing a magnifying glass from his pocket. "This passage, the one that speaks of a rose, the one we have been translating as, *'look under the rose for what you seek.'* Are you certain it says to look under the rose? Could it mean below the rose?"

Androlitis pondered her question. "That is a strange interpretation. Why do you ask?"

"I will tell you why. Look closer at the passage."

The line with the rose commentary was blurred as if something had spilled and soaked into its fibers, bleeding ink around its edges.

"Yes, I see it," DeLarussa said, his eyes moving closer. "There was something here, below the words. It appears to be another letter, or perhaps another word. Someone tried to remove the stain, or is it an imperfection in the parchment itself?"

Androlitis interrupted. "There is nothing in Fitzwalter's commentary to indicate anyone tampered with the parchment. I am beginning to believe this is a well thought out hoax, Irina."

Kazakov contemplated his comment with skepticism, starting to doubt Androlitis' motive. "Perhaps, but allow me to see Fitzwalter's diary again."

In Nigel Fitzwalter's own hand she read the words aloud. "'The rose shows the way at sunset,' dated, July 25th, 1933."

DeLarussa watched her eyes, focused and determined, move across the parchment. In her head, she made imaginary additions, flourishes, and serifs to the words.

"Here, this one," she said, her voice rising with anticipation. "This I believe is what was under the stain."

Kazakov picked up Fitzwalter's diary. "His last entry," she said to Androlitis. "Tell me what you see."

He stared, flipping back and forth from page to page. "Oh my God, Irina, Nigel Fitzwalter did not write this?"

The handwriting, while similar to the rest of the diary, had been written in another hand, fancier with more flourish.

"Entry 67: 'Kazimir Petya, in a chamber above, lowered a rope for Sir Nigel to climb out. Before he could free Sir Nigel a large rock fell from the cavern roof striking him, causing him to fall back into the darkness. I fear Petya is dead.'"

She turned to the final entry. "'I hear rumbling sounds. The grotto is collapsing. Sir Nigel is trapped. Father Koshenko shouted for Sir Nigel to tie the rope around his waist. With great effort, he was able to hoist his broken body to the opening and pull him free just as the final rumbling brought down the entire cave burying Kazimir Petya. Sir Nigel is dead. Koshenko administered last rites.'

"His wife, Daphne, wrote this from a description given to her by Koshenko." Kazakov closed the book. "It is the only explanation that makes sense."

Faruq Abdalla, certain this meant the end of their quest, lashed out. "So we are on a wild goose chase. Is that what you are saying, Irina?"

Androlitis placed his arm over the younger man's shoulder. "There are things we are not meant to know, Faruq."

Kazakov pulled DeLarussa to the side. "Come, Father, help me pack the vehicle."

The tailgate lifted and Kazakov, out of Androlitis' earshot, whispered, "Something is not right, Antonio. Do not share anything more with the abbot."

CHAPTER THIRTY-FOUR

Hans Richter got his first glimpse of civilization as his crippled Range Rover limped into a tiny Arab village twenty kilometers from the city of *Abu Rudeis* on the Sinai Peninsula's western coast along the Gulf of Suez. The fresh scent of clean ocean air became palpable a respite from the dry, scorched Sinai they'd traveled for hours. They needed to stop, find someplace to repair the damaged Rover torn apart by the dust storm. Miserable, he and Jeremiah drove on a donut-size-spare tire without a windshield to protect them from the elements; their faces were sunburned, red, and caked hard with layers of sand and sweat.

Richter shook loose sand from his hair, touched his cheek and shuddered as his fingertips brushed against the flaking skin of his face. Disgusted, he turned to Jeremiah. "Find a repair shop to replace the fucking glass and secure us a new tire." He made a guttural sound, spitting sand grains from his teeth.

Jeremiah grumbled incoherently but said little else.

A mile from *Abu Rudeis* Jeremiah pulled off-road into an area that had promise. He drove past several dilapidated stores, a few ramshackle dwellings, and a sad looking park with ill clothed children scampering over rusted playground fixtures, but nothing resembling a repair shop. He asked Richter if it was safe to stop and ask someone.

Richter, emphatic, said no. "I do not want our presence here known. Better we continue south. If you see a place, pull in. If not, continue to the city. We will have to take our chances."

Jeremiah drove in and out of a half-dozen side streets, until, on a dead end, unpaved dirt road, he spotted an Esso sign, a filling station with a single garage bay and lift. A sign, in Arabic, above the door, said *Gamal Sabura, Proprietor.*

Jeremiah, his Arabic language skills not much better than Richter's, called out from the Rover. "*As-salām 'alaykum,*" he said, butchering the pronunciation. When the mechanic made no response, Jeremiah shouted louder, "*Min fa□lik,* excuse me." It got the old man's attention. He nodded to the mechanic in coveralls standing underneath a ten-year-old Volkswagen van up on the lift in the sole repair bay.

Sabura pulled an oily rag from a back pocket, wiped his hands, and, for good measure, rubbed his still filthy palms against his greasy coveralls and smiled through a mouth devoid of two front teeth.

"*Sprechen sie Englisch, Herr Sabura?*" Richter asked. The man shook his head. "*Russen?*" Another head shake. He tried French, Italian, and Hebrew, all with no recognition.

Jeremiah pointed to the Rover, and a glimmer of understanding came across Sabura's face.

All three stood in front of the hole that was once a windshield. Sabura whistled, finally understanding, his head shaking. He spoke in Arabic, but nothing was understandable to either Jeremiah or Richter.

Jeremiah pointed east toward the desert, "*Habūb,*" he said. The man's face lit with recognition. He managed two words in English, "*Habūb* bad."

Richter nodded, agreeing that *habūbs* were bad. He pointed at the Rover's windshield, and walked to a parked van with a price sticker on the dashboard. He tapped the windshield, and pointed to his vehicle.

Sabura ran a hand over the van's windshield and shook his head. He made a motion with his hand, indicating that it would not fit the Range Rover.

Richter pulled Jeremiah to one side. "Make this idiot understand that I do not want to buy his goddamn windshield. I want the goddamn van."

"In what language Hans?"

Richter cursed under his breath, opened the van front door and removed a dashboard For-Sale sign. "*Addesh*? How much?" he asked.

Sabura grinned through his toothless mouth, answering in Arabic. Richter shook his head and said, "I do not understand."

Sabura knelt and drew a number in the dirt, 80,000.

"Egyptian?" Richter asked.

Sabura nodded.

He did a fast calculation. "He wants ten thousand American for that piece of *drek*."

"We do not have that much cash, Hans."

"You think I do not know that? I will negotiate."

Richter knelt and drew a number in the dirt, 50,000, knowing they had less than 1000 Egyptian dollars on hand.

Sabura shook his head and started to walk away.

Richter followed, tapped his shoulder and countered—65,000.

Sabura smiled and nodded. He motioned for Richter to follow him into a small office behind the repair bay.

Following the mechanic, Richter motioned to Jeremiah.

His eyes riveted on the office door, Jeremiah positioned himself so he could see both the garage bay and the Esso pumps near the roadway.

Sabura pulled a ring binder from a shelf and produced what Richter thought were the vehicle's registration papers. He reached for a grease-smeared shoebox and pulled out a set of keys. Before handing them to Richter, Sabura held up six fingers, then five, confirming the agreed upon price.

Richter nodded, but when Sabura started to sign the registration slip, he pulled a Glock with a silencer from under his shirt. Two rapid pop-pops and Sabura fell, dead.

"Get in here," he called to Jeremiah. "Stuff this piece of dog meat into the back of our old vehicle."

Richter strolled casually to the petrol pump and filled a plastic gasoline can. "Follow me in the new van. We find a place and set both him and the Range Rover on fire. We leave no trace of Herr Sabura."

"Where are we going, Hans?"

"South, twenty or thirty kilometers, then east, back to Santa Katerina, another hundred kilometers. That is where we will find Kazakov and the stones. I am sure of it."

Chapter Thirty-Five

Father Odonio emerged from a door in the outer wall of the monastery and watched Irina Kazakov climb out of the one remaining SUV. "Where is the second vehicle?" he asked as Faruq Abdalla shut off the engine behind a secluded cluster of palm trees on the north side of Santa Katerina.

Before anyone could answer Odonio's questions, Androlitis acted quickly to stop him before he ssaid something to alert Kazakov about a series of underground tunnels hidden beneath Santa Katerina.

"The sandstorm caught us by surprise and the Egyptians Irina hired as porters ran off with our second vehicle." He opened the door and stepped down, motioning to Kazakov. "Go with Odonio, quickly."

"I did not expect you to return so soon, Father," Odonio whispered.

Androlitis heard the panic in the priest's voice.

"Tell me, Father, what happened in my absence?"

"Murder."

Kazakov heard the remark and turned with urgency mixed with fear. "Richter?"

"Soon after you left we had visitors. Two Mossad agents, and I believe, two Americans, both FBI."

"I spoke with an American before we left," said Androlitis. "His name was Lansing."

Excited, Odonio took hold of Androlitis' arm. "Yes Father.. He asked us questions about this Richter person. The Israeli agent named ben Yehuda, implied Richter was responsible for murdering Father Demos—may he sleep in the Lord's embrace. But for now, you must come with me. We go to the *adyta*," he said, using the Greek word for a hidden room within a cathedral's walls, in medieval times a place of sanctuary from invading hoards.

"I have prepared quarters for the night. No one must know you have returned, and you must remain out of sight."

Behind the main altar, inside a private reading room reserved for the Abbot, Odonio approached a massive bookcase against the far wall. He grasped a shelf and pulled forward. The entire bookcase moved sideways revealing a room behind it.

Shelves lined with books, the room was furnished with a half dozen chairs and tables. In the far wall a second door led to a steep narrow set of descending steps. In single file, they started down. When Kazakov reached the top step she hesitated, her heart rate accelerated, sweat formed on her brow and lips. Warily she fought her claustrophobia with controlled breathing and closed eyes as she followed them down. At the bottom step, still hyperventilating, she eyed the narrow passageway.

Odonio led them to a circular chamber off the main passageway, its only furnishings a large table with six chairs on each side and a single high-back chair at the table's head. She ran a hand over its rough-hewn surface, her eyes taking note of multiple carvings, letters in languages a thousand years old etched into the dark wood. Suspended above the table was an ornate chandelier, now electrified, its candleholders still visible.

Androlitis lowered himself into the high-backed chair at the table head. "We stay here only until morning, Odonio."

"Only until morning? Why Father? Where do you go? You are safe here."

Androlitis lowered his eyes. "Because we have deciphered both the parchment and the diary of Nigel Fitzwalter."

"Does that mean…?"

"Yes, Odonio. We know the location of the grotto Nigel Fitzwalter found in 1933. The grotto where he first discovered the stone keys Irina has carried with her from Rome."

"It is here on the mountain?" Odonio was incredulous. "How is that possible? Men have searched for centuries, looked for clues to the Hebrew Law on every inch of the holy mountain."

"The answer is on the parchment, Odonio. One only needed to know where to look. A single word, a word lost to antiquity due to an unfortunate accident, a spill that hid the parchment's true meaning."

"I do not understand," Odonio asked. "What spill?"

"That I do not know, but we have Father Demos to thank. Do you remember what the American, the large black man, the detective named Drew, said when he found Father Demos' body in the basilica?"

"Yes, he scratched some words on the underside of a pew in his final seconds. It said, *under the rose*."

"Yes, come Odonio, we have much to prepare and little time to do it."

Chapter Thirty-Six

Driving at speeds that made Lansing uneasy on the poorly maintained roads of the Sinai, The Ford Explorer turned the Ford Explorer turned southeast toward Santa Katerina, sixty kilometers away. They followed a crisscross pattern of paved and unpaved roads built into dry riverbeds until they reached *Ein Khudra*, the Green Oasis, a desert paradise northwest of *Dahab*. The terrain between *Ein Khudra* and the monastery, far too mountainous and more conducive to pack animals than vehicles, was the only way to catch up to Richter before he found Kazakov and the stone artifacts, she carried with her.

Approaching Mt. Sinai from the west, Bilboz drove down into a wadi running alongside the western edge of the mountain. "What is that?" Lansing asked, eyeing a tour bus.

"*El-Bustan*," Bilboz said, never taking his eyes from the rock-strewn riverbed. "There is a small chapel there, it is the site believed to be the place *Moshe* struck a rock to provide water to the fleeing Israelites, or so the legend says.

"How do you want to play this when we reach the monastery?" Bilboz asked.

"We are tourists," ben Yehuda answered. "We go in separately, one at a time."

He turned to Lansing. "Here," he said, handing him a map of Santa Katerina's inner compound. "We will blend in among the pilgrims but be vigilant. Odonio knows us by sight—who we are and who we are looking for. Better he does not know we have returned."

He pointed to a spot on the map. "There is a garden here," he said, his finger tapping the paper. "There is a small fountain with a statue of the Virgin in the center. Visitors often meet there in the late afternoon for tea served by the monks. We will be inconspicuous. One hour."

Teacups and small plates in hand, pilgrims to the monastery gathered near a fountain in the monastery garden. Monks carried trays of moussaka and cheese phylos as they stopped to speak with pilgrims, engaging them with subtle pleas for monetary donations.

Ari ben Yehuda entered the courtyard now in late afternoon shadow. The sun low in the sky framed the bell tower with Mt. Sinai rising in the distance. He took a triangular phyllo from a tray offered by a monk and took a position at the rear of the courtyard where he could observe everything.

Lansing and Drew entered from the opposite side and joined ben Yehuda near the fountain. They exchanged glances but said nothing to indicate they were together. Lansing checked his watch, and looked back at ben Yehuda. There was no sign of Elon Bilboz, and it was nearly a half hour past the time when they'd agreed to meet. He moved closer to ben Yehuda and whispered, "Something is wrong, Ari."

Elon Bilboz knelt behind a pew at the rear of the church. He peered down the nave at the altar where he caught a fast glimpse at a lone figure in a black robe disappear behind the altar's main table. In a crouch, he waited for the figure to re-emerge. When it did not emerge, he inched forward and waited.

From the shadows, Hans Richter motioned to Jeremiah. "There is someone here," he whispered. "I saw movement, only for a second."

"Yes, I see him, Hans." Jeremiah checked the clip in his gun, but Richter slapped at his hand. "Idiot. You will alert the entire monastery?"

Jeremiah re-holstered his weapon and pulled a switchblade from his pocket. He held it in his palm, and with a quick flick of his wrist, the six-inch blade locked into place. He crouched and began to creep to a side aisle, never taking his gaze from whomever was hiding in the shadows farther up the main aisle.

Bilboz, now half way down the nave, stopped when he heard voices coming from a side door. He watched two priests make their way onto the altar and down the marble steps behind it.

Weapon in hand, Bilboz followed. He crept up onto the altar and found the steps leading down. Both priests were gone, vanished.

Richter moved closer, positioned himself behind a marble column and eyed Bilboz.

The Israeli agent pushed on a door that opened into what looked like a library. He entered, stood in the center of the room and gazed around him. The room had no doors or windows. No way in or out except the solitary door he'd come in through, but who belonged to the voices he'd heard and where did they go?

Bilboz walked the room's perimeter, a palm flat against the wall, tapping, feeling for anything to suggest a way in or out.

Richter motioned to Jeremiah. He moved onto the altar and peered in through the open library door Bilboz left ajar. He stepped inside, felt a rush of air and spun around. Bilboz stood behind the door, a gun in hand.

Jeremiah's leg came up in a violent karate kick that caught Bilboz off guard. He reeled, toppled backward and lay there exposed as Jeremiah plunged his blade deep into Bilboz's side. Blood gushed from the wound.

Bilboz tried to stand. He clawed at Jeremiah's shirt. But Jeremiah's hands wrapped tightly around the Mossad agent's neck choking the life from his body.

Bilboz groaned, gasping, pain from the stab wound searing through his midsection. He tried to pull the blade free, but with consciousness fading, the room spinning, he fought to just stay alive. Jeremiah let go, twisting the blade deeper before shoving Bilboz to the ground.

The toe of Jeremiah's boot slammed into the side of Bilboz's head. He tried to stand again, but the church began to spin around him. He got as far as one knee, fell and crashed into a table. Its contents scattered, a crescendo of metal and glass goblets, wine bottles, and candelabras crashing onto the marble floor.

"What was that?" Androlitis said from inside the *adyta*.

Kazakov pressed an ear to the door leading up the steps to the church. "Someone is there. We must use the escape tunnel and get out of here." She started for the only door that led out of the hidden rooms of the *adyta*.

"No. Stop!" Androlitis shouted.

"Why?" Kazakov questioned. "It could be Richter. How long do you think a hidden door will fool him? If he finds us, we will be all be killed and the artifacts gone, forever."

Her fear of Richter was genuine, but to Father DeLarussa, Androlitis' face said something else entirely. It was fear, but not fear about whoever was outside the *adyta*, instead, what they might find in the escape tunnel.

DeLarussa scooped up the leather sleeve holding the parchment, Fitzwalter's diary, and Kazakov's canvas rucksack. Abdalla slid a panel away in the *adyta* wall revealing a tunnel leading out of the room, but to where?

Kazakov entered the narrow passage, made her way to the end and pulled on the lever acting as a door handle. The heavy portal slid back revealing another set of steep stairs carved from solid granite. "What is this?" she asked, warily eying Androlitis.

"It is a dead end, Irina. It does not have access to the outside."

"Then where does it lead?"

The abbot remained silent.

Richter found the library door and burst in, losing his footing in a puddle of wet blood, Elon Bilboz's blood. "*Sie sind ein verdammter. Dummkopf,*" he snarled at Jeremiah. "Why do you not use your brains, for once. We must get out of here now, before someone finds this dead Jew."

Richter tapped Jeremiah and pointed to a side aisle. "*Schweigen,* silence," he said. They knelt in the shadows and waited.

Odonio came down the center nave, went up the altar steps, turned and looked back before starting for the library and the hidden *adyta*. He'd seen the Israelis mingling with pilgrims in the garden and needed to warn Androlitis. Seeing Bilboz's body he ran screaming into the monastery garden. A hundred eyes turned in his direction. Over and over he sobbed, "*eínai nekrós, eínai nekrós.* He is dead. He is dead."

Hearing the cries, Lansing took off running.

CHAPTER THIRTY-SEVEN

Angered by the brazen murder of Elon Bilboz at the hand of Hans Richter, but still needing direction from Tel Aviv, sben Yehuda took the chance and used his SAT phone. He needed clarification on how Mossad wanted to proceed. Not only did the agency and the Americans have no official authority in the Sinai, being caught trying to spirit a piece of antiquity out of Egypt would bring more problems than ben Yehuda or Mossad needed.

Israel's clandestine service rerouted his call via a second satellite to avoid Egyptian interception. Anyone monitoring radio transmissions would discover its origin out of sub-Saharan Africa. A second murder at the famed monastery in less than a month was certain to bring the Egyptians back to Santa Katerina, something ben Yehuda or Mossad could not risk.

Lansing continued his attempts to make Odonio understand the danger posed by Hans Richter. The Orthodox priest remained closed mouthed whenever the subject of the absent abbot, and his 'guests,' Kazakov and company, came up. A mounting distrust, not just for Odonio, but for Androlitis as well, nagged at Lansing. The priests were hiding something and he was certain about it.

Lansing paced in a circle around Odonio who remained silent behind the abbot's desk in a private office off the rectory. "What should I call you, Odonio? Is it Father or Brother Odonio?"

Odonio held a rosary tight between his fingers, and looked up at Lansing. "You have no authority here, over me or my brethren." There was a resignation in his voice, a dismissal of Lansing and the Israelis.

"You must listen," said Lansing. "Your community has already had one murdered priest, and now an Israeli agent is dead at the hand of the same person, Hans Richter. He will kill again and again until he gets what he is after. You and your brothers are not safe while he remains at large. This Richter is a German national working for the Russians. He is ex-KGB, now FSB and before that East German Stasi. He's followed Irina Kazakov around the world for months and has left numerous bodies in his wake, not just here, but in Washington, and another murdered priest at the Vatican."

Lansing's words, though impassioned, had little effect on Odonio. He remained still, his rosary in hand. His fingers moved deftly along strands made of knotted wool as he repeated, "Lord Jesus Christ, Son of God, have mercy on me a sinner."

Arlen Drew took Lansing's arm and led him away. "Let me have a crack at him, Ted."

"Crack at him? No, Arlen," Lansing scoffed. "He's a priest for God's sake, not a perp, and technically he's right. We have no authority here. I'm going to appeal to his higher angels."

"Higher angels? What higher angels?"

Lansing turned, eyed Odonio still praying, and then looked back at his partner. "I'm going to beg."

Satellite phone in hand, Ari ben Yehuda came through the rectory door. "I reached Heifetz. She is unable to send assistance at this time. She believes the Russians tipped the Egyptians that something was about to go down here. The chatter is all over the Internet about a pair of dead priests."

"Elon was not a priest," said Lansing.

"These are the Russians, Lansing. Truth is an illusion to them. Heifetz is certain Hans Richter sold them a bill of goods; embellished the narrative for his superiors, about our presence or the reason we are here."

"For what purpose would he keep our presence a secret to his superiors in Moscow?" asked Drew.

"It makes perfect sense," said ben Yehuda. "One word from Richter about Mossad and the FBI being here and all hell breaks loose. The Egyptian authorities swarm in, Mossad is forced to send covert assistance at the least, and Richter has more FSB eyes on his ass than he can handle. If he intends to waylay Kazakov he needs to do it with as little fanfare as possible. The Russians will see it as a botched mission if he fails for any reason."

"What is Mossad's assessment?"

"Egyptian military will be here by morning at the latest."

Ben Yehuda looked first at Odonio still praying his rosary, then back at Lansing who shook his head in resolution. Odonio was not going to cooperate.

Ben Yehuda sat on the edge of the desk and leaned into the priest. "Please, Father Odonio, the lives of your abbot and the people he is with right now depend on it."

Odonio's expression changed for a brief second, and then he turned back to his rosary.

Lansing took the beads from his hand. He offered no resistance. "We know what Irina Kazakov is here looking for," he said.

Odonio's head came up. "I do not believe you."

Lansing got a nod from ben Yehuda to continue. "They are searching for the lost tablets of the Ten Commandments, are they not?"

A light came on in the priest's eyes. He nodded. "Yes."

"Thank you for your honesty, Father. Believe me, when I tell you we are not here to prevent Irina Kazakov from finding the tablets. We are after Richter for the murder of a museum curator at the Smithsonian Institution in Washington, and for ordering the killing of a twenty-year-old woman, an innocent graduate student from Massachusetts."

Odonio remained stoic.

Ari stepped in. "All right, Father Odonio, here is the truth, as we know it. If I say anything that is incorrect please stop me."

Odonio nodded.

"There are no secret artifacts leading to the Ten Commandments."

Ben Yehuda waited for a response. Not getting one he continued. "The Russians have been blackmailing, sorry, wrong choice of words, threatening the monastery for decades, 1967 to be precise. Am I wrong?"

Odonio whispered, "No you are not."

"Will you elaborate, Father?"

"Yes, Agent ben Yehuda, it is time you all knew the truth. The Russian military came to Santa Katerina on the eve of the 1967 war with Israel. They had a weapon that needed hiding until the time came to use it on the Israelis. I assure you it was not a request. Father Anatole Petrakis, our abbot at the time, at first denied permission and said no to the Russian barbarians, but after a short meeting with a Russian commander he relented. Their threat was destruction of the monastery during the coming war. Stray munitions, a bomb misguided, they had many ways to accomplish this."

"Where is this hidden weapon now?" Lansing asked.

"Father Petrakis removed it from the location where the Russians hid the device, a small silver canister, and moved it someplace the Russians would never find it, but circumstances changed. The Arab invaders of Israel lost the war, the Soviet Union eventually collapsed and the Russians forgot all about their hidden weapon."

"Until now," Drew said from across the room.

"Yes, Agent Drew, until now."

Lansing made no mention that capturing Hans Richer was his priority, the FBI's priority, not Mossad's.

Odonio focused on ben Yehuda, his eyes questioning what he'd been told.

Lansing intervened, lied. "Mossad is here to prevent Richter from accomplishing his mission," he said, trying to convince himself as much as Father Odonio.

The priest glared. "And what is Richter's mission, if you know, Mr. Lansing?"

Ben Yehuda stepped forward. "The Russian belief that the artifacts have religious value is a ruse. They want their canister back, plain and simple, and Richter has been tasked to use whatever means necessary, including killing your brothers and anyone else who get into his way."

"If as you say this entire mission is a ruse, why does Mossad not do what Mossad does with men like Hans Richter?"

"I do not disagree, Father. But if Richter succeeds, neither you nor I, nor anyone else, will ever be safe from whatever is in that canister, and Father Androlitis along with Irina Kazakov will be dead. That is Richter's MO."

Odonio pushed himself up from the chair and moved across the room. "What is this thing, MO? I am not familiar with the word."

"Killing is what Richter does. He does it well, with efficiency, and he loves his work."

Odonio, silent for several seconds, blurted, "They left several hours ago."

Lansing let out an audible sigh. "Finally! Thank you, Father. Do you know where they went?"

Odonio strode to a window and pointed. "To the Holy Mountain. They follow a path set forth by a British archeologist named Fitzwalter. There is a map and an ancient parchment that they follow."

"To where?" asked Drew.

"According to Fitzwalter's diary, there is a grotto, hidden from sight somewhere on the mountain, where God first gave His law to the Hebrew slaves. The parchment shows the way, but if what you tell me is the truth, the way to what, I no longer know."

Three kilometers from Santa Katerina, ben Yehuda knelt and looked up at the mountain. He collected his bearings and spread a hastily drawn map across the sandy ground. He scanned the route Odonio had drawn before they left.

Lansing, alongside him, opened a slick sales brochure he'd taken from a wire rack in a monastery souvenir shop. He opened the pleated pamphlet that showed the approved and safe paths up the mountain, as well as the location of way stations, small chapels, and Byzantine ruins along the route. Odonio gave them strong admonitions against attempting to reach the sites without a guide, because once off the approved routes, dotted with modern solar lights for night walks, he warned of treacherous fallen-rock formations, unseen crevices, and frequent landslides.

"They have several hours' head start," said Lansing. "They could already have reached wherever that damn map is directing them."

"Always so impatient, you Americans." Ben Yehuda laughed. "Always in a hurry to get someplace. Things in this part of the world have been buried for thousands of years. Pharaohs and kings, tyrants and conquerors, invading hordes, and still there is the land and still there is the eternal God of Hosts."

"I know Ari, but..."

"No Ted, you do not know. Where can Kazakov and Androlitis go? What will they find on the mountain? With hundreds, no thousands of tourists and scholars coming here every year, it surely would have been discovered centuries ago."

Drew stood over them, shaking his head.

"You think we are wrong about this, Arlen," said Lansing.

He nodded. "Yes, I think we've been played."

"Played?" said ben Yehuda.

"Yes, by Odonio and Androlitis."

CHAPTER THIRTY-EIGHT

Father Odonio peered down the set of steep, narrow stone steps. Hewn from solid granite, illuminated by a string of low-wattage bulbs, they led to an elaborate maze of underground tunnels below the monastery where Kazakov, DeLarussa, and Faruq Abdalla anxiously waited. How long before the American agent, Lansing, realized he'd been duped and started back to the monastery? Odonio knew time was short and he needed to hurry.

In his short conversations with Lansing he knew the man was nobody's fool, nor was the nosy Mossad agent, ben Yehuda. Odonio's main concern now was more urgent—how to keep Kazakov from discovering the monastery's secret—a secret they hoped would remain for all time.

At the bottom step, Odonio hurried down the passageway ending at a massive oaken door. Carved into the wood was a depiction of *Christ Pantocrator*, the image of Jesus, his face stern—a revered icon. Most often depicted holding a copy of the New Testament, this icon showed the Savior grasping a pair of stone tablets clutched tightly to his chest.

Odonio genuflected, rapped three times and waited. When the door opened Androlitis was there, grinning. "You have done well, brother," he said, embracing him.

Odonio stepped inside the chamber. "For now," he said. He took Androlitis' arm and whispered, "We do not have much time. What does she know?" he asked, referring to Kazakov.

"She is in the sleeping quarters now, pouring over that parchment."

Both priests continued down the tunnel to a second door. Androlitis placed a metal key into the lock, turned and pushed. The heavy portal creaked as it opened. Kazakov and DeLarussa were huddled around a table in the middle of the room.

The leather parchment lay unfurled, next to it Nigel Fitzwalter's diary open to a page dated, August 9th, 1934. Androlitis peered over Kazakov's shoulder.

"What have you discovered, Irina?" he said.

Kazakov stared at him, took the diary and flung it across the chamber.

DeLarussa gasped, confusion in his eyes.

Androlitis backed away, and then, calmly, without emotion he asked, "When did you first know?"

"Here," she answered. "Look at the sketch Fitzwalter made, if there ever was Fitzwalter."

***

"This is not good, Hans," said Jeremiah. Uneasy, his gun dangled at his side. "We should not have returned."

"You do not have to like it," Richter snarled.

"But, Hans, I killed a Mossad agent and an innocent priest."

Richter laughed. "No, Jeremiah, you murdered two priests. You forget Father Angelico, the old fool. There are no innocents here. And so what?"

"So what?" Jeremiah was incredulous. "We need to be out of here before the Egyptian authorities return, or worse, Mossad. Mossad does not take kindly to the killing of one of theirs. They will never stop coming after us, ever, no matter how long it takes. Do you not remember Munich, 1972? We must cut our losses; tell the Russians we are not able to complete the mission."

Richter ignored his plea and entered the church through a rear portal. He shoved Jeremiah into a dark shadow behind a column. "Listen to me and listen good. If you for one second believe the Russians will simply say too bad and allow us to go on our way, then you are a bigger fool then I thought. I know these Russians. Return empty handed and both you and I will disappear, never to be heard of again. They no longer call themselves KGB, but whether they are FSK or FSB, and wear tailored suits from Savile Row instead of Russian crap, they are still the same thugs. Believe me, I know because I am one of them—and so are you."

Emerging from the shadow Richter peered down the nave. Certain the church was empty he pointed to the altar steps. "Go, there, now," he ordered Jeremiah.

Kazakov paced the floor. Twice she started to speak and twice she stopped, fuming. Spinning around she faced Androlitis. "Why, Father, why this elaborate hoax. Where did the diary come from, and what of the parchment? Is it also a fraud?"

Androlitis sat in a chair across from her and considered the question. "No, Irina, you are correct. The parchment is not genuine. It was prepared in 1978 by one of our scribes, a most talented forger. Sadly, Josephus died several years after."

Kazakov lashed out again. "So it is not the real diary of Sir Nigel Fitzwalter either?"

"Not entirely."

"Now I am at more of a loss, Father. What does that even mean, not entirely? Either a man named Fitzwalter discovered the sacred tablets or he did not."

Odonio came to the table, looked at the abbot and nodded. "It is time she knew."

Chapter Thirty-Nine

Jeremiah pushed against the library door. He entered the sequestered room and stared at the furnishings. His eyes went first to a massive bookcase against a far wall, and then to a large table with several chairs in the center of the space—his look, one of confusion. The room, empty, appeared to have no other way out except the door they'd just come through.

Richter, close behind, strode to the bookcase, placed his fingertips against the wall and tapped, listening for a hollow sound. He moved to his left and repeated as Jeremiah lifted a rug from underfoot, and looked behind each painting on the walls. "There must be another way out of here, Hans. I know I saw someone with my own eyes."

Richter scowled. He too had seen someone or something disappear up the altar steps and not return. He moved to the middle of the room and stared long at the bookcase again. He strode forward, reached in and began to push handfuls of books onto the floor. Jeremiah reached for the higher shelves out of Richter's grasp, tossing a dozen more leather-bound tomes at the German's feet.

The bookcase empty, Richter ran his hand along the top and bottom surfaces of all the shelves. There were no hidden latches or levers.

He backed up and stood amid a pile of old books. He kicked them aside, looked down and spotted scratch marks etched into the wood floor near the right-hand edge of the bookcase.

"That is where they went."

Jeremiah stared first at the scratch marks, and then at the empty bookcase. When he looked up again, Richter had a smug grin on his face. "Go," he said to Jeremiah, pointing to the far side of the bookcase.

Jeremiah positioned himself, and leaned a shoulder against the wood as Richter pulled out from the opposite side. The bookcase slid sideways revealing the hidden door behind it.

Richter snarled, his smug grin now wider. He drew his gun and peered down into the darkness. At the bottom of the long stone staircase, he saw a dim glow illuminating a passageway. He started down, weapon drawn, with Jeremiah on his heels.

Abbot Androlitis led the group through the underground labyrinth. The interconnected tunnels crisscrossed below the monastery. Lit by a generator humming softly somewhere in the distance, it supplied enough electricity to power the low-wattage lights strung along the tunnel roof.

Odonio came to Androlitis' side. "It is in God's hands now."

Odonio continued to whisper. "What of the others," he asked. "DeLarussa and Abdalla?"

Androlitis, resignation in his voice, said, "We must place our faith in God if we are to be rid of this Russians vermin."

Kazakov stared at the tunnel walls and the white tiling that coved it from the entrance where they'd started to where they were now standing, by her calculations at least two hundred yards in. She eyed a grouping of tiles that had broken loose and fallen. Androlitis, still engrossed in conversation with Odonio, had moved off to one side. She inched closer to investigate the broken tiles.

She pointed a flashlight at the granite walls under the tiles. She had explored dozens of underground caves, early Christian catacombs, and medieval passageways for decades. From Rome to Egypt, to South America, she'd seen them all, but these markings, she was certain, had not been made with simple hand tools. People who lived before the age of power tools did not excavate this passage. She decided not to confront the abbot now. She would wait until she had DeLarussa alone to relay her misgivings.

DeLarussa, twenty yards behind the group, slowed his pace and gazed up at the tunnel walls. On the ceiling above his head were icons, frescos that depicted scenes from the Old Testament—Moses receiving the Law, Abraham offering Isaac to God. He marveled at their delicacy and intricate detail, rivaling old masters he'd seen in Rome.

"How much farther?" Kazakov asked the abbot.

He pointed ahead. "Soon, Irina, soon."

Odonio led them into another tunnel, and then several sharp turns into yet another passageway. DeLarussa saw Kazakov's breathing become labored as the path narrowed and the ceiling got lower. Perspiration formed on her forehead. He recognized the start of a claustrophobic panic attack.

He came up alongside her. "I have you."

Disoriented, Kazakov fought her phobia as the passage narrowed around her. She took short, deep, gulping breaths and closed her eyes.

Odonio held up a hand and stopped in front of a massive arched door. Clad in copper with a green patina from decades of oxidation, it had an elaborately detailed bas-relief of Mt. Sinai. He pulled an old metal key from his robe pocket.

Kazakov remembered seeing one like it once before, in Rome. Odonio's key was identical to one Jeremiah used to gain entrance into Father Angelico's workshop below St Peter's Basilica. She shuddered, remembering the old priest's face, his body writhing, Jeremiah's knife protruding from his side. The key Odonio used contained the same two letters engraved on its head, a Greek Chi and Rho, the first two letters of the word Christ, superimposed one above the other.

Androlitis knelt in front of the door before entering. He lowered his head, mumbling a prayer, before he stood and turned to Kazakov. In a soft voice he said, "I will need the stones you brought with you, both of them."

Richter, now less than twenty yards behind them, heard Androlitis' voice. He held up a hand and motioned to Jeremiah. Richter checked the magazine in his gun, pointed two fingers, first at his eyes and then to the tunnel ahead. Jeremiah nodded he understood and moved to the opposite side of the passageway and knelt in a crouch.

Richter motioned again. The voices up ahead were now moving, the volume lower with every passing second. When they trailed off, almost inaudible, Richter motioned again. He peered around the wall into the passageway. "We will let them lead us to it, then strike."

Jeremiah nodded.

<u>**CHAPTER FORTY**</u>

A full moon illuminating the desert landscape, Lansing stopped the SUV in a small copse of fruit-laden date palms that overlooked the monastery. He remained quiet, composing himself for several seconds before stepping out of the vehicle. He'd driven like a man possessed, at one point losing a muffler pipe when they bottomed out and skidded into a rock-strewn wadi. He'd barely avoided a massive boulder blocking the road ahead. Even strong admonitions from ben Yehuda to slow down on the treacherous terrain, roads in name only, were ignored, but the Mossad agent saw the fire in Lansing's eyes, a look of angry determination. He backed off, opting instead to hang on. He'd known Lansing for only a few weeks, but one thing was clear, Theodore Lansing did not like being played by a sociopath like Hans Richter, nor a gang of priests pleading ignorance of everything.

Sweating in the rear seat, Arlen Drew, silent through the entire hair-raising sprint back to the monastery, kept one hand on a grab-bar above the door.

"Check your weapons," Lansing barked.

Ben Yehuda came alongside him and pointed down at the monastery walls fifty feet below the rise. "We need to be very careful from here on, Lansing," he warned. "The abbot knows we are here."

"How could he know?" asked Lansing. "An hour ago I didn't know myself."

The Israeli agent handed Lansing a pair of binoculars and pointed down the rise at a small light visible on a parapet high on the monastery wall. When Lansing looked through the glasses, a camping lantern came into focus and a man holding a pair of binoculars came into view. Whoever it was, his face remained hidden.

"Richter?" Lansing asked.

"I do not think so," ben Yehuda answered. "More likely, one of the monastery priests. But yes, they know we are here, and be certain he will warn the others."

"Arlen," Lansing ordered. "Move that SUV closer to the ridge line, but keep it far enough back so that spotter on the wall can only see the top of the roof. Point the nose east and turn on the headlights. I want a beam of light illuminating the ridge line all the way to those rocks over there." He pointed to an outcropping fifty yards east of their position. "I need the lookout to believe we are making camp for the night. It may buy us time to get down there without them realizing we're coming."

Lansing tossed a backpack over his shoulder and started for the ridge. Ari and Drew followed.

A carillon inside the church's campanile held nine huge copper-clad bells, gifts from the Tsars over many centuries. Each pealed in synchronized octaves. In the Sinai's stillness, the booming chimes echoed off the nearby mountains, reverberating in a decrescendo of dying volume. Deep resonant sounds filled the still night air as ben Yehuda, Arlen Drew, and Ted Lansing reached the monastery's far side. It was past midnight.

"Over there," ben Yehuda pointed. "A door."

They sprinted across the open space. Lansing grabbed the door handle, a wooden lever meant to move up and down, but it would not budge.

Ben Yehuda screwed a silencer onto the end of his gun. He held it against the lever and fired three quick rounds. Dry wood chips exploded around him.

Lansing saw a light coming through a stained-glass window of the church. In single file, they sprinted across the open space to an archway leading inside to the main sanctuary.

Shadows cast from a chandelier above the altar created eerie shapes along the cathedral's floor and walls. They continued down the nave, hugging the aisle, staying low as they moved.

Arlen Drew stopped to glance at the location Demos' body only days before had been found. All traces of t0f a grisly murder cleaned.

Lansing crouched behind a pew and whispered, pointing up at the altar. "There."

Drew crept up the marble steps and moved behind the altar to the sacristy door.

Inside, he tapped the walls, lifted rugs and pushed a heavy cabinet aside. He rummaged through desk drawers tossing papers aside when Lansing's voice called to him in a low tone.

"Arlen, get in here, now."

Drew and ben Yehuda followed the sound of Lansing's voice to a small library with an bookcase swung partially out from the wall—its contents strewn in a pile on the floor. Behind it was a steep stone staircase leading down.

In a tunnel below the library, ben Yehuda stared at the blue and white tiling affixed to the walls. Lansing pointed up at icons and friezes on the tunnel roof.

"What is this?" Drew asked. "Could this have been dug by hand, even with a couple of hundred years to get it done?"

"It would be some marvel of engineering," said Lansing.

Lansing took a small knife from his pocket, went to the wall and pried a tile loose. He held it in both hands and slammed the porcelain square across his knee, splintering the ceramic.s

The broken edge was powderedwith pieces flaking away. It looked cheap, as if it had come from a Home Depot in Georgetown.

"This piece of crap is not very old, Ari," Lansing said.

Lansing directed his flashlight at the granite underneath the tiles. He ran a finger across the gouge marks. "Feel this, Ari," he said to ben Yehuda.

"What's your take?"

"Take on what?" asked Drew.

"The markings made by the tools used to excavate this tunnel, their depth—and in particular their length."

Drew ran a flat palm over the markings and placed his index finger into a groove.

"What do you feel?" Lansing asked.

"Nothing, it's smooth, like it was sandblasted."

"Precisely."

"If this excavation took place prior to power tools, those markings would not be smooth. Whomever excavated this tunnel, and whenever it was done, I doubt it was monks in the third or fourth century."

Lansing turned his attention to ben Yehuda. "But you knew that already, Ari, didn't you? This was not engineered by priests or monks, was it?"

His tone was accusatory.

"Where are you going with this, Ted?"

"Stop the bullshit, Ari. Something's been off since we first started this little romp through the desert. Every time we came close to nabbing Richter another roadblock appeared. First Mossad loses him at the airport in Tel Aviv—how does that happen in your own backyard? Then after Demos' murder, I thought we had him in our sights again, but you convince me to go for a joyride into the Sinai."

Lansing hoped for a reaction from the Mossad agent.

"And what about your boss in Tel Aviv, Colonel Heifetz? She shows up in Washington, contacts the assistant director and redirects the investigation with some cock and bull story about the Ten Commandments?"

As Lansing spoke, anger grew. "Just what in the hell is Mossad really after here, my friend, because it's sure not chasing after some phony religious artifacts."

CHAPTER FORTY-ONE

Felicia Albreda reached into a desk drawer in her ofice She opened a bottle of Tylenol and placed two smooth white caplets on the desk next to a bottle of single malt Scotch she kept for just such nights. She held the acetaminophen between her fingertips and placed them on her tongue, poured two fingers of the twelve-year-old Balvenie and downed them with single swig. She glanced A desk clock; its LCD snapped to 2:35 a.m. She started to thumb through a log of Lansing's every move since he first arrived in Israel two weeks before.

Each of Lansing's report, date and time stamped, was automatically recorded and cataloged by the bureau. Worrisome, was the number of times Lansing's Mossad partners came close to nabbing the Russian operative, only to have him to slip from through their fingers.

Through FBI Director Walter's office inquiries were made to several of the United States government's most secret alphabet agencies. Cryptic and vague, each response confirmed that Mossad rarely missed any opportunity to secure a timely takedown of a suspect they were closing in on. No plausible explanations were given on how or why, but it did question Mossad's fervor without commenting one way or the other.

Red flags went up in Albreda's mind. Could Mossad and the FBI be at cross-purposes? How odd was it that Aviya Heifetz, a high ranking Mossad colonel, flew to the United States under a pseudonym, met her in an unofficial capacity and convinced the Assistant Director to allow

Lansing to join the Richter manhunt? She remembered the matter of a dead Vatican security officer at a townhouse in Georgetown with a lot of unexplained, but inconclusive evidence that Mossad had ordered a hit.

Director Walters, using off-channel contacts, assured her that if, in fact, Mossad was involved in the townhouse incident, little of what transpired matched their standard protocol. The bureau's best analysis: Mossad had its own agenda, and one not necessarily shared by the bureau.

Lansing's reports arrived once in every forty eight- cycle, and all Albreda knew from his last filing, dated five days ago, Ted and Arlen Drew were working the case somewhere in the Sinai. For the fourth time, she looked at a written transcript prepared by her staff from Lansing's last transmission.

Sidearm, Ari ben Yehuda's code name, *has no partner today. He left and is not expected back. Suspect Merlin.*

Agent ben Yehuda's partner had been killed by Richter, code name Merlin. She thumbed through a stack of transmissions looking for the name of possible Mossad agents she suspected of being Richter's latest victim, a news clipping or an obituary in a local newspaper. Ari ben Yehuda's name did not come up in any database, not unusual, or the name of anyone who might have been Mossad. She did not expect to find anything.

One short chime, and a light on Albreda's desk phone started to blink. "Director Walters for the assistant director, ma'am."

"David?" she said, glancing at the desk clock. "You're working late."

"I called your house, Felicia, but your housekeeper, Rosaria I believe, told me you were here, still at work."

"Not much I can do at home," she said. "Ted and our son Joshua are on the other side of the world. What's this about? Because whatever it is, it must be urgent at 3:00 a.m."

"It's about that case, the one you wanted inquiries made about."

She felt her heart start to race, and a band tighten around her head. She closed her eyes and held her breath. "What's happened?"

"Easy, Felicia. Yes, as far as I know Ted is fine."

"So why does fine not ease my mind, David?"

"I don't want to talk about this on the phone. Come to my office now. Colin Macpherson is here waiting for you."

Macpherson, Albreda wondered—*a spook, meeting with the director, at the Hoover Building, and in the middle of the night no less.*

Something was up.

On the elevator to the director's office, Albreda's mind conjured all manner of scenarios that might bring Gregory Macpherson to the office of the Director—none of them good.

Angus Macpherson, number-two at Langley, directed the CIA's International Anti-Terrorism Unit. As she approached the director's office, all Albreda could think about was her husband, six thousand miles away and in danger, the kind of danger that drew the attention of the CIA.

The only illumination in Walter outer office was a single library-style desk lamp equipped with an ordinary old-school pull-chain and a green plastic shade. She made her way past a receptionist's desk and maneuvered around the furniture to an L-shaped corridor.

"David? Are you here?" Albreda whispered.

"Yes, Felicia, come in, it's not locked."

She made her way to his inner office and entered without knocking.

Angus Macpherson rose from his chair. He stood rigid and came forward to greet her, a hand extended.

Albreda had never met Angus Macpherson in person before, but the first thing anyone noticed upon meeting himsthe first time was his size. The diminutive assistant director, barely 5'3" tall, craned her neck upward at the 6'7" Macpherson.

He wore a blue jogging suit, complete with a tie-dyed sweatband around his head and pair of Adidas running shoes. Macpherson made an imposing figure.

A quick up and down glance made it clear to Albreda that the man took good care of himself. Not just tall, the forty-year-old CIA anti-terrorism chief looked buff, his thighs and leg muscles well defined in the too-tight pants of his jogging suit.

"Please, Felicia, sit," said Walters, pointing to a chair in front of his desk. MacPherson sat next to her.

"About a month ago, Mr. Macpherson…" she said.

Walters stopped her. "Angus is up to speed, Felicia. Hear him out."

Macpherson reached under his chair and came up with a leather diplomatic pouch. He undid the straps, lifted a flap and withdrew a bound folio.

Albreda thumbed through every pagee. On top of page-one the words, Biologic Devastation Potential, were printed in large bold type. Below was a bulleted list. She recognized the entries, a who's who of nasty microorganisms.

"What is this, Mr. Macpherson?"

"Angus, please," Macpherson said. "They are extremely dangerous, and deadly, and antibiotic-resistant strains of bacteria, each with potential for use in biological warfare if aerosolized."

"I am not following," Albreda said. "What is their relationship to the Kastianich murder that my husband is investigating in Israel?"

"Turn to page three," Macpherson said.

She stared at the Russian words with their English transliteration. She read aloud pronouncing them phonetically, *D'la Bartovik.* "What does it mean?"

Macpherson waited several seconds, adding to the unfolding drama.

"From December of '79 to February of '89 insurgent groups in Afghanistan fought the Soviet Army and the allied Afghan forces. Damn thing nearly bankrupted the Kremlin."

Albreda stood up and poured a cup of coffee from a carafe on Walters' desk. She turned and faced Macpherson again. "Why do I have a feeling that another shoe is about to drop, Angus?"

"Because it is, Felicia. *D'la Bartovic* is part of an intercepted transmission between an Egyptian outpost and Moscow. At the height of the conflict in Afghanistan, the Russians were taking heavy losses on the battlefield and needed a way to stem the tide. We were never able to confirm *D'la Bartovik* until recently.

"From where in Egypt did this coded transmission originate?" asked Albreda.

Macpherson directed her to the last page of the dossier—a set of GPS coordinates.

David Walters picked up a remote and turned on a flat screen TV monitor affixed on the wall across from his desk.

A satellite view of a walled structure appeared, and in the background black mountainous terrain.

"This is Saint Catherine's Monastery, Santa Katerina, official name, the Sacred Monastery of the God-Trodden. It sits on the Sinai Peninsula, at the mouth of a gorge near the foot of Mount Sinai, in the city of Saint Catherine, Egypt."

Albreda gasped. "David, that is where Ted and Arlen Drew are right now."

"Just what is *D'la Bartovic?*" she pressed, now stone-faced with no emotion to give away her fear.

"I'll answer that, David," said Macpherson. "In a clandestine lab outside the city of Omsk, near the Kazakhstan border, Russian scientists developed a biological weapon of some kind—a virus, maybe a bacterium. We never knew for sure, or if the entire story was a hoax."

Albreda, confused, asked, "I am not seeing the Sinai connection here?"

"In '91, when the Soviet Union collapsed, the old guard of the KGB, we believe, sought out a place to hide the weapon their scientists developed at Omsk. A large sum of money, estimated at five million dollars, was transferred from an account in a Swiss bank to an entity called DBHS."

"What is that?" she asked.

"Not what, who?" Macpherson answered. "It is an acronym for the corporation that administers the Monastery of Santa Katerina. Does the name Androlitis mean anything to you?"

Chapter Forty-Twos

Albreda placed a canvas travel bag at the foot of the stairs in her Georgetown house and checked her hair and makeup in a full-length wall mirror. An antique grandfather clock chimed off the hour. She checked her watch again; it was 11:00 a.m.

With Director Walters dead set against the trip, it but she had convinced her boss to okay a request that she travel to Israel by herself, unescorted. There were a thousand reasons not to go, prime among them, the lead agent on the case was her husband. She understood there were limits, safeguards against personal feeling interfering with bureau business, but on this one she was adamant, implying that she would go, with or without David Walters' blessing.

Director Walters relented. She could go, but not in any official capacity. Instead, his office booked her on a commercial flight and used her personal American Express card to pay for the ticket. It put up the fewest red flags. Both agreed it was imperative the Israelis, Mossad, and Aviya Heifetz in particular, not know in advance she was coming.

The late-night meeting with Macpherson in Walters' office did not break up until after 5:00 a.m. giving Albreda barely enough time to get home, shower, change clothes, and have her housekeeper pack a bag. Macpherson, on Walters' request tasked a CIA operative in Jerusalem's West Bank to shadow her until she made contact with Heifetz. Reluctant, Albreda agreed to all of Walters' conditions.

The doorbell chimed. She gave herself one last look in the hall mirror. Her chic, gray business suit, with its knee-length skirt, thin gold belt, and a matching jacket was perfect. A dark gray pocket-square peeked out from the jacket's lapel pocket. Her silk blouse with a top button left casually undone completed the look—serious businesswoman with a flirty side. She glanced at her left hand. Instead of her diamond wedding band with its circle of not so small diamonds, a simple cocktail ring took its place. The only other jewelry she wore was a simple pearl necklace.

The limo driver took her bag, placed it into the trunk of a black Lincoln Town Car and held the door open for her.

"Reagan National?" the driver asked.

Albreda nodded into the rearview mirror.

"What time is your flight ma'am?" He asked.

She saw the flash of a leather strap under his suit jacket and removed a cellphone from her handbag on the floor of the car. She logged into her FBI mail and s entered the director's personal email address.

"David, thank you, but I did not need a babysitter to the airport."

The Delta Sky Club at Reagan National had several passengers waiting for flights or on layovers when Albreda arrived a few minutes before noon. A flight information board showed departure time for Tel Aviv at 2:00 p.m. was on time. A Sky Club hostess asked Albreda if she wanted anything from the first-class lounge lunch menu, which could be delivered on the plane.

The glass-enclosed room off the main concourse had floor to ceiling drapery to provide privacy from people walking by on the concourse.

Albreda picked up a card on a round bistro table, a reminder that the Sky Club offered complementary public WiFi. Afraid that her cell phone transmissions could be intercepted on public WiFi she reached into he handbag and turned hers off.

The Sky Club hostess returned with coffee and a toasted bagel, placing them on the table in front of her. Albreda watched the woman walk away and turned her attention back to eying the other people in the room.

Nothing looked suspicious, but in the back of her head was Director Walters' voice. He'd been her mentor and advocate, pushing her career forward from behind the scenes.

Albreda first learned about David Walters behind the scenes advocacy when a clerical employee at the bureau with too much 'holiday cheer' at an after-hours get-together tried to ramp up his importance with a coworker. The woman, a computer tech in Operations, laughed off his lubricated advances, but shared his clumsy attempt at seduction with a coworker who just happened to be the sister of Albreda's confidential assistant. Felicia kept the information to herself, not even sharing it with her husband.

Albreda's eyes continued to scan the people around her in the lounge. One of them, she was certain, had to be an agent David Walters placed on her flight. She looked for telltale signs, shoes inconsistent with their clothing, FBI shoes she euphemistically called them, more utilitarian than fashionable, or FBI issue haircuts, whatever that meant, but she would know it when she saw it. Nobody in the Sky Lounge looked suspicious.

Sipping her coffee Albreda wondered if the agent could be a woman. That would make more sense, she thought. A female agent could stay closer and have better access to restrooms and lounges.

***

Albreda awoke on the plane at 3:00 a.m. Washington time. She curled her knees under her and pulled a blanket to her chin in the tight business-class pod. She reset her watch to 10:00 a.m., IST, Israeli Standard Time. She reached up and pushed the call button for something to get her blood sugar up.

A twenty-something flight attendant wearing a Delta apron over his uniform appeared in the aisle. She asked for a glass of orange juice. He nodded, turned and started aft toward the First-Class galley.

Albreda sat up in her pod, but when an 'occupied' sign on the lavatory door flashed, she laid back down and waited. The darkened aisle leading to the aft galley was empty, the dark cabin silent, except for an ever-present drone of the aircraft's engines.

Albreda eyed a male passenger in a Delta sleep-smock. His slippers, soft-soled, stuck out into the aisle. When he stood up and started toward her she removed a compact from her bag, opened the mirror and watched him approach. As he neared, Albreda keyed in on the ten rows between them. Reaching her seat, he placed a hand on the seat back for a brief second, tapped it once and continued forward.

Albreda kept focus in the small hand mirror. A man's leg, almost imperceptibly, started to rise from a seat three rows behind, and then drop back down when the man in the smock reached the occupied restroom. She leaned back in her seat. She had found her agent.

Albreda slid out of the pod and stretched in the aisle before starting aft toward the galley. When she passed the man she'd followed in her mirror, back in his seat and now sitting upright, she took mental note that even now, at 3:00 a.m., he had not placed his pod into sleep mode.

He made direct eye contact as Albreda passed. She recognized the haircut, FBI standard issue. David had her back.

Albreda's flight landed at 11:00 a.m. IST and made her way through the terminal to Israeli customs. There would be no governmental courtesy usually usually afforded foreign law enforcement and diplpmats because today she was not FBI. Her ID and passport documents contained her real name but no indication of her actual identity, or her position at the bureau. She was simply Felicia Albreda, VP of a DC advertising firm called Vista Images. She was in Israel on business, estimated to be three weeks' duration.s

As she stood in the customs line, Albreda looked around her, impressed with the tight security, unlike anything she'd experienced in the United States. Armed military, with automatic weapons slung over their shoulders, many with dogs, patrolled, stone-faced and vigilant. Other men and women, she took for plainclothes Shin Bet agents eyed everyone in line, profiling, searching for tells.

Through customs, her canvas bag carried by a porter, Albreda stood at the curb outside the terminal. A police officer in a black uniform wearing white gloves motioned to the first car in a queue several meters away. It started forward. The white VW sedan with Hebrew lettering on the side stopped in front of her, on its roof a lit yellow dome light with Hebrew lettering, pulled up.

"Good afternoon," the driver said as she slid into the rear seat, thankful for the air conditioning. "Your first time visiting *Eretz Yisrael*?" the driver added in perfect English. Albreda handed him a slip of paper. Written in Hebrew was an address.

***

After a thirty-minute ride, the driver pulled onto a residential street someplace in suburban Tel Aviv. The area appeared not what she'd anticipated. In her mind she expected a modern structure, something akin to Langley, but on a much smaller scale. This place looked like an old decrepit building.

Set back fifty yards from the road, surrounded by an ornamental fence, it had seen better days but knowing Mossad, and knowing how they operated, she was certain the deception was purposeful.

"You are sure this is the correct address, madam?" her driver asked.

Albreda began to question herself and the address supplied by Macpherson. On the roof three metal structures of varying sizes were spaced equidistant from each other. Mossad's off-site satellite building appeared to be an ordinary house on an ordinary suburban street refitted for communications.

Standing in an empty lobby Albreda looked up at building's directory. The idea that there would be a listing for Mossad mad her laugh. She pressed an elevator button and waited.

When the elevator door opened two men in khaki slacks and white shirts with open collars stepped out. The taller of the pair had a conspicuous bulge under his shirt.

"May I be of assistance?" the he asked.

"Yes, you may," Albreda answered in a firm voice. "I am here to see Colonel Aviya Heifetz. I do not have an appointment"

The second man interrupted. "I am sorry, Madam, but I believe you are lost. You are an American tourist? Are you not?"

She looked up at the elevator's ceiling, knowing someone was monitoring the conversation. She smiled at the man. "Do us both a favor and tell Colonel Heifetz that Felicia Albreda is here and needs, no insists, on speaking with her at once."

"As I told you, Madam, I believe you are lost, mistaken. There is nobody here by that name."

Albreda took her cell phone from a pocket. "In five seconds, I am calling the American Embassy. Perhaps they will send a car to this location to get me. Better yet, I have the U.S. Ambassador on speed-dial."

A series of short beeps came from the man's front pants pocket. He removed a two-way device and listened for before pressing the elevator button, summoning the car back down to the lobby.

The two men positioned themselves on either side of Albreda as the elevator rode up to the fourth floor. Neither man took his eyes off her for a second, comical she thought; where could she go?

The elevator door opened and one of the men pointed to a door at the far end of a long corridor. Together they led her to it, flanking her, moving in lockstep.

Aviya Heifetz, seated behind her desk, stood up and pointed to a chair. "I have been expecting you, Felicia. If may I still call you Felicia?"

Albreda stared at the Mossad colonel. The transformation was amazing. When they'd first met in Washington, Heifetz looked, acted and spoke like someone's kindly old grandmother. Today, here in her office, she wore a pair of crisp khakis and a matching military style shirt open at the collar. On the shirt's epaulets were rank insignias. Heifetz' hairstyle in Washington a grandmotherly gray with a curly perm, was now dark with a short, cropped haircut.

Albreda sat quietly for several seconds "Between you and I, Aviya, if I may call you still call you Aviya, just two women with tough jobs, two women being honest with one another…"

The volume of Albreda's voice rose incrementally, tinged with anger she'd bottled up, thought about and rehearsed during the long flight to Israel. She'd rehearsed in her head what she would say a dozen times, but here, now, she lost it.

"Let's just cut the bullshit, Aviya. I do not like being played for a fool. Woman to woman, what kind of shitstorm have you involved the bureau in, because it certainly is not about some relics from the time of Moses. And where the hell are my agents, Lansing and Drew?"

CHAPTER FORTY-THREE

Irina Kazakov followed Father Odonio through a wooden door with a copper-clad bas-relief of Mt. Sinai affixed to it. Inside was a circular chamber she estimated to be five meters in diameter, which was no a tomb or grotto built by monks with hand tools.

Gone were the cheap, crude blue and white ceramic tiles that lined the passageway, replaced here by clean, stainless-steel panels. Along the curved walls an extension, two meters high and four meters wide, protruded like a shelf into the open chamber.

The Russian linguist approached the shelf and peered down at its top surface. There were no seams between it and the wall. Etched into the top surface, in Greek lettering, was the word *Iēsoús*–Jesus. Below it, also in Greek, she translated an inscription, paraphrasing, *"May the Lord in his divine wisdom protect our sacred vow, so mankind may be spared."*

"Spared from what, Irina?" asked DeLarussa.

Kazakov stepped back and pondered the strange metallic extension protruding into the circular chamber. She commented on its lack of anything identifying it as Russian. No inscribed CCCP, obsolete since 1991 after the post-World War II, Cold War regime collapsed. At the far edge of the shelf's top surface was an odd-looking depression formed in the surface.

DeLarussa came alongside her. "What are you thinking, Irina?"

She ignored him, instead, placed a hand into the depression. She estimated its depth at ten centimeters, four inches, with a pair of molded T shapes facing in opposition to each other with, their vertical bars abutting each other at the bottom. At the crossbar of each letter were three upward projections of different lengths she estimated to be three or four centimeters long, spaced unevenly giving it the look of grinning Jack-O-Lantern. She turned to Odonio, and back to Androlitis. "Do either of you have any ideas about what this is?"

Odonio answered meekly. "No Dr. Kazakov, I do not. I have never been in this place before."

Odonio's gaze met Androlitis'. "What is this place, Constantine?" he said, using the abbot's given name.

Androlitis interrupted. "No, Irina, he has not. Only Father Petrarkis, the abbot before me, and I know the truth."

Kazakov took another look at the steel walls. She looked glared at the Abbot, her anger building. She uttered two words, so low that it was difficult to hear. "Why me?"

Androlitis came alongside her. "Because I needed the stolen artifacts to rid ourselves, once and for all, of these godless Russians who have blackmailed and threatened the brotherhood for fifty years."

DeLarussa came forward. "The parchment and the map, Fitzwater's diary describing the Commandments, the original tablets, was it a hoax, a ruse?"

"Yes," Androlitis answered. "And I am truly sorry for that."

Kazakov eyeballed the Abbot. "Are you sorry about the deception, Father, or sorry you have been exposed? Why was I brought into this fiasco?"

Faruq Abdalla, silent until now, shouted across the chamber, "Because we needed someone with gravitas, Irina, someone who would lend credence to their scheme! If you were actively seeking the Commandments, Irina, then they were real. That's why. Is it not, Constantine?"

"Yes, Irina, you were chosen precisely for that reason."

There was sadness in his voice but not contrition. "We needed the Kremlin to believe you were on a wild-goose chase that would lead nowhere, giving them time to retrieve whatever they buried in the Sinai fifty years ago."

Kazakov went silent before speaking again. "So, is this all about recovering the stone artifacts?"

Meekly, Androlitis replied, "Yes Irina, but please, do not blame Odonio. The fault lies with me and me alone. Until this very minute, neither Father Odonio nor any others in our brotherhood knew of this place's existence beyond believing it had been excavated in a true search for the genuine Commandments. We have kept the myth of the tablets alive since 1967 and have been paid handsomely by the Russians to do so."

Abdalla, exploded, "So this a marketing plan to bring the faithful to your monastery in hopes of finding the Commandments. It is at the end of the day only about the money!"

"No, my son, it is about survival, our brotherhood's survival."

"I am sorry too, Father," Kazakov answered. "But that is nonsense and you know it."

"Irina, please hear me out. You need to understand, know the entire story."

"All right, I am listening."

"With war about to rage in the Sinai in 1967, a convoy of twenty or more trucks with Russian military and civilian engineers arrived here. The trucks carried heavy equipment for excavation. Father Petrarkis was Abbot then and the Russians at first intimidated him with threats. It was a tumultuous time. Santa Katerina lay at the crosshairs of a dozen Arab armies. They told Petrarkis that if he did not allow them to excavate under the monastery when the fighting broke out the Russians would see to it that Santa Katerina became a casualty of war."

"And he complied?" asked Kazakov.

"No Irina, he did not. Petrarkis convinced them that placing whatever they needed to hide under Santa Katerina, which was never disclosed to Petrakis, would be a foolish tactic. Too many outsiders, he argued, came to Santa Katerina. If they believed for one minute that such an important piece of history lay beneath it the secret could not remain a secret for long.

"Instead, the Russians on Petrarkis' advice went fifty kilometers south to a series of caves. The Russian commander, in a hurry to hide the weapon and get back to war planning, did the expedient thing without informing his superiors. They hid the device deep inside a cave and sealed the entrance with explosives. The Russian expected to retrieve it as soon as the war broke out."

"Then why build this place, with its elaborate winding tunnels?" Kazakov asked.

"To further proffer the myth of the original stones Moses carried down from Sinai and divert attention from whatever the Russians hid," Androlitis answered.

"After the Six-Day war in 1967 Egyptian tanks lay scattered across the desert, Arab armies fleeing from the IDF, and the Russians gone forever, Father Petrarkis prayed."

Abdalla moved toward the Abbot. Androlitis backed away until his legs felt the steel box protruding out from the wall.

"What the hell is in there?" Abdalla shouted, pointing at the protruding shelf. "And why do the Russians want it so badly that they dispatched a murderer like Hans Richter to retrieve it?"

"That, Constantine, is a question I would like an answer to as well," said Father DeLarussa.

"I now believe it is a weapon of some kind," Androlitis said, sheepishly.

"What kind of weapon?"

"That I do not know."

Kazakov, now blind with rage, lashed out. "In the name of Christ, Constantine, how could you not know? In all the years since 1967, you never thought to look—to rip the walls away and find out? Who built this place?"

"Father Petrarkis built it with the financial assistance of a Greek oligarch named Bernardakis Matsoukas," Androlitis said pointing to the walls. "They are made of reinforced concrete. It would take powerful explosives to remove it. Dynamite below the monastery would risk destroying religious treasures thousands of years old, not to mention that we do not know the nature of whatever the Russians stored here. For all we know it could be a nuclear device they planned on using against the Israelis."

Kazakov's demeanor softened. She understood. "The artifacts are the key to getting inside that thing and finding the weapon. Am I correct?"

"Yes, Irina. Matsoukas started the excavation in 1970 and completed the construction of this tunnel in under a year."

"Where is this thing that Hans Richter is so hell bent on retrieving, and why now?"

"Father Petrarkis with Matsoukas' assistance breached the cave where the Russians hid the weapon," said Androlitis. "The cavern was resealed and the weapon, a metallic cylinder of some kind, was moved here and an elaborate set of keys made."

"The stone artifacts that were stolen from the Smithsonian in Washington that led to Kastianich's murder?" Kazakov asked.

Androlitis nodded. "Without the stone artifact there is no way to retrieve the stone key.

"Faruq," Kazakov said said, resignation in her voice. "Hand me my backpack."

She lifted the two stone artifacts from her backpack and handed them to Farther Androlitis. "How do they work?" she said.

Androlitis held them in his hands. He shook his head from side to side and whispered, "I do not know."

"Liar!" Abdalla screamed.

"Say or do what you want, my son," said the Abbot. "I cannot help because I truly do not know."

Faruq Abdalla reached for Androlitis. The Abbot backed away from the younger, stronger Egyptian.

"*Genug*! Enough!" a voice boomed in German.

All eyes turned. "*Anschlag oder ich beenden sie beide*. Stop or I will kill you both."

Hans Richter, framed in the doorway, had a gun pointed at them. Standing next to him, Jeremiah waved a semi-automatic.

Chapter Forty-Fous

Richter pointed his weapon tat Irina Kazakov's head. Gesturing, he herded everyone against the far wall of the chamber.

"You will hand them to Jeremiah… *bitte*," he said, adding sarcasm.

Kazakov started to comply until Androlitis shouted . "Do not, Irina. This madman is going to kill us all once he has them."

Richter laughed. "Madman, I will show you madman, you insipid fool!" He fired a single round into Odonio.

The wounded priest grabbed at his chest and fell, silent. Kazakov gasped aloud and started for the fallen priest, now on the ground.

"Touch him and another of your little band will die, *liebchen*!"

Richter snarled and Kazakov backed away. "You and I, we have such a long history, Irina. It would be a shame to kill you as well." He grinned, exposing a gold tooth in the corner of his mouth. "You more than anyone knows what I can and will do it, and never lose a second's sleep over it." He pointed the muzzle of his gun at her head again.

Kazakov knelt, never taking her eyes from Richter, picked up both artifacts and handed them to Jeremiah.

"Here, use this," Richter said, giving Jeremiah a small geologist's hammer.

Jeremiah placed one stone on the edge of the steel box protruding from the wall, turned to Richter, and said, "Are you certain of this, Hans?"

Richter nodded, remembering what Anton, his Russian handler told him before leaving Moscow—*double tap, one soft hit at each end of the stone, and then harder, just above the lettering on the top surface.*

The method of extracting whatever was hidden inside had been drilled into Richter over and over.

Jeremiah placed the hammer over the stone and double tapped once at each end, and harder over the archaic lettering in the center. The outer stone broke away, revealing a T-shaped metallic object embedded inside. He handed it to Richter.

"*Gekommener blick, Irina*, come look," Richter said. "It is ingenious what these priests did."

Kazakov, eyes wide, stared at the object in Richter's hand. The top of the T had inward grooves machined into it and small outward notches spaced unevenly apart. The bottom of the T had a two-inch screw extending outward.

"Now the other one," Richter ordered.

Secreted inside the second stone was a nearly identical T-shaped object with the same inward and outward projections. At the bottom of the T, instead of a projecting screw, was a narrow groove.

Richter fit the two pieces together, turning the screw inside the groove until both pieces interlocked into one continuous piece, two letter Tees set end to end.

Richter extended a hand to Kazakov. "Since you have been so instrumental in recovering this for us, Irina, I give you the honors."

She took it from Richter's fingers and turned her head toward the box projecting from the wall. He nodded to, pointing. "*Gehen Sie*, go."

Kazakov stared into the depression. Her eyes went back to the object in her hand. Carefully, she lowered the joined Tees. The grooves and notches in the depression fit like pieces of a jigsaw puzzle. She now understood. She looked back over her shoulder at Richter. He laughed, his shiny gold tooth mocking her.

"Exert gentle downward pressure," he said.

Kazakov pressed. There was a series of short clicks as the back of the shelf slid forward several inches, revealing a hinged lid.

"Open it," Richter ordered.

Kazakov did as she was told.

"All of you, and you as well Irina, get up against that wall. Jeremiah, do not take your eyes or your gun from them for even one second."

Richter reached into the open box and removed a metal canister resembling a Dewar flask a half-meter long with the diameter of a baseball bat. On its side, painted in bright red, were three interlocking rings, a symbol, circa 1970s for biohazard.

Richter lifted a backpack from the ground and prepared to transfer the canister when a loud voice stopped him.

A defiant Androlitis was holding something in his hand.

"Stop now! If you try to take that canister we will all die."

The Abbot took a step toward Richter. Jeremiah recognized the object secreted in the priest's hand and backed away, frightened. He lowered his weapon.

Richter laughed. "You are a bigger fool than even I believed, Father. What do you plan doing with that thing? Blow us all up?"

Androlitis held a hand grenade in one hand, the pin in his other hand displayed above his head.

"I do not know where you got that thing, Constantine, but if you believe for one second that it frightens me, you would be mistaken. Look around you, where you are. If you detonate it, we may all die, and perhaps even bring your precious monastery down around our ears."

Lansing continued down the narrow passage with Drew and ben Yehuda behind him, all with drawn weapons. Hearing voices from below he stopped. Ari ben Yehuda moved to the opposite side of the tunnel and hugged the wall. Arlen Drew moved behind ben Yehuda as Lansing peered around the bend. There was an open door. He motioned to ben Yehuda. They retreated to formulate a plan.

"There's at least fifty feet of open space between that last turn in the tunnel and the door. How do you want to play this, Ari?" Lansing said

"Element of surprise," Drew piped up. It's the best way to go in unless one of you has a better idea?"

Lansing looked at ben Yehuda who nodded. "All right then, surprise it is."

Abbot Androlitis dropped the grenade pin onto the ground and waved the explosive at Jeremiah. "I will not warn you again!"

Jeremiah stood his ground, waiting for Richter's orders.

In Russian, Richter tried to convince Jeremiah that Androlitis was bluffing. He would never jeopardize the monastery. Jeremiah was not convinced.

He took a step in the abbot's direction but stopped when Androlitis began to recite a prayer in Latin. Jeremiah recognized as the words, *Yea though I walk in the Valley of Death.*

"No. Hans, he is not bluffing. Look at his eyes? Rapture… he is prepared to die."

"No, Father!" DeLarussa pleaded with Androlitis. "Do not do this. No matter the reason, it remains a mortal sin, murder and suicide. Dying accomplishes nothing."

Kazakov took DeLarussa's arm just above the elbow and pulled him back. "Do not push Richter. I know the man well. There is nothing he will not do, even die to complete a mission."

Androlitis' attention turned to Kazakov, and back to Richter. He grabbed Abdalla's outstretched arm, his huge fingers smothering the back of Androlitis' hand. He pressed hard, invoking a cry of pain as the Abbot's reed thin fingers jammed tight against the grenade handle preventing it from detonating. Jeremiah's other hand clasped Androlitis' wrist. He pressed his bald head into Androlitis' chest and drove the crown of his skull upward into the priest's lower jaw.

Androlitis staggered into the wall with Jeremiah still holding tight to his wrist. The much larger Jeremiah slammed his body into the wall, pinning him as they struggled for the grenade. Richter moved sideways, his weapon waving at Kazakov as Abdalla, keept them at bay.

Three figures came barreling in through the open door; Lansing upright, ben Yehuda in a low crouch with Arlen Drew behind them.

Jeremiah drove his shoulder into Androlitis' midsection lifting his body off the ground.

The Abbot moaned as air left his lungs. He doubled over, gasping. The grenade fell from his hand and rolled across the ground.

For Androlitis, everything started to move in slow motion. He stared at the small pineapple-shaped explosive, seconds from detonation, wobbling like a dying top coming to rest against the far wall. Both Richter and Jeremiah dove for cover, their arms clasped tightly over their heads.

"*Get out!*" Lansing shouted, but Ari ben Yehuda was already face down, his body flat against the floor.

There was a huge flash and a deafening blast. Arlen Drew went airborne, his body blown out of the door. His head slammed against the granite wall, and everything went black.

Ten minutes later Arlen Drew opened his eyes. A trickle of blood ran down his face. He stood up slowly, tentatively, his vision blurred.

"Ted?" he called out. "Ari?" His voice sounded like it came from inside a soundproof room, garbled like it was far away.

The tunnel was filled with choking smoke and the door to the inner chamber gone. In its place a pile of debris from floor to ceiling blocking entrance.

Staggering onto the pile Drew tried to dislodge a large boulder. From above his head a fine powder continued to rain down. He was covered in soft, white dust. Again, he tried to pull rubble from the pile as a huge chunk of granite fell from the tunnel roof missing—then, another, and another. The labyrinth was coming down around him.

Drew climbed down from the pile of shattered granite up against the door. He felt lightheaded, his lungs exploding. He took a step, felt woozy and dropped to one knee, fighting to stay conscious. The tunnel walls swirled in his head. He came to his feet, shaky, staggering toward where he'd first entered the tunnel from the monastery above.

Through thick dust, Drew spotted a sliver of light coming from the stone stairs leading up to the library. Falling rocks sounded like he was in an echo chamber. On his hands and knees he started up toward the light.

Drew staggered from the library onto the altar and stared down the nave. The church was filled with acrid smoke, airborne particles visible in beams of light streaming through the stained-glass windows. Through the haze, at first only disembodied heads, a dozen people were running toward him.

Drew stumbled down the altar steps. "I… I need to get help," he choked, before falling into the arms of someone in a black caftan. The last thing Arlen Drew remembered was a gold Greek cross dangling from the man's neck.

CHAPTER FORTY-FIVE

Arlen Drew opened his eyes. Still disoriented, his head pounded and his body felt like he'd gone fifteen rounds, and lost. He remembered the bright flash, and a sensation of hot air rolling over him. Everything else was a blank.

He turned his head and looked around the room. A small writing desk with a straight-backed wooden chair sat across from him, alongside the desk a bookcase filled with leather-bound texts. The only light came from a small window high on the wall above his head. Mounted on the ceiling, an overhead fan turned slowly. Affixed to the wall across from his bed was a crucifix. He squinted for a better look. The foot-high cross painted gold and red had a life-like figure of Jesus, arms spread, head bowed in supplication. Drew attempted to sit but a gentle hand pressed him back onto the narrow cot.

A smiling face removed a moist compress from his forehead and replaced it with a fresh one. A gentle voice spoke. "You must remain still, my son. You have suffered a terrible blow to the head. You have sustained a nasty concussion. I thought at first that we were going to lose you."

"Are you a doctor?" asked Drew.

"No, I am Father Zachariah, one of many who do God's work at the monastery."

Drew tried to sit up, and again was admonished to lie back down.

"I need to get down to the tunnel," Drew pleaded.

"Shhh," Zachariah whispered. "We are well aware of the explosion."

"No, you don't understand," Drew argued, pushing Zachariah's hand away.

Zachariah pressed harder. "Please, there is nothing you we can do for them."

"No," Drew shouted, his voice louder. "You don't understand."

He placed one foot on the floor alongside the bed and tried to stand up. He felt his knees start to buckle and grabbed hold of Zachariah's shoulder.

In the hallway outside the room, with Father Zachariah close behind him, Arlen Drew looked down a long narrow hallway. On both sides were doors spaced several feet apart, ten in all. He was in the priests' private residence.

Outside in the courtyard, Drew saw the basilica on the opposite side of the compound. A cloud of dust still lingered above the cathedral. He asked Zachariah, "How long was I unconscious?"

"Over an hour," he said.

Drew draped an arm over Zachariah's shoulder as they moved across the courtyard and into the church.

Lightheaded, using pew backs for support, Arlen Drew made his way down the central nave toward the altar. The closer he got to the front of the cathedral the thicker was the fine dust still floating in the air.

Zachariah helped him up the altar steps and into the library behind the altar.

A line of priests in black robes, two maintenance workers, and even kitchen staff in food stained aprons had formed a bucket brigade passing pails of debris up the stone steps from the tunnel below. Drew pushed past them and peered down. A man stood on every other step handing off pails of sand and rock from the person below him to the man on the step above.

Drew turned his body sideways, his back pressed against the wall and inched down past them.

At the bottom, aghast, he saw that there was no tunnel. The entire labyrinth had collapsed. Even working as hard and fast as they could their efforts were fruitless. There was far too much devastation, too many huge blocks of granite blocking the way. The hand grenade, though small, had set off a chain reaction bringing the mountain down on top of them. Lansing and Ari ben Yehuda were trapped, entombed if they were even still alive.

Drew grabbed the arm of a worker standing on the pile. "Have there been any sounds from inside, any cries for help?"

The Orthodox priest covered in fine white dust looked like a ghost. He shook his head and said something in Greek that Drew did not understand, but his body language told the story.

"I am sorry," Zachariah said, "Father Dematrakis speaks only Greek. And, no, there has not been a sound. Were you there, inside, when it happened?"

Drew nodded.

"What caused the explosion?"

Drew shook his head, denying he knew. The last thing the brotherhood of the monastery needed to hear now was that one of their own, the Abbot, had detonated an explosive and blown the place to smithereens.

"Has anyone contacted the authorities?" Drew asked. "We need heavy equipment if we are to gain entrancc."

"No, my son," said Zachariah, "we cannot call the Egyptian authorities."

"For God's sake, why not?"

"They would ask too many questions. Who is trapped behind the debris and why are they here? For years the Egyptian government has looked for a reason to close the monastery and replace it with a mosque. There are always problems with the Egyptians."

"Is there a satellite phone in the monastery?" Drew asked.

"Yes," came Zachariah's quick reply. "The Abbot keeps one in his room."

Colonel Heifetz and Assistant Director Felicia Albreda rode an elevator down to the *Tea Garden*, an atrium below ground level. Heifetz led Albreda to a small round table in a corner of the open space.

"In here we are as secure as possible," Heifetz said, assuring Albreda that she could speak without fear of being overheard or the conversation intercepted by anyone on the outside.

"Just what does the FBI think they know about this case, Felicia? If I may call you Felicia."

Albreda, from long experience questioning suspects felt that the Mossad colonel was wanted information from the FBI director. She would be as forthcoming as she could be without revealing too much information.

An antiquities curator at the Smithsonian in Washingtom was murdered in his laboratory. A female summer intern purported to be a graduate student was questioned at the scene as a suspect. She not charged or taken into custody. The woman we interviewed at the Smithsonian turned out to be an imposter who had murdered the real Gretchen Bell, was a known Russian operative. The imposter's body turned up dead on a golf course in Washington."

Heifetz nodded, "Please, Felicia, continue."

"You appeared at my office in Washington, out of the blue I might add. The timing did not go unnoticed. You related a story about a Russian operative, an ex-Stasi officer named Richter, with an implausible narrative about a search for missing artifacts that would lead to a location of the actual tablets of the Ten Commandments. You must admit, Aviya, it sounded farfetched, but you convince me, and I convinced my Director to dispatch two agents halfway around the world to track down this Richter person. I am sorry but I now believe the FBI has been played. Both my agents are missing someplace in the Sinai. How accurate is that Colonel?"

Two women in military khakis khaki pant came through the arched entrance to the atrium. Heifetz motioned them away and leaned forward.

"You are right, Felicia. There are no tablets, no lost Ten Commandments. There never was."

"Albreda grinned. "So why don't you tell me the truth?"

"Yes," Heifetz said, "you deserve the truth. Two weeks before five Arab armies invaded Israel in 1967, the Soviets wanted to hedge their bets on the outcome of the war, a war, I might add, that to their chagrin lasted six days. Russian scientists had developed a virulent strain of something called Marburg V12."

Albreda weighed telling Heifetz about her meeting with CIA terrorism chief Angus Macpherson.

"The night before I left for Israel I was briefed by one of our WMD specialists. He knew of a clandestine lab outside Omsk, near the Kazakhstan border, where the Russians developed a biological weapon of some kind, a virus he believed, or possibly a bacterium. He never knew for sure, or if the entire story was a hoax cooked up by the KGB."

Heifetz took a long deep breath. "It was not a hoax, Felicia. After the USSR collapsed in 1991, the old guard of the KGB sought to recover their weapon hidden somewhere in the Sinai thirty years before. A large sum of money in cash and gold, estimated at ten million dollars, was transferred from an account in a Swiss bank to an entity called DBHS on Grand Cayman Island in the Caribbean."

"What is DBHS?" Albreda asked.

"It is an acronym for the European corporation that administers the Monastery of Santa Katerina in the Sinai. Does the name Constantine Androlitis mean anything to you?"

Before Albreda could answer, Heifetz felt her cell phone vibrating. She looked at the readout, excused herself and went to the opposite side of the atrium.

Albreda read the expression on Heifetz's face—concern mixed with worry, wrapped in fear.

"Come, Felicia, back upstairs to the operations room."

"What happened, Aviya?"

Heifetz did not answer.

The Mossad colonel led Albreda through a door marked *OpCom*. At a computer terminal, a young man who looked to be about her son's age age was typing at a keyboard.

Heifetz introduced him as Samuel. Behind the young man, watching intently over his shoulder, stood another man Albreda judged to be in his fifties. Heifetz introduced him as Levi Brooks, Major, IDF.

Albreda saw the look on Brooks' face. Deep furrows creased his upper brow, and deep-set brown eyes shouted disaster. Albreda saw Heifetz's face change.

Brooks held a computer printout in his hand. "He is in trouble, Aviya."

She tapped Samuel's shoulder. "Where did this printout come from?" Heifetz asked.

Samuel swiveled in his chair.

Brooks looked down at the long printout. "Thirty minutes ago, a satellite communication arrived at a CIA listening station in Morocco. The call came from a satellite phone in the Sinai."

"Who was the originator?" Heifetz asked.

"He identified himself asd to be an FBI agent named Arlen Drew. We do not know if it is a code name or if the call was a hoax."

Albreda stepped forward. "The call was genuine. Arlen Drew is one my agents. You said it came from Morocco?"

"Yes, ma'am. Arlen Drew referenced you directly. The communications officer in Morocco did not get much more because the satellite went out of range in the final minutes."

Albreda's heart was racing and he blood pressure rose.

"I am sorry, Director Albreda, but that is all we have."

Heifetz interjected. "Levi, Ms. Albreda is not an agentl. She is an Assistant FBI Director."

"I apologize," embarrassed Brooks said,

"Forget the damn apology," said Heifetz. "Give me what you have."

"Based on Drew's short call and what we are able to glean there was an underground explosion followed by a cave-in. Agent Drew was thrown clear, injured, but able to function. However, several others were trapped inside the collapsed tunnel with an American named Lansing and Ari ben Yehuda, Mossad, among them."

Albreda felt her legs go wobbly.

They were buried along with an assortment of other, as of now unidentified. OpCom lost the signal before Drew could say who they were. He did not know if anyone survived the blast."

Heifetz took the printout and motioned for Albreda to follow her.

In Heifetz's office, Albreda sat across from the Mossad colonel, her face ashen, a reaction Albreda did not expect.

"What is wrong Aviya?" she asked. "That is not the steely-eyed look of a Mossad colonel."

"Am I that obvious?"

"I am afraid so. What is it you have not told me?"

"The Mossad agent trapped inside that cave-in, Ari ben Yehuda, he is my son."

Heifetz picked up a telephone on her desk. "Find Daniel Elman, now. I do not care where he is, just find him."

Thirty seconds later her phone rang.

Chapter Forty-Seven

Disoriented, and in total darkness, Lansing sat up and pulled his cell phone from a pocket. He checked the readout—battery life was at 100%. He accessed the phone's flashlight and illuminated the chamber. For the first time he saw the destruction, collapsed walls with bomb debris strewn around.

In the gray soupy-white haze of fine suspended particles. In several places, the steel walls that once lined the chamber were gone and a substratum of black granite was visible where the metal plates were torn away by the hand grenade blast. Exposed rebar formed a mass of twisted metal. The grenade that Androlitis used could not have caused the extensive damage. A cascade of events brought the mountain crashing in on them. An unstable configuration above the tunnel had collapsed.

Lansing tried to take a deep breaths but his lungs felt caked in the fine airborne particles. Inhaling was painful and labored, and one of his legs was caught under a slab of fallen rock.

Lansing pressed the heel of his free boot against the confining boulder and pushed. He felt a sharp pain as it rolled off his leg and away. He tried to stand, stopping part way, changing his mind, thinking maybe not and sat back down.

"Ari," he shouted into the smoke. "Where are you? Drew, can you hear me? Is anyone here?"

From somewhere in the gray haze, a gravelly voice, barely audible, called out.

Lansing made another attempt to stand, fighting through the pain. stood up, fighting through the pain.

"Oh my God," Lansing said aloud, remembering that someplace under all this rubble was a canister of deadly Marburg virus. Was it still in one piece or had the biological agent been released?

Lansing heard a faint moan, this time certain it was Ari's voice. He crawled toward the sound, calling as he crept, "Keep talking, Ari, Keep talking."

Lansing crawled to a mound of dark soil jammed against the far end of the once circular chamber. "Ari?" he shouted again.

"Here, Ted. I'm trapped. There is a large boulder above my head forming an open space below me. I can barely turn, and I don't know how long it will hold."

"Are you hurt?"

"I don't know. There is a lump the size of a baseball on the back of my head and dry blood is caked over my face. Truth, I am starting to feeli sick to my stomach."

Lansing's thought: a concussion at the least.

Part of the boulder trapping ben Yehuda was visible above the mound of dirt and debris. Lansing cleared what soil and rock he could. If the integrity of the boulders failed, Ari ben Yehuda would be crushed to death.

Using hands and fingers, Lansing cleared the smaller rocks that held ben Yehuda prisoner. He worked methodically an inch at a time, careful to retain stability before pulling the next rock free. Each time a piece of rock came loose, ben Yehuda called out to Lansing. The slabs of granite above him mase a grinding sound. The manmade cavern that held ben Yehuda reconfigured its already tight dimensions making it smaller and more dangerous as Lansing worked to free him.

On his belly, legs extended behind him, Lansing dug with a fury. With each stone removed it risked the integrity of the space even more. He knew he was out of options.

It took an hour, but Lansing could finally see through a small opening into ben Yehuda's crypt. A hand emerged first through the hole and Lansing, instinctively, placed his fingers across ben Yehuda's wrist. The Mossad agent's pulse felt weak.

"Can you widen the opening from your side?" Lansing asked, his mouth inches from the hole.

From both sides, they scraped the packed sand away from the edges, just enough for ben Yehuda to fit his head and one shoulder through the opening.

"Can you turn sideways?" Lansing said.

Lansing dug his fingertips into the fine powder at the edge of the opening and cleared another six inches. He took a firm hold of ben Yehuda's exposed shoulder and rotated his body slowly, ninety degrees until Ari's shoulder slid through the opening, followed by his chest, hips, and legs. One last tug and Lansing pulled him free.

In the silence of the cavern, ben Yehuda saw for the first-time what Lansing had known for an hour.

Before the explosion, the chamber had been twenty-five feet in diameter. It now looked half that size with large, jagged pieces of granite strewn around; they were trapped.

"Have you heard anything from Arlen?" ben Yehuda asked. "And what about the others?"

Lansing started to speak, but when he looked up at ben Yehuda, his eyes were glazed, his eyelids fluttering.

"I don't feel so good, Ted," were the last words ben Yehuda uttered before toppling into Lansing's outstretched arms. He'd stopped breathing.

Lansing laid him on the ground and started chest compressions, pumping at one-second intervals followed by exhaling into ben Yehuda's open mouth.

CHAPTER FORTY-EIGHT

The telephone on Aviya Heifetz's desk buzzed once. "Please hold for General Ellman," said a voice on the other end.

"Shalom Aviya, Daniel here. It is good to hear your voice. It has been a while. My aide said you sounded worried. Should I also be worried? Because when Mossad is worried, I have good reason to be as well."

"Yes, Daniel, We have a problem—a big one. Are we on a secure line?"

"Always," said the general.

"I am in a bind, the kind only you can help with."

"Yes, I got that impression. What kind of trouble have you and those spooks of yours gotten yourselves into?"

Heifetz laughed. "I'll tell you, David, like a heart attack, Daniel. What I am about to reveal goes no further."

"Yes, go on."

"My son, Ari was on a covert operation with two Americans agents, both FBI. They have been pursuing a German national named Richter, Hans Richter, for several weeks now."

"I am not familiar with that name," Ellman said.

"Richter works for, we believe, the Russian FSB. He is wanted by the Americans as well, the FBI, and Interpol, for multiple murders in both the United States and in Europe—three we know for certain. The trail of bodies runs from Washington to Rome and here in Israel as well."

Ellman, hesitation in his voice, asked, "Where is this covert operation of yours taking place?"

"In the Sinai."

"Ah, so our good friends the Egyptians are a part of this. Exactly where in the Sinai are they?"

"Near the mountain, Daniel." Heifetz stopped and corrected herself. "Technically, they are trapped underground in a tunnel or labyrinth of some kind underneath a monastery."

"Saint Catherine's?" Ellman asked.

"Yes, Daniel, I am afraid so."

Heifetz knew that General Ellman, even though a close personal friend and a confidante, would never sanction what she was about to propose without full disclosure.

Slowly, and with precision, leaving nothing out, Heifetz read the general into Ari ben Yehuda's mission, from Kastianich's murder in Washington, to tracking Hans Richter across the globe, and as much as she knew about events that took place at the monastery, including two dead priests, also at Richter's hand.

"Daniel, do you remember an operation several years ago, code name *Vampre*, an acronym for a program the Russians named *Virus Amplification using a Monopolymerase Protocol - Resistance Experiment?*"

"Of course I remember. If my memory serves it had something to do with a Russian attempt to infect the 67-War battlefield with a deadly strain of virus. But nothing came of it. It was determined that the entire story was hoax." Ellman went silent for several seconds. "Oh no! Please, Aviya, do not tell me we are going to do that again?"

"Yes, Daniel, I am afraid so. But this time it is worse, much worse. It will have international ramifications if we do not act."

"What kind of operation are you talking about, Aviya?"

"An extraction."

"And who is it we are extracting?"

"Ari and an American a named Lansing, and, we believe with high confidence, *Vampre*, or whatever is left of it."

"Your son Ari served under my command many years ago, a captain if I recall."

"Yes Daniel, my son, Ari. I am sending to you the last GPS coordinates we have for their location. It came via a satellite phone communication from an FBI agent named Arlen Drew by way of a CIA listening station in Morocco."

"Why is this Arlen Drew in Morocco?

"He is not in Morocco, Daniel. Drew is the partner of the American agent trapped underground with Ari. His name is Theodore Lansing. It is a long story, but I need a plan to extract Lansing and my son along with whatever they have recovered from *Vampre*."

Hearing a soft rap on his office door, Feneral Ellman looked up.

An Air Force captain entered and saluted. "Captain Isaac Rabin, sir. You sent for me, sir?"

"Sit, Isaac, please," said Ellman, He held up a printout. "Look at these locations and tell me how close to the GPS markers referenced could the IAF safely land a helicopter, undetected. This aircraft needs to be large enough for a team of six fully equipped commandos, technical personnel and two, possibly three civilians, maybe as many as four who may need medical attention."

Captain Rabin studied the numbers and placed the paper on the general's desk.

"These coordinates are in Egypt, sir. If I triangulate using Dahab on the Gulf of Aqaba and El Tor on the Gulf of Suez it puts the location somewhere close to the monastery of St. Catherine near Mount Sinai."

"Very good, Captain. But is that the best you can do, somewhere near the monastery?" Ellman asked.

"I am sorry, sir, but there are elements missing from these coordinates. The colons and dashes indicate that whatever device sent the communication was low on power. There are missing keystrokes. If I may, what type of device sent this?"

Ellman did not answer, instead, thanked Rabin with a curt, "You have been most instructive, and helpful, Captain."

Rabin gone, Ellman picked up his phone. "Get me Heifetz again."

"To say we have a problem, Aviya, is understating the obvious. You are asking me to extract two operatives from a location we are not even certain about, in a place we have no business even being, and do it all covertly. Impossible!"

"That is precisely why I called you, Daniel. You are master of the impossible. But, yes, that is precisely what I am asking, but there is something else."

Heifetz heard a groan.

"Of course, with Mossad, there is always something else. What is it that will make this operation even more difficult?"

"They are underground, buried in an explosion of some kind."

"Are they even alive?" Ellman asked. "Do you have proof of life?"

"No, Daniel, but one of them survived the blast, Lansing's partner, Arlen Drew, so I am hopeful."

"All right, Aviya. Perhaps we can do this off-channel—maybe. There are a few favors due me from the Prime Minister's office, but the last thing Bibi needs right now with the Iranians breathing down his neck, is an incident."

Ellman put Heifetz on hold and called Air Operations in Haifa. "I need the name of all the presenters at a recent drone conference. There was a paper delivered by an exceptional young American concerning a new technology developed at MIT. It had to do with an experimental underground Infra-Red locating device."

Ellman reconnected to Heifetz. "I will send you a preliminary extraction plan in a few hours, Aviya."

Chapter Forty-Nine

A mile from Haifa a black Mercedes pulled up to a large hangar. Joshua Lansing peered from a side window and spotted an Israeli Air Force insignia above the entrance. A woman in a blue jumpsuit approached his car and slid in next to him.

"Shalom Joshua," the woman older than his mother said. "I am Aviya Heifetz, Colonel Heifetz."

Like the ground crew crawling over a helicopter parked nearby, her flight suit bore no flag, insignia or rank. "I am Mossad," she said.

Her admission stopped Joshua Lansing cold. The call from his mother in the middle of the night now made sense.

"Pleased to meet you, Colonel. I spoke with my mother a few hours ago. She's an Assistant Director at the FBI. She told me to listen and trust what you have to say."

Heifetz made no mention of Joshua's mother being there, being in Israel. Both Heifetz and Albreda agreed that Joshua did not need to know her current location.

"Yes, Joshua, I spoke with your *Ima* today as well."

Joshua nodded. "I will do whatever I can, Colonel."

"Good. I need you to listen carefully. It is about your father."

"I know he's here, somewhere in Israel. He's on assignment, but I don't ask too many questions about his work."

"Yes, his work is what this about." Heifetz touched his shoulder. "There was an explosion and…"

"Oh my God, is he…?"

"No, no, Joshua, but he does need our help."

Joshua's breathing increased, his pupils dilated. Heifetz detected a slight tremor in his left hand. The young man was frightened. He took a deep breath to compose himself. "Whatever you need, Colonel Heifetz."

"Excellent. But first, I want you to go with that soldier there." She pointed to an IAF corporal standing in front of Mercedes. Corporal Dávid will outfit you in a flight suit and flack vest."

She saw Joshua's face when she said flack vest. "It is only a precaution," said Heifetz.

Her assurance brought him little comfort.

"Can you tell me where we are going, Colonel?"

"First to an Israeli Air Force installation in Eilat. You will land there temporarily to add crew and equipment to the aircraft's electronic array before we continue south into the Sinai."

"Sinai? Aircraft?" he asked.

Heifetz pointed to the US made Blackhawk helicopter. "I will remain there in Eilat to oversee operations. During the flight, a team on board will assist in uploading an experimental GPS locating devices to that UAV of yours. The team will then link into the signals put out by your experimental drone. The initial coding took place last night before we brought the device here to this location."

"My UAV is here? How? When?"

Heifetz gave him a sly smile. "Suffice it to say, Joshua, it is here, now."

"But Colonel, syncing a GPS device to my vehicle is redundant. The prototype already contains a built-in transmitter to synchronize outgoing signals with any receiver in the proximity of five miles, depending on terrain. I designed it to be similar to a WiFi discovery module built into commercial devices and cell phones. It seeks a partner automatically."

"And that, Joshua, is our problem. Your UAV was not designed for covert military operations. Do you know Doctor Gabriel Ganz?" She saw the recognition in his eyes. "Ah, so, you do know him."

"By reputation only. You say he did this at the experimental facility in Haifa?

"Yes. Last night. Ganz took your UAV through its paces and soon discovered the omnidirectional signals your program code emits. The signal becomes discoverable as soon as the onboard communication package activates."

"Yes, ma'am, that's how I designed it."

Heifetz touched his shoulder. "Your design, as elegant as it is, was not meant for the operation we are about to launch."

Joshua understood the breadth of Mossad's reach and beamed when she told him how impressed Gabriel Ganz had been while playing with the UAV's controls and saw first-hand the degree of resolution its images transmitted. However, the outgoing signal was a problem that needed solving.

"Dr. Ganz's experimental GPS code, unlike yours, is discoverable only to the computers on board our aircraft. He can explain it far better than I when you meet him, but all outgoing communications are shielded from devices without the correct receiving codes. During this mission we cannot risk anyone asking questions about why we are in their air space, or what we are doing there. It is bad enough we must execute in daylight because time is not our friend here, Joshua, and we are running out of options."

Chapter Fifty

Joshua Lansing pressed his forehead against a window and stared down at the azure water moving below the Blackhawk helicopter. On their first hop from Haifa to Herzliya they'd hugged the Mediterranean coast. He now watched the ground come up as the large helicopter started its descent, landing on a small peninsula jutting out into the Mediterranean.

The landing area appeared desolate with a nondescript blockhouse and a corrugated steel hangar. Quonset-shaped. The hangar stood in stark contrast to Herzliya in the distance, a modern city with gleaming high-rise buildings and a bustling port.

Heifetz led Joshua into the hangar where Gabriel Ganz sat hunched over a circuit board connected to a control panel with an array of oscilloscope images on a computer monitor.

He wore a baseball cap with a peeling New York Yankees logo turned backward on his head. In his mid-forties with a shock of salt and pepper hair, Dr. Ganz looked at Joshua.

"Ah, wonderful, you finally made it, kid. Glad to meet you. Let me say that I was blown away by your presentation in Haifa a few weeks ago," said Ganz with a Midwestern accent.

He saw the odd look on Joshua's face.

"Born and raised in Wisconsin," Ganz said, "still a farm boy at heart. Yale undergrad—doctorate from MIT."

"You were there, sir, at my talk in Haifa?"

"Absolutely. You've built one hell of an' ass-kickin' vehicle here. You should be proud of yourself."

"That is high praise, sir, especially from you. I've read everything you've written on the subject, including your doctoral thesis. Your work is an inspiration not only to me but my colleagues at MIT."

"I had the opportunity to fly that little bird of yours around the test facility in Haifa before retrofitting my GPS location module. There is a beauty in your design, one that I found…"

Heifetz made a loud *ahem*. "Gentlemen, please, we do not have time for shop talk."

"Yes, of course, Aviya," said Ganz. "The colonel is right. Come, Josh, I'll show you how to upload this module patch to your UAV's existing software."

Heifetz went to the far end of the hangar, spoke briefly to a young officer and motioned to Ganz. "It is time, Gabriel, come. They are ready for us in preflight."

"We'll can do this onboard the Blackhawk," Ganz said.

Joshua Lansing's idea of a pilot's preflight briefing room came from what he'd seen in Hollywood movies. This preflight room was not much different.

Eight rows of plush leather armchairs faced an eighty-inch flat screen monitor displaying a static circular logo—a seven-branch blue menorah on a white field encircled by Hebrew lettering—Mossad. An empty podium stood in front of the room.

Joshua took a seat in the second row and stared at a set of toggle switches embedded into an armrest. Heifetz sat next to him, Ganz on the other side. He pushed a toggle, embarrassed when the seat started to recline. He brought it quickly back to an upright position. In front of them were four men and one woman, all in identical flight suits like his, also without flag or insignia. He leaned over to Heifetz and whispered, "Our flight crew?"

She nodded.

"Special Forces?" he asked.

She saw his angst, reached across and patted his shoulder. "Just listen, Joshua, just listen."

From the rear of the room a flag-rank officer strode down the center aisle. Joshua recognized the three-sun-cluster insignia of a brigade general. Tucked under a shoulder epaulet was a blue beret with IAF markings. Behind him walked another pair of officers, also IAF, both majors.

The general nodded to Heifetz who whispered to Joshua, "General Daniel Ellman."

"Good morning gentlemen, ladies. For this operation, we are call sign, Eagle Talon. I must impress on you the importance of this mission's covert nature. Once you leave this building, please know that Eagle Talon does not exist on any documents the Israeli government will admit to having." He motioned to the officers alongside him.

"Major Davíd Baratz is the mission commander and Major Zel Aufman will sit co-pilot on the Blackhawk." Ellman nodded to Baratz. "Major, if you will?"

Baratz strode to the podium, lifted a TV remote and clicked once. A slide appeared on the monitor—a map without markings or borders. Joshua recognized the Sinai Peninsula. A second click and a grid identifying latitude and longitude superimposed over the map's surface. A third click and the image on screen zoomed in to show topography in high definition.

"These images have been uploaded to our onboard computer," Baratz said.

Another image appeared. "That is the monastery of St. Catherine's, or Santa Katerina as the locals call it," Baratz said before moving the pointer again. "And this is Mt. Sinai, southeast of the monastery. A community of Greek clergy runs it, all males. I wish that I could tell you that residents of the monastery are friendlies, but recent intelligence tells us that may not be the case. We will improvise based on what we find after we land."

Baratz's eyes went to the intelligence report. "At 1100 hours last night we confirmed that our targets for extraction are below ground near or directly under the monastery. We are not yet certain of their precise location or their physical conditions. There is an array of highly sophisticated, classified, and experimental equipment on board the aircraft that will assist in locating where they are trapped after we arrive at the extraction point. This equipment cannot fall into anyone else's hands, especially the Egyptians. Should that become a possibility, there is an encrypted file to render the entire array useless. Before we take off Dr. Gabriel Ganz is going to explain how the program is activated from the helicopter's cockpit. Once on the ground the key word will be improvise. There are too many unknowns here, but you have been selected for this mission because Mossad has full confidence in your abilities."

Ground personnel swarmed over and inside the Blackhawk making final preflight checks before the crew came on board. Major Baratz settled into the pilot's seat and linked his onboard communication package to Mossad Operations in Tel Aviv.

"I read you Eagle Talon. Tracking modules are up and functional—satellite link is secure. Outgoing signals are tasked from Kanaf 4," referring to the *Kanaf 4* Air Force base in central Israel near kibbutz *Hatzor*. "Kanaf will have you from liftoff to air insertion over the Sinai at 28.49° N by 34.50° E. Once in Egyptian airspace move to frequency 637- 4XZ UHF."

All communications originating from the Blackhawk would be relayed first to a Mossad listening post in the Egyptian resort city of Sharm El-Sheikh on the Sinai's southern tip. From there, the signal would be handed off to a satellite, recoded, and then relayed back to Haifa Naval Command, and only then rebroadcast to the Blackhawk crew.

To the Egyptians, the signal would appear to be a secret communication originating out of central Israel. They would spend hours or even days deciphering the message, and when they did, all they would find was misleading chatter about a fictitious IDF troop maneuver, more than sufficient to make the Egyptians believe they'd stumbled onto something important, drawing their attention from the mission and the Blackhawk's true position. It bought time, hopefully enough.

CHAPTER FIFTY-ONE

B aratz banked the helicopter to the west and Joshua felt a sudden increase in the G-Force as the corrugated hangar and blockhouse below him shrunk in size. The rapid maneuver forced him into the seat back, a simple canvas and metal folding device attached to a bulkhead wall. He reached for a grab-bar above his head, and pulled his safety belt and shoulder harness tighter, grateful he'd passed on the scones and donuts in the briefing room. His belly churned as the Blackhawk moved out over the Gulf of Aqaba and climbed rapidly to twenty-five hundred feet. He now understood why his father hated helicopters.

In the seat next to him, Gabriel Ganz saw Joshua's discomfort. "Close your eyes and take deep breaths, Josh, it'll pass."

Midway to their insertion point, Major Baratz unsnapped the latch on his shoulder harness, stood up and started aft to give one last set of instructions to his commando team.

"Isaacs, I need visuals of all maritime traffic moving below us. Anything looks suspicious, or military, I want to know, and fast. Look for assets visible on the decks. Assume all are potentially hostile."

Back at the Blackhawk's controls, Baratz maintained sufficient altitude to make the aircraft's radar signature appear normal to the Saudis on their east and to the Egyptians to the west. He kept the chopper over international waters above the Gulf of Aqaba. He knew the Egyptians, and probably the Saudis as well, would monitor them until certain they were not a threat. Programmed into Baratz's onboard computer was a turn west to the city of Danab on the peninsula's west coast.

The route took them inland, east, another sixty kilometers to the monastery of Saint Catherine. It meant increased scrutiny by the Egyptians, but the plan was to stay low enough and avoid detection by local radar.

North of Danab the Blackhawk descended to one hundred meters and moved inland over the Sinai coastline. Commandos took positions on both the starboard and port sides. Binoculars scanned the horizon for anything or anyone that might give away their presence.

"Eagle Talon is approaching the nest," blared through the aircraft's loudspeaker. Mt. Sinai appeared on the horizon.

Ganz unsnapped his harness and started for the cargo bay. "It's time, Josh."

Joshua followed Ganz aft.

"I have a visual," came a cry from the port side door.

Below them, a Bedouin village with five cinder block structures, several brilliant white tents, and a flock of sheep, appeared.

"Assess," Baratz said from the flight deck.

Focusing, the spotter responded. "Five subjects on foot, sir." He scanned the village in a systematic left to right pattern and stopped suddenly when a glint of light flashed up from below.

"Wait, sir. I have something."

He brought the glint into sharp focus. An Arab boy peered up at them through a pair of binoculars. "Bedouin herders, Major. They know we are here."

The Blackhawk veered south and climbed out of range before descending again with Mt. Sinai between them and the Bedouin village.

Ganz lifted a handset from the cargo bay wall. "I'm ready to send the first burst, Major."

"That is affirmative," Baratz answered, switching on the communication software. A coded sequence, answerable only on the Mossad frequency assigned to ben Yehuda's satellite phone, went out in five blasts, two seconds apart—if the Mossad agent could respond, the return would be in under a minute. They waited.

In the Bedouin village, the boy still holding his binoculars rushed into his father's tent. "*Abi, Abi.* Did you see it? Did you see it? A helicopter low in the sky."

"What kind of helicopter?" the old man asked his son. "The kind that brings tourists to the monastery?"

"No *Abi*, it was bigger. Much bigger."

"Did it have markings?"

"No *Abi,* no markings. Not Egyptian or American or Israeli."

The old man grabbed the binoculars He looked up scanning the sky in a three hundred sixty-degree circle. He saw nothing but a cloudless blue expanse. "Are you certain, my son?"

The boy pointed west. "Yes *Abi,* it was there."

The old man walked across the compound to the small cinder block building. He entered and sat down in front of a short-wave radio.

"Stop," Ganz shouted. The computer screen monitoring signals emitted from the drone's communication package pinged. The burst had been received by ben Yehuda's satellite phone somewhere below them. He got up from a crouch and turned to Joshua. "I want you to send another burst every thirty seconds." He slipped a pair of headphones over Joshua's ears. "It will sound like crystals dropping on a tile floor. There," he pointed, "in the upper left corner of the computer screen an icon will appear if the signal is acknowledged. Click on it and the originating GPS coordinates appear."

Twenty minutes later with no return signal, Ganz, still working on the UAV, continued to make code changes to the infrared program hoping to increase its surface penetration. He pulled an intercom phone from its cradle on the bulkhead wall. "Anything, Josh?"

"No sir, not yet."

Ganz pinged the flight deck from the intercom phone. "Major, can you take us higher?"

"That is affirmative, Dr. Ganz."

The Blackhawk climbed to three hundred meters.

CHAPTER FIFTY-TWO

"Eagle Talon, do you copy?" Major Baratz authenticated the incoming voice communication from Eilat. The monastery of Santa Katerina was ahead on his horizon. He rechecked the encryption codes again. Only then did he respond.

"I copy, Mama Bear."

"Have you located the package?"

"Negative on that. We are currently at our extraction site, but we are working on it."

"I copy that, Eagle Talon, but you need to wrap the package and bring it home. We have five vehicles moving west toward your position, ETA forty-five minutes. Do you copy?"

"I copy, Mama Bear. Can you slow them down?"

"Negative, Eagle Talon. Satellite imagery confirms bogeys to be Egyptian military vehicles. We have no assets currently in the area and scrambling F-16s from Eilat is not an option. Do you copy that?"

Baratz switched to the onboard intercom. "Dr. Ganz, how fast can you get that UAV flying?"

Baratz eyed Joshua.

Fully absorbed, rewriting code, deleting code, altering the UAV's output signal and return capture, Joshua did not hear a word Ganz said to him.

Baratz came back over the intercom. "I need an answer, Doctor Ganz, and I need it now."

Ganz lifted Joshua's arm away from the computer keyboard. "Joshua," he shouted.

He looked up.

"I asked you how much longer?"

Joshua lost it. "Damn it! I don't know. I'm working as goddamn fast as…" Then, "Oh geeze," he cried out. "It was here all the time. My God, I'm such an idiot. Check this out, Dr. Ganz. Tell me what you think. If we increase the outgoing power the IR signal should penetrate deeper below the surface, and if we simultaneously increase the incoming contrast…"

Ganz stared at a paper readout with Joshua's primary coding. His face lit up. "My God, Josh, you're right. If we work in tandem, you on the outgoing code while I recode the contrast setting, we can get it done in less than…"

"Tell Major Baratz, twenty minutes," Joshua said.

The voice from the cockpit came back. "I heard him. You have fifteen."

"Captain." Baratz spoke via headphone to the commando team leader sitting aft with his six-man assault team. "Secure for descent. You will deploy to that ridge on our west. Mama Bear has a convoy of vehicles, Egyptian military, headed toward us. They cannot reach our position."

Code sequences altered, Joshua ordered the Blackhawk back down to one hundred meters—the precise distance he and Ganz calculated for maximum clarity of the unmanned drone's return signal. Together they unscrewed four bolts holding Joshua's UAV secure to the helicopter floor. The four propeller-driven mini engines started as they released the drone through an open side door. It hovered in place, static, alongside the Blackhawk's open door.

Joshua switched on the thermal sensors and the video capture program. Images appeared on his computer monitor. The monastery courtyard came into high-definition view as the UAV soared above Santa Katerina. Ganz activated the ground penetrating Infra-Red program. Using data supplied by Arlen Drew about the tunnel's most probable location in reference to the cathedral, Joshua kept the UAV in place, hovering, sending burst after burst of infrared signals.

Multiple images from below ground, hazy and tinted green, appeared on his monitor. One showed an odd looking, thin vertical red line running from ground level to a depth of ten meters. The red line was five hundred meters from the church putting it well outside the monastery wall.

Joshua touched the screen, his finger superimposed over the line. "That's heat emanating from someplace below. Someone or something is alive down there."

CHAPTER FIFTY-THREE

Profuse sweat formed on Ted Lansing face as he continued CPR on ben Yehuda. Lansing always thought of himself as cool under pressure but the longer he continued CPR the less sure of himself he became. Above him he heard the rocks shifting. How long before the entire tunnel came down on him killing them both.

Lansing looked down at Ari ben Yehuda and breathed a long sigh of relief when the Mossad agent finally opened his eyes and looked up at him.

The Mossad agent took a long, raspy breath and tried to sit. He'd been unconscious, not breathing when Lansing first pulled him from the rubble with a nasty gash on the back of his head and blood caked to his face.

After finding ben Yehuda unconscious he shined his cell phone flashlight into ben Yehuda's eyes. He watched his pupils react. *Good or bad?* He could not remember if pupils were supposed to react. It had been years since Lansing took the mandatory First-Aid refresher course. "You scared the crap out of me," Ari.

Ari mumbled incoherent

"What happened?" One second, I'm talking to you, and the next… I don't remember a next."

Lansing held a finger in front of ben Yehuda's eyes. "Follow it," he said, again not sure what was supposed to happen.

Ari first followed the finger as it moved horizontally across his field of vision, and then vertically. Still unsure, Lansing repeated the finger movements three more times. Each pass showed ben Yehuda's left eye following evenly, but there was sluggishness on the right side. What that meant, Lansing had no idea, but he knew it was not good.

"Lie still," he said.

Lansing looked at his cell phone's flashlight, the only illumination between them and total darkness. The power readout of the battery had dropped to 65% in a half hour. He believed what he said about finding a way out, but they needed a miracle.

ben Yehuda's eyes close again, his breathing became shallow. He placed two fingers on his wrist—his pulse was weak. Whatever hit ben Yehuda's head, and even without much medical training, Lansing knew the Mossad agent needed a real doctor, and fast.

Lansing struggled to his feet using a fallen boulder for leverage and tested the ankle. The pain had subsided. He limped across the bombed-out chamber and crawled up a mound of collapsed earth pressed against a wall. It felt soft underfoot.

Dropping to his knees Lansing began to push the soft dirt aside. Every few seconds, he turned to check ben Yehuda who now appeared to be asleep, his chest rising and falling rhythmically.

Lansing crawled down the mound, knelt at ben Yehuda's side and shook him awake.

"Ari, Ari, wake up. You can't go to sleep. I need you to stay awake." He helped ben Yehuda to a sitting position with his back propping him against the wall.

The hole now almost four feet deep. As he dug Lansing encountered rock, at first small pieces of granite that had broken loose from the walls. He remembered Androlitis holding the hand grenade above his head, grappling with Jeremiah, and the damn thing falling and rolling across the ground..

Redoubling efforts Lansing began to lift pieces of rock from the expanding hole.

As he moved soil and rock he suddenly recoiled recoiled when he touched something soft. At first a finger, and then, as he continued to shove dirt aside, a hand and a wrist—Richter's wrist. On the wrist was a watch, an expensive *Glashütte*. Alongside Richter's dead body a canister with a biohazard symbol and Russian lettering, *BHNMAHNE, Warning!*

Chapter Fifty-Four

Joshua, hunched over the computer terminal, tweaked the incoming infrared data from drone pulses emanating from below ground. He worked furiously, hurrying, mistyping, backtracking; his fingers felt like mallets on the keyboard, his eyes continually drawn to the mission-clock set into the helicopter's bulkhead.

He'd never worked this fast or under this much pressure. He powered up the software, and then powered it back down. He executed test runs of the incoming data, racing, rewriting code on the fly, re-tweaking over and again.

Ganz reviewed the final computations of the signal output and asked, "How wide a field do we now have at ground level?"

"It's still problematic. I won't know for certain until I have it up and flying with data streaming in real time—best guess, between ten and twenty feet—not great but we can get by with that."

At their current altitude, by the time the drone's IR signal reached ground level its field of vision narrowed to a four-foot radius. If the helicopter flew higher the field widened, but the return signal would be decreased by an inverse square ratio. At two hundred meters no discernable signals would reach the onboard computers.

Joshua scanned a printout, hoping to see a way, but the longer he looked the more unsure he became. He sat upright and asked, "Is it fixable?"

"Maybe," Ganz answered as he lifted the intercom microphone. "How long can those commandos hold off that Egyptian convoy?"

Baratz responded to the commando team leader sitting aft with his men.

"Get us on to that ridge, Major, we will keep them at bay for as long as it takes."

Ganz turned back to Joshua.

"It's a go. Retrieve the UAV," Baratz ordered. "Isaacs, have your team ready to deploy on my command."

Joshua flew the UAV up alongside the Blackhawk's open door where it hovered just out of reach making soft beeping sounds barely audible over the helicopter's roaring engine. He maneuvered the hovering vehicle into the open door of the chopper until the device floated, static, six inches above Ganz's outstretched hands. Another deft maneuver and it landed, softly, at Ganz's feet.

"Capture is secure," Joshua said.

Baratz's voice, followed by a warning bell, rang through the aircraft. "Prepare for rapid descent."

Joshua felt dizzying nausea when the Blackhawk executed a pair of perfect yaw maneuvers, changing direction twice. He closed his eyes, white-knuckled fingers gripping an overhead bar.

The Blackhawk's dive was terrifying as Baratz brought the helicopter above a crest overlooking the monastery, with a long unobstructed view of the roads leading to it from the east.

The Israeli commandos rappelled from the helicopter door and in seconds positioned themselves along a narrow ridge and waited for the Egyptian convoy.

Joshua placed a screwdriver on the UAV control access door, removed a four-inch square panel and extricated a pair of logic boards. Dr. Ganz spread a schematic on the floor. "What are we looking at here?"

Ganz jotted notes on a pad as Joshua identified areas of the circuitry that controlled angles of view at varying altitudes and their relation to the return signals. He explained the complex circuitry.

Ganz tossed out questions and possible solutions, most of which Joshua rejected, not because they would not work, but because they either did not have the right components on board or were too time-consuming.

"What would happen, Joshua, if, let us say, we widened the outgoing field and compensated by decreasing the incoming resolution? Would we not have the best of both solutions?"

"But that defeats our purpose," said Joshua. "The detail, the definition, would be lost."

"Maybe extreme detail is not necessary. All we need do is locate those underground heat signatures you saw before. We do not need to see detail, just proof of life. What we need now, and fast, is a location that will not put us in the middle of a collapsed cave in."

Baratz pinged the intercom from the flight deck. "How much longer? That convoy is getting close, too close. It is about to get hot down there. We need to excavate the package and be out of here before all hell breaks loose."

Joshua, his face inches from the logic board, a mini soldering iron in hand, made a final connection to the circuitry. He swiveled to face the computer terminal and entered new code.

He sat back and sighed. "Done!"

"I heard him, Dr. Ganz," came Baratz' voice over the loudspeakers.

At one hundred meters Joshua and Dr. Ganz lifted the drone from the helicopter floor. All four propellers running, they launched it out of the side door, where it waited for a command from the Blackhawk's onboard computer.

Joshua hunched over the console activated the UAV cameras. Ganz read off coordinates captured on the UAV's first run.

He switched on infrared visualization, and the thin red line that indicated heat rising from below reappeared, its lowered resolution apparent. The once bright red color with sharp lines of demarcation at its edges now looked dull, almost pastel, and out of focus. A Vernier scale superimposed over the screen indicated a field of view less than three meters wide. Joshua's changes had more than doubled what the UAV could see. He manipulated the joystick and moved the hovering drone along what he hoped was the tunnel's underground path. He stopped suddenly.

"Look at this, Dr. Ganz."

Glowing fissures, not seen on the drone's first run, were spaced at varying distances along what he and Ganz assumed was the tunnel's underground path. Each vertical fissure ran downward from the surface with heat emanating upward from below.

Joshua continued to adjust the controls, enhancing the IR sensitivity in small increments. What first appeared to be single red lines descending below ground were now multi-hued—deep red toward the center with cooler shades of red at its edges. An air vents measured a meter in diameter, wide enough to get a man down into the tunnel, or someone back up to the surface.

"Over there, to the east," Baratz's voice boomed over the engine roar. A cloud of dust was rising from the desert floor less than five kilometers away. "That's them, Egyptian military. We are out of time gentlemen. Get that damn thing in the air or I need to pick up Isaacs and his team and get the hell out there."

Joshua flew the UAV along the presumed path of the tunnel collapse until Ganz shouted, "Stop Josh! Backtrack, twenty meters."

The UAV changed direction retreating over its last pass above the cave in.

A pair of Infra-Red heat signatures appeared, one of them moving. "It's them!"

But who were they? Ganz wondered. Did the heat signatures indicate Lansing and ben Yehuda or could it be Richter?

Ganz recorded the precise GPS positions of the signatures.

Captain Isaacs, poised on the ridge, looked up when Major Baratz's voice came into his earpiece. "Do you copy, Captain?"

"I copy, Major.

"It is a go. We have a location on our target."

Joshua switched from infrared back to daylight vision and zoomed in on the two commandos running full clip toward the location they'd seen the heat signatures. The explosive specialist carried a huge backpack.

Hovering low in the Blackhawk, all eyes zeroed in on the computer screen, Ganz relayed Isaacs' position in relation to the glowing fissures. "Two meters west, Captain."

Isaacs slowed until Ganz shouted for him to stop. "You are directly over the vent."

"Hand me a temperature probe," Isaacs said. On his knees, he started to clear sand and rocks until he could see saw into the opening. "I need the fiber optic."

Jacobson pulled a coil of fiber optic cable from a spool in his backpack. Isaacs connected a thermal probe band and lowered it. Temperature in the vent, a foot down, read five degrees warmer than at the surface air.

Ganz at his computer screen saw the readout. "Can you go deeper?"

Isaacs lowered the probe several more meters. The temperature climbed one-tenth of a degree per foot.

"How far away are those moving heat signatures?" Isaacs said into a shoulder microphone.

Ganz came back. "Three meters to your west. They appear to be in a circular chamber of some kind with an earthen wall of rock between them and the collapsed tunnel. They cannot get out through the tunnel without heavy machinery. They are at a depth of eight meters, give or take. Miss the mark by a few meters and you will need to dig through the collapsed earth and stone."

Isaacs looked off in the distance at the high wall surrounding Santa Katerina. He saw the campanile and spire of the cathedral behind it. From what Arlen Drew told his debriefers at the hospital in Eilat, Isaacs visualized the path Lansing and ben Yehuda took after entering the underground labyrinth from a door behind the church's main altar.

Drew told his debriefers that he and Lansing followed the tunnel, first north for what he estimated was less than one hundred feet, and then west another two or three hundred, all with a downward slope. He said Lansing, ben Yehuda, and five others were trapped when a bomb went off inside the chamber and he was thrown out into a passageway, barely escaping before the entire length of the tunnel collapsed on those trapped behind a door.

"How stable is the ground under us?" Isaacs asked.

Ganz came on. "You can widen the fissure with a series of low impact shape-charges, but it's a crapshoot on whether the whole place collapses. Direct the charges east, away from the heat signatures."

There was a long silence waiting for Baratz to make the final decision.

"No explosives until I give the word, Captain. Get down there and bring them up," said Baratz.

Major Baratz spoke into the intercom. "Hold on Dr. Ganz, you too Joshua. I need to take us down, right now, and fast."

Joshua pointed out of the Blackhawk's open door. White muzzle flashes were now visible from the ridge where Isaacs had deployed his commandos. The Egyptians were engaging.

The explosive expert opened a pack containing two small shape-charges. He connected detonators to them, positioned the packs according to Baratz' orders and lowered them into the vent.

Isaacs hit the firing switch. A plume of dust exploded upward from the vent.

CHAPTER FIFTY-FIVES

Isaacs dropped his backpack, pulled on the Velcro straps and laid it flat on the ground. Inside a zippered compartment were nine, foot-long aluminum tubes, each with threaded ends.

In seconds they had the foot-long sections locked together creating a tripod.

He slid a top cap over the tripod's apex and locked the device in place, positioning it over the vent opening. He then secured a motorized lift.

The commando team leader stepped into a leather harness attached it to the servile motor and positioned himself above the opening. The lift motor and held the cable wire steady as Isaacs descended. An LED attached to his belt illuminated the vent hole below him.

Partway down, blocked by a large rock protruding into the narrow space, Isaacs kicked hard until the jagged obstacle broke loose and fell.

"Did you hear that?" ben Yehuda said, his eyes darting toward the dark end of the chamber. "I heard something."

Unsteady, Lansing came to his feet, aimed his i flashlight and started toward the sound.

He stood directly under the vent hole. A tangle of small rocks and loose debris was on the ground. He peered up into the opening. A bright light in the narrow space blinded him.

Isaacs let out cable a few centimeters at a time allowing the hoist to control his controlled descent.

Lansing first saw a foot, and then a leg, emerge through the opening above him.

Isaacs tugged twice on the cable, signaling to the commando above that he was all the way through. From a pocket, on the legs of his pants, he grabbed a handful of light sticks.

One at a time he held them in his hand, bending each one until it was activated and glowing. He dropped them to the cavern floor. The chamber took on an eerie look in the green glow.

Ted Lansing held the *Vampre* vacuum flask close to his chest.

Isaacs reached for it, but Lansing pulled it back. "Sorry sir, *Vampre* stays with me."

Isaacs reached again. "As much as we all want you out of here, Lansing, *Vampre* is my prime objective; not you."

Lansing handed him the canister. "What took you so long to get here?" he joked, embracing the Israeli commando. "Just get us the hell out of here."

"Shalom to you as well." Isaacs laughed. "Who else is down here except you and Ari?"

"Just me and Ari ben Yehuda. The others are all buried somewhere under this rubble."

"How badly are you hurt?" Isaacs asked.

"My leg is pretty banged up, but it's Ari I'm worried about. He took a bad blow to the head and has been in and out of consciousness since I dug him out from under this crap."

Isaacs spoke into a shoulder microphone. "Relay back to Mama Bear that *Vampre* is secure—I repeat, *Vampre* is secure. Ari and the American agent are both alive. Lansing looks to be in okay shape, but ben Yehuda is not so good. No other survivors." He turned back to Lansing. "Your partner, Arlen Drew, he made it out. He's in a hospital near Eilat, and he is the reason we found you."

Captain Isaacs shined a small flashlight into ben Yehuda's eyes and felt for a pulse. "Ari goes first. I don't like his color and this place does not look stable." He spoke into his shoulder microphone again. "Getet the team off that ridge and over to our position, ASAP, with a litter. I'm sending ben Yehuda up to you now."

Harness secure, ben Yehuda, limp body, rose to the surface where commandos helped him out of the harness and laid him on the ground.

Arriving at full run, Shana Mogen, Eagle Talon's medical officer, and four Israeli commandos knelt alongside the litter and secured the injured Mossad agent for evac.

Next, Isaacs fitted Lansing into the harness, tugged twice on the cable and watched him rise into the vent.

Major Baratz landed the Blackhawk in a dry wadi twenty-five meters below the ridgeline. An automatic weapon at his side, Baratz took a position at a side door and waited for the commandos to carry ben Yehuda's litter down the slope with Lansing behind them, an outstretched arm draped over Isaacs' shoulder.

On Captain Isaacs' signal, the commandos lifted ben Yehuda's litter into the Blackhawk as an Egyptian mortar round detonated behind them.

"They are firing blind," Baratz shouted as he settled into his seat on the flight deck. "Get everyone inside before those bastards get lucky. Gentlemen, we have to go!"

Two commandos took positions at the open doors on both sides of the aircraft. The helicopter rotors picked up speed and the Blackhawk started its ascent.

"Dr. Ganz," Baratz shouted. "Get that flying bug into the air. I need a visual of the hostiles before I clear the ridgeline. Once exposed we are sitting ducks."

Joshua, his shoulder harness pulled tight, watched from his jump seat, torn between seeing how badly his father was injured and getting the drone airborne. He sat frozen, terrified, unable to move.

"Josh… Joshua!" Ganz yelled.

A glint of recognition appeared in his eyes. Ganz was calling him.

"You heard the major? It was not a suggestion. Get that damn UAV airborne."

Joshua freed himself from the seat harness.

Ganz stared at the image on screen. The Egyptian patrol convoy came into view in high definition. "Thirty degrees to port—range, seventy meters."

The UAV went dark, exploding in a hail of gunfire from a fifty-caliber machine gun mounted on the rear of an Egyptian jeep. The onboard computer screen.

In a rapid ascent, the Blackhawk made a run for it, but as soon as they cleared the ridge again, gunfire pinged off the helicopter's undercarriage, several rounds piercing the outer skin. Narrow beams of light streamed in through the openings making a dotted pattern on the bulkhead wall.

Baratz brought the Blackhawk down again. We need more cover and I need time to get us up and clear of that .50 caliber."

Visible to the Egyptians, machine gun fire tore through the Blackhawk's outer skin. A commando positioned in the open door fell, blood pulsing from an artery.

Shana Mogen crawled over and pulled him back inside. She tore away his flack vest and cut his shirt free with a knife secured to her ankle. She pressed hard against the soldier's wound but was not able to stem the flow of blood She turned to Ganz, her head shaking.

With no warning, an ear-piercing whine filled the air above them. A jet fighter painted in camouflage came in low, split the air, and executed into a vertical climb. The IAF pilot made a tight turn and started back down toward the ridge.

Lansing peered out of the open helicopter door and looked up. He recognized the vintage aircraft, a French-made Mirage Dassault circa 1973. It carried no markings or flag designation.

The unmarked fighter jet swooped back in, went vertical again, did a barrel roll and started back to engage the Egyptian convoy.

Onboard cannon fire tore up the desert floor less than fifty meters from the Egyptian Jeep carrying the .50 caliber machine gun.

Seeing the fighter turn back for another run, the Egyptian commander started to bug out.

A voice speaking in Hebrew came into Major Baratz' headset. "Welcome back, sir. Your bogeys are leaving and I do not believe they will be a problem much longer. Do you need further assistance?"

Baratz answered the pilot, "I need the closest medical facility."

"I copy that Eagle Talon. Change your heading to 144, target 41 North by 34 degrees East. I will provide cover."

Baratz checked his map coordinates. "Those coordinates put us in the Red Sea. Reconfirm heading and position."

The fighter pilot reconfirmed. "You are correct, sir. CVN 72, USS is standing by to receive you, Major. They are the closest medical facility.

United States aircraft carrier USS Abraham Lincoln, designated CVN 72, was part of the US Fifth Fleet currently on maneuvers in the Red Sea.

Gabriel Ganz made his way to Lansing lying on a fold down cot suspended from the bulkhead wall by a pair of chains, his injured leg in a makeshift sling.

Ganz moved to ben Yehuda in the next cot where Shana Mogen was wrapping a clean bandage around his head wound, monitoring his blood pressure and watching for signs to indicate the severity of his head injury.

Lansing touched Ari's shoulder as he passed. "You hold on my friend. We are almost home."

Ganz turned back to Lansing. "You have a most remarkable son, sir. Without his unique expertise, none of this rescue would have been possible."

Lansing started to sit up, supported by an elbow. "Where is Josh?"

Ganz turned and pointed. Joshua Lansing, seated a few feet away, was slumped over, his flack vest soaked in blood and his eyes closed.

CHAPTER FIFTY-SIX

Colonel Heifetz sat absently twirling a pencil between her fingers as she sipped tea from a paper cup, her third in an hour. Her foot tapped the floor making soft pitta-pat sounds.

Felicia Albreda, sitting across the table, held an unlit cigarette between her lips, a habit she'd kicked years ago. She dropped it unlit in an ashtray, stood up and started to pace. Heifetz reached for her arm.

"Felicia, please, sit. Making yourself crazy does no good. Let me get you a glass of wine? It will calm your nerves. Believe me when I tell you I have the utmost confidence in Daniel Ellman. The team he sent to find them is our best. They will bring them both out alive."

Heifetz was not sure she believed a word she'd just said.

Both women turned when a young naval officer appeared in the doorway with a folded piece of paper in his hand. Heifetz read as Albreda settled back into the seat next to her. "Are they alive?"

"I don't know yet. Come with me, they're waiting for us in Operations."

In Naval Operations three men and two women sat at computer consoles in the darkened room, their faces bathed in green light from the screens. The LED screens had real-time images of military operations going on concurrently throughout the Middle East. Satellite feeds monitored ports from the Caspian to the Black Sea. In the top left-hand corner of each feed was a coded identification marker that Albreda recognized. The images streaming into Israeli Naval Intelligence originated from American satellites.

Air Force colonel, Emmanuel Saalzer, Chief of Operations, came in.

Heifetz greeted him and introduced Albreda, adding, "Agent Lansing is her husband."

Saalzer's face spoke volumes. "Is Joshua Lansing, is your son?"

"Yes, Colonel, Both his father and I are very proud of him."

"Please, Director Albreda, sit. Allow me to bring you up to date on where we are at this time. The initial extraction did have a few glitches," said Saalzer. "But Joshua, your husband, and Ari ben Yehuda are now en route to the Red Sea and the United States Carrier, Abraham Lincoln." He looked at his watch. "Their ETA is 21 minutes."

None of what Saalzer said made Albreda feel better. "What are you not telling me, Colonel?"

"The aircraft they are on took fire from Egyptian ground forces and I am afraid that Joshua has been wounded. There is a Shayetet -13 medical officer onboard the helicopter with him."

"Shayetet -13?" Albreda asked.

"It is what you Americans would call Delta Force, Special Ops. Dr. Shana Mogen, the team medical officer, made the decision to divert from Eilat, and instead head for the US carrier. The ship has full medical facilities onboard and a trauma team."

"Do you know how badly he's hurt?" Albreda asked, her mind going to a worst-case scenario.

"No, Director, we do not know the medical condition of any of them because after the decision was made to divert to the Lincoln, Major Baratz the Blackhawk commander, ordered radio silence. When ths medical officer aboard the Lincoln does an evaluation and breaks radio silence we will know."

Heifetz walked Saalzer away from the computer array. "Can you get us out to that carrier?"

"You know if it were possible I would, Aviya. But the nature of the extraction makes that impossible at this time. We cannot land an Israeli aircraft on the Lincoln. Too many eyes are focused on us now. Egypt already suspects us of violating their airspace. The evacuation helicopter they are in has no Israeli identification."

Heifetz returned to the consoles and extended her hand to Albreda.

"They are being triaged on the Lincoln. After they have been evaluated and stabilized they will be airlifted to the Hadassah Medical Center at Mt. Scopus. General Ellman arranged for both you and me to leave for Scopus now. A plane is being readied as we speak."

The USS Abraham Lincoln turned into the wind to ease the carrier's rolling action and facilitate the incoming helicopter's approach. On the carrier flight deck, in ever decreasing light, eight seamen from the medical unit wearing body armor knelt under an overhang and waited. With night closing in, the Blackhawk's nose light visible twenty degrees above the horizon was a mile out. A boatswain mate stood on deck with a pair of strobing light-sticks in his outstretched arms to guide the approaching Blackhawk. the Blackhawk hovered above the deck, and touched down.

A landing crew from the Abraham Lincoln's Air Operations blocked the helicopter's wheels, locking them into position and securing the aircraft on deck as Major Baratz shut down the rotors.

The Lincoln's triage officer, Lieutenant Commander Louis Connolly, climbed aboard.

Commander Connolly, a trauma surgeon, went first to ben Yehuda, and then to Lansing who waved him away with, "I'm fine. Look at Joshua first."

Connolly lifted a bandage from Joshua's shoulder. Shana Mogen had packed his shoulder wound and inserted a drainage tube. The collection bag was already half filled with blood.

She briefed Commander Connolly she'd already administered Ampicillin 1.5 grams IV and 0.5 mg of Demerol IM. Connolly placed his stethoscope on Joshua's chest. He listened for a few seconds and said, "Sickbay, now."

The Abraham Lincoln's medical facility, although cramped, resembled a modern-day hospital ER. Navy personnel in blue scrubs circulated in the tight quarters. They went about their jobs with crisp efficiency, placing surgical instruments onto trays, rolling monitors into place, and waited for the injured to arrive from the receiving deck.

Two corpsmen wheeled Ted Lansing into a curtained cubicle.s

Alone in the curtained bay, Lansing shouted, "Where is Joshua?"

No one answered. He shouted again, sat up and stepped down off the bed. His knee buckled.

Lansing reached for a steel cart for balance. The instrument-laden rolling cart tipped sideways and crashed, medical instruments strewn everywhere. Heg lay sprawled on the floor, more embarrassed than hurt.

Commander Connolly pushed the curtain aside and glared. "What in Sam Hill is goin' on here? Y'all may be a civilian, Lansing, but make no mistake. I am in charge of this triage bay, not you." He pushed the curtain farther back. "I need some help here."

Two Shore Patrol officers appeared.

"Get this man up off the floor and back into that goddamn bed." Connolly's eyes, focused, riveted on Lansing.

"Your son is in surgery right now. As for his injuries, he's suffered substantial loss of blood and the surgeon, Lieutenant Commander Fallon, tells me he's had major trauma to his left shoulder. Dr. Fallon is our most experienced orthopedic surgeon. He stabilized the injury, did a temporary repair to stop the bleeding, and the medical staff is preparing him for evac. They are currently transfusing two additional units of packed cells, O-Negative. When Fallon deems him stable enough, he will be airlifted to Hadassah Hospital at Mt. Scopus. You and Agent ben Yehuda will be prepped for the flight to Scopus as soon as I have an aircraft ready."

Connolly checked his watch. "2200 hours at the latest. Joshua needs imaging of his shoulder that we are not equipped to do here on onboard. You, however, do not appear critical, but the medical staff at Hadassah Hospital will make that determination."

"With all due respect, sir, I'm not going anywhere without my son."

Connolly, angry at his command order being challenged, took one step, turned and faced the corpsman. "As soon as triage gives the okay prepare Agent Lansing for evac."

Lansing sat up, slid to the edge of the bed and tried to stand.

"Stay where you are, Lansing," Connolly ordered, and then addressed the Shore Patrol officer. "If he gives you a hard time, use restraints."

Lansing started to object when the corpsman snapped to attention.

"Ten-hut, Captain on deck."

Connolly saluted the Lincoln's commanding officer.

Captain Waylin Stewart stood alongside the cubicle's partially drawn curtain.

"At ease, gentlemen—some privacy, please. Corpsman, find Agent Lansing some clothes. I want him in the Wardroom—thirty minutes."

"Aye-Aye, sir."

Stewart closed the curtain and came alongside Lansing's bed. "I came down because this matter is highly classified. I need to know what the hell is going on here. You and I, we need to talk."

CHAPTER FIFTY-SEVEN

Lansing, in a wheelchair, escorted by a corpsman, stood outside the Wardroom door. The young ensign knocked once. "Permission to enter."

"Come," came a crisp reply from inside.

Sitting at a long table were the ships commanding officer and its security officer.

During Lansing's five-year stint in the Navy after graduation from Annapolis, he'd had eaten meals in rooms like this with its low ceilings, exposed conduit, and harsh fluorescent lighting.

Two flat-screen monitors, hung on a wall above the table. An aroma of freshly brewed coffee wafted to his nose.

The Lincoln's captain opened a folder and scan several pages before he looked up at Lansing..

"The commanding officer of the extraction team, a Major Baratz, Israeli Air Force, and the body of one of his men killed in the rescue, have already been airlifted to Eilat at 0900 hours along with the rest of Major Baratz's team for debriefing. I don't know who is pulling strings here, but those strings have aslong reach, Lansing, a very long reach. I also see there was a civilian on board, a Dr. Gabriel Ganz."

"Dr. Ganz is a computer programmer, sir, an aeronautical engineer. Beyond that, you will have to take it up with the Israelis."

Stewart slid a sheet of paper across to Lansing who stared at a fuzzy digital image.

"Where did you get this?" Lansing asked.

Captain Stewart did not answer "shatever you were sent to find in that collapsed tunnel is important enough for Mossad to get its hands on, that they are willing to…" Stewart stopped, searching for the right word. "Let me say, share."

Lansing stared at the image again, sepia and faded, the focus blurred, a metallic cylinder with a biohazard symbol. Underneath it the biohazard symbol was word, superimposed over the picture, in bold red paint, A hand drawn circle with a single word inside it, *Vampre*. It was the canister Lansing had hauled out of the collapsed tunnel.

"A cylinder, identical to this one, was found inside a backpack belonging to Major Baratz," Stewart said.

Lansing stiffened. "Where is it the cylinder now, sir? Did anyone open it?" There was urgency in his voice.

"No, Lansing, we are not reckless. It's safe," he said, "in a secure location on board. When the evac craft landed in Eilat, the missing cylinder was noticed by Mossad, and USsCentCom notified me."

Stewart passed another sheet of paper across to Lansing. In vague terms, the nature of the *Vampre* project was outlined. Highlighted in yellow marker were the words, hazard, virus, fatal, and hemorrhagic fever.

Stewart's demeaner change to anger. "Just what in hell did you bring aboard my ship?"

"I must apologize, Captain, but again, that is classified and you need to take it up with CentCom."

Fuming, Stewart stood up. "Jesus Christ, Lansing, I checked your background. You're ex-Navy and we are a Nimitz Class carrier with six thousand personnel. Do the math. Is my crew at risk from whatever that thing is?"

"I'm not being cute, Captain, but I truly do not know."

Stewart shoved another communication across the table. "Maybe this will jog your memory."

Lansing read the document with a Mossad heading and a signature at the bottom, Aviya Heifetz.

Stewart leaned forward, his palms on the table. "It appears to me that Mossad wants whatever this *Vampre* is returned badly enough to give clearance for Agent ben Yehuda to take possession once you are evac-ed. Right now it's in an explosion-proof safe and ben Yehuda is in no condition to take possession of anything, much less whatever this *Vampre* thing is. That leaves you, Agent Lansing."

Lansing considered his options, how much should he, or could he reveal to Stewart without compromising *Vampre*. "It is not an explosive device," he finally said.

"Comforting, but not helpful."

"When are we being airlifted out, sir?"

Stewart grabbed the phone from the table. "Is the XO ready with that evac craft?"

"Aye-Aye, sir. The Israeli, Ari ben Yehuda, has been cleared medically and is prepared for evac. He's in sickbay sir, but the FBI agent, Lansing, is not in his quarters."

"Lansing is here with me in the Wardroom."

"Then evac is a go, sir. I have a C-2A Greyhound on its way up to the flight deck. We can launch in twenty minutes, sooner if need be. A squall is closing from the west."

"I want to know the second that aircraft is up on deck and ready to fly."

Stewart closed the folder. "I still don't like this, Lansing, but I have my orders to transport you and ben Yehuda aboard my beautiful new C-2A, along with whatever is in that canister. I only hope that I am not being bullshitted here."

"Not by me, sir."

"Again, Captain, I am not being obtuse. I really do not know what Vampre is."

Stewart became all business. "You will be met in Eilat by an Israeli specialist who will take custody of the canister before you go on to Mt. Scopus."

"Aye-Aye, sir." The words came by habit.

Stewart smiled. "I checked your Navy record, Lansing, quite impressive."

"If you say so, sir. I left the service with the rank of Lieutenant Commander."

"You're too modest," Stewart said. "A Navy Cross and a Purple Heart."

"Thank you, sir, but just wrong place at the right time. Sometimes you do whatever you need to do so you don't get yourself or the men under your command killed."

Stewart reached for a phone on the table. "I want an update on a patient in sickbay, Joshua Lansing. He's a civilian."

"There's been a delay on the evac—a catapult problem," Stewart the lied. "It'll be another forty minutes."

"What's going on here, Captain?" Lansing asked.

"Ensign Corwin will escort you to sickbay. Your son is there, resting comfortably. The surgeon has him ready for evac to Scopus."

"OR Recovery is straight ahead, sir." Ensign Corwin pointed down a narrow passageway

The surgical recovery area of sickbay was in subdued light. Lansing could hear soft beeping sounds coming from a heart monitor. A curtain opened and a Navy nurse in blue scrubs came out. A stethoscope hung around her neck; her face framed by short brown hair.

"Are you Theodore Lansing?"

He nodded.

"Captain Stewart called down to sickbay, sir. I'm Lt. J.G. Donaldson. I've been taking care of Joshua since he came out of surgery. He's been asking for you."

"Thank you, Lieutenant. Can I get a status update?"

"Joshua sustained a serious injury to his shoulder. Lieutenant Michaels removed pieces of shrapnel that was driven from a machine gun round that pierced the helicopter's bulkhead and landed in his left shoulder damaging the lateral thoracic artery. Dr. Michaels repaired the laceration and stopped the bleeding. Bone fragments from the damaged humerus head were removed. The orthopedists at Hadassah Hospital will do the final repair. He's still a bit groggy from the anestheis. I administered a shot of morphine a half hour ago."

Above Josh's bed, a heart monitor beeped softly casting a soft green light into the tight space.sLansing leaned over and kissed his son's forehead. He held his hand, feeling the pulse oximeter clamped to an index finger. A huge bandage ran from Joshua's left shoulder covering most of his chest. He moaned and opened his eyes.

"Don't try to speak, kiddo. Just rest."

A small smile came across Joshua's face. "Did you get the bad guys?"

Lt. Donaldson laughed. "You've got a real fighter there, sir."

Lansing took Josh's other hand. "I am so proud of you," he said, his eyes glistening. What you did, getting that drone of yours…"

Josh lifted a finger. "It's called a UAV."

"Yeah, but it's your UAV. None of that matters now. What's important is that you're going to be okay. I bet there's a certain cute Israeli corporal who can't wait to get her hands on you. In fact, I would not bet against your mother finding herself a ride to Mt. Scopus."

"Me neither, Dad. Mom does have some pull down at the bureau."

Lt. Donaldson stepped forward. "I'm sorry, sir, but it's time. I do need to prepare Joshua."

Chapter Fifty-Eight

Ari ben Yehuda lay awake and alert on a stretcher aboard the USS Lincoln's evacuation aircraft as the plane flew north over the Gulf of Aqaba. Across the narrow aisle, asleep from the effects of a morphine drip, Joshua Lansing lay with his chest rising and falling at regular intervals.

Ted Lansing leaned over in a jump seat alongside his son. He watched anxiously as a corpsman monitored Joshua's vital signs and adjusted the IV drip.

In a forward area of the aircraft, in an explosion-proof compartment behind the flight deck, the *Vampre* canister was held secure by layers of duct tape, cushioned by wads of bubble wrap hastily commandeered from the USS Lincoln's galley.

"How is he doing, Ted?" asked ben Yehuda.

Lansing came across the aisle. "All things considered, Ari, lucky. I'll know more once we get to Mt. Scopus. How are you feeling?"

"Been better," said ben Yehuda. "My head is still killing me."

From the flight deck, a voice blared over the intercom. "Secure for landing. Corpsmen, ready your patients. We will be on the ground for only as long as it takes to hand off the package and injured personnel. Ordinance officer, give that thing in the box one last look and confirm."

The Navy C-2A Greyhound taxied from the runway to a hangar at the edge of the air base where an Israeli Chinook waited.

Parked a short distance away, an unmarked SUV waited with two passengers.

The Chinook's aft ramp opened and a team of medical personnel was first to board the C-2A, behind them, two civilians in Hazmat suits. One carried a large metal case.

Israeli technicians made their way to the bombproof compartment behind the cockpit door.

Lansing, leaning on crutches, found himself sandwiched between the C-2A's pilot on one and an Israeli bomb expert on the other. He watched them open the safe and cut bubble wrap away from the *Vampre* canister.

The C-2A pilot handed Lansing an iPad. "I need positive confirmation, sir, that this is the same canister recovered from the collapsed tunnel."

Lansing nodded, tapping a screen icon. "I'll need a signature as well, sir. Use your finger."

Lansing scribbled his name on the small screen.

The Israeli medical team transferred Joshua Lansing to a rolling stretcher, carried him to the waiting Chinook, and returned for ben Yehuda.

In the darkened hangar, the black SUV, its engine idling, Heifetz and Albreda climbed out and walked to the waiting Chinook, boarding through the open ramp at the rear. Heifetz took a foldout seat next to Ari, Felicia alongside Joshua. "Where is Lansing?" Heifetz asked.

"I'm right here, Colonel," Lansing said, his voice coming toward them from the forward cabin.

Heifetz motioned. "Follow me aft."

She led him to a small galley at the rear of the helicopter.

"The *Vampre* canister is being transported to a DNA sequencing lab in Tel Aviv." Her voice just above a whisper, we have consulted with your CDC in Atlanta, and a team is on route to Tel Aviv now."

"Who is we?" asked Lansing.

"We are Mossad. I do not fully comprehend the plan, but you will be briefed after you have been cleared medically. One more thing, Lansing, this information cannot be shared."

Lansing moved next to Felicia, leaned down and kissed her cheek. She brought her arms around his neck. "How is Joshua, Ted, really? I haven't been able to get a straight answer from anyone."

CHAPTER FIFTY-NINE

Forty-eight hours after surgery to reconstruct his injured shoulder, Joshua Lansing reached for a trapeze bar suspended from a rail above his hospital bed. He used his good arm to pull himself up into a sitting position. He winced, his face contorted.

Hana Erlich, siat in a chair across the room, "Do you need me to call the nurse, Joshua?"

She'd been at his bedside since the surgery, leaving only to sleep on a couch in a nearby lounge or grab something to eat from a vending machine.

She stood alongside the bed with backlight streaming from a window behind her.

"No," Joshua said. "Come closer."

He'd been taken directly from the helicopter landing pad on the roof to a triage unit adjacent to the surgery suite, where doctors first assessed his injuries before moving him to an operating room. An orthopedic team and a vascular surgeon took over three hours to repair the damaged artery and graft bone where shrapnel had chipped away a good portion of his left humerus head.

Hana brushed her lips against his forehead, but before she could move away, he lifted his free arm and pulled her close, kissing her, softly.

The door to the room opened and both Felicia and Greta Erlich, Hana's mother, came in.

"Joshua, clasped her hand. "If I lost you now, I would…"

Hana, her face reddening, shushed him, gesturing with her eyes, *you will embarrass me.*

"I think we may something thing going on here," Greta Erlich laughed.

Felicia laughed. "I was thinking the same thing, Greta."

The door opened again, and Ted Lansing stood there on crutches with an odd look on his face. Albreda recognized the look. "What's wrong Ted? Is it Ari?"

"No," Lansing answered. "Ari is doing fine. They put a few stitches in that cement head of his and did a full neurological workup. He's on his way back to Mossad headquarters. But something is up and I need to go to with Colonel Heifetz, to Tel Aviv."

"Right now?" she asked.

"Yes, today."

"Do I or the Bureau get a read in?"

"Not now," he said. "Colonel Heifetz was emphatic. Better the Bureau has plausible deniability for the present time."

The ride from Hadassah Hospital to the Chaim Sheba Medical Center's Advanced Technology Lab, seven kilometers east of Tel Aviv, took under an hour with Heifetz behind the wheel driving like a lunatic.

The blue Hyundai sedan barreled north on Route 1 toward the facility that housed a discreet, top secret military installation for identifying, sequencing and altering DNA.

Heifetz entered the medical complex through its East Gate and drove down a ring road past several modern buildings, some with ornate sculptures adorning the grounds in front of them. Every medical specialty from obstetrics to rehabilitation to pediatrics had its own freestanding structure. Behind the Eye Institute a small two-story building, partially obscured by trees and hedges, had signage declaring it *Administration Offices - A.*

A doctor in a white coat met them. Heifetz recognized the man from previous meetings

"Shalom, Aviya, and to you as well, it is Agent Lansing, is it not?"

Lansing nodded,

"Ayla is waiting upstairs with that other American agent."

"Other agent?" Lansing asked. "No one told me anything about another agent assigned to this case."

Heifetz laughed. "Because, Theodore, it is a surprise."

Ayla Yalom greeted Heifetz with a hug and soft cheek peck. Lansing made her to be close to his age.

Tall, nearly six-foot, with salt and pepper hair cropped close to her face, a deep tan and olive complexion, Ayla Yalom made an imposing figure.

One wall of her office had photographs of Yalom with several Israeli faces Lansing recognized from newspapers and television. On a second wall were several additional images of a much younger Yalom in combat gear, one with her head sticking out of a tank turret—written across the picture, in bold black marker, Golan Heights, 1994.

Lansing followed her into an anteroom. A semi-circular grouping of chairs occupied the center. Ari sat across from Lansing, and in the seat next to him, Arlen Drew with a toothy grin. Lansing turned to Heifetz and gave her a thumbs-up.

Yalom moved behind the group. "Agent Lansing, do you know the name, Anton Vassily?"

Lansing shook his head indicating no.

"What about Anthony Dustman?"

"Never heard that name either. Who is he?"

Yalom opened a folder and sat next to Heifetz. "Anton Vassily is my Russian counterpart. A year ago, maybe longer, Mossad placed an operative undercover Anton Vassily, AKA Dustman's office in Moscow. Our female mole entered into an intimate relationship with a young clerk in Vassily's office, where he gained access to sensitive information. It was then that Mossad first learned of Vampre's existence."

"And now I suppose the Rusians want it back?" said Lansing with a mocking tone.

Yalom turned to Heifetz. "You were right Aviya. He is very good."

Lansing stopped smiling.

Yalom turned her attention back to Lansing. "I know you meant that in jest, but there is more truth there than you know. In 1978 the Russians captured an Israeli agent named Aaronson. Dr. Aaronson is still in prison somewhere in Russia."

"1978? Jesus. That's almost forty years for God's sake, before the damn Soviet Union collapsed."

"Yes, and we think forty years is enough time in prison, do you not?" said Heifetz.

Lansing nodded his agreement. "And this Vassily character can get Aaronson out of Russia?"

Yalom had a strange look on her face. "Not wittingly."

"I don't understand," said Lansing. "How can you…"

An intercom on Yalon's desk buzzed. "Professor Mondschein is here."

Dr. Russell Mondschein entered carrying a blue folder. In his early fifties, wearing a white lab coat, Mondschein was bald, his head shaven.

A small *kipah* sat on the back of his head and knotted fringes of an *arba kanfot*, the undergarment worn by orthodox Jews, dangled from his waist. Yalom introduced him as a co-recipient of the Nobel Prize in Genetics.

"Sit, please, Dr. Mondschein. Allow me to lay this out for our friends here." Heifetz turned her chair to face Lansing. "You were correct in your assessment. The Russians do want *Vampre* back and we want our long-incarcerated spy back. Dr. Aaronson is now in his late seventies, in poor health and of no further use to the Kremlin. We have communicated our wishes to the Russians through back channels that we might be willing to return *Vampre* if the price was right. Our negotiator allowed them to make the first offer, which we, of course, turned down, and a second, and a third, until Aaronson's name came up."

"Smart negotiating tactic," Lansing said. "Make them believe Aaronson's return is their idea."

"But why would you return something as dangerous as a deadly pathogen that has no known cure?" asked Drew.

Dr. Mondschein interrupted. "Please allow me. By early next week, My lab, will have completed sequencing the genome of the *Vampre* virus. This particular strain is not new to us. The Russians, however, stumbled on to it by accident in 1965. The science of virology has come light years since then. We now understand precisely where in the viral genome it lives and the precise locus of the DNA sequence that makes it so deadly. We have synthesized a patch to insert the altered sequence into the DNA rendering it no more dangerous than influenza. In my opinion, a good tradeoff."

"Won't the Russians know their virus has been altered the minute they get their hands on it?" asked Lansing.

Mondschein closed the folder. "Colonel Yalom. Ladies, gentlemen, I shall take my leave for now. There is much work to be done. Ayla, you can explain it to them.s

Yalom took a remote control from her desk and turned on a TV monitor mounted to the wall. The first image to appear was a well-dressed man in an expensive blue suit about to get into a black Escalade parked outside a magnificent mansion in Washington, a house Lansing recognized—the Russian Ambassador's residence.

Yalom zoomed in on the figure standing outside the Escalade. "I give you Anthony Dustman, aka Anton Vassily."

CHAPTER SIXTY

Lansing and Drew flew separately to Paris from Tel Aviv. Both carried identification meticulously prepared by Mossad. In Paris, they boarded separate flights on Turkish Air arriving at Istanbul's Ataturk Airport an hour apart. Heifetz and Ari ben Yehuda made similar covert flights, first to London, and then to Ankara, via British Air. On arrival they rented separate vehicles and drove three hundred kilometers east to Istanbul where they met with Lansing and Drew at a cheap hotel near a sprawling network of indoor souks peddling leather, jewelry, and gifts.

A week after spiriting *Vampre* out of the Sinai, Heifetz received a cryptic message over a back channel from Anthony Dustman, the Russian agent who first engaged Richter. He hinted that a deal could be made concerning the deadly virus.

Dustman sounded urgent, not from the standpoint of retrieving the canister but saving his own ass for Richter's botched attempt. Heifetz kicked the request to her superiors in Israeli Intelligence who gave her the go-ahead to see what the Russian wanted. In every dealing heifetz had with Russia's clandestine service duplicity always remained on the table as a possibility.

Agreeing to Dustman's meeting, Heifetz insisted on a public space for the actual exchange of *Vampre* for Dr. Aaronson, a so-called Israeli spy held by the Russians on trumped up espionage charges since 1978.

Dustman reluctantly agreed to the wide-open courtyard of the Blue Mosque.

Heifetz knew the popular tourist attraction would have an abundance of tourists present.

Mossad knew that Russia's modern spy organization, now the FSB, an incarnation of its original KGB, was formidable. In a retrofitted compartment in ben Yehuda's rental car, an Israeli friendly auto mechanic in Ankara built a hidden compartment to transport *Vampre* to the exchange location.

The Blue Mosque in Sultanahmet Park, a short distance from Haga Sophia, was not as tourist-laden as Heifetz had hoped. Dark gray skies and a threat of rain kept the tourism down. The courtyard looked deserted when they arrived.

Lansing and Drew, dressed in Arab garb with long white *dishdashas* and woven *kaffiyehs* atop their heads, blended in with the few Arabs visiting the holy shrine. Heifetz donned a long skirt and a *Hijab*, her face partially obscured.

Anton Vassily, Dustman, and several FSB agents held Solomon Aaronson in a minivan just outside the mosque walls. The exchange was scheduled for noon.

In a second vehicle, a step-truck that looked like it had once been used for mail delivery, Russian technicians waited with everything needed for a rapid, positive identification of the *Vampre* virus. Equipment filled the mobile lab set up for genome identification.

Heifetz entered the courtyard carrying a small suitcase containing five separate vials, each with a minute sample of the *Vampre* virus separated at the Chaim Sheba Medical Center.

She stopped and glanced around looking for anything unusual before proceeding into the open space.

Five women in black burkas hurried past her, looked her up and down and proceeded to the mosque entrance.

Heifetz stopped in the middle of the open courtyard near a domed hexagonal structure.

Israeli geneticists led by Dr. Mondschein had replaced the original virus taken from the monastery tunnel with a genetically altered strain. Heifetz knew Vassily would demand proof and she was ready.

Doctor Mondschein assured her that no field test, especially one done hastily, could be sensitive enough to differentiate his altered phenotype from the original virulent genetic strain. The Russians would not realize the replacement until they had *Vampre* back in lab in Moscow, too late to do anything about it and in no position to admit they'd been duped. Their Kremlin bosses wpuld seek retribution.

Arlen Drew took a position several meters to Heifetz' left, and Lansing across the courtyard maintained line of sight. Both armed, they waited.

Ari came alongside the mosque's foutain engaging a group of pilgrims in perfect Arabic.

"South entrance," he said into a wrist microphone.

Lansing spotted a man, tall and lean, wearing traditional Arab robe. He made his way toward Heifetz. When the figure was less than twenty meters away, she laughed into her wrist microphone. Sticking out from the bottom of his white *dishdasha* were a pair of John Lobb oxfords that sold for seventeen hundred pounds in London. "Idiot," she muttered under her breath getting a laugh from ben Yehuda.

"Positive ID?" asked ben Yehuda.

"It's Vassily," Heifetz answered.

Anton Vassily came alongside her. "It has been a while, Aviya. You are looking very…"

Vassily paused, eying Heifetz's *hijab*, "good," he said facetiously.

He peered around the courtyard. "And where is that handsome son of yours?"

"If you know that Vassily, then you also know that if you try to pull a fast one you will be dead before your body knows it."

"Aha, it is so nice that you still have a sense of humor. It always was one of your finest attributes."

"Stop the delay, Vassily, where is Dr. Aaronson?"

"He is nearby, close. Where is my virus?"

Heifetz pointed to the case she'd placed at her feet.

Vassily took a step forward.

Heifetz held up a hand. "Proof of life."

Vassily spoke into a hand-held device. "Bring Aaronson to the edge of the courtyard, but no farther."

Two FSB agents in ill-fitting wool suits appeared from under an arch.

Aaronson. Old and stooped over, supported under each arm, he was literally held erect by Vassily's thugs. He looked fragile.

Lansing whispered into his wrist mic. "I could take them both out. Quick and quiet."

Ari's voice came on. "No, Ted. Hold your position. Let it play out. We are playing a long game."

"I am handing over *Vampre*," Heifetz said loud enough for her team to hear.

"How do I know you are giving me the real virus, Aviya? Pardon me for not trusting Mossad."

"You can trust me because you will get to choose."

"I do not understand," he answered.

Heifetz opened the case. Nested inside five foam cutouts were tiny vials.

"We have separated *Vampre* into five subsets. All are identical. You may select any two and take it to wherever you have hidden your testing laboratory. I know it is someplace closeby. Dr. Aaronson remains where he is now, in open sight. After you have confirm *Vampre's* authenticity, only then will you receive the final three vials. I will then take Doctor Aaronson, and our business is concluded. One more thing Vassily, that small sample is one-fifth of what you need, or so I am told by our scientists."

The Rissian nodded, selected a pair of the vials and hurried from the courtyard.

Heifetz spoke into her microphone. "Nobody takes their eyes from those agents holding Aaronson. If they make a move to take him anyplace you are authorized to use whatever level of force needed to keep it from happening.

Ari, and Drew, move in closer to Lansing."

Lansing glanced down at his watch. Vassily had been gone for almost an hour, and the men propping up Dr. Aaronson had not moved in over forty minutes. They looked like animatronic statues, their eyes focused on the mosque courtyard, their heads moving from side to side in a rhythmic cadence.

"He's back." It was Ari's voice now in their earpieces.

"Is good, Aviya," Vassily said. "It appears, Aviya, you have kept your word for once." He turned to his men holding the old man. "Bring him here."

Ari and Lansing followed behind the Russians, their hands gripping weapons concealed under the long *dishdashas*. Aaronson moved slowly, his captors supporting him under each arm.

"Do not intervene," Heifetz said, her voice emphatic. "If he falls, then move in."

The Russians brought Aaronson to Heifetz and released him. The old man's knees started to buckle, but Heifetz held up a hand. Ari, about to move in, stopped. He spoke into his wrist mic. "He's all right. Hold your positions until the Russians are gone."

Anton Vassily scooped up the remaining vials of virus from the case open at Heifetz's feet. He carefully placed them in another case with Styrofoam compartments. He bowed to her with a foppish flourish and a grin that said, *you just traded a useless old man with no value for a Russian military asset.*

Heifetz grinned back, with a face Vassily had seen before, smirking. He stared at the case in his hand, wondering what his superiors in the Kremlin would do to him if it were not actually *Vampre* in the remaining four vials. It was too late to do anything about it.

CHAPTER SIXTY-ONE

Six months after returning from the Sinai, a warm June breeze and a cloudless sky over Cambridge promised a beautiful day for Joshua Lansing graduation. If not for Felicia Albreda's connections at DOJ, securing tickets might have been a bust.

With her son's recovery in an Israeli rehab hospital, by the time Albreda got around to even thinking about graduation, finding hotel accommodations in Boston or Cambridge, it was too late.

A sweet sounding, but ineffectual woman on the phone at the MIT president's office informed her that parents of graduates made plans the day their son or daughter first enrolled at the university.

Today, six months after the 'incident,' as it was referred to by the few FBI personnel who knew about it, Albreda and Lansing were making their way along the Charles River to Killian Court on the MIT campus to see their son receive his doctoral degree in engineering.

At convocation the previous evening they saw him gowned in his gray robe with crimson arm stripes, academic hood, and a red-tasseled tam. The traditional hooding ceremony at MIT recognized the enormous effort and dedication it took to earn the prestigious degree. No one in the audience suspected what additional trials the young man with his arm still in a sling had endured to get there.

Killian Court in front of MIT's Great Dome held thirteen thousand seats, and every one of them appeared occupied. Albreda handed the crimson striped tickets with a large V printed over them, to a young man in a crimson blazer with a lapel sticker that said, *Staff.* He smiled and spoke briefly to a nearby usher.

"They were led down an aisle and seated three rows from the stage.

Lansing felt a tap on his shoulder and turned around to see who it was behind him. In the row were three familiar faces—Abraham and Greta Erlich, and, in a short, sleeveless polka dot dress, Hana Erlich.

"You made it," Lansing said extending a hand. "When did you arrive in the US?"

Greta Erlich took Felicia's hand. "How could we not be here today to share the day with Joshua. We landed at Logan Airport too late for last night's convocation. It was close to midnight, so we checked into the Hilton near the airport."

Felicia smiled and squeezed Greta Erlich's hand. "As soon as the graduation ceremony is over, I am are getting you out of the Hilton. No hotels. You are all coming back to Georgetown with us and I will not take no for an answer."

Felicia smiled at Hana, remarking how beautiful she looked.

Hana thanked Felicia as she craned her neck, looking first left and then right.

Felicia pointed to the famed MIT dome. "If you are looking for a particular graduate, I suspect they are lining up for the processional. Josh is there someplace."

"Oh, I wasn't looking for…" Hana stopped, her cheeks turning a soft pink.

Lansing leaned over and whispered in Felicia's ear, "Something's up."

"Up with who, the Erlich's?"

"No, Aviya Heifetz." Do not turn around."

Lansing excused himself and made his way to the aisle and peered up at a small knoll several yards to his left. A pair of familiar faces looked back, Heifetz and Ari ben Yehuda.

Heifetz motioned for him to follow them.

In the doorway of a secluded building.

"We have Anton Vassily stashed in a safe house near Alexandria. He's requested political asylum in Israel, but our new right wing government will not grant such a request."

"Why?" Asked Lansing

As the words left his mouth he knew why. It took six months for the Russians to realized they'd been duped. Whatever value the *Vampre* virus had as a weaponized organism was now gone. According to Dr. Mondschein, it might take years, if ever, for the Russians to identify his genetic alterations in the viral genome.

In Moscow, rats abandoning ship claimed it was all Anton Vassily fault. Vassilu learned that President Putin wanted him removed from his security post at the FSB, and in Russia under Pthe present regime remove had an ominous connotation.

Anton Vassily chartered a flight, transferred as many bank accounts as he could to a bank in Zurich.

Vassily then hid his wife's extensive collection of expensive jewelry in a false-bottom suitcase, and fled to Tel Aviv, hoping for asylum. After learning that Israel would not accept him as a political *émigré* Mossad spirited him out of the country to Washington using a forged diplomatic passport to gain entry into the United States.

"How safe is he in now?" Lansing asked. "Can he remain here for a while I try to work a deal with the our State Department?"

"How long will that take, Ted?" Ari said.

Lansing thought for a moment. "A week, maybe longer."

Settled back into his seat as the commencement speaker, industrialist entrepreneur Elon Musk, completed his address and received a standing ovation from a waving sea of gray and crimson.

"I'm going to miss dinner with the Erlichs tonight. I have to get back to Washington."

"What's happened, Ted? Who was that?"

"Aviya and Ari," Lansing said. "Right after the ceremony, I am going to make my excuses—urgent bureau business. I'll take a cab to Logan and fly back to DC this evening, early. I need you to call the Director and get me in to see Jorgensen at State. I also need the White House on standby to sign off on something. We might just have the biggest military intelligence coup of all time."

"Anton Vassily?" she inquired.

Lansing nodded.

"Joshua, Javier, Albreda, Lansing," boomed over the loudspeakers. Felicia reached across for Lansing's hand.

Beaming theu their strid across the stage, his arm still in a sling hidden under his doctoral gown. He accepted the diploma, turned and looked out at the audience.

Hana was standing, shouting and whooping, "Joshua, Joshua, Joshua." The late afternoon sun illuminated her face, her hands cupped around her mouth.

Joshua continued across the stage, reached the end and blew a kiss in her direction.

"Oh yeah, something is definitely going on here, and not with Anton Vassily."

Lansing arrived at the State Department complex at 8:00 in the morning. He stopped at the guardhouse surrounded by strategically placed anti-terror concrete barriers. He presented his FBI credentials and was immediately escorted to a secondary entrance where a young man with a State Department ID hanging from a lanyard around his neck showed him to a third-floor office.

Stepping from the elevator Lansing met Phillip St. John, Chief of Staff to Secretary of State, Neville Conroy. "I apologize, Agent Lansing, but the assistant secretary was called away on important business today. I have full authority to set the terms for Anton Vassily's entrance into the United States. He is currently waiting in my office with two Israeli diplomats, but may I assume they are not really diplomats?"

"Wouldn't know anything about that," said Lansing.

Was he getting the runaround?

Lansing's first look at Vassily since the Blue Mosque was a surprise. He expected the Russian spy to be thick-bodied with bushy eyebrows and a bad suit.

Instead, sitting comfortably in a chair, wearing a designer suit and expensive dress shoes, the Russian spy looked like he just stepped from the pages of GQ. He'd dropped forty pounds.

Phillip St. John moved everyone to a conference table and opened a set of typed pages affixed by a metal clip. "I will make this simple, Mr. Vassily."

St, John placed two identical documents on the table across from Vassily. The terms of the Russian's defection had been hastily prepared by the Department of State.

"Mr. Vassily, the conditions set forth here are non-negotiable. You will be transported directly from here to Fort McNair. It is a military installation on a peninsula at the confluence of the Anacostia and Potomac Rivers. For three months you will be available for debriefing by NSA officials. They, and only they, can approve a final determination of the veracity of your information. In particular, FSB operations currently going on worldwide. Do you understand what I told you?"

Vassily nodded.

"At the end of three months, if and when we are satisfied, you and your wife will be relocated, given new identities, a place to live, and a job. You will have no further contact with anyone from your previous life in Russia."

"I have a son," said Vassily.

St. John opened a folder. "Yes, I am aware. Andrei, age 26. He is currently in the Russian military, Intelligence I believe."

"Yes, Andrei is training in Crimea now."

St. John closed the folder. "I am sorry, Anton, we cannot have a Russian Intelligence officer in our witness protection program."

"Katya, my wife, will never agree to that."

"That is certainly her prerogative, Anton. I can have her on a flight back to Moscow by this evening."

Vassily lowered his head. "That shall not be necessary. I canl convince her that this is the only way. She knows that with me gone the FSB will look for their pound of flesh elsewhere, and they are not selective about who they get it from."

CHAPTER SIXTY-TWO

Lansing pulled into the driveway of his Georgetown colonial at 4:00 p.m. that evening. He reached above his head and pressed the garage door transponder. Felicia's SUV was already there. A quick look at his watch told him she must have left Cambridge early to make the seven-hour drive back to Georgetown.

In the den, Rosaria, their housekeeper, was pouring coffee from a silver carafe. Greta Erlich sat on the leather couch alongside her husband, and across from them, in a two-seat divan, Joshua and Hana were cuddled together.

Felicia came across the room, kissed Lansing on the cheek and whispered in his ear, "Just don't freak out."

Confused, Lansing gave her an odd look, welcomed the Erlich's and sat next to his wife.

"Dad," Josh said. "There's no good way to say this so, here goes. I've been offered a job."

"Fantastic," Lansing said. "By who? C'mon kiddo, details."

"By Dr. Erlich."

"In Haifa?"

Joshua nodded.

Lansing turned to Abraham Erlich. "For real?"

"Yes, Ted, we have offered Joshua a three-year contract."

Felicia came across the room and stood behind Josh and Hana. "Ted, there's one more thing."

Lansing's eyes went to Hana's hand, her ring finger was moving up and down with a diamond ring—a small solitaire in a simple white gold setting. It was the same ring he'd put on Felicia's finger more than twenty years ago.

About Howard Gleichenhaus

Author, Howard Gleichenhaus was born in Philadelphia, Pennsylvania and grew up in the Bronx, New York City and Spring Valley, New York. He earned his Bachelor's Degree in Biology from Southern Connecticut State College, a Master Degree in Biology and a second Master's Degree in Psychology from Fairleigh Dickinson University in Teaneck, New Jersey.

He spent a few years doing neurochemical research at the Nathan Kline Institute in Orangeburg NY and polymer chemistry research at Reichhold Chemicals in Sterling Forest, New York, before settling in to a 35-year teaching career in the Clarkstown Central School District in New City, New York.

Howard, retired, lives in Delray Beach, Florida with his wife, Fredda. They have been married for 49 years.